MISTER TENDER'S GIRL

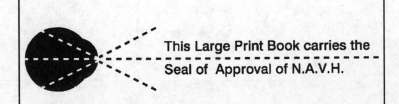

This Large Print Book carries the
Seal of Approval of N.A.V.H.

MISTER TENDER'S GIRL

CARTER WILSON

THORNDIKE PRESS
A part of Gale, a Cengage Company

Farmington Hills, Mich • San Francisco • New York • Waterville, Maine
Meriden, Conn • Mason, Ohio • Chicago

GALE
A Cengage Company

LIBRARY OF CONGRESS CIP DATA ON FILE.
CATALOGUING IN PUBLICATION FOR THIS BOOK
IS AVAILABLE FROM THE LIBRARY OF CONGRESS

ISBN-13: 978-1-4328-4898-9 (hardcover)

Published in 2018 by arrangement with Sourcebooks, Inc.

Printed in the United States of America
1 2 3 4 5 6 7 22 21 20 19 18

For Ed Bryant
We all miss you here

Come, dip on in
Leave your bones, leave your skin
Leave your past, leave your craft
Leave your suffering heart.
— JAMES, "SOUND"

■ ■ ■ ■ ■

PART I
ALICE

■ ■ ■ ■ ■

ONE

Thursday, October 15
Manchester, New Hampshire
Deep, deep in the morning, sirens.

I peer out the window of my coffee shop, waiting to see the flashing lights, the blur of brilliant, pulsing red, the rush of an ambulance blistering toward the horrors of others. I see nothing, and the sound fades, as all eventually do. Perhaps it was never there at all.

"Miss?"

I snap my attention back to the man at the counter. Older man, salt-and-pepper beard, deep-green eyes, the color of jade. Charcoal suit, no tie.

"I'm sorry. What would you like?"

"Cappuccino. Small. To drink here, please."

His voice is deep. Enchanting.

"Of course."

When he hands me the crisp five-dollar

11

bill, I catch his stare, and his gaze is locked on me. There's an endless longing to it, as if I'm the ghost of someone he once loved. This has happened before.

"Can I get a name?" I ask, holding eye contact for only a moment.

He thinks on this for a moment, as if I've asked a deeply personal question.

"John."

I write this on a sticker and place it on the lip of a ceramic cup.

When I give him his change, he looks only at my hands. John takes his money and leaves my space as quickly as he entered it.

Sometimes I meet a person and my paranoia insists they already know me. Know everything. Where I live. How many scars I have. My real last name. It's a game my mind likes to play when it thinks I'm getting complacent, or cured. Happy, even. I meet people every day at the Stone Rose, the coffee shop I own. Customers rarely give me this feeling.

But John does. I dismiss it, knowing my past has chiseled and shaped my mind into something that favors fear over sense. Paranoia over logic. I take a deep breath, hold it to the count of four, then release. Repeat.

Sometimes this helps.

Two

Paranoia is also the reason I keep no knives in my house, which makes for practical concerns. My diet at home consists of things I can eat with a fork and spoon, and even when I want a slice of butter on my bread, I reach for an individually wrapped packet, the kind you find in restaurants. Spread it with a fork.

It sounds mad, I know. If someone wanted to hurt me, they wouldn't need to use a knife. On my dining room table alone are things that could maim or kill. Fork in the eye. Ceramic plate smashed over the skull. Wineglass, broken to a fractured stem, sliced across the carotid artery. Cloth napkin shoved down the throat, fingers used to pinch the nose shut. You might even argue that if someone wanted to stab me, why would they bother relying on *my* knife? Surely they would bring their own.

I'd tell you those are all reasonable points.

But I don't have to rationalize my horrors to you.

I pour another glass of merlot. The chicken on my plate is tender, and the tines of my fork slide easily into the spongy flesh. I've developed a friendship with the Hannaford Market butcher, and he always cuts my meat and poultry at the counter for me. His name is Jesus, and he's never asked me why I make this request. I plan on giving Jesus a nice tip at Christmastime.

I drop the fork, my appetite not reaching critical mass. The wall clock reads just past eight, and my stomach tightens at the thought of the coming night. Music from the little Bose player fills the room, but I hear the silence behind it, the vacuum that grows like a cancer as it draws closer to bedtime. In bed, the weight of the night will sit on my chest until it threatens to crush me altogether.

Sometimes I wish it would. Sometimes I fall asleep with that thought in my head, a wish for death, and there's a kind of dark peace to it all, like a shipwreck victim floating gently to the bottom of the ocean floor.

Dinner over, dishes done. My one-hundred-and-twelve-year-old compact colonial house is now as clean as it was one hour ago, things back where they should be, not a fiber or dust mote in sight. I straighten a picture on my wall that probably isn't even crooked. A photo I took of London a decade and a half ago. Street scene, at night, a couple on the sidewalk holding hands and looking into a dimly lit storefront. I was with my father that evening, just after he'd given me that camera for my birthday. It was the first photo I'd taken with it. I was thirteen.

I miss England sometimes — the smell of London, the aroma of time, moisture, and car exhaust swirled together in a blend only big cities can produce. But mostly I try not to think of the place I grew up. I almost died there when I was fourteen.

Beams from car lights sweep along my windows, temporarily highlighting my living room wall like prison searchlights. Richard must not be working the overnight shift at the hospital tonight. He rents the room on the third floor, above my bedroom. I call it the Perch. It has its own small kitchen, bath, and separate entrance, for which Richard pays me five hundred dollars a month. I rarely see him, and I won't deny he's somewhat odd, but he causes me no trouble, and his rent pays nearly a third of my mortgage.

There's a comforting energy to Richard, one I don't feel with many people, where having him living here makes me feel safe.

Well, perhaps not safe, but in some way less panicked. Knowing he's up there makes me feel less alone, I suppose.

The car door opens and closes, footsteps on the exterior stairs, upstairs door hinge squeaking, then silence. He's quiet as a cat. Never even a dribble of music, a foot stomp, or a squeaking bed. Sometimes I imagine that, as Richard passes the threshold into the Perch, he turns into vapor until sunrise.

In my room. Teeth brushed, flossed, gleaming to perfection. Pajamas of the flannel variety, which hang loosely around my thin frame. I haven't eaten enough, I know, and the hunger may wake me if I'm lucky enough to fall asleep. My hour at the gym this morning was intense, as it always is, and I haven't taken in enough calories to account for those I've burned. I'll eat more tomorrow.

I look down at my left arm, which is lean and toned, both bicep and tricep visible if I flex just right. I like what I've become on the outside. But as strong as I am and with all my training, the things with neither form nor mass scare me the most. Like silence. And memories. Nighttime.

If I had been stabbed during the day, would I dread the sunrise every morning, like a vampire? Maybe. But I wasn't stabbed

16

during the day. I was stabbed late on a half-moon night, a few days before Halloween. So I suppose all this wondering doesn't really matter for anything.

In bed. Grab my phone, which someone who has trouble sleeping shouldn't do. But my sleep issues go beyond my brain's reaction to a little glowing screen.

Facebook, Twitter, Pinterest, Instagram.

Two-second glances at unrestrained propaganda. The triumphant struggles of super-moms. The political rants. The photos of the perfect kids, the great vacations, the most exhaustive meals. It all makes me so sad, mostly because I don't believe any of it. But I also realize a lot of this is me, my cynicism. I rarely post but often lurk.

An email from my brother, Thomas. It's good to see his name in my inbox, the last name I used to have. I changed my last name from Hill to Gray when I turned eighteen, but just seeing his last name makes me think of the best parts of my childhood. Thomas is bitching about Mom. This doesn't surprise me.

I almost put the phone down and turn off the lights, but I decide to check my Blind-Date account. I signed up for the dating site a year ago on the advice of a friend who worried I would die from loneliness. She doesn't know about my past. She doesn't know the name Alice Hill, only Alice Gray. But I did sign up, checked it for about a week, then lost most of my interest. I've never been on a date through it but still stray back to check the activity every now and then. I don't know what I'm hoping for.

Now I scroll through a month's worth of matches, swiping them away like mosquitoes. But the last one freezes my fingertip in mid-rejection. I stare at the screen name, the man some algorithm has determined me to be compatible with. This match, this man, doesn't know my real name, just the random screen name I created a year ago. Perhaps he would recognize me from my profile photo, though I don't know how. I've changed so much since I was fourteen.

Still, his screen name glows at me, seeming to pulse like a heartbeat on the screen. I whisper it aloud just to convince myself it's real.

"Mister Tender."

THREE

Mister Tender made my father famous, at least among fans of graphic novels. My father wrote and inked them. Not comic books — never call them that. *Graphic novels.* My father created Mister Tender, and Mister Tender nearly killed me.

My father was the sole owner of Mister Tender. He wrote the stories, he drew the panels, inked the artwork, colored all the bold and beautiful violence. No one else helped bring that monster to life.

The Mister Tender series ended its run fourteen years ago, shortly after I was released from the hospital. There was no final volume, no end to the story. My father simply refused to ever draw that character again. He also refused all future royalties, assigning them to a local women's shelter, and shunned all interview requests. We never again said the name of that demonic bartender in our household, which we didn't occupy together all that much longer. Two years after the final image was drawn, my parents' marriage fractured, and my mother swooped up Thomas and me and moved us to the States. My father was left a shell of a man, riddled with depression, his hands bloodied in his own ink.

I visited him as often as I could, which wasn't enough. If it had been up to me, I would have chosen to live with my father, but a child has no recourse when the law proclaims a parent's right to custody as "untenable."

My father was stabbed to death three years ago in London by an Islamic extremist; this is, at least, the common belief, for the single eyewitness (an elderly pedestrian over two hundred feet away) described the assailant as having worn a black, robe-like outfit, which he referred to as "Muslim garb." The murderer was never caught.

Dad had very stupidly drawn a political cartoon showing Mohammed, and despite Mohammed having been made into a rather appealing figure, the cartoon was a death warrant. The murderer's blade pierced my father four times: twice in the chest, once in the stomach, and the fatal blow to the neck. So now, because God apparently finds such things amusing, two members of the Hill family have been brutally attacked with knives, and I stand as the lone survivor.

Mister Tender was a bartender — part human, part demon — and he was excellent at lending an ear to stories of woe. Then he'd convince his customers to do very bad things. The thumbnail image of him on my dating app is not a photograph of a real man but the character himself. Just the sight of him roils my stomach, even though, in truth, he's a beautiful creature. Thick, dark hair, swept back 1920s style; preternaturally smooth, white skin; strong, high cheekbones; dark, jade-green eyes, a gaze that pierces into your deepest, most hidden places. He'd fix that gaze on you as you slid up to the bar. Then he'd slide over a new cocktail of his own devising, a mixture of some unknown liquid, bubbling and smoking, a kaleidoscope of colors. As you considered the logic of actually drinking it, he'd lean over and, with just a touch of Cockney, say, *So, then, what's your fight against the world today, love?*

That's Mister Tender.

And Mister Tender always pours heavy.

My thumb twitches to delete the match suggestion, but I don't. I'm drawn to it, the way a person might reach out to open a closet door, checking for a hiding intruder.

21

I press on the link.

He has the same traits as my father ascribed to the character in his debut. Unknown age. Occupation: bartender. Likes: making wagers, watching people lose. Dislikes: teetotalers. Yet there's one bit about this Mister Tender's profile that is markedly different from his deceased namesake. The Mister Tender of my father's creation resided in the West End of London.

Here, on this little screen, Mister Tender lists his hometown as Manchester, New Hampshire.

Mister Tender has come to America to find me.

FOUR

Friday, October 16

The man in the gym keeps staring. He's in my direct line of sight as I do my lunges, but I look straight ahead. I'm a regular at Steeplegate Fitness — hell, I should have my name on the wall — and I don't get approached often. But I won't say it's never happened.

Real gym rats keep to themselves, and you can always tell them apart from the trolls. Rats have their routine, their headphones, their focus. They'll leave you alone, because *they* want to be left alone. Trolls, meanwhile, always have bad form and are prone to spending most of their time doing bicep curls and checking themselves in the mirror, secretly hoping you're paying attention to them. They'll slowly begin encroaching into your space, eventually finding some reason to say something to you. Usually something like "Are you a fitness coach? I could use some advice." Or "I haven't seen you here before. Is this your regular gym?" Once, someone walked up and asked me about my scars, which I don't always bother to conceal at the gym. I'm neither proud of nor ashamed of my scars; they are just a part of me.

My answer to the trolls is always the same. I remove one earbud, ask them to repeat the question just to make sure they haven't said something worth hearing, then tell them I would like to concentrate on my workout. If they press on, I tell them to fuck off.

This man sharks in a bit closer, eyeing the abductor machine next to me. He's stocky but not quite muscular, and his pajama-like sweats and T-shirt don't suggest the image of someone who frequents gyms often. Both of his ears are pierced and full of colored gems, which adds contrast to his smooth white face. He gives me a smile and a nod, which I ignore, and climbs into the machine. The abductor machine consists of two cushions that rest against your knees, and you can choose whether to open your legs out against resistance, or close them together against resistance. Either way, you're opening and closing your legs a lot, and I can feel him grunting next to me, knowing

24

he set the weight too high but is unwilling to stop and lower it. Perhaps his groin will tear.

I could move to another area of the gym, but I was here first. It's not my nature to yield ground.

I thumb the volume higher on my music.

Then he says something. *Goddamn it.*

I hear his voice but not the words. I ignore him, and as I'm in mid-lunge, he gets out of the machine and stands directly in front of me. My head is level with his waist, so I straighten. Sweat trickles down my forearms toward my hands, each of which is holding a fifteen-pound weight. He gestures for me to remove my earbuds.

For a moment, I fantasize about beating him senseless. He's got six inches and sixty pounds on me, but unless he has trained in MMA or boxing as much as I have, I could probably take him. I want him to give me a reason to sweep his legs out from under him.

I lower one weight to the floor and remove an earbud.

"What?" I say.

"You're Alice, right?"

I stare at him, unable to answer, because it all suddenly makes sense. It's my paranoid fantasy becoming reality: that some of the people you meet in the world already know you. Know every last detail about your life. Have been following you.

This must be Mister Tender from the dating site.

I drop the other weight and shift into a striking position. He holds up his hands.

"Hey, take it easy. We have a mutual friend. Jimmy. You remember Jimmy, right?"

I put my fists up.

Jimmy.

Yes, I remember Jimmy.

FIVE

If this guy found me, that means Jimmy knows where I am. I shouldn't be surprised; I didn't take great lengths to cover my tracks from my ex-boyfriend. He was never abusive, never threatened me, and there were actually elements of a sweet man in that junkie's body. I've had a total of three romantic relationships in my twenty-eight years, and the one with Jimmy was the longest and most recent. But I had to leave him, and I did so in the middle of the night. In the middle, in fact, of a drug deal gone terribly wrong. There were no goodbyes, and he's never tried to make contact with me since.

Back then, Jimmy and I were criminals. He probably still is.

"I don't keep in touch with Jimmy," I say, keeping my stance and fists in place.

"He didn't tell me you were this hot," the gym guy says.

I stay silent, eyeing his kneecap.

"No disrespect," he adds. "I'm just sayin'."

I was convinced I'd rid myself forever of Jimmy, but now it appears I was only in remission.

I put my earbud back in and turn away.

Then he lightly grabs my left arm to get my attention. Apparently, he thinks our conversation isn't done.

I spin and seize his throat with my right hand and grab his testicles with my left hand. I want to slam my heel into his kneecap, but we're not at that level. *Yet.* Instead, I squeeze with all ten fingers. He's immediately disabled, as if struck by lightning. Gasping, arms at his side. He could swing if he wanted to, and I'm prepared for that, willing to release to duck his fist. But he'll miss, and then he'll pay for that, too.

The music thumps in my ear, and I can't understand his desperate words, which suits me fine. I squeeze harder.

He collapses to one knee, and I finally release. As he looks up from the floor, his face is flushed, his eyes narrowed in pained rage. His moving lips leave little room for misinterpretation.

Fucking bitch.

Movement in my peripheral vision. I glance and see Samuel, one of the owners, rapidly closing in. I pop my earbuds out.

"Jesus, Alice, what's going on here?" He pronounces it *heyah,* more Boston than Manchester.

"This asshole grabbed me," I reply.

Sam glances at the man on the floor, comes very close to smiling, then looks back at me.

"I'd ask if you're okay, but maybe he's the one I should be asking. You want to call the cops?"

"No," I say.

He jerks a thumb at the man and says, "You, out of here, and no coming back."

"I was just trying to talk to her," the man says. "We have a mutual friend, and I wanted to ask her a few things."

"I don't care what you wanted," Samuel says. *"Out."*

The man doesn't protest. He rises, smooths his hair and shirt, then winks at me — not in a flirty way, but rather a shared-secret way. As if we're coconspirators and we're about to be taken into separate rooms for questioning, and he's telling me to just *go with the story.*

He turns and walks away, and as he does, he says something that gets lost in the clashing of weight plates on the other side of the

gym. But if I had to guess, I think he said:
See you soon.

Six

In 2003, we left Old England for New England. We left, in fact, the day after the courts granted my mother sole custody of my twelve-year-old brother and sixteen-year-old me. I was gutted to leave my father; it seemed I was the only person who didn't blame him for what happened. *He* didn't stab me, and he had no idea the character he created was going to be able to twist the minds of two disturbed teen girls.

His face when we left that day . . . God, I can still see it. In my whole life, I'd never seen such despair in someone's eyes. I used to dream of running away in the middle of the night and setting myself adrift on a raft, floating back across the Atlantic toward him.

We moved to Arlington, a snarky little suburb just outside Boston, all cramped in a flat too small to escape my mother's constant bouts of self-pity.

I spent two miserable years completing

my high school education in a Massachusetts public school. Friendships had already taken root years before my arrival, and there was little social room for the likes of a pale, scared, and scarred British girl who wore long sleeves on the hottest of September days. I was teased, called a freak. The more I hated school, the more I missed my father and blamed my mother for shoehorning me into a new world. And how I hated the sympathy she craved.

I don't like to discuss this much, she would tell anyone she had met for more than five minutes, *but poor li'l Alice, she's the victim of a horrible crime. Stabbed multiple times when she was only fourteen, poor, poor dear. And by two girls possessed by a cartoon character Alice's own father created. Let me tell you, it's no easy task raising a child with the issues you can only imagine she has. I never do get a break . . .*

When I turned eighteen, I was ready to leave. I had been accepted into a university in San Diego, which seemed wonderfully distant and exotic. It was to be my chance for a new start, one that I could do on my own terms. I fantasized about making friends, true friends, ones in whom I could confide. I thought about the beach, the smell of the sea. The sun tanning my pale skin. Of not being so conscious of all the scars I carried.

A month before I was to move to California, Thomas got sick. His world changed in a day, changing the rest of ours with his. I couldn't leave. I had to stay and help my fourteen-year-old brother. Medication after medication, none of which seemed to work for very long before Thomas would descend deep within his own world, a world of suffocating darkness that he would emerge from screaming and punching. Then he'd be perfectly fine for a spell, sometimes months. And then, not.

I remained in Arlington with my mother, who seemed constantly hanging on to life by her fingertips, and my brother, who at times frightened me. I studied general business at a community college and discovered fitness, but it wasn't long before I yearned for a more significant escape.

When I was twenty-one, I met Jimmy in a Boston bar and began my own descent into darkness.

As I walk, I scan the streets, wondering if Jimmy's 1970 charcoal Challenger will rumble and purr down the chilled asphalt, pulling alongside me. But the streets of Manchester are quiet this morning, and for a moment, I only hear the whisking of the fall breeze, which rattles crisp, fallen leaves and straightens the hairs on the back of my exposed neck. It's a three-block walk from the gym to the Stone Rose, a stroll characterized by a collection of hundred-year-old colonial homes, most of them decorated for Halloween. Shiny pumpkins and plastic bones.

I enter through the back of the Rose, the coffee and sweets shop I purchased two years ago with insurance and estate proceeds I received after my father died. I love my coffee shop. There is a good energy here, and within its walls, I have a community of employees and customers that makes me feel normal. In the end, I suppose feeling normal is the best anyone can hope for.

There are three knives in the Rose, because we sell pastries and some things that need cutting. My employees don't know my history, and I couldn't figure a logical explanation for not having knives in the shop, so I tolerate the few we have. But I never use them. I haven't picked up a knife in over a decade.

It's just after ten in the morning, and I spy a dozen or so customers, most of them regulars. I come in for about six hours most days, though I rarely open or close the shop myself. I leave that to my staff, who I try to

34

keep as happy as possible so they stay. There's one thing about a coffeehouse: people come for the faces as much as they come for the coffee. So I try to keep the same faces around.

The aroma of espresso calms me from my encounter at the gym, and as I walk behind the counter, I find myself steadied. Three years ago, fleeing Boston for Manchester, I never would have imagined myself trading heroin for coffee beans. If I look hard enough, I can still see track marks on my arms, like the faintest of ancient, dried riverbeds on a satellite photo of the desert. Funny, with all my fear of blades, I had no issue sticking myself repeatedly with needles. That's the power of the drug. The irony is that one of the reasons I left Boston was to get away from heroin, only to find Manchester steeped in it. But I'll never use again.

"Morning," Brenda says as she steams milk. She's been with me for the two years since I opened the Rose. She's a favorite with the customers and has called in sick only once.

"Good morning. Busy today?"

She shrugs and smiles. "Manageable." Brenda is two years younger than me and could pass for a modern version of Audrey Hepburn (if Hepburn were a crunchy liberal). It took me some time to pinpoint what makes Brenda so likable. It's the eyes. When she looks at you, you feel there's no one else she could possibly be more interested in talking to. Fixed, focused, unwavering gaze.

I tie on my purple apron and walk into the seating area, clearing cups and greeting my customers. Most of them know me, and I spend a few minutes of the usual talk with them. The weather is a favorite, especially as we crawl through the last months of the year. Charlie tells me the *Farmers' Almanac* calls for a hard winter. Charlie is a thousand years old and quotes the *Farmers' Almanac* like the New Testament. I don't have the heart to tell him I haven't the faintest clue what the *Farmers' Almanac* even is.

Maggie is nose-deep in her laptop, working on her book. It's either her second or third, and she writes cozy mysteries. I read her first one. I learned a cozy mystery involves a pleasant little murder framed around a lot of cooking and eating. Sometimes the book even gives you recipes. Kyle, armed with his computer and Bluetooth headset, is busy conquering the world of Manchester residential real estate. He greedily guzzles the free Wi-Fi and uses the Rose as his office three hours a day for the price of a large Americano. Jim and Linda sit next to each other and read their books in silence, which, I would suspect, is what most of their relationship consists of. Carla cradles a mocha and tells me her twin boys are dressing up as some Star Wars characters for Halloween. Some names with an abundance of vowels.

Then there's the man, the one from yesterday. John. Cappuccino. He sits in the best chair in the house, a tall-backed, velvet-lined beauty rescued from Craigslist and lovingly restored. It stands like a throne, giving those occupying it a full view of the Rose, small as my place is. He smiles at me, and I reply with a tight-lipped nod, and after a moment, he returns to his book. I push away the nervous edge I get from him, the sense he's watching me, but my paranoia at least seems justified given the events of the past day.

As I make my rounds of the room, John is the only customer I choose not to talk to.

My thoughts snap back to Jimmy. What he wants. I wonder if Jimmy *is* Mister Tender, trying to provoke me. If so, he's smarter than I ever would have credited him. Jimmy doesn't even know the real reason I have the scars, doesn't know anything about my father and his famous creation. I haven't told a single person the truth about my past since we moved to the States.

I head into my office, which is small but has a window looking out onto the street, giving the space a cozy light on all but the most dismal of New Hampshire days. Some prior tenant lined the walls in the office with dark wood paneling, and despite its ugliness, there's a tree-fort feel in here. It makes me feel safe. Protected.

I sit at my desk among the clutter of bills paid but not filed, free samples of coffee beans, a stray case of sugar packets, and a scattering of pens, paper, and notes to myself.

An envelope atop my desk catches my attention.

This wasn't here yesterday. White, thin, with *International Air Mail* blazoned in a red font on the side. My instinct tells me it's some kind of literature from a European purveyor of coffee beans looking to expand overseas. Sometimes I get these. The small wholesalers representing boutique coffee plantations are too expensive for the big boys — Starbucks, Peet's, Dunkin' — so they target the higher-rated independents, like the Stone Rose.

But I've never received a parcel from a

purveyor where my name and address are handwritten in exquisite calligraphy. I look at the return address. No company or personal name. Just the words *London, England.*

England.

I pick it up, suddenly not having a good feeling about this at all. Last night, Mister Tender came to me, and today, Jimmy resurfaced in my life via a creepy proxy. Now I have a mysterious envelope from the city I limped away from years ago. At least the name on it is my new one.

I take a pair of dulled scissors and tear along the top of it. The envelope has the weight and shape of a children's book: hard, square, thin. As I pull out the contents, I realize my guess is right. It *is* a book, and I see colors emerge as I slide it out from the envelope.

There is no correspondence. There is only the book.

I drop it immediately on the top of the desk as if it bit me. In a way, I suppose it did.

The cover shows the bartender who destroyed me throwing back a shot of what looks like blood. He laughs as he tilts his head back, and some of the shot misses his mouth and streaks the side of his face. He

looks like a fucking jackal.
  The title is simple.
   Mister Tender: Last Call

SEVEN

This is a book that does not exist.

After my attack, my father put away all the inks and pens that went into the bartender's journey to fame and never created another panel with Mister Tender in it. The carnivorous graphic-novel fan community screamed for more, wanting to know how the artist would treat the story line when life not only imitated his art, but nearly killed his daughter in the proccss. Reporters from around the world clamored for the exclusive interview, but my father never spoke of what happened to me. Thousands of pounds were thrown at him to create one last book where Mister Tender could be held accountable for his crimes, but my father refused. Mister Tender simply ceased to exist.

As I reach out to touch the book, I have the sense I'm being watched, as if someone wants to see my reaction to this exact moment. I look out the window of my small office. All I see is an empty street. Red and orange leaves litter the sidewalk beneath bony, barren trees.

I leave the book on my desk and go out to Brenda.

"The envelope in my office. Did you put it in there?"

She looks up at me and squints in confusion. "Envelope? The one with the nice writing?"

"Yes. That one."

"Came in yesterday's mail. About an hour after you left. Why, what's wrong?"

"Did you have to sign for it? Was there anything else with it?"

"No, it just came with the rest of the mail. Just catalogs, mostly. It's all on your desk. Was I not supposed to put it in there?"

"It's fine," I say. "I'm just trying to figure out who sent it, is all."

"Alice, you look shaken up. What was in the envelope?"

It's just a book that shouldn't exist and probably came from Hell. That's all.

"It's nothing." Then, I amend the answer. "Well, it's actually something bothersome, to be truthful. But I don't really want to discuss it."

"Okay," she says, giving me my space.

Damn it. I want to tell someone about my past, about what happened when I was fourteen. About the things I did when I was with Jimmy. About my sleepless nights, or trying to cook dinner without a knife. But I shove everything down, cramming it smaller and denser, deep within my chest, and now it's all but collapsed into itself, creating a black hole so strong, the truth can never escape. I tell no one, and the worst part is I don't even understand why.

I go back to the office and eye the book from the doorway. Should I take it to the police? Have it fingerprinted? That glossy cover would be a perfect flytrap for prints. But my instinct tells me whoever did this wore gloves. Meticulous. Careful. Just like the handwriting on the envelope.

I won't deny I want to look at it, crack its spine and see what horrors wait inside. But I also know that whatever is on the pages in this book, once I look, it can never be unseen. Whatever is inside will forever be in my mind. And since I constantly struggle against triggers of panic attacks in my daily, routine life, I can only imagine what will happen when I read this book.

I should toss this thing directly in the waste, but I don't. I shouldn't look inside, but I know I will. But I won't look at it alone. I shove the book into my purse.

It's been two weeks since I've seen my mother and Thomas. They're less than an hour away, but it feels like worlds separate us. Despite all the things wrong with my family, they know my history. I will look at this book with them.

I grab my purse, tell Brenda I won't be in the rest of the day, and walk home. As I climb into my Jeep, I look up in the sky and see the gathering white-and-gray clouds to the west. The forecasters were right.

There's something coming, and it'll be here soon.

EIGHT

I slow my car as I turn onto Webcowet Road in Arlington, the small Boston suburb just northwest of the city. There is a quiet here that seems unnatural, as if a glass cake cover has been lowered over this suburban neighborhood. Sometimes when I come here, this quiet is embracing and comforting. Other times, it's oppressive and suffocating. There is no middle ground here. This is where my mother and brother live.

Gone is the cramped flat in which I spent my high school years, replaced with an oversize, four-bedroom home purchased with my father's insurance money. Though he cursed my mother for taking his children from him, my father still carried over two million pounds in life insurance, and after Thomas got sick and couldn't be trusted to care for himself, my father included her as a beneficiary.

Thomas and I also received proceeds from

my father's estate — Mister Tender money, ironically — and I used my share to purchase the Stone Rose. My mother manages all of Thomas's money, since he has little interest in doing anything but sitting in his room, playing video games all day.

I pull into the driveway and get out of the car. The air seems heavier here, and sometimes I think that's due to the few thousand bodies buried in my mother's backyard. From her patio, I could throw a rock over the fence and hit a grave in Mount Pleasant Cemetery, and on occasion, I have done just that. Some people think a cemetery is peaceful and a good place to go for a spell to think. I never have. I don't need my thoughts surrounded by ghosts any more than I need knives in my kitchen drawers.

I walk the steps to the porch and hear the shouting. Mostly muffled behind the old house walls, but it's definitely her. She's shouting at Thomas, which, while not unusual, tightens my skin every time I hear it. I hear snippets of her tirade, chunks of anger like *You can't do anything!* and *If it wasn't for me . . .*

Normally I walk right in, but I don't want to walk into this. I tend to allow her these episodes, and by *allow* I mean stand by and simmer inside as she vents all her anger on my twenty-four-year-old brother, who seems perpetually on the cusp of being able to care for himself but somehow never makes that final leap. If he were fully mentally disabled and completely dependent on her, I wouldn't stand for any of her verbal abuse. But Thomas is more like a fourteen-year-old trapped in a man's body. So when she unleashes on him, it's like she's yelling at a sullen teen, and somehow that becomes acceptable to me.

Or perhaps I'm a coward. After all, I'm the one who finally moved out so I wouldn't have to hear it all the time.

There's a ccase-fire in the shouting, so I take a long, meditative breath and open the door.

"Hello? Mom?" When I was a child in England, I called her *Mum.* I have since dropped that and many other terms.

I stand in the entryway and listen. It's coffin-quiet in the house.

A little louder. "Mom? Thomas?"

Footsteps. A door opening upstairs.

"Alice, dear, is that you?"

I want to ask her what other woman would be shouting out *Mom* to her, but I simply call out, "Yes."

Seconds later, she races down the stairs. Well, more like lumbers. My mother is not a small woman. She's enlarged since moving to America, as if taking advantage of the greater land mass here.

She comes to the door, gives me a smothering hug, then pulls back and studies my face.

"Darling, is everything all right? What's wrong? Why are you here?"

"Everything's fine," I say. "I just wanted to see you."

She holds my face as if I'm a child, then tugs down beneath my right eye with her thumb. "You're not using, are you? Please tell me you're not on that awful poison again! My heart couldn't bear it."

"No, Mom, I'm not. Really." She asks this from time to time, usually in those rare moments when I feel the need for her emotional support. "I just . . . needed to see you. How are you?" I nod upstairs to where the shots were fired just moments ago.

She exhales so loudly, it seems as if it's her last breath ever.

"I'm just tired, Alice. Thomas has been *so* spotty today and won't let me do anything. I was just upstairs trying to get him to take his medication, and he just sits there like a zombie in front of his Xbox, killing things. It's not right, Alice. It's not right. Bloody games."

I read the barely concealed subtext here. *Since you've moved out, I have to deal with him alone.*

But I didn't come here to let her guilt-trip me.

"Mom, you need help. I always tell you that, but you never do anything. Even when I lived here, you barely let me help."

She scoffs at this. "The last few years you were here, you weren't ever around. You were always with Jimmy."

She pronounces it *Jeh-may.*

"Mom, you can leave Thomas alone for a while. He's perfectly capable of taking care of himself."

"He needs me, Alice. And he needs his medication. If I'm not here, he won't take it."

"And you need your sanity. Why don't I stay here today? Go see a movie. Go shopping."

I'm actually excited by the idea. I'd rather look at the book alone with Thomas anyway.

"No, dear. I've got too much to do. Maybe another time. You should really ring first before you come over."

I want to pound logic into my mother with a sledgehammer, yet I remain silent. I want to tell her she doesn't have to be a martyr. But the truth is, she was born to play that role, and if she didn't have Thomas to take care of, she'd find something else. Self-induced stress is her fuel.

"You just . . ." I don't quite know how to say this, so it comes out exactly as it formed in my head. "You don't seem happy with life."

"What?"

"We all struggle, Mom. But there should be room for happiness, right?"

I mean these words as an honest reflection, but the way her eyes narrow tells me she's taken this as an insult.

"I used up my allotment of happiness a long time ago," she says.

"God, that's depressing."

"My role in life is as a caregiver, not a frivolous harlot bouncing around from one party to the next."

"Who's talking about parties? I'm just saying you could use a break."

"Idle hands are the devil's workshop."

I've touched on something here.

"Are you saying you don't trust yourself to be happy?"

She inches closer and assesses me. "We're not all that different, you and I," she says, which I think is meant as a barb. "We don't do well without focus and direction. When you became aimless, you ended up addicted to heroin, now didn't you?"

"I wasn't aimless. I was damaged."

"We are *all* damaged, Alice. Just in different ways." She wipes her hands on her hips. "Now let's stop talking about me needing a break when there's work to be done."

"I'm just trying to help, Mom. You should let me."

She smiles at me, and her eyes almost disappear into her fleshy face. "You've enough going on with your little coffee shop and all. You're not working today?"

The conversation has now shifted, and suddenly I'm aware of the purse over my shoulder. I reach in and hand her the book.

"This came in the post for me. From London."

She looks at the cover.

"Oh my God," she says. "Who sent this to you?"

"I have no idea. There wasn't a note. Have you ever seen it before?"

She doesn't answer. She doesn't even open the book. She's transfixed by the bartender staring directly into her eyes.

Then, another voice. It comes from Thomas, who looks down on us from the second floor.

"I have."

NINE

When Thomas's medical problems began at the age of fourteen, we all thought he had the flu, a heavy malaise that kept him in bed for several days. To be honest, I didn't think too much of it at the time, or bother to wonder why the flu was going around in the summer. I had turned eighteen, just finished high school, and was three months from moving to San Diego. I was going to be on my own, far away from the small, dark Arlington flat that always smelled vaguely of decay.

On the fifth day, we took him to urgent care. The doctors noticed the red welt on the side of his thigh and quickly confirmed Lyme disease, most likely from the woods nearby. Not uncommon, they told us. Should be better with a potent course of antibiotics, they said. Only Thomas never really got better.

He seemed all right for a while, but in the

final month before I was due to go to California, he took ill again. The malaise returned, followed by horrible digestion issues, compounded by night terrors. My mother took him back to the doctor, who said it could be side effects from the Lyme disease and ordered another round of antibiotics. After that round, Thomas physically rebounded, but he was never the same person again. He grew sullen, and not just in a teenager way. Distant, brooding, prone to intense focus on one thing (like video games) while shutting out the world around him. He slept twelve to fourteen hours a day, barely ate, lost weight he couldn't afford to lose.

My father came out to see him, a painful experience for all of us. My mother barred him from the house, and Thomas barely expressed interest in his presence, so I was the only one who spent time with him. He stayed in a nearby hotel for three days, and we had dinner each night. I had visited with my father often since moving to the States, and this was the first time I struggled to find things to talk about with him. We had both changed. I remember my father brooding during his stay, angered at being so close *to* his family but unable to be a part *of* it. He cursed my mother, just once, but that was once more than I had ever heard before.

I remember that moment so clearly. He took me out to dinner, and after ordering, he looked up from the table and said to me, "Alice, you've suffered more than anyone ever should, but I hope you never know what it's like to have your children ripped from your chest by the fucking devil." His eyes had such sadness in them, and he said nothing more on the subject. We ate that night in a thick and dreary silence, with one notable exception.

"I wish I could live *now,*" he said, tossing his napkin onto his empty plate.

"What do you mean?"

"*Now.* Right now. Not in the past. Not thinking about anything else. Just here. You. This." A considered pause. "Forever."

"I don't understand," I say.

But I did understand. He wanted a life without a past — something I'd been chasing since I was fourteen. I remember thinking, *All these broken little people wishing for their bits to be glued back together.*

There was little else spoken between my father and me. At the end of his stay, he gave me money and told me to get Thomas properly diagnosed.

I handed the money to my mother and relayed his wishes, to which she simply said,

"He doesn't know the first thing about protecting his children." But my mother did take Thomas to a specialist, who claimed his symptoms were likely a mixture of his hormones and mild neurological side effects that sometimes accompany Lyme disease. The symptoms should subside.

So we were told.

Thomas was no longer the little brother I knew. He'd turned into a different person, an angry boy who didn't want to be cared for or to care for himself. He seemed unmanageable, and my mother was unwilling to seek any extra help. She pleaded with me to stay, just for a little while. *Maybe a year,* she said. *That's all, until we get things straightened out with Thomas. San Diego won't be sinking into the ocean anytime soon.*

I reluctantly agreed, and that one year turned into many more, and I eventually traded the idea of San Diego State for Bunker Hill Community College.

Now, Thomas stares down at me from the second-floor balcony, the look on his face a smug knowingness.

"I've seen it before," he repeats. His British accent is more faded than even mine.

"What is it?" I ask.

"Hello to you, too, Alice."

"Thomas. *Hello.* Now, what is this?"

He shuffles down the stairs, his hair an unruly mess of tangles and clumps. He wears a T-shirt of some death-metal band I'm grateful not to know, and sweatpants cling lightly to his bony hips. In the last three years, he's been officially diagnosed as having bipolar schizoaffective disorder, which, without his meds, can result in delusions, hallucinations, manic and depressive episodes, and potentially suicidal behavior. I look at him as he ghosts closer to me, wondering which, if any, of these things he might be experiencing in this moment.

Thomas takes the book from my mother's hands.

"It's the final book," he says. "I don't think he ever completed it."

"There was no other book," I say. "He stopped drawing."

Thomas shakes his head. "That's what he told you. What he told everyone. But I saw it right before we moved." He looks over at my mother and tilts his head. "Remember that fun period of time?" he asks her. "I was eleven, and you told me my father tried to kill my sister, and we had to leave. Not just leave him . . . We had to leave the fucking country. Remember that, Mom?"

"You watch your insolent mouth, Thomas," she says. "I never claimed he tried

56

to do any such thing. But he did create . . . *this.*" She points at the book like a prosecutor spotlighting the defendant. "He created the story that nearly killed her. He was not a *fit* father."

Thomas laughs and runs his hands though his hair. "Jesus Christ. How is it that I'm the least crazy person in this room?"

"Thomas —"

He suddenly screams, his lips gnarled in rage. "*He* didn't stab her! She was attacked by two psychopathic teenage girls — her *friends* — as some kind of tribute to a work of fiction! And you yanked us away from him because you had to blame someone else after the girls went to prison!" His expression falls flat, as if he's an actor breaking character. "Well, he's dead now. So I suppose it all worked out in the end. You have nearly all his money, and he's six feet under. You have *officially* won."

She turns to me. "Do you see what I have to live with? Every day. I give every ounce of my soul to my sick boy, and he turns on me like a rabid dog every bloody chance he gets."

"Why do you hate him so much?" I ask.

"What? Don't be mad. I don't hate your brother."

"No. *Dad*. You always hated him so much."

She snorts. "Because of what he created. It destroyed our family."

"No," I say. "Even before that. I remember all the times the two of you fought, ever since I was little. You were never happy together. Why did you even stay married?"

Maybe my system is jolted from everything that's happened, but I shock myself with my own question. I've never asked about this before. But I truly want to know, and though my words are soft and earnest, she tenses as if cornered by a pack of wild dogs.

"Don't tell me I was never happy. You don't know what my marriage was like."

"Because you never talk about it. You both just seemed miserable all the time."

She takes a deep breath, bracing herself against a growing anger. "There were happy times," she says, her words clipped and brittle. "In the beginning. But we . . . grew apart quickly."

Her previous words ring back to me. *I used up my allotment of happiness a long time ago.* I've almost forgotten about the book. I truly want to know the answer to this question: "So what happened?"

Her eyes narrow and her face relaxes, and I sense she has a very specific and truthful answer to my question. But then her expression suddenly reverts to her default cloak of haughty defiance, as if deciding I don't deserve the truth.

"We had a family," she says. "That's what happened. We had *you,* and that meant responsibility. I could handle all that responsibility, but your father couldn't. I had to do everything."

"Oh, for fuck's sake," Thomas says. "What a load of horseshit. He was a great dad."

She turns to him, her face so red, I think the top of her head may explode open with spewing lava. But she doesn't yell. Her voice is a shaking whisper, which makes her all the more frightening. "Thomas, you will *not* use those words in this house, and you will treat your mother with *respect.* You're a wicked, ignorant boy, and you wouldn't even be alive if it weren't for me."

"Exactly," he says. "That's why I resent you."

I need to stop this. I wanted even the smallest insight into my mother's past, but I've just made things worse. "Thomas," I say. "Enough with the arguing, *please.* Can you just tell me about that?" I point to the book, which is still in my brother's hands.

It takes him a second to pull his anger away from my mother, but Thomas finally opens the book and studies the panels. Suddenly I'm itching all over to see it, panic attacks be damned. "I never actually saw the book," he says. "Just that cover art. In Dad's study, about a week before we moved out."

"You never told me," I said.

"Of course not. He said he'd never draw Mister Tender again, and then he did. I didn't want to give you a reason to be angry with him."

"She already had *plenty* of reasons to be angry with him," my mother says.

"Mom, *stop*. Dad loved me. He didn't want any of this to happen."

"Yet he had to keep drawing, didn't he?" She shakes a meaty finger at the book Thomas holds. "He said he never would, and look what we have right here. He couldn't *help* himself."

"It's the final book," Thomas says. "I asked him about it the day before we moved out. Told him I saw the cover. He actually cried." Thomas's voice is suddenly so, so soft. "He said it was something he wanted to do to help him process what had happened to Alice, but he told me he only drew a few panels." Thomas looks up from the book, and for a moment, his eyes are perfectly clear, free from the clouds of medication and the blackness of judgment. They are sad, beautiful eyes, a deep, soulful brown. He says, "He was a good man. He didn't deserve what happened to him."

"No," I say, "he didn't." And for that moment, until I hear my mother release a frustrated sigh that snuffs the silence, Thomas and I are connected by an energy that is both tragic and lovely. It's been years since we've had three seconds like the ones that have just passed, and I fear it might be years until it happens again. Poor, poor Thomas, the river of his life run dry by the bite of a tick.

"He couldn't let it go," my mother says. "He could never let anything go, and he ended up getting killed over his stupid cartoons."

My father never drew graphic novels again, but he didn't give up his calling as an illustrator. In the last two years of his life, he worked for a political satire magazine with its office in the Southwark area of London. Three years ago, one of his colleagues, Brett Simonson, wrote a scathing essay about the disturbing trend of wealthy young London girls running away from home to Syria and joining ISIL, usually as sex slaves. My father illustrated the piece, which included a drawing of Mohammed looking down from the sky and weeping at the sight of Islamic extremists beheading Christians. The office received threats and

61

demands to take the piece off the website. Management refused, and my father had a quote in the *Guardian* about their stance.

We are equal-opportunity satirists. We target all races and religions, not just Muslim extremists. Why is it that these fanatics insist everyone in the world, most of whom are non-Muslim, follow the laws of their religion? A devout Jew couldn't care less that I, an atheist, don't observe the Sabbath. Why should these Muslims care if I draw a picture of Mohammed? Yet the world bows to their demands, time after time, because of fear. I say this: It's a cartoon. Relax.

It was the only time I ever recall my father referring to his work as cartoons. Two weeks later, my father was stabbed to death as he exited the office building. The perpetrator was never found, and no group ever claimed credit.

"Mom, stop, *please.*"

I often think that, in her own way, she's sicker than Thomas, infected with emotional extremes, ping-ponging constantly between illogical defiance, doting, enabling love, and miserable self-pity. Before she can launch into whatever tirade she has planned,

Thomas speaks first.

"There's an inscription," he says. "Look."

He hands me the book, and I look inside its pages for the first time. My skin is flushed with excitement, because no matter the origin of this book, there is a connection to my father here. And the connection is even more personal than I could have guessed, for on the title page just after the cover, there is indeed something written in ink. It's written, in fact, to me.

In my father's handwriting.

Alice, what did the penguin always tell you?

TEN

It's familiar.

It makes sense only in a vague, comfortable way. I *should* know what this means, but its meaning is just out of reach.

I look at the letters, the familiar half cursive, half print. The steady hand of an artist, the swirls of each *s,* the half-crossed *t*'s, the offset dots over each lowercase *i.* This is his handwriting, the ink patterns I've known since I was old enough to read.

If it didn't have my name on it, it would trouble me less. But he wrote this to me. The book was sent *to me.* By a man murdered three years ago.

Thomas takes it from me and holds the pages close to his face. My mother peers over his shoulder and reads the inscription aloud.

"What does that even mean?" she asks.

"I have no idea," I say.

"He's a loon," she says. "He always was.

What kind of sick joke is this?"

"Mom, stop."

"I will *not* stop, Alice. He's been dead for three years, and somehow he's arranged to have this sent to you from the grave?"

"That doesn't even make sense."

But she didn't hear me. "What a sick, sick man," she said. "Good riddance, is what I say. You should take that book and —"

"It's from our stories." Thomas says this as he continues to stare at the words on the page.

My mother snaps her head to him.

"What do you mean?" I ask.

He looks up at me, and I see life in his eyes, a liveliness most often buried deep inside him.

"Remember, Alice, when we were kids? The stories he used to tell us? Chancellor's Kingdom?"

Chancellor's Kingdom.

"Yes," I say, finally making the connection. "I remember."

As children, Thomas and I shared a bedroom, and each night at bedtime, my father would tell us a story. He never read us books; the stories we heard were the ones he made up on the spot, the most epic of which was about Chancellor's Kingdom, a faraway world throughout which little Alice and her younger brother Thomas journeyed on the back of an impossibly gigantic penguin. Every night was a new adventure, and as much excitement as Alice and Thomas had in discovering this world, all they really wanted to do was come home to their parents.

But there was always an obstacle, a challenge to overcome, an enemy to defeat. The story took months to tell, all revealed in fifteen-minute chunks every night. Shortly after the story ended, after the fictitious Alice and Thomas found their way safely home again, the real Alice and Thomas moved with their parents to a new house, one a few streets away, next to Gladstone Park. That house was bigger than the previous one. Thomas and I got our own rooms. We never heard of Chancellor's Kingdom again.

"The penguin," Thomas says. "What was his name?"

"Ferdinand," I reply, the ridiculous name immediately coming to my lips after years of dormancy. "The penguin's name was Ferdinand. And he was twelve feet high and was all white, with only wisps of black at the ends of his wings. And he could fly."

Alice and Thomas rode on Ferdinand's back high into the skies above London, just as Wendy, John, and Michael had soared after Peter Pan. But the similarities between Neverland and Chancellor's Kingdom had ended there, and although the former had plenty of scenes of action and suspense, it was nothing compared to the darkness my father could command. Chancellor's Kingdom contained entire cities of ruin, graveyards with the bodies of heroes only mostly buried — heads rising above the dirt — and a vast amusement park full of flesh-eating zombies. My father's stories always enthralled and frightened me, and I sometimes wonder how life would have turned out had he just been content penning a trite and toothless Sunday comic strip.

Then another jolt of a memory. Mister Tender *was born* in Chancellor's Kingdom. He lived as a character in my bedtime stories before making the leap into the world of graphic novels, evolving from the stories meant to put me to sleep.

"Alice, dear, you look ill," my mother says. She gives my arm a little squeeze, more of a pinch, just below the elbow. "Let me get you some tea."

She leaves the room, and Thomas says, "Do you understand what he wrote? What did the penguin always tell you?"

I do remember now. I can hear him saying

the words, and my father always used an almost-American accent when speaking as Ferdinand. Several times, in situations when Alice and Thomas were about to face a rather tense situation in Chancellor's Kingdom (which was almost every night, because Dad knew how to pace a story), Ferdinand would look down at them with a very serious face and say, *Now then, if you get the sudden urge to start trusting someone, be smart and do away with it.*

Ferdinand never wanted us to trust anyone. One time, the Alice of the story asked Ferdinand why, if that was his advice, should they indeed be trusting him, to which Ferdinand simply replied, *Perhaps you shouldn't be.*

I go back to the beginning of the book, turning each page with care. There's the title page with my father's inscription. A blank page follows. Then another title page, this one with a more demanding font, with the words *LAST CALL* stretching side to side. No publisher information, no copyright date. But at the bottom of the title page, in a font so miniscule, I have to bring the book close to my face, there's a website address.

www.mistertender.com

Beneath the address is a single word: *gladstone.*

Nothing else.

The scent of the book hits me. It's so familiar. It makes me think of my father's office, of those times he'd receive boxes of his advance copies. He'd open them up, and the room would fill with the incense of fresh ink and binding glue. The heady scent of glossy art.

I now realize I've already forgotten about getting fingerprints on the volume; we have all now handled the book. My second realization has a more visceral impact, because I flip through to the next few pages and see they are completely blank. Is there some kind of hidden ink I need to detect, or is this just an extension of a cruel joke? Why bother setting a hundred blank pages into a bound volume?

But the following page isn't blank. I recognize the characteristics of my father's art: bold, straight strokes; angular, shaded faces. White eyes, no pupils. The first panel is a double panel, stretching from one side of the page to the other. There are a little boy and a little girl, and they cling tightly to the back of a penguin, a miraculously large and airborne penguin, which descends into a heavenly plane of clouds holding gleaming white castles.

This is not the usual gritty setting in which Mister Tender dwells. This is Chancellor's Kingdom. Thomas and I are those children, and that impossible penguin is Ferdinand. I read the perfectly straight lettering in the white dialogue box.

What is this place? the little version of myself says to Ferdinand.

This is Cloud City, he says. I remember now. Cloud City was the capital of Chancellor's Kingdom.

Why are we here?

Because, young thing, there's nowhere else to be at the moment.

I realize Thomas is now reading over my shoulder, and I turn my head just enough to see his face. He looks desperately tired, but I think there's more than just fatigue in his eyes. The inception of tears.

The next panel shows Ferdinand landing on a cloud, and a rat in an immaculate yeoman warder uniform stands guard before an unwelcoming spiked steel gate.

"I remember the rat," I say.

"Me too," Thomas whispers.

The rat challenges Ferdinand with a riddle, which must be answered to gain entrance.

Step aside, Ferdinand says. *I've no time for*

your puzzles. Can't you see I'm carrying precious cargo?

The rat draws his sword.

Look out! little Thomas yells.

Then, with one swoop of his wing, Ferdinand smacks the rat, sending him sailing right off the edge of the cloud.

I turn the page. The three adventurers pass through the gates of Cloud City, and once again little Alice questions Ferdinand as to why they are there, and the penguin tells her they must find someone to help them get home. *That's the point of it all anyway,* Ferdinand says. *If you can't get home, why bother exploring to begin with?*

That page ends. The one adjacent to it is blank.

I flip past two, three, four more pages. They, too, are blank, and for a moment, I think my father's brief, incomplete story is a tiny, solitary island surrounded by empty, white gloss sheets. But then I turn to the next page, and this one is not blank.

Not at all.

As I take in the first panel, I can already tell something's a little off. It takes me a moment, but then I realize this is not my father's work. It is impressively close, and probably to the casual observer, the differences would be indiscernible. But I know how my father would hold his pens, the angles from which he approached every blank canvas, the trajectory of every stroke, and while the artwork here is a beautiful imitation, it is an imitation nonetheless.

The first panel shows a woman, who, despite the exaggerations of the face, is most clearly me. She's walking along the street at night, scarf snaked tightly around her neck, eyes down, her frame caught in the moment within a focused pool of street light. This light illuminates the thing in her hand, which, on closer inspection, is a movie ticket.

A wave of goose bumps peppers my arms.

The ticket displays the name of the movie.

I remember that movie. I saw it two weeks ago.

ELEVEN

My gaze sweeps the rest of the page, the other few panels.

I turn the page.

Blank.

They are all blank, the rest of the book.

"What is it?" Thomas asks. I can't tell what he's been able to see, and I snap the book shut.

"Nothing," I say.

My mother walks back into the room. "Give the tea a few minutes, then." She clearly sees the fear on my face. "What's wrong?"

If I tell her what I just saw in the book, she'll freak out. Perhaps even more than *I'm* freaking out, and I'm the one with panic attacks. Then she'll launch into a furious tirade against my father, worse than before, and I don't want that. This house is toxic, and I don't want to add to it.

"It's nothing," I say, a lie so obvious I

wonder why I bothered with it at all.

"Alice —"

"Mom, please, just let it go."

I shouldn't have come.

She looks at me, her small eyes set back in her meaty face. She wants to assail my father more, reminding me why she tore me from him. She wants to justify her actions, wants to remind me my only chance at normalcy is thanks to her. But, in a sweet and seldom moment, she doesn't. She lets it go.

Instead, she switches to small talk, her second language after her native language of complaint.

I last two more hours at the house next to the cemetery. Two agonizingly slow hours, and the whole time, my mind whirs about what I saw in the pages of that book. My mother carries on about things like Thanksgiving plans, a holiday we've adopted but that still feels like forced, manufactured happiness to me. I tell her, *Of course I'll be there.*

Finally I escape. On the drive home, I keep checking my mirrors, feeling as if a ghost has stowed away in my backseat.

As I pull up to the curb of my Manchester home, I feel pricks on my skin and cold metal in my stomach, like an impending flu just beginning to dig its claws into me. It's shortly after dusk, and the sky hangs heavy, barely holding in its guts. As I walk up the steps to my house, my tenant, Richard, descends the exterior steps from his upstairs unit. He's tall and gaunt, his shoulders perpetually slumped forward, a sunflower too heavy to keep its face skyward toward the sun. His hands are burrowed in his baggy jeans, and an Army coat wraps his thin frame. Richard is perhaps my age, but age is somehow difficult to guess on someone who rarely smiles. As he sees me, his dark eyes brighten a tad.

"Hey, Alice."

"Hi, Richard."

I'm in no mood to talk, which is fine since Richard rarely says more than *hello.*

But this time, as I pass him on the walkway to the house, he calls to me from behind.

"Are you okay?"

Pricks on my skin again.

"It's just . . ." He stammers to find his words. "You don't look great. I mean, you don't look *bad,* you just —"

"I think I'm coming down with something," I say. "I'm fine. Thanks."

He nods and then looks back to the ground, his black, stringy hair falling over his left eye.

"Have a good night," he says and keeps walking to his car.

"You too," I mumble.

Richard works mostly nights at Elliott Hospital as an RN. I'm happy to have him gone tonight, because I don't want him pounding on my door in concern if he hears me gasping for air or sobbing in exhausted fear.

I fumble with my keys and barely seem able to let myself in the door. The security system chirps its thirty-second warning, and I manage to punch in the code on the illuminated pad. I race to every light switch and flip them all on. Along the way, I drop the book on the kitchen counter, facedown.

Then the tingling begins in my fingertips, tiny stings of frozen extremities plunged into hot water. A sign of an impending panic attack. Sometimes I can force it down, but I have the sense this one has come to play. You can't battle a million firing synapses that force your brain to relive suffocating dark moments for hours on end. Well, actually, there is a way, and it's called medication. I've tried them all — legal and illegal alike — and have given up on every single one. Medication is life's CGI — a fancy trick that makes everything beautiful and surreal, yet astoundingly flat and hollow.

The attack barely even bothers flirting with me. I'm in my kitchen when I get a stronger sense of it creeping up on me, like a ghost that just passed through the nearby wall and into the room. I cannot hurt this thing coming for me; it can only hurt me. All I can do is suffer its blows and assure myself I'll come out the other side. Sometimes, I don't want to come out the other side. There are times when I want to be swallowed by it and suffocate into sweet nothingness inside its belly.

My breathing tightens. A thousand pounds of memories crushing me, forcing the air from my lungs and keeping me from taking in any more. *I'm dying.* It's always my first thought, though I've been having these attacks since I was fifteen. I always get a chance to breathe again, but I never know how long this monster will sit on top of me before finally letting up.

My skin starts to burn. Eyes squeeze closed. I fall to the hardwood floor of my living room and stretch my arms above my head. Sometimes this helps.

Breathe, Alice.

But I can't. I'm helpless against the thoughts in my head. I desperately try to relax, but desperation never begets any kind of peace. I tell myself I'm safe, that this can't hurt me, but it does no good.

This is happening; I'm beyond the point of stopping it. I will go through this as I always do, immersed and yet detached from it. Acute, prolonged horror peppered with chunks of missing time, moments where my mind shuts down entirely.

My scars pulse with heat. I struggle to still my mind and count them, because even counting can help. *One, two, three* on the back, *four* on the left shoulder, *five* on the forearm, *six* on the clavicle —

And then I see them, as I always do. Sylvia and Melinda Glassin, the twins who wanted to walk me home through the park that night. It's all here, playing in my mind like a movie I've watched a thousand times. Gladstone Park. The little bridge over the creek. All the twins talk about is Mister Tender. How handsome he is. How he can fulfill wishes.

I tell them he's just a character. Make-believe.

It's so dark that I can't see Sylvia's hands, but I know what she is holding. She attacks me first, from behind, and she cries out as the knife blade slips so easily into my buttery, fourteen-year-old skin.

On the floor of my house, I open my eyes and manage to suck in the smallest pocket of air. It's not enough, but it's a start. It's a sign I will at least survive tonight, but not before Sylvia and Melinda have their way with me. I have never been able to stop them, not even with the medication. But I have learned how to dull my mind against their faces, harden my skin against their blade. I look at the faux antique clock on my wall, its bronzed second hand ticking at a glacial pace. I count the seconds, knowing they will turn into minutes, and praying the minutes won't turn into hours.

There's nothing in this world more trapping than one's own mind.

Forty-two minutes later, the initial rush of ease sweeps through me. It's delicious morphine signaling the worst is over. I'm on the floor, stripped to my bra and underwear, slicked in sweat and tears, my paper-white skin splotched in heat rashes, my heart beating as fast as a hummingbird's wings. The shortest attack I've had lasted seven minutes, the longest nearly three hours, and I'm grateful this one leaned toward the merciful.

I peel myself from the hardwood floor, noticing the sheen from my body's imprint as I stagger to my feet. I feel like I've gone eight rounds in a cage match, and now all I want to do is sleep.

The book is on the kitchen counter where I left it. I reach to it with weak limbs, lift it with shaking hands. Turn it over, look at the cover, open and turn to the inscription.

Alice, what did the penguin always tell you?

"Don't trust anyone," I say. I turn the page over, and I imagine my father's cologne as I turn to the first bursts of color.

I thumb past my father's artwork and get to the second story, the one responsible for tonight's attack. The imposter's artwork. Again, the first pane, the one of me clutching a ticket to a movie I saw just two weeks ago.

I inhale deeply, count to four, hold my breath, count to four again, and exhale, count to four. Repeat. Repeat. Repeat. Sometimes this helps.

The second panel depicts me sitting at my kitchen table. Nighttime. I stare off into nothing, my face a blend of fear and gut-stabbing loneliness. A glass of red wine sits in front of me. The rest of the bottle is close by.

It's the third and last panel that gets me the most. It shows me sleeping in my bed, and the clock on the nightstand reads just after two in the morning. The details of my room are exactly as they truly exist: same bedside table, same lamp, same artwork on the walls. Even my comforter is correct in its pattern detail. This is my cold-weather comforter, which I just brought from the closet to my bed earlier this month. And perhaps most unnerving of all, the point of view of this scene is not from my bedroom window, but rather on the opposite side of the room, near the door, as if the artist came into my house, up the stairs, and into my bedroom. Drew me as I slept. I realize a person wouldn't actually have had to be standing in my doorway to capture these details; they could have just looked in my bedroom window and imagined the perspective. Still, the choice to draw the point of view from inside my house is especially unnerving.

Whoever did this was able to find these lost panels of my father's work, the only depictions of Chancellor's Kingdom that exist, and append them with their own copycat art. Moreover, whoever sent me this book is clearly watching me. Following me. I arm my security system every night, so I'm certain no one is standing in my bedroom as I sleep. Yet someone still knows the intimate details of the room itself.

The name *Jimmy* pops in my head, but again I can't make sense of any connection. I would never credit him with the creativity and skill needed to accomplish sending me a hand-drawn graphic novel postmarked from England. Jimmy is a criminal and a heroin addict, or at least he was when I left him. He's back in my mind, but it's a stretch to title him Mister Tender.

And then there's the creep from the gym.

I set the book down, labor upstairs, and crawl into bed, reaching over and turning off the lamp before collapsing my head onto the pillow. I grab my cell phone and launch the security system app. In it, I can see all the events for the last thirty days. Anytime I armed or disarmed the house, any time movement was picked up by a motion sensor. I look at each event and try to correspond with what I remember but quickly get lost. I can be up at all hours, so I can't be certain if a motion sensor event was me or not. But nothing sticks out as unusual. And the arming and disarming events correlate with what I recall of my daily routine.

From the app, I arm the system for the night, then pull up my sheets and close my eyes.

I keep the light on.

It will be some time until sleep comes tonight, if at all.

TWELVE

Saturday, October 17

Morrissey bleats about horrible loneliness as I drag myself through the back entrance of the Rose. The Rose features music primarily from Manchester (UK) bands. A typical lineup playing over the sound system includes the Smiths, James, Oasis, Joy Division, and of course the shop's namesake: the Stone Roses. Once in a while, you might even hear the Bee Gees in my coffeehouse. Yes, even the Bee Gees hailed from Manchester.

I remove my coat, which is freckled with the corpses of a thousand melted snowflakes. An early snow, the first of the year, and it's just beginning. At least four inches have already fallen, and there's plenty more to come. The chill stays with me.

I pass my office and glance at the desk, relieved no new envelopes are waiting for me. Behind the bar, Brenda writes the daily specials in different shades of chalk on a blackboard canvas. Next to the words, she's rendered a simple but beautiful image of a cappuccino: strong, bold strokes shaping the porcelain cup, a topping of creamy froth, wisps of steam. Brenda even designed the logo for my place, which depicts a red rose growing from within a coffee mug. She should be in art school, not working in a coffee shop.

She doesn't look up. "It happened again."

"Simon?"

"Yup."

"What was it this time?" I ask.

"Knocking on the ceiling."

"He likes you."

Simon is the ghost that supposedly haunts our building on Elm Street. I've never heard anything, but then again I'm rarely the one opening the shop at five thirty in the morning. That's left to Brenda, and she swears she hears footsteps, dragging sounds, knocking, and occasional indecipherable whispers. On one hand, I think, *Hell, the building is over a hundred years old. What do you expect?* On the other hand, Brenda is the only employee who's ever heard anything, and everything she describes is out of a clichéd ghost handbook, so maybe she's just a little bored. Looking for attention.

"There are four other references online to this building number and paranormal activity," she says, her gaze still glued to the phone screen.

"I know," I say, because she tells me this every time.

"You should add hazardous duty pay to my check," she says.

"Well, if Simon ever actually does something to you, I'll consider it."

"Someday you'll hear him."

"I hope so," I say, meaning it. I'm intrigued by the idea of ghosts. It's the living I do my best to avoid.

I notice the Band-Aid on her forearm.

"What happened?" I ask.

She shrugs. "Nail sticking out of the wall in my place. Little gash, not too bad."

Little gash, not too bad. I can't imagine.

The front door opens and two cats walk in. Teenage girls with heavy gray makeup, whiskers, cat ears and tails, and matching yellow cat backpacks. It's eight on a Saturday morning, and I'm guessing these two are just winding down from a Friday night costume party. Halloween is still nearly two weeks away, but I suppose some like to celebrate all month long. Cat One orders a latte, Cat Two a large coffee, no room for cream. They brush heavy, wet snowflakes from their leotard-clad arms.

Brenda sets about making their drinks as Dan walks in. Dan has worked here less than three months, and I'm doubting he'll make it to his fourth. He's only ten minutes late today, and he whisks past me, grabs his apron off the hook, and hurriedly ties it on as he steps behind the counter.

"Sorry," he says. "My phone died, so the alarm didn't go off."

"That's why you plug it in," I say.

"And the snow made things more difficult."

"Don't you walk here?"

He smiles and shrugs, and I decide at that moment he will have to go. I'm maybe five years older than him, and his sense of entitlement grates on me. He starts *oh my god the night I had*-ing to Brenda as I walk into the sitting area and wipe down the tabletops with a damp terry cloth. The two cats wait by the bar for their drinks, each still looking a bit drunk.

The door opens again, as it will many more times before the morning rush is over. Frigid air sweeps in and ices briefly around my neck. I turn my head and see him, the man from the gym, walking inside the coffee shop. *My* coffee shop. He ignores my gaze and heads directly to the counter.

Brenda looks up at him as she does everyone — with complete focus, attention, and interest — and it angers me, because this asshole doesn't deserve any of it.

He looks different, but perhaps it's because he's not in gym clothes. He looks bigger, fuller, more sure of himself. A leather jacket wraps snugly around his sturdy frame, and his hands are adorned with large gold rings, each of which gleams with shiny little stones. He looks taller than I remembered, over six feet for certain, but moreover he seems more of a threat. Maybe it's because he's so relaxed, so certain that walking in here is his right, that he can just saunter in and I'll say nothing.

He's wrong.

I approach him from behind, and he turns just as I near, sensing me. His sudden smile suggests he didn't know I would be here, that this chance meeting is a pleasant surprise. I don't buy it.

"Well, look who it is," he says. "Little Miss Kick-Ass." He holds up his hands in mock surrender. "No need to attack, darling. Just getting my morning caffeine."

"You need to leave."

He tilts his head just a fraction toward mine. "That so?"

"This is my place, and I don't want you here."

"Take it easy, pretty thing. I already paid for my drink. Should be up in just a moment."

Brenda looks at me, her wide eyes full not of fear, but of excitement. I've never kicked anyone out before.

"Give him his drink, and then he's leaving," I say.

Dan, pulled toward drama like a pig to truffles, walks over to the front of the counter. He says nothing but wants to watch everything.

"Sure thing," Brenda says, then tells Dan to fill a large decaf coffee.

"Thought you needed caffeine," I say.

"Well, now, maybe you caught me in a little lie," he says. He folds his arms across his chest, and his rings point at me. It's not hard to imagine them as little brass knuckles. "I actually lie all the time. I find it helps in life. Don't you find it's easier to get what you want when you lie, cheat, and steal, Alice?"

I backpedal a few paces, and he follows me, bringing the conversation away from my staff, who watch me with curious expressions. "You can tell Jimmy I don't want anything to do with him," I say.

He smiles. "You think Jimmy sent me?" he asks. "No, darling. No one sends me anywhere. I sent myself."

"What do you want?"

"You have no idea who I am, do you?"

"I don't care who you are."

For a moment, I picture his fists coming toward me, his golden knuckles smashing my jaw, splitting my head open. I take a step back, and he takes a step forward, but nothing in his stance suggests violence. Yet.

"I'm the guy you stole from," he says. "Three years ago. You remember that, don't you, sweetheart?"

"I don't know what you're talking about," I say.

But it's not true. I know exactly what he's talking about.

In early 2012, Jimmy taught me how heroin can transform pain to beauty, can create a new world of the mind, a place of infinite escape. All it took was that first bump, and I knew I'd never be at peace again unless I was high — and I'd do anything to keep it going. That included stealing from people who didn't care to be stolen from.

I hit bottom the night we stole nearly eight thousand dollars from Nick, our regular dealer. It was Jimmy's idea, and he'd been tipped by a mutual friend that Nick was carrying "excess funds" with him that night. I accompanied Jimmy to the deal, and any judgment I had was clouded by my overwhelming need to stick a needle in my arm as soon as possible. In the motel parking lot, Jimmy pulled a gun and held it to Nick's head, demanding the cash. Nick insisted he only had the drugs, nothing more. Then Jimmy lowered the gun and shot him in the stomach. I'm not even sure he meant to do it. But that's what happened.

It was the moment I woke up. That window was probably only going to be open for a few seconds, but for those seconds, I had a clarity birthed by fear, a fierce vision of my short and dismal future: if I stayed with Jimmy, I was headed for a certain, bleak death, if not at that moment, then soon. So I ran that night, fast and hard, away from Jimmy, away from the heroin. I sprinted out of that motel parking lot and never turned back, never saw Jimmy again, and never touched anything harder than alcohol since. I went to my mother's house in Arlington, back into her caring, suffocating arms. After three days of withdrawals, I knew rehab was the answer, despite my mother's insistence that only *she* could make me better. I checked myself into Column Health in Arlington and did my twenty-eight day tour, after which I refused my mother's offer to move back in with her and Thomas and opted for Manchester, a comfortable distance away from Arlington and that much farther from Boston.

"Alice, if you're going to lie, you need to do it a lot better than that. Otherwise, what's the point?"

I wonder if there's a gun beneath his jacket. Probably.

"I left that night. *I* didn't take anything. I don't know anything about what Jimmy may or may not have taken from you. I haven't seen him in three years. You need to talk to him, not me."

Right then, Brenda calls out his drink.

Freddy, large decaf.

He turns, walks a few steps back to the counter, and picks up his coffee. In that moment, both Brenda and Dan look over to me. I think, *What if this guy decides to pull a gun from his waist and start shooting everyone?*

Do I attack, call the police, or continue the conversation?

He turns and walks back to me, drink in hand. Unnervingly casual.

"So that's the thing," he says as he reaches me. "I *have* talked to Jimmy, and that conversation didn't go so well. My fault, really. It took me three years to find out who stole eight g's from me and shot my boy, so I was unrealistic to think there would be any of the cash left. And of course there wasn't, but that's not really the point." He air pokes me. "The *point* is I can't let people steal from me. Hurts business. So even if it takes me three years to track the thieves down, it *behooves* me to do it. Do you know that word? Behoove?" He takes a sip of his coffee, squinting against the heat of it. "Great fucking word."

"Yeah, I know that word."

He nods. "So I had this chat with Jimmy, and he didn't have anything left. But you both owe me. With interest, I've rounded the figure off to ten thousand. Now, Jimmy, being the strung-out, wormy piece of shit he is, can't afford a used condom in a whorehouse. But he tells me you were with him that night, so using my master investigative powers, I tracked you down. Here you are, owner of this fancy coffee shop, with a nice little house in the better part of this shithole city, and it's got me figuring you could come up with the ten thousand. Oh, and I'm adding in five thousand for the loss of my dealer. You know he's dead, right?"

He says it so casually, but the news punches me in the stomach. Oh God. I always wondered what happened to Nick, and now I know. Oh God, oh shit.

"Jimmy killed him, and you were there, so that makes you what they call an *accessory to murder.* Now, *I* know who killed Nick, but the police still don't. They didn't investigate real hard, Nick being a dealer and all. But a murder is a murder, Alice. It doesn't ever go away. The police *will* arrest someone if they think he — or *she* — is a suspect. So if you have it in your mind you want to go to the police now, you do what you gotta do. But I'll make sure they know all about what you and Jimmy did that night. So the way I figure it, fifteen thousand dollars is an awful cheap price to pay to avoid either prison or whatever I decide to do with you. A bargain, really."

"The police will never believe you," I say.

"As far as you should be concerned, honey, I *am* the police. And judge. And jury. Now it's up to you to determine if I'm also your executioner. And I don't even give a shit about Nick — I've got a dozen guys like him — but he was my property, and you destroyed something that belonged to *me.* I'm going to get my fifteen grand from you."

"I don't have that kind of money."

He smiles, and I wish he hadn't.

"Well, now, that's exactly what Jimmy said. Things didn't end up well for him. Do you want to see a photo?"

He pulls his phone from his jacket pocket and starts swiping along its screen.

"No, no, I don't," I say.

"You sure? It's amazing how a lack of teeth changes the way a person looks. You really gotta see this."

"No, please."

"You sure?" He lowers the phone, and his smile disappears. "Look, Alice, I'm a busy man, and fifteen thousand is a small amount of money for me to be spending my time on. But the thing is, I *like* retribution. I would be doing this even if you only stole a dime bag from me. So I'm not going anywhere. It would *behoove* you to put together that money. You've got two days, and I'll be close by during that time."

Close by. Like watching me through my bedroom window. Sketching me.

The question just comes out.

"Are you Mister Tender?"

"What?"

I repeat my question, though I can already see from his face he has no idea what I'm talking about.

He spins his cup around so I see Brenda's handwriting.

Freddy.

"You should already know my name."

He walks around me toward the entrance. I turn my head as he opens the door, but before he walks out, he turns and says one more thing. This time it's loud.

"And your coffee? It's a little bitter, Alice." He holds up his hand and pinches his thumb and index finger together. "Little bitter."

THIRTEEN

As the fear drains, it's replaced by prickly, heat-generating anger. I want to chase after Freddy, sweep his legs out from under him, smash his face with my fists.

Fucking Jimmy.

My chest pounds, and I force myself to draw in long, slow breaths in an effort to calm myself. Brenda and Dan are watching; I can feel their gazes heavy on me. Though I doubt they could make out most of what Freddy said to me, his body language spoke volumes.

I turn and walk back toward them, trying to appear like everything is fine. Just fine.

"Who *was* that guy?" Brenda asks.

"I don't know," I say. Which at least is the truth. "Freddy, I suppose."

"What did he want?"

"I don't want to discuss it." I figure that's the best way to discourage further questions. And it works, though both of them keep staring at me, wanting more, until finally accepting my silence with visible disappointment.

I go to my office, thinking, *I don't have fifteen thousand dollars.*

Well, technically I do, but it would leave me very tight. I have a cash reserve of about eighteen thousand I use for my monthly expenses, the idea being that, hopefully within the next six months, the Stone Rose will finally be a source of income rather than a drain on it. With my share of my father's money, I had enough to buy my house and the coffee shop. If I got rid of fifteen thousand now, I'd have about two months of reserve left to cover what the coffee shop and my tenant's rent doesn't. If I paid the creep fifteen grand, I'd have to seriously look at a second mortgage on the house or a business loan.

But . . . no. Even if I did have the money, *no.*

I didn't shoot anyone or steal anyone's money. I *left* that night. That was all Jimmy, and I'm done paying for the mistakes of others.

Also, I have a feeling that if I give Freddy everything he wants, he'll keep coming back for more.

Still, all my resolve will hardly make

Freddy leave me alone. He's here now, and I have to figure out what to do about him.

Goddamn it.

I shut the door, and the room closes in on me. As my mind reels, I force myself to breathe. Deep and slow. Deep breath in, count to four, hold, count to four, let it out, count to four. I do this until I feel back in control, if even just a little. Out of control is the last place I ever want to be, but lately that seems to be where I exist the most.

I turn to my computer, as if the answer might be as simple as a few clicks away. I check the balance in my bank accounts, seeing exactly what I expect.

Then I have an impulse, one that I've pushed down for a long time. But this time it comes on hard, almost painfully. I don't even have control over my fingers as I type, and in a dizzying, desperate way, I feel like I'm shooting heroin again.

I stare at the five words I've typed in the Google search bar:

sylvia melinda glassin mister tender

For years, I've managed to avoid searching out information on the twins who stabbed me. Since testifying against them as a fifteen-year-old, I haven't wanted to see their faces or know anything about their miserable lives. I remember them sitting in the defendant's docket, their expressionless faces, smooth skin, bright, lifeless eyes. I could barely tell them apart, but to me that hardly mattered anyway. They never spoke, they never defended themselves, and Sylvia even cracked a smile when they were found guilty. They were whisked from court, and I never again saw their faces, except nearly every night when I close my eyes.

Attempted murder is treated as the same as murder in England, with a mandatory life sentence. The minimum requirement of prison time before the possibility of parole is up to the discretion of the judge, and though English judges are often viewed as too lenient, this was not the case for the Glassins. The judge deemed the twins' crime "heinous, willful, and most particularly vile." They were ordered into detention at Her Majesty's pleasure for a minimum term of twelve years before even the possibility of stepping outside prison grounds. A harsh punishment for their age, or so I was told. Good.

The case was sensational in England and had traction around the world, but once I assumed a new name in America, none of my few friends or coworkers ever knew my connection to the Glassin twins. So it's been easy to avoid any news about the twins; all I have to do is not seek it out. Once in a long while, my mother will make some comment about an article she's read concerning them, but presently I know nothing more than they are slowly aging within concrete-block walls.

My index finger hovers over the Enter button for a moment, as if it's the trigger of a gun pointed at my own head. Then I fire.

There are over one million results, but the one grabbing me immediately by the throat is the very first news-feed result, dated just three days ago.

Glassin Twins Seek Privacy after Prison Release

The article is from the *Daily Mail,* and the thumbnail photo accompanying the teaser is one I've seen before, one I remember from the papers in the days leading up to the trial. In it, the adolescent twins wear matching summer dresses (apple-red with mustard-colored flower petals) and they're standing shoulder to shoulder in a park, the sun shining brightly on their pale, smooth faces. Their long, brown hair falls flat and straight past bony shoulders. Neither of them is smiling. There's a chill to this image, and the casual observer would likely use the word *creepy* rather than *cute,* even before they were told what the girls did.

I click on the story.

Sylvia and Melinda Glassin were convicted of attempted murder in the famous "Mister Tender stabbing" in London's Dollis Hill suburb in 2001, and on Thursday, the twenty-eight-year-old identical twins walked out of prison for the first time in fourteen years. They had first been eligible for parole in 2013.

Both women were paroled under strict terms, including rigid curfews, frequent check-ins with their supervising officers, and a permanent surrender of their passports. Their crime was sensational not only because of its brutality and the ages of all involved, but also because of the victim. Alice Hill, also fourteen at the time of the attack, was the daughter of Reginald Hill, the creator of the vastly popular Mister Tender series of graphic novels.

In the series, the eponymous main character had the ability to convince his victims to commit violent crimes, usually with the promise they would be rewarded with whatever they most wanted. Life imitated art when Sylvia and Melinda — themselves devoted fans of the series — attacked Alice Hill with a kitchen knife in a deluded attempt to please the fictional character and be rewarded.

At their trial, the defense attorneys sought to convince the court the girls both suffered from temporary delusions brought about by the ingestion of psychotropic mushrooms. However, they were found criminally sane and were sentenced to life in prison.

In their time in prison . . .

I stop reading when I see the photo of the adult Glassin twins. It's a hurried image showing them stepping into opposite sides of a car immediately after their release. Both have long hair, well past their shoulders, and are draped in similar gray overcoats. One of them — Sylvia, if I had to guess — has her face half turned toward the camera and seems startled, like a nocturnal animal suddenly caught in the beam of a flashlight. Melinda looks down into the car, her focus clearly on just getting out of there. And as I look at this photo, I wonder, *Who are these women now? What's inside them? Is there anything that's carried over from their teenage selves?*

The rest of the article says the twins had both been model prisoners, a primary reason for their early parole, and that each had expressed genuine remorse, blaming drug use for their actions.

They *did* offer me mushrooms that night. I refused.

A few paragraphs on me, my family, my father's murder. But not my new last name. The article states I am now living in the United States and did not respond to requests for commentary on this story.

No one ever tried to contact me.

I scroll to the comments, of which there are a few. Most say something to the effect that the Glassin twins should be boiled in oil, and I'm not going to disagree with this. One person inexplicably writes how he's had sexual fantasies about the twins for years. The final comment, which chronologically was the first one posted, was placed there by a user named Mr. Interested.

Alice is beautiful and Alice is scarred. She is the embodiment of all of us.

God, who are these people? I hate that there are creeps talking about me through internet commentary.

Then I remember something from the

book I received. The website. I type into the address bar:

www.mistertender.com

Do I want to go down this rabbit hole?
I hit Enter. The page loads instantly.
All white, with one sentence in a beautiful and familiar swooping script.

Alice, what did the penguin always tell you?

Exactly as it appears in the book sent to me from London. Nothing else on the home page. Then I hover my mouse over the words and see they link to something. I click again.

A small dialogue box pops up, asking me for a password to continue. I remember the word written beneath the web address in the book. How could I forget the name of the park where I was stabbed?

gladstone

I press Enter.
A new page.
On it are the same colored panels as in the book, the ones drawn by my father. The

little versions of Thomas and me, flying on the back of Ferdinand, demanding entrance into Cloud City.

I doubt my father made this website.

Scroll down the page, no links to anything else. Back to the top. There I notice a word in an impossibly small font in the corner of the screen. I lean toward the display and squint to read.

Tendertalk

I've gone this far; I may as well keep going.

Click.

A message board, one dedicated to all things Mister Tender. The top of the page tells me there are close to two hundred active members of the board, and further down are forum topics with titles including *MT Discussion Thread, Where to Buy,* and *Fan Fiction.* But the one that gives me immediate pause is at the bottom of the list, and it simply says *Alice.*

Another click, and now I'm in a world I never actually believed existed, but always feared.

Fourteen

My new name.
My address.
The name of my coffee shop. My gym.
Photos of me.
Fucking *photos of me.*
Two hundred people keeping tabs, as if I'm some kind of freak who needs to be studied. A science experiment.

Alice Hill is now Alice Gray.

She lives alone.

Here's her house. Her bedroom is on the second floor, window on the right.

Alice at the Stone Rose. See the scar on her shoulder?

Sharp stings in my chest, needles of an impending panic attack. My hand shakes as

I scroll through the pages, the book of my life as seen through the eyes of stalkers. They know everything about me. Perhaps I even know them. Maybe they are regulars at the Rose.

All these years of paranoia. But it's real. It's all desperately real.

These people. What are they, some kind of fans? Does the victim of every sensational crime have their own cult following?

Most posts are from one person, this *Mr. Interested.* His latest just three days ago.

She is beautiful. Her scars only make her more so.

That's the extent of the post, no comments following it. I read a few others, as many as I can stomach. Posts from Mr. Interested usually consist of one sentence, often followed by a photo. Most have a creepy protective undertone.

We should do more for her.

Alice is lonely.

I want to hold her. Keep her safe.

I study each picture, try to think where I

was in that moment. Most photos are me walking outside, taken from a distance. There is even one of me outside the movie theater a couple of weeks ago, the exact image that was later drawn into the book I received. Each photo is a candid one, and I have no memory of anyone being near me in those moments.

Only Mr. Interested posts photos. The others simply comment.

Mr. Interested must be here. In Manchester.

Yet the book I received was from England. *What is happening?*

I look closer at the picture of my house posted a few months ago, my nose an inch from the screen. Trees in full bloom, my lawn green and lush, the sky a brilliant blue. Middle of the day, I'm guessing, so I'm likely at the Stone Rose. Everything seems perfectly normal about my house, but as I look closer, there's something off. It takes me a moment to realize what it is, and then I see it. In the Perch window, the curtain is pulled to the side. Richard's room. His curtains are always closed. But the picture is too small, and I can't zoom in on the message board. So I right-click and save the photo to my hard drive, hoping Mr. Interested uploaded a large version. I open the saved photo and zoom in using the photo viewer app. The photo becomes grainier, but not so much that I can't see what's in that upstairs window.

It's Richard.

He's looking down. Directly at whomever took this photo.

I can't take any more. I've only been in this world for twenty minutes, but I can't survive another minute in it, at least not now.

I slam down the lid of my laptop, which I toss into my bag. Then I grab my coat, leave my office, and tell Brenda I'll be gone for the rest of the day.

"Is it because of that guy?" she asks.

"No," I tell her. "I mean, yes and no." I'm out of breath.

She stands in front of me with Hepburn eyes full of worry. "Alice, you can share with me, you know. You're so . . . coiled up all the time. Maybe it'd be good for you to talk." Then she breaks eye contact and looks at the floor. "I'm sorry. I don't want to pry. Obviously it's your life. I just want you to know I'm a good listener, is all."

I look at Brenda and suddenly want a friend more than I've wanted anything in the world. I *do* want someone I can talk to. Share my worries, so that maybe they'll erode just a bit. Maybe it's okay to tell people what happened to me. Hell, apparently there's a whole community out there already feasting on every detail, so why not let someone of my own choosing into my life?

I walk to the counter, grab a pen, and pull a flyer off the bulletin board. I turn it over and write on the back — *www.mistertender .com password: gladstone* — then I hand the paper to Brenda.

"I'm very private, Brenda. You know that. But five minutes ago, I learned privacy's an illusion. So if you want to know more about me, just go here."

She looks at the paper and reads the back.

"What is this?" she asks. "Who's Mister Tender?"

That's a question requiring a lifetime of answers, so I don't give her any. As I head to the front door, I sweep my gaze through the coffee shop. Every face I see is a familiar one, customers I've served for months. Years, even.

The man with the salt-and-pepper beard and green eyes isn't here.

FIFTEEN

My house is only five blocks away, but the
snowstorm makes my destination feel impossibly distant. I trudge east on Harrison
Street, sucking in chilled air while tumbling,
puffy snowflakes act as a million tiny sound
dampeners, rendering my world as silent as
the inside of a snow globe. Or coffin.

I pass a house fully prepared for Halloween. Bony arms reach out of the snow-
covered lawn. One of the hands grips a
bloody, plastic butcher's knife, a jarring
departure from the smiling bats and googly-
eyed witches along the front porch.

I bury my hands deeper in my pockets and
keep moving. I imagine faces in windows,
watching me pass. Gazes tracking my direction, hands scribbling down what I'm wearing. What direction I'm headed. The mood
on my face. Reporting back to their coven
what has become of Alice today. And I can't
argue with the fascination. Who wouldn't

want to know what became of that girl nearly stabbed to death by her own friends, the little twins who were convinced a comic-book character was controlling their minds? Throw in a brother with some kind of wasting disease and a mother addicted to martyrdom, and you have a fully fleshed-out television serial.

I finally reach my house. Richard's car is here, but he's probably sleeping after working the night shift. I'm not in the mood to go up to the Perch, wake him, and ask if he remembers someone standing in my yard taking a picture of the house months ago. So I head inside. Turn off my alarm and go room to room, opening each closet door. No monsters. I also look under my bed, finding nothing but a thin layer of dust coating the hardwood floor.

The tingling begins. Incoming panic attack.

God, please no.

I can't do this.

I'm not strong enough.

I can't spend another night in a sweaty ball on my floor, wondering if each struggle for breath will be my last.

If I do nothing, the attack will come. In fact, it's already started. On rare occasions, I've been able to stave off the attacks, but that window's closing fast. I run down the stairs and grab my car keys and the gym bag I always have packed and at the ready. Out the door, into my car, and I wrestle through snow-packed streets to the gym, which is only a half mile away. Sliding. Floating. I don't even bother with the seat belt, because, at this point, it seems laughable I should care about plunging through the windshield.

I make it.

Run my membership card through the digital reader with barely a hello to Tim. Race to the locker room, where I set a record time in changing. The tingling is strong now and moving up my fingertips to my hands, my chest tightening. *Focus, Alice.* I take the hand wraps from my bag and unravel them to the floor, black snakes. With a precision and speed borne from years of practice, I bind my hands and wrists into tight, powerful rocks.

Hair pulled back into a whip. Shoes and socks off. Grab my water bottle, stow the bag in an empty locker, and run to the back corner of the gym, the hundred-square-foot stamp where the boxing equipment stands.

No one is using this area, and if they were, I would have fought them for it. Fought and won.

I start with the heavy bag, working combinations in a smooth, steady rhythm, focusing only on what's directly in front of me, pushing against the creeping madness edging into my mind.

Jab, cross, hook, *kick.*

Jab, cross, hook, *kick.*

I set the round clock. Three minutes on, thirty seconds off. In moments, sweat slicks my face, my arms, my thighs. It's a good sweat, leaching the toxins from my body. I switch moves.

Jab, jab, left hook, uppercut, *knee.*

Keep going. Ignore all other thoughts.

I slip into a trance, transport into another world, one in which I'm in complete control. The bag resists me, but I hit it harder, cause it pain, defeat it one blow at a time. This bag is everyone who watches me. This bag is telling me I owe it fifteen thousand dollars. This bag is posting my real name and address to the world. This bag is a junkie ex-boyfriend.

Jab, cross, elbow, punch high, then low.

One round. The thirty-second rest is an eye blink. Begin again.

Sweat flies from my body and rains onto the heavy bag with every punch and kick. Round after round. I go until my muscles beg me to stop, then I go longer. I don't care. If I die doing this, I'd be proud. Finally, I turn to the speed bag, then start hitting it one hand after the other, first using the backs of my hands and then the sides. I'm sloppy at first, and my exhaustion keeps me from establishing a smooth rhythm, but I find it. It's here I finally feel the panic attack retreating, taking shelter against the force of my will, waiting to come out again when I'm more vulnerable.

Not today. You won't get me today.

Over and over, two hits right hand, two hits left, repeat, repeat, repeat. The bag slams against the wooden drum with a hypnotic percussion, and soon, I'm locked in with it, unable to do anything else but lock in and keep going.

Thucka, thucka, thucka, thucka.

War drums. Those words flash in my mind, and then I see imagery. Armies on the horizon, moving toward each other in a slow, machinelike march. Suddenly, all I can think of is death. I can see it, even smell it. Crisped, rotten meat. Ripped, exposed bowels. Burned hair.

There are no guns in this battle — only weapons that cut. Broadswords, daggers, bayonets, hatchets.

I don't stop hitting. I want to pound this bag until the seams burst apart.

Harder, harder, faster, faster.

They can't get you, Alice.

They *will* get you, Alice.

They can't hurt you anymore.

They've never stopped hurting you.

They are ghosts.

They are *everywhere.*

I'm screaming. Not in my mind, but in the gym, above the sound of my fists and my rage, I am screaming. Screaming at everything that has ever done anything to me, because all I want is to be left alone.

I close my mouth. As I let my swollen hands drop to my sides, and as the last trail of my voice fades to silent, the bag wobbles and then rests still. It's in the same condition as when I started. I haven't hurt it. I haven't seemed to change it in any way.

Tim stands across the room. He stares at me with hesitation and concern, as if I'm an escaped animal who needs to be very carefully lured back into its cage.

"Alice," he says. "Are you okay?"

My chest heaves with exhaustion. Sweat runs into my eyes, turning my world into a glassy haze. The tingling sensation is gone.

"For now," I say.

Sixteen

Sunday, October 18

Today is the fourteenth anniversary of my attempted murder. I had almost forgotten, but my phone screen reminds me. October eighteenth. I remember it mostly as it was referred to in court, the solicitors repeatedly saying, "On the night of October 18 . . ." I will hold no memorial on this day, carry no special reflections. I'll just try to get through it as I do every other.

I rise from my bed and place my bare feet on the cold floorboards. Light streams around the closed curtains, and I walk over and crack them open an inch. I used to throw them open wide.

It seems at least a foot of snow came down. It certainly won't bring Manchester to a standstill but will surely slow it to a New England crawl. Brenda is opening the Rose today, and I know she'll be there because she's within walking distance. I text her, telling her she can open the shop a little late. Sundays we open late anyway.

Okay, she replies. Will you be in today?

I think on that for a moment, then reply, Not sure yet.

Truth is, I have no idea what I'm doing today. Ideally, curling up in a ball and hiding, or disappearing down some magical tunnel leading me to some other world. My own Chancellor's Kingdom, where even the scariest things can't hurt me.

That would be wonderful.

You doing okay? she texts.

I don't reply.

Back at the window. My car is blanketed by snow. Next to it is Richard's, behind which fresh tracks indicate he came home from work not too long ago. He's up there in the Perch, likely sleeping.

Or maybe there's a little hole in the ceiling, one through which he's threaded the tiniest of cameras, the kind with the fish-eye lens that can view an entire room. Maybe he's up there now, laptop open, watching me. He sees me in my loose cotton shirt that barely covers my underwear. Maybe he's been watching me in my sleep, waiting for me to stir.

I move to the bathroom, where I grab my robe and cinch it tightly around me. Back in the bedroom, I scan the ceiling but see nothing more than smooth white plaster.

Down to the kitchen. The coffeemaker has a fresh pot waiting for me, and I pour a cup and stir my laptop to life. The local news site tells me not to drive unless it's an emergency. I wonder if a drug dealer named Freddy coming after me counts as an emergency. I'm an easy target at home. Maybe he'll come knocking on my door this morning, seeing if I have his money, which of course I don't.

No, he said I had two days. I have until tomorrow.

Why am I taking him at his word?

And what good is another day if I'm not going to give him what he wants? Then what happens? Then he pushes in my door and bursts inside the house. *Nice place you got here, Alice.* I'll attack and hope for the best. But it won't be that easy, will it? He'll have a gun —

(or a knife)

— and he won't hesitate. He'll hurt me before I can hurt him. Because his is a world of violence, and despite all my self-defense, mine is a world of fear. I was able to strike first in the gym because he didn't expect it. But when he comes back for me, he'll be prepared.

The sinister book sits on the counter, and I reach for it. I inspect the inscription once again and this time lick my thumb and smudge the ink. It smears. The words are truly handwritten, not printed. I'm convinced my father wrote these words, but when? And, more importantly, why?

An idea hits me. More of an impulse, really. Maybe an act of desperation.

Back to the laptop.

www.mistertender.com

On the screen, the same inscription as in the book, a simple scan of the original. I type in the password and navigate back to the forum, back to the thread titled *Alice*. No new posts since yesterday.

I find what I'm looking for, a link to register. To become a member. Hell, I'll become a member. The most famous one of all.

Members can post.

I choose a random username and password, and when I'm told I need to provide an email to complete my registration, I jump over to Yahoo and create a new email account under a false name.

Minutes later, I'm a user on Tendertalk, but all I do is stare at the message board. I have no idea what I'm going to post, but a few things come to mind.

FUCK YOU is one of them. *LEAVE ME ALONE* is another.

But I don't actually want anyone knowing who I am. I want to do a bit of trolling myself. Maybe post a comment or question that might reveal a bit about who is watching me. Perhaps I'll pose as a newbie who has recently became obsessed with Alice Hill. Maybe Mr. Interested will take me under his wing and guide me into his underworld, show me this deep, dark web of stalkers. This is like the goddamn *Phantom of the Opera.* Christine in the bowels of the Paris Opera House.

But before I type a single thing, a direct message appears in the inbox of this forum. It's from the master of ceremonies himself, Mr. Interested.

I click to open it. The message only has two words.

Hello, Alice.

SEVENTEEN

I snap my head and look out the kitchen window, convinced Mr. Interested has a pair of binoculars trained on me. I see nothing, but that doesn't stop me from pulling all blinds closed. The kitchen falls into a soft darkness, and I flip on the lights, then sit back down at my laptop.

Who are you? I type.

Seconds later:

I'm an observer.

An observer of what?

Of your struggles.

An instant queasiness overtakes me. Ice filling my guts.

I just want to be left alone.

I don't think that's really true. None of us really wants to be alone, Alice. We all need each other. We all need help.

I don't need help.

Yes, Alice, I think you do. How are you going to pay Freddy Starks his money?

I don't know who that is.

Yes, you do. Your visitor from Boston.

Are you him?

No, but I know he was looking for you. Could be, perhaps, I led him to Jimmy. And then to you.

I stand and push the chair back. Race to the front door and make sure it's locked. It is. Check the alarm, which is still set to Stay. Any door or window that opens will trigger it.
Back to the computer.

Are you watching me right now?

No.

How did you know it was me on the message board?

This time, his reply takes nearly a minute to come.

I know the range of IP addresses used by your computer. An address within that range was associated with your registration. An educated guess, call it.

Breathe in, count to four. But I can't do it. My heart is racing too fast. I get to three before I have to gasp for air.

What do you really want?

I want to take care of you.

But you sent that man to find me. Why?

It doesn't matter now, Alice. He's here. So what are you going to do about it?

I pause a moment. Then:

I'm not going to pay him.

In an instant, he replies.

Then you have to kill him.

I'm very close to shutting off the computer, but I don't. His last words seem to pulse on the screen, and though I don't respond to him, I keep looking at the chat, wondering if he will write more.

Moments later, he does.

He's coming for you, Alice, and he won't go away until he gets what he wants. You should see what he did to Jimmy.

Oh God.

Is Jimmy dead?

No, but he probably wishes he were.

How do you know all this?

I follow things that interest me.

Then he posts a link to a page within the Boston Globe website. I click on it, and it takes me to a brief article, dated one week ago, about a man found beaten outside a bar in the North End. There's very little detail, but the man was identified as James Haskill, 29, of Boston.

How do you even know about Jimmy and me?

Because I've been watching you for a long time, Alice. I know you better than anyone. Which is why you won't go to the police. You know if you do, I'll make sure they know about what you and Jimmy did three years ago. The murder you committed.

I had nothing to do with that.

I suspect Jimmy would be happy to blame it all on you.

I pound the keys.

I don't know what you want from me. I just want to be left alone.

Mr. Interested ignores this.

Check the planter box just outside your front door. Dig a few inches down, and you'll find a plastic bag with a gun in it. The gun cannot be traced. When Freddy comes for you, shoot him. Tell the police it was self-defense and that you took his gun off him.

What the hell?
There are so many things to ask, but I before I can type another word, someone knocks on my front door.

Eighteen

I might not have knives in the house, but I do have a baseball bat. Youth sized, aluminum, light and strong. I race upstairs and grab it from beneath my bed. I'm confident in my self-defense abilities, but I don't know who's waiting on the other side of that door. Better to have a weapon other than just my own fists and feet.

(Check your planter box just outside your front door)

I peer out onto the front porch through a crack in the curtains. Some, but not all, of the tension in my shoulders slides away as I see Richard standing there. I hold on to the bat as I open the door. Frigid air washes over me.

"Hi, Alice, sorry to bother you so early. I heard you moving around . . . figured you were awake."

Monitoring me. Listening to me.

"Hi, Richard."

His gaze darts to the bat and then back to my face.

"I didn't mean to startle you."

"It's okay," I say. "I was already startled before you knocked."

"Everything okay?" His dark eyes register concern. A day's worth of stubble molds his cheeks and neck, and his dark, stringy hair hangs over his forehead, giving him a haggard look. He's at least a half foot taller than me, but his frame is so slight, it wouldn't be unreasonable to think he'd topple easily with a light shove. Or breeze.

"What do you need, Richard?"

"Well, like I said, sorry to bother you, but the hot water's out again. Would you mind checking the pilot light on the heater?"

I relax a little. The heater is a constant problem. But I keep holding the bat.

"Yes, of course. Sorry about that. I really need to get that fixed."

He offers a thin smile and shrug. "Just got home from my shift. I like to take a hot shower before I get some sleep."

"I'll relight it," I say. "But it'll probably take an hour or so to get the water hot again."

"It's no problem. Just thought I'd let you know. Thanks, Alice."

He turns to head back to the Perch.

"Richard," I say.

"Yes?"

He's already here. And I don't think he's part of this, so I may as well ask. "Do you remember . . . Well, this would have been in the summer, I think. Do you remember someone taking a picture of the house? It's a weird question, I know. But I saw this picture of my house online, and you were up in the Perch, in the window, looking down. I–I was just wondering if you remember that. If you saw someone."

He pushes his hands deeper into his coat pockets, bundling against the cold. He's wearing thin sweatpants, maybe even pajamas, tucked into untied snow boots.

"Huh," he says. "No, I can't say I remember that exactly. In the summer, you say?"

"Well, the trees were full, but I don't know exactly when."

"No, sorry, I don't remember seeing anyone around the house. Certainly not taking pictures."

"Oh, okay. No problem, then. Just thought I'd ask."

Richard seems about ready to turn away but decides against it. He looks at the ground as he speaks.

"Alice . . . I mean, really, it's none of my business, but you tell me you're okay, and

I'm thinking you're not."

"Richard, I —"

"I hear you, you know?" Now he looks up, and when his gaze locks onto mine, it's powerful. Perhaps because he so rarely looks me directly in the eyes. "Sometimes, at night. Not often. I hear you upset. Crying. Once in a while I think . . ." He searches for words.

"What do you think, Richard?"

"I think maybe you're hurting yourself or something. I mean, again, none of my business, but you seem . . . just . . ."

"Just what?"

"Just so *alone.*"

And here is where I lose it. The word *alone* stabs me in the heart, and I'm stunned by how much it actually hurts. I nearly lose my balance, then walk back a few steps into my house, sit on the bottom step of the stairs, and start crying. *Weeping.* I don't care that Richard is staring at me through the open doorway as cold air floods my house. I don't care I'm a disheveled mess in a robe that barely conceals me. I don't care if Richard is actually one of the stalkers. All I feel is the pain of that word, because it is so desperately true. Of all the words anyone could ever use to describe me, there is none more honest than that simple, solitary adjective.

Alone.

"Oh, oh God, Alice. I'm so sorry." He walks inside and puts the lightest of hands on my terry-cloth shoulder. "I didn't mean to . . . You know. I'm such an idiot. You're not alone. I'm sure you have lots of friends. I mean, God, look at me. I don't ever go out or anything. I'm the loner, not you. I mean, you're not a loner, I'm just —"

"Shut up, Richard," I say into my hands.

"Right, of course." He removes his hand, but I can see his feet through the gaps in my fingers. He doesn't know whether to stay or go.

I allow myself some more tears, and it feels cleansing. For some reason, I'm comfortable with being vulnerable in this moment. But I don't let it last too long. I wipe my face, stand, cinch my robe tight, and square my shoulders.

"Do you know anything about computers?" I ask.

He seems startled by my change of direction. "Um, a little, I suppose."

"How can I find out who owns a website?"

He shrugs. "You can check WHOIS."

"Who what?"

"*W-H-O-I-S.* You do a WHOIS lookup on

132

any website, and that tells you. You know, like 'who is the owner of whatever.com.' "

"Okay," I say. "Hang on." I walk over, grab my laptop, and sit back on the bottom step again. "Close the door, Richard. It's freezing in here."

As he reaches back to close the door, I spy the corner of the planter box outside. Snow is piled on top of it, a big loaf of white bread. Is there really a gun there?

The door shuts, and I refocus on the laptop screen. I Google *whois* and immediately find the site I need.

"So I just enter in the website I want to look up?"

Richard peers over my shoulder and looks at the screen.

"That's right."

My instinct is to pull the screen from his view, but I don't. Living with secrets hasn't worked out for me anyway. I type in www.mister-tender.com and click Enter.

"What's that site?" he asks.

"Long story."

The page loads with technical terms, but it doesn't take me long to find what I'm looking for. Halfway down the page, I see *Registrant Name.*

Next to that, it says *Registration Private.*

Damn it.

Richard leans in closer. "Yeah, no surprise," he says. "You can pay an extra ten bucks a year or so to shield all your info. Most websites are private, I would expect."

"So now what?"

"I have no idea," he says.

"Well, thanks, Richard."

He stands upright. "You know, I like listening to long stories."

I sigh. "But that doesn't mean I like telling them."

"Okay, I won't pry anymore," he says.

When he looks at me, why do I simply trust him? There's really no reason I should, except that he pays his rent on time and otherwise leaves me alone. Just earlier, I had a moment of panic that Richard was spying on me through my ceiling, but now, as he stands here, I sense his energy, and it's *good* energy. I have no logical reason to think he's not Mr. Interested. But he's not. I just know it. He is just Richard.

"Are you working tonight?" I ask.

"No, I'm off."

"Then come over for a glass of wine," I say. "Maybe I'll tell you a long story."

His face brightens, and for a man I've never considered particularly attractive, it's lovely.

"I'd like that," he says. "What time?"

"Let's say five."

He nods. "Sounds good." When he looks to the ground, he blushes. I don't want him blushing, because that means he might be thinking tonight is a date. Tonight is not a date. Tonight is me being able to connect with another human being, something I do far too seldom.

"And look," I add, "you're probably going to go check out the website when you get back upstairs. If you do, you'll need a password. *Gladstone,* all lowercase."

"Alice, I'm not trying to —"

"It's okay, Richard. I'm realizing it's healthy for me to share some secrets. Look at the site. It'll be a good starting point for our conversation later."

He only nods at this, then turns and walks away. I partially close the door and listen until he's back in the Perch. Then I open the door, check the street to confirm it's empty, then dig through the planter box with my bare hands. The snow daggers my fingertips, but it takes only a moment before I feel the slick plastic of a Ziploc bag. The hard metal inside. I don't pull the gun out of the planter. I don't want it inside my house. I don't even want it this close to me, but I'm not touching it more. I pile the dirt and snow back on top, then retreat back into the house.

Door locked.

Alarm panel armed to Stay. Ice crystals melt and drip from my numb fingertips. I walk to the basement, where the water heater lives. As my bare feet press down the cool, wooden steps into the darkness of the unfinished space, a sudden thought comes to me. A certainty, even.

The water heater is working just fine.

What if I'm wrong about Richard and my trust is misplaced? Maybe he made up that story about the water heater just to have an excuse to knock on my door at the moment it would unnerve me most.

I make my way in the tight space, reach up, and pull the chain on the solitary light down here. The bulb has little effect.

Aroma of damp brick and musty wood beams.

The cold of the concrete floor bites into the bottoms of my bare feet as I walk to the water heater. Again, another certainty washes over me. The moment I check the water heater and confirm it's working just fine, I'll hear the basement door close, followed by the sound of someone descending the old steps.

I force myself to keep moving forward. Finally, I reach the water heater in the back corner of the room. I bend down and slide the cover to the pilot light over to the left. As I do, I touch the metal exterior of the heater itself.

It's cool.

I peer at the pilot light.

It's out.

The muscles in my back relax, and as I reach inside to ignite the pilot, I think that I'm looking forward to that glass of wine with Richard.

NINETEEN

Midmorning, and my morgue-silent house fills with a brilliant light that only occurs this time of day and year, when the low winter sun hits my southern windows and bright, dusty beams flood my downstairs. This sudden burst of sunshine makes me realize there are some curtains I haven't closed, so I do.

Then, I think, *What the hell am I going to do?*

Should I call the police to tell them about the gun in my planter and the man stalking me? Tell them about another man named Freddy Starks who is looking to exact a pound of my flesh?

In the lowest points of my life, police were involved. I remember the sirens of their cars in the distance as I was bleeding to death exactly fourteen years ago today. A vague notion of one of them looking over my body and saying "bloody hell" over and over. I don't want to call the police. What can they really do, anyway? Arrest me in connection with a drug dealer's murder, and probably little else.

So I just sit here, rattled with indecision, impotent to effect change. This lasts literally hours.

Change instead comes to me, and it does so with the ring of my doorbell. In my years here, I don't think I've ever had more than one visitor in a day.

Freddy Starks. It has to be.

I grab the bat. There's no way I'm opening the door, but he'll find a way in. He knows I'm here.

Another ring. Impatient, only seconds after the first.

Shouting erupts on the other side of the door.

"Alice! Open up!"

That's not Freddy Starks. I know who it is, and it's the last person I would expect on my doorstep.

I drop the bat and race to the door, then open it.

Thomas is standing on the porch. A red welt paints an imperfect circle around his left eye.

He very nearly smiles as he says:

"Happy anniversary."

TWENTY

"Thomas, how did you get here?"

He jerks a thumb back at my mother's Toyota Highlander parked across the street.

"Is she in the car?"

"Nope. She's at home."

"You're not supposed to be driving. And . . ." I reach out and touch the side of his face, which, despite the blaze of the welt, is chilled. "What happened to you?" And then I put it together before he even has a chance to answer.

"She hit you," I say.

"Jesus, Alice, it's cold as a bitch out here. Can I come in?"

"Yes . . . sorry." I stand aside as he shuffles in.

"It's two in the goddamned afternoon," he says. "You're still in a bathrobe? Must be fuckin' nice."

I shut the door and wonder for the thousandth time what happened to the Thomas

140

I grew up with. We were never alike, and it was a rare occasion when someone would tell us we resembled each other. Our personalities were just as disparate: I was the shy one, borderline withdrawn. Thomas was always outgoing, friendly to a fault, the golden retriever of the family. Even when he was thirteen, a full year before he got sick but at a time most boys turn into real shits, Thomas was always the sweet one.

This was after my assault, so I was detached from the world, disappearing into my room at every chance, but Thomas would come to my room and talk to me through my door, trying to get me to come out. He'd sit on the floor in our apartment and read me the most stupid knock-knock jokes he could find, playing both the asker and the answerer. The jokes were like smoke grenades: deployed effectively, they always succeeded in flushing me out. He was annoying but sweet. Always cheerful. And he never swore.

I force myself to remember he can't control who he is, and I need to dig deep into my patience.

"I'm not working today," I say. "I can't believe you drove so far in this weather. I can't believe you drove at *all*. You don't even have a license."

"I had to get out of there, since she sure doesn't want me the fuck around. I had nowhere to go. Thought about wrapping the Toyota around a few utility poles along the way, but I ended up making it here un-scathed."

"Did she really hit you?"

"What does it look like?"

"Why?"

"Who the hell knows? We were arguing, and I might have called her a filthy whore."

"Thomas!"

He shrugs. "I meant it ironically. I mean, who would even touch that? I guess she doesn't have a sense of irony. She sucker punched me."

"Did you . . ."

"Hit her back?" he asks. "Of course not. But not because I didn't want to." He shakes snow off his long, unkempt hair. "I'm just afraid if I start, I won't be able to stop. That I'd just fucking kill the bitch, right there. *Boom.*"

"Thomas, quit talking like that."

"It's true," he tells me.

"Thomas . . . she's trying, you know? She had no right to hit you. Of course not. But she has a lot to deal with."

"You mean she has to deal with me."

"Well —"

"You're right, she has to. I know. I'm a goddamn mess. I *get* it. But she's never done this before. She usually just yells."

I turn from him and grab my phone, dial.

"Are you —"

"Shhh," I tell him.

My mother doesn't answer. I leave a message.

"I wanted to tell you Thomas is with me, and what you did to him is inexcusable. I can't believe you hit him. He's staying with me at least until we can figure this mess out."

I disconnect the call, wondering if she'll even bother to call back. I have a sudden urge to smash my phone against the wall, then run into the kitchen and smash plates, glasses, breaking everything that can possibly be broken. The desire to see the shards of shattered objects makes my mouth water.

"Can I really stay here?" he asks me. His face softens, and for a moment, I see my brother, my real brother, the one buried deep beneath the disdain.

"For now," I say. "But . . ." I decide to tell him, not to protect him, but in a hope he will protect me. "There are some things going on with me right now. I'm not sure this house is the safest place to be."

"Are you having your panic attacks? I

mean, it being the anniversary and all."

"God, Thomas, stop reminding me. No, it's not that."

"Dad's book," he says.

"That's part of it."

"What else?"

The antique clock on my wall chimes. I hate that clock, but I don't get rid of it because it was my grandmother's. Every time it chimes, it make me think of a heart's last beat. I glance over at it. God, is it really already two?

"Let me get dressed," I say. "I need to get out of here."

Minutes later, I'm back downstairs, and we head out the front door. I pause to look at the planter box with the snow scraped off one side of it. I must stare too long, because Thomas asks, "What is it?"

"Nothing," I say.

We trudge through the snow, which has finally stopped falling. Thomas only has sneakers but doesn't complain. It's a short but messy trudge to the Rose, and this time, I walk in through the front entrance, not the back. James is playing on the sound system. The song's title is not lost on me. "Out to Get You."

Brenda stands behind the counter. She looks at me, and it takes me a moment to remember I'd told her about the website. I bite off the regret I feel, forcing it down. Screw it, I think. It's okay for her to know.

I walk up. "How's it going today?" I ask.

"Quiet. Postapocalyptic quiet. Lucky for me, since Dan called in sick and it's just been me here."

Goddamn it. I'm glad I didn't smash my phone, because now I get to use it to make a very satisfying call. Dan doesn't answer. It seems he and my mother are hiding from me. So I leave a message for him as well.

"Dan, it's Alice. In case you don't remember, you've already used up your sick days. So don't bother coming back in. And I know this little job wasn't your career aspiration, but I hope getting fired motivates you to think about what you want to do with your life. And if it doesn't do that, I hope it just pisses you off."

I disconnect.

"Wow," Brenda says.

"Brenda, I'm sorry. I can't help you today. I know it sucks, but I just can't. I need to spend some time with my brother. There are things going on."

She nods, and in her expression, I can tell she's up to speed with the history of my life.

"It's okay, Alice. Really."

145

"And I'm adding a five-hundred-dollar bonus to your pay this week." Much better to give the little money I have to her instead of an extorting drug dealer.

Her eyes widen, she smiles, and I realize how beautiful she truly is. "Oh my God. Thank you, Alice."

"You've earned it. And put the word out we need another barista. Let's find someone reliable."

"Sure. I can help with that. Absolutely."

I ask her for two black coffees. As she hands them over, she asks if I'm okay. *Really okay,* she puts it.

"I'm not okay at all," I say. "Not even a little, and someday, maybe even soon, we'll talk about it all. But not today."

Honesty feels good.

Thomas and I grab two of the six cushioned chairs in the Rose. We sit in a quiet corner, and I look outside. No one on the streets.

"I don't know where to begin," I say, turning to my brother.

He thinks on this for a moment, then leans forward and says, "What are you scared of?"

This actually makes me laugh. "Everything."

"Really, Alice. What scares you the most?"

The way he asks makes me think his question alone is right up there on the list.

I answer, "There are things I'm scared of and things I'm worried about. Worried? I'm worried a man is coming to hurt me because he says I owe him money. But scared?" I pause only for a moment. "I'm scared of all the eyes watching me."

"Alice, what are —"

"Just let me tell you. And don't interrupt."

And, perhaps for the first time in my life, I open up to my brother and share. I'm brutally honest and open, telling him all the things haunting my life and what all of them do to my mind in the long, piercing hours of the night.

I'm naked, scared, vulnerable, and it feels good.

TWENTY-ONE

"Don't go to the police," he says. These are his first words when I finish. The comment surprises me, though I'm inclined to agree.

"Why?"

"Just like the penguin says, Alice. Don't trust anyone."

"That was just a story."

"This is all a story," Thomas says. "Everything is a story. Nothing is real."

"Why do you say that?"

"Because if this life were all real, it would just be so fucking heartbreaking."

A small bit of my own life slips away with his comment.

"Thomas, this is all real. What happened to you was real. My . . . my stabbing was real." I reach out and touch the welt on his face. "Our mother is real. The key to it all, I think, is how we find beauty in any of it."

He actually chuckles at this. "When's the last time you've found beauty in anything?"

"In the walk over here," I say, happy to have an answer. "There were a few leaves that had fallen on top of the snow. Red and brown, resting on the soft white. I thought that looked exquisite."

"I didn't see them," he responds. He takes a sip of the coffee, looks out the window, then focuses his gaze on me. "Is the gun really there? In the planter?"

"It is."

"You need to take it."

"I want nothing to do with it."

"What happens when he comes back? Are you going to give him the money?"

"I can take care of myself."

He shakes his head, almost like an uncontrolled twitch, then reaches across and grabs my wrist. His fingers are still cold. "We can go, Alice. You know? We can just leave. You and me. I can help. I'm not the burden Mom says I am. I can contribute. I know I have challenges, but I can contribute. Let's just *go.*"

"Where?"

"Anywhere. I don't care." Then he thinks. "No, I take that back. Let's go somewhere warm. I ruined your chance to go to San Diego. Let's go there."

How I wish it were all so easy. In this moment, I love my brother so dearly, almost jealous of the childish lens though which he sees the world.

"There are things that stick to you, Thomas. They're like your skin. No matter how fast or far you run, they accompany you. They are forever a part of you."

"Wow."

"Wow what?"

"That was a line from Chancellor's Kingdom. The Skeleton King. You don't remember?"

I want to say I do, but I don't, and the fact I'm quoting my father's decades-old stories without realizing rattles me.

I shake my head. "Doesn't matter. It's true. Leaving solves nothing. We moved all the way to America years ago, and I still have nightmares most nights."

"So what do you do, Alice? How do you get to a place of happiness? With all you've told me, with everything happening to you, how do you find a way to enjoy life?"

Enjoying life, not just surviving it. I think he's not just asking me, but himself as well.

"I haven't the faintest clue," I say.

"You seize control."

"How?"

"You take care of the guy looking to shake you down. Then you deal with this *Mr. Interested* shit. You fight back, Alice. You *fight.*"

"Thomas, I'm tired of punching at ghosts. This is real life. This isn't a video game."

"Like you said, Alice, there are some things you can't escape. Just like your skin, they are a part of you. So just wear them. Make them fit your body."

"Thomas, it's not that easy."

My phone lights up and vibrates. I look down and see my mother's photo. It's from three years ago, Christmas. She's wearing ridiculous snowball earrings, which is the precise reason I chose this for her contact image. But in this moment, it's not amusing.

"Hello," I say, holding a finger up to Thomas.

"You have a wretched brother," she says.

"You had no right to hit him," I reply.

"Keep him. And you'll see. You'll start to get scared of him, too. You think he's a child, Alice, but he's not. Wait until you wake up, finding him staring at you from the doorway of your bedroom. Like a lion looking at a piece of meat. You wait until that day, then you tell me what an awful mother I am. You just wait."

I glance up at my brother and try not to picture a carnivore.

"I'm going," I tell her. "We'll talk tomorrow once we've all had a chance to cool down some."

Her voice is lower, almost hissing, and I think of Gollum. "Good riddance to the lot of you. You've both caused me a lifetime of heartache." And then she is gone.

I stare at the phone, and though she's disconnected, her picture remains. I place the phone facedown on the table.

"Sounds like she misses me," Thomas says.

I change the subject, focused on something else.

"Thomas, what do you remember of Chancellor's Kingdom?"

"Everything. I remember everything."

"Do you remember how Mister Tender came into the story?"

"Yes," he says.

"I think I remember, but tell me what you know. Because whoever Mr. Interested is, maybe he knew Dad. And the more we remember, the better chance we have of finding him."

Thomas smiles. For the briefest of moments, I think maybe he's actually happy, and if that's the only positive thing I've accomplished today, or even this year, it's enough.

"Mister Tender worked at the hotel on

Halloween Island, where we went right after Cloud City. Ferdinand took us there. Remember?"

I do. The characters of little Thomas and Alice were trying to find their way back home from the otherworldly realm of Chancellor's Kingdom, a world unto itself, complete with bizarre and wondrous provinces. Every place Alice and Thomas went answered some questions, but usually created even more. There were always clues to follow.

"It was October when Dad told us the parts about Halloween Island. I remember that, because I hadn't heard of Halloween before. You had, but I hadn't. I asked if it was like Guy Fawkes Day, and Dad said no, that it was much scarier. That it was a celebration of the dead. Ferdinand took us to Halloween Island because we needed to find some key or something, I think."

"Yes," I say, the stories flooding back into my mind. "A key to a chest we found in Cloud City. There was supposed to be a map inside, but the key was with some skeleton thief."

"That's right. And he was staying in the hotel where Mister Tender worked."

I recall my father's voice dropping an octave when he talked about Mister Tender.

Not in an overplayed, melodramatic fashion, but with the tone of a man offering a serious warning to those who would listen. He would stare deeply into my eyes when he spoke of him, as if truly trying to convince me of this character's existence. Mister Tender is charming, he'd say. Good looking. Men want to be him. Women just want him. But if you listen to him too carefully, Mister Tender will pull you in, and from that there is no escape. He'll give you advice, usually just the exact words you need in the time of your greatest desperation, but there is always a price for his wisdom. And that price is usually for you to hurt someone. Someone innocent.

Mister Tender earned his tips in the blood of others.

"And of all the characters in that story, Mister Tender had one of the smallest roles," I say to Thomas. "Why, years later, was he the one character Dad chose to create a whole series of books around?"

Thomas leans back in his seat and looks up at the ceiling.

"He started drinking more," he says.

"When?"

"When he was drawing the novels."

I'm amazed Thomas remembers this, but he's exactly right. I was probably ten when my father stopped telling us the stories of Chancellor's Kingdom, and Thomas would have been six. I was twelve when the first Mister Tender book came out, and my father *was* drinking more at that time. His drafting table was always garnished with a glass of whiskey late at night, something I can't recall from his earlier days when he focused on political cartoons and corporate graphic-design projects.

"I never really thought about it," I say, "but you're right. It's as if the creation of Mister Tender was when he started drinking."

Then Thomas says the exact thing I'm thinking.

"Maybe that was the price he had to pay to become successful. Maybe there *was* a real Mister Tender somewhere, telling Dad to create this character to become wealthy. Maybe alcohol was the price."

"No," I whisper. "I think *I* was the price."

The coffee shop door opens, and a ghost washes over my skin. Two teenage girls enter. For a second, I think they are twins, but they aren't.

"He wasn't an alcoholic," Thomas says. "I don't remember him like that."

"No," I say. "But I probably remember more than you. I remember that when the first book became successful, I was excited for him. I didn't really understand the book, and he didn't want me to read it, but he told me it started as an idea from Chancellor's Kingdom. I also remember Mom and Dad fighting more than they ever had."

"That's all a blur to me."

"That's because of how they were after my attack. Things were so bad, that's all you remember. But things weren't so good even before that. I remember turning thirteen and Mom and Dad fighting so much, we almost canceled my party. She would yell at him for spending too much time drawing, and he would yell back that she resented his success. I can remember one time he said, 'You like my money, but you don't want to pay the price for it.' I always wondered what he meant by that."

Thomas looks dumbfounded. "I feel like I've blocked a lot of that out."

I have nothing to say to this.

Thomas crosses his legs and leans back into his chair. "So someone is following you, this Mr. Interested asshole. He's drawing pictures of you, doing a pretty good job at mimicking Dad's style."

"That's right."

"And this other guy — this drug dealer — is coming after you for fifteen thousand. But he's not the same guy."

"I suppose he could be. But I don't think so."

"But they know each other," Thomas says. "Didn't you say Mr. Interested told Starks how to find you?"

"Right. 'Pointed him the right direction,' or something like that." Thomas is processing everything that's been happening, and I pray he comes up with some idea for what I should do next.

"And you haven't talked to Jimmy?"

"No."

"So Mr. Interested tells Starks how to find you, but then gives you a weapon to defend yourself with."

"I saw it in the planter."

"And the book you got was postmarked from London and included unpublished cover art and an inscription from Dad."

"So it seems."

"And on top of all this, the Glassin twins were recently released from prison."

"Right."

Please, Thomas, tell me what to do.

He uncrosses his legs and stares right into me. "And I thought *my* life was fucked up."

Hope drains from me.

"I know, Thomas. I specialize in being fucked up. The question is, how do I un-

157

fuck everything up?"

"Well, take this in order of priority," he says. "Your most pressing problem is Starks."

"So it seems."

"I can help, you know. I have money. I mean, Mom manages it, but it's mine. Hell, I hardly spend anything as it is. I can give you the fifteen grand."

I had resolved not to let Freddy Starks get any amount of money from me, but when Thomas says this, it brings both tears to my eyes and the sense of a massive weight lifting off my chest.

"I . . . Oh, Thomas, that's so kind of you. I mean, it's not like I don't have any money at all, but I didn't take this man's money. I'm just not sure —"

"Alice, all in all, it's not that much. I mean, what else are you going to do when he comes back?"

"But Mom needs that money to help with expenses, doesn't she?"

"She's got plenty of her own."

"Thomas, I don't know what to say. I —"

"Just say you'll take it, and we can cross one major problem off your list."

The brother who I struggle to relate to is making more sense than I can muster myself.

"Thank you, Thomas. So much. Yes, I will take the money. I can pay you back."

He waves it off. "Don't worry about it. It makes me happy to be giving money to you rather than Mom."

"We need it soon, though."

"It's Sunday. Banks are closed. I'll have to go in the morning. There should be a branch around here."

"Do you need Mom to sign off or anything?"

"I'm pretty sure the savings account is in my name and hers. Either one of us can make a withdrawal."

"What will you tell her? She'll surely see the money is gone."

"I'll tell her I needed it for hookers and coke."

I laugh again. My brother is making me laugh, which is wondrous.

Thomas places his coffee down and shifts in his chair. "The other question is what are you going to do if you find Mr. Interested? If you find out who he really is?"

"I don't even know how to find him," I say.

"But say you do. What's your plan?"

"I haven't thought it through that far."

"But you must have a sense of it. Say you found him. Say, even, you knew who he was, and you saw him sitting here. In your coffee shop. What would you do?"

I think of Freddy Starks standing in the Stone Rose, threatening me. How I wanted to protect my staff. How I wanted to stop the threat before something bad happened. But yet I just let him walk away.

"I would tell him to stop."

Then there's a glimmer in Thomas's eyes. Almost excitement.

"You already told him to stop when you messaged with him. He's not going to stop, Alice. He's obsessed with you. Addicted, maybe."

"Well, you think I can't go to the police," I say. I think the same thing, truthfully. "So what options am I left with?"

"You could run," he says. "Just take off. Like I said, maybe take me with you."

I know he wants this. Wants to start a new life, but he doesn't know what I know, which is that starting new doesn't fix your problems.

"Thomas, I agree we need a change. *You* need a change, and I want to be in your life more. But I can't run from this."

"So what, then? What are you going to do, Alice?"

And I know, because it's been in my mind ever since I first saw Mister Tender on the dating app, taunting me.

"I need to hunt him down. And then make sure he doesn't ever come back."

TWENTY-TWO

As we walk back to my house from the Rose, it's clear my role as an aggressor needs to begin immediately.

Freddy Starks sits in a silver Land Rover outside my house. His engine is idling, and the SUV's breath wisps in a white cloud from its twin tailpipes. I have to pass him to get to my house, and for a moment, I consider turning around.

"It's him," I say to Thomas.

"Him who?"

"Starks."

"But I thought he gave you two days. That's tomorrow."

"I guess you just can't take the word of a drug dealer anymore. Come on."

I don't look over as we walk by, though I'm tempted. After we pass, I hear the car door open and close. I'm nearly at my door when he calls out.

"Did you know someone died in your house?"

I turn.

"Go away," I say.

He starts walking toward us, hands buried in the pockets of a gray wool overcoat.

"It's true," he says. "I did a little research, mostly out of boredom. Manchester is a shit-boring town, but you can find some interesting things in the local newspaper archives of the library." He wears a smug expression. "Looked up your address. There was an article from the fifties about a woman who died in there. Lived alone, so it took a couple of days to find her. They think she stroked out. You ever hear her at night, Alice?"

"You said two days," I tell him. "Now get off my property."

Starks gets within ten feet of us and stops. "Who's your boyfriend?"

"I'm her brother, asshole."

"Whoa, some mouth on this kid."

I whisper to Thomas. "Take it easy."

I take two steps toward Starks. *Be the aggressor.*

"Careful there, sexy." Starks lifts one hand halfway out of his coat pocket, enough so I can see the handle of a gun. "You might be able to use your kung fu shit on me, but a

163

bullet wins every time."

"You said two days," I repeat.

He shrugs. "So I lied. What the fuck you want from me?"

I can hear Thomas breathing heavily behind me, and I'm aware that I'm effectively shielding him from Starks's line of sight.

"Go in the house, Thomas," I say.

"No," he says.

Starks says, "I'm bored here, Alice. I want to go home. The way I figure it, you made a decision whether or not to pay me in about five minutes after I left you. So another day doesn't really matter, does it? You either have my money or you don't, and me spending another night here isn't going to change that."

"We're getting the money for you," Thomas says. "But we can't do anything about it on a Sunday. You'll have to wait."

Starks loses his smug expression in an instant. Stripped away, all that's left is the snarl of an animal.

"Don't you fucking tell me what I have to do, kid," he says. "I do what I want, and if I'm saying you pay now, then you pay now."

I inch forward, weight on my back leg, trying to let my years of training control my movements. Trying to fight the fear, or at

164

least use the fear to focus me. I've taken self-defense classes where I've bested large men with weapons; the key is getting close enough to have a chance. I shift my focus between his groin and trachea; either one of those will do.

"We don't have fifteen thousand dollars in cash today," I say. "And no number of threats is going to make that happen. If you want it, you need to wait."

Now Starks takes the gun out of his jacket and holds it by his side. It's late afternoon, but I don't see anyone else on the snow-caked street. Then I wonder about Richard. Is he watching from upstairs?

"Maybe I don't really want the money," Starks says. "Maybe I've got plenty already, and I don't need yours. Maybe all I want is to hurt someone."

Starks takes another step. I need him about five feet closer before I have a chance of striking first.

"Get in the house," he says. "We'll talk there."

"No," I say.

He wiggles his gun in his hand. "Are you fucking blind, bitch? Or just stupid? Get in the fucking house, and move slowly."

I hear Thomas moving behind me. "Alice," he says. "Let's just go in the house. I'll get the key from the planter."

"You see, Alice? Just listen to your brother. Maybe he's the smart one of your family. Though he don't look it."

I turn my back to Starks, the last thing I want to do. But this way, I can see Thomas's position and adjust my body to block Starks's view of what Thomas is doing. Thomas leans down and scrapes through the top layer of snow in the planter. I step toward him and a bit to my right. Thomas finds the plastic bag and opens it up.

We need to get into the house without Starks. *Don't shoot him, Thomas,* I think. *Just point the gun at him long enough for me to disarm him. Once we get inside, we'll be safe.*

Thomas slowly pulls out the gun. Suddenly I see this all going horribly wrong. Thomas doesn't know how to use a gun, and we don't even know if it's loaded. The moment Starks sees it, he'll kill both of us before Thomas can even point the gun at him. I need to do something. If I stand here, we're going to die.

I turn and charge at Starks.

His expression changes into one of surprise, but that doesn't keep him from bringing his arm up and leveling his weapon at me.

I'm closing in fast. Another second and I might have a chance to knock his arm before he can fire. I plant on my right foot and swing my left leg around in a sweeping arc. Starks pulls back his arm before he fires, avoiding my kick. He takes a step back, just out of my range, and brings the gun up again.

"Stupid bitch," he says.

I lunge at him.

A single gunshot smashes my eardrums.

Just before I reach Starks, an invisible force sends him reeling backward. His gun skitters along the ice as he collapses on my driveway.

Blood pools, coating the top layer of snow like cherry syrup on a snow cone.

It almost looks pretty.

TWENTY-THREE

"Thomas!"

"He was going to shoot us, Alice! You saw that. I *had* to."

Starks on the ground, writhing and groaning, blood leaching into snow. Stomach wound, I think.

I scan the street, seeing no one. A small miracle. I peer up at my house. No Richard. Then I realize his car isn't even here, so he must have gone out when we were at the Rose.

"Thomas, we have to get him inside. *Right now.*"

"Alice, I don't think —"

I spin toward him. "Thomas, put the gun away and help me get him inside. *Now.*"

Thomas tries the door but can't open it.

"It's locked."

I toss him the keys from my jacket pocket, but he doesn't know which one is to my front door. He tries one at a time, and my head nearly bursts from frustration.

Finally, the door flies open. Alarm chirping.

"Four seven six five three," I tell him. "Turn off the alarm."

"Wait, what? Four seven what?"

"Goddamn it." I race past him and disarm the system. "Put the gun inside."

He does.

Then we both run out to Starks, who's trying to stand but failing. His gun is out of reach, but I still grab it and toss it inside my house.

"We'll each grab an arm and drag him," I say.

Thomas nods without saying a word. He looks like he might vomit.

"You fucking shot me, you goddamn . . ." Starks scrunches his face in a fresh volley of pain and doesn't complete his sentence.

I grab one of Starks's arms, and he yanks back with only weak force. Thomas grabs the other.

"Hold tight," I say.

"Fuck you," Starks moans. "I'll kill both of you." Then he pulls back hard, releasing both of his arms from our grips. He manages to twist onto his side, offering me a perfect opportunity.

I kick him directly in the stomach, perhaps

on the entry wound itself. Starks howls. Loud. I should have thought of that.

Miraculously, we are still alone on the street.

We grab his arms again, and this time, Starks offers no resistance. We flip him onto his back and drag him to the door. Up, over the threshold, into the entryway, across the hardwood, and onto the thick, cotton area rug, colored not too differently from the blood beginning to spill onto it. I look back at our path and see a few dribbles of blood along the way, though thankfully not an abundance of it. This all strikes me as a scene from a movie. Certainly not reality. Perhaps that's why I'm as calm as I am. None of this can be real.

"Go outside and cover up his blood," I tell Thomas. "Use the snow shovel near the door."

"What are we going to do with him?"

"I don't know," I say. "Just go."

And he does. While he's outside, Starks uses the opportunity to threaten me more, but his venomous hatred slowly becomes peppered more and more with pleas for help. He says it hurts. He says he doesn't want to die.

"I'll help you," I say, standing over him. "But first you have to help me."

He swipes at my leg with his hand, but I sidestep it easily, then deliver another kick, this time to his side. More blood on my rug. I don't care. I'm zoned in.

"Anything. Jesus, just call an ambulance. I'm bleeding out here."

I lean over him.

"How did you find me?" I ask. "Someone told you, right?"

He places his hand over his stomach, and the cracks between his fingers are quickly breached by a red stream.

"Oh God. Oh Jesus."

"Listen to me," I say. *Who told you where I was?*"

"I-I don't know. Some guy came . . . up to me. I didn't know him. Just named you and Jimmy, and gave me your address. Then took the fuck off."

"What did he look like?"

"I dunno." Another wince of pain. "White guy. Older."

"That's it? How old?"

"Fuck, bitch, I'm *dying* here."

How old?" I ready myself to kick him again.

"No . . . no. Okay, shit, maybe fifty, sixty. Who knows?"

"But you went to Jimmy first, even though you didn't have his address?"

"He wasn't hard to track down, and he was in Boston. Can you help me now? *I don't know anything.*"

Some older white guy tracked Starks down and told him about my involvement that night. This man is certainly Mr. Interested. But the question is, how does Mr. Interested even know about that?

Starks lashes out with his legs, a swift and clean arc sweep, and I'm too late to react. I crash to the ground, knocking the back of my head against the hardwood floor. The impact stuns me, and in an instant, I taste the salt of warm blood in my mouth, flowing from where I've bitten the inside of my cheek. I try rolling away, but Starks snakes his thick arm around my neck from behind, squeezing me in the crook of his elbow. I swing an elbow back, which lands on his ribs. He grunts but does not let up. He is wounded but strong. I try to fight the fear, try to relax my body and understand which parts of his body are vulnerable and how I might attack them.

But I can't breathe.

My throat threatens to implode at any moment. Panic is here, and it paralyzes me as much as Starks's power.

I exhale but can't bring in fresh air to replace it. The helplessness of this moment is beyond any panic attack I've ever had.

I try the elbow again, but I may as well be fighting underwater. All that training, all my strength, and how quickly it evaporates. Seconds.

Starks's voice in my ear. Hot breath on my face. "*This* is what I came here for, Alice."

I kick, but my legs don't connect with anything. My fingers claw at his arm, digging impotently into his overcoat. I swing for his head. It's out of reach.

I try screaming, but nothing comes. The only sound from me is a rattle deep in my lungs. My eyes feel like water balloons filled beyond capacity, ready to burst any moment.

Then a *crack,* a crunching sound. A wet, gagging sound comes from Starks, lasting only a heartbeat. His grip releases from my neck, and his hands mercifully slide from me. I gasp. Jump to my feet, spin around.

Starks doesn't move.

Thomas stands over him, the snow shovel held in both fists, the business end hovering a foot above Starks's head. There's fresh blood on the blade.

He's not dead. He's still breathing. Pulsating blood bubbles on his lips.

"Thomas," I say. My voice is a croak. I

don't know what to add. This is too surreal for coherent sentences.

"Are you okay?" he asks.

I reach up and touch my neck, raw and burning.

"I-I think so."

"He's still alive," Thomas says.

Just then, two things happen. Starks's right arm starts twitching, the only part of his body that does so. And my phone rings.

Thomas looks down at the coffee table where my phone vibrates and scoots along the smooth wooden surface. He reads the contact on the screen to me.

"It's Mom," he says.

"Oh, good God."

"Should we answer it?"

"*No,* we don't answer it. There's a man bleeding to death in my living room."

The phone vibrates a few more times and then falls silent.

"Alice, what do we do?" Thomas drops the shovel to the floor and closes the front door.

"Is the blood outside covered up?" I ask.

"Yes."

"Did anyone see you out there?"

"I don't think so. But what do we do about *him*?"

"I don't know." But I do know, don't I?

We do nothing, and by doing nothing, he dies. It's what we do *afterward* that stumps me.

"He was killing you, Alice. I had to do something."

I take three steps over to my brother, and I hug him. He seems little more than a scarecrow, skin so cold, it's a wonder blood flows through him at all. Neither of us is equipped to deal with what's happening now, but it suddenly hits me how little of the real world Thomas ever has to handle.

"Thomas, it's okay." I rub my hands on his back. "You saved me. He would have killed me for certain. You . . . you did the *right* thing."

"I think I'm gonna puke," he says.

"Don't puke. We've got enough to clean up."

He gives a small laugh, which might just be enough of a pressure relief to keep both of us from collapsing under the weight of all this.

My brother releases from me and runs his fingers through his hair. As he does, my phone buzzes a second time.

"It's Mom again," he says. "You should get it. Otherwise, maybe she'll come here."

He's right. She has a second car. As much as I don't want to talk to her right now, I answer the call.

"Hi."

"Oh, Alice dear, thank God you're there. I've made a terrible mistake."

Those words coming at this time make me clench all my muscles.

"What do you mean?"

"I was so awful to you and Thomas. I'm so sorry. And I need him to come home. There's no telling what type of problems he'll get into without me. He needs his medication. Alice, I *need* to take care of him. Can I talk to him?"

"He's . . . busy right now."

"Just send him home, Alice. Will you do that for me? Very soon."

"Mom, I think he needs to spend some more time here. Maybe a few days."

"Oh, I couldn't bear that. You don't know how to take care of him like I do."

"He's twenty-four years old. He *drove* here. He's got" — I look at the bloody snow shovel on the floor — "capabilities."

Her voice is softer, almost a whisper. "Oh no, Alice. He's just a boy. Just a helpless, innocent boy. He can't survive without me. Like a cub alone in the woods."

At that moment, I look over to my brother, and as I do, the antique wall clock chimes the five o'clock hour in its hollow, lonely tone. Thomas looks down upon Starks, wearing spray from the man's blood on his coat. Thomas is still, a ghastly mannequin, his head tilted slightly to one side, as he gazes at Starks with wonder.

"He's fine, Mom," I say, not believing it at all.

"He needs his medication," she replies. "He's not right without it."

"He can go a couple of days without it."

"He *can't*," she says. "I'm coming there to get him."

"No." *God no, not that.* "He has your other car anyway — he would still need to drive it to get back home. Let him spend the night here, and he can come home tomorrow morning."

Thomas snaps out of his reverie, looks to me, and shakes his head. I hold a finger up and mouth, *It's okay.*

"Alice —"

"Mom, it's okay to have a break. For both of you. It will make things better. Just give it a night, and we'll call you first thing in the morning."

Suddenly, Starks makes a low, moaning noise. I turn and look at him, and his eyes shoot open. The noise lasts maybe two seconds, but it petrifies me. Thomas grabs the shovel and holds it over his head to strike again, but I wave him off. The moaning stops, but Starks's eyes remain fixed open, like a creature futilely trying to see in the dark.

"Oh, Alice," my mother says, "I suppose one night is all right. But I'm telling you, he's not going to sleep a wink in any place other than his bedroom."

"He'll be fine."

A long sigh from her. "All right, dear. And I know he's standing there but doesn't want to talk to me. You never were good at fibbing, you know."

I say nothing to this. There is nothing to say.

"Call me in the morning, okay, dear? First thing, Alice."

"First thing," I say, then tell her goodbye and hang up the phone.

I'm turning to say something to Thomas when the only sound worse than a ringing phone fills the room.

Another fucking knock at my door.

TWENTY-FOUR

"Who's that?" Thomas hisses at me.

I raise my finger to my lips.

Shhhh.

Silence. Then, another knock.

I look at the two guns on the floor. I assume Starks's gun is loaded, but I know for sure the one from the planter box is.

I slowly creep toward the guns, trying not to make noise on the freshly bloodied floorboards.

"Alice?"

I know that voice.

"Alice? Are you in there?"

Richard. God, what does he want? Is the damn water heater out again?

Then I remember.

It's five o'clock. I invited him over at five, promising a glass of wine and a long story. I was going to spill my guts tonight.

I look over at Starks, thinking he's the one who spilled his. He's looking directly at me but not moving. Eyes wide open, likely paralyzed in shock.

"Don't answer," Thomas whispers.

"I know," I whisper back.

Richard's car wasn't here when Thomas shot Starks, so he couldn't have heard the gunshot. He must've pulled up just a few minutes ago. Did he see Thomas covering the bloody snow?

Richard knocks again. He knows I'm here.

"Hi, Richard," I call out. "I'm sorry, I have to cancel tonight. I'm not feeling well."

A pause. "Oh, okay, sorry to hear that. Is there anything I can get you?"

"No. No, thanks, Richard. I just need to rest."

"Okay, I understand." The disappointment in his voice is obvious. "It's just that, well, I want you to know you can talk to me if you want to. I'm a good listener."

"I'm sure you are, Richard. Another time, I promise."

Then I realize Richard must have seen Thomas's car in the driveway, a car he doesn't recognize. He probably thinks I found a better option for company tonight than him and am now feigning illness to get rid of him.

I almost feel sorry for him, but goddamn it, I have a dying man and at least a quart

180

of blood covering my living room rug. I have no capacity for sympathy at the moment.

I know Richard is still there because my squeaky wooden porch betrays the slightest shift of weight on it. He hasn't moved. He's wondering if he should say something else. But he's not the one who speaks next.

"Help me!"

Starks's voice jolts me. I turn, and Thomas holds the shovel high above his head, ready to strike again.

"Thomas, no," I say.

Through the door: "Alice? Alice, are you okay?"

"Get help before these crazy fuckers kill me! I'm hurt!"

Thomas doesn't hit him with the shovel, but he kicks him in the ribs. Starks yells out.

"Alice, what's happening? Should I call the police?"

"Yes!" Starks screams through gritted teeth.

"No, Richard," I say.

In an instant, I realize that if I let Richard walk away, this all falls apart. He calls the police, the police come, we plead self-defense. But we clearly tried to cover up the shooting. And the story will come out about why Starks was after me to begin with, and that will all tie back to Jimmy murdering a small-time drug dealer. I was there that night. I could be facing prison when this mess gets sorted out.

Then I remember something else.

Richard works at the hospital as an RN. He knows how to treat wounds.

It's a choice I don't want to make, but I have to.

I open the door.

Richard stares at me wide-eyed, but it's nothing compared to the expression on his face after I grab his arm and yank him inside, and he takes in the bloody chaos of my living room.

"I'm sorry," I say. "You're a part of this now."

TWENTY-FIVE

"Holy cow, Alice," Richard says. "We need to call an ambulance."

Holy cow. He actually said *holy cow*.

"Yes," Starks moans. "Do that. Ignore anything this crazy bitch says and call an ambulance." He tries to push himself off the floor but manages only a few pained inches of elevation before Thomas collapses him with another kick to the side.

"Richard," I say. "Listen to me." Richard continues to stare at Starks, so I grab his shoulders and turn him to me. "Listen to me, okay?"

I feel the tension in his shoulders as he nods.

"This man came here to kill me," I say.

"Which one?"

"The one on the floor. The other is my brother."

Thomas offers a weak wave. "Hey."

Richard returns a wide-eyed nod.

"Bullshit," Starks wheezes from the floor.

This time, Thomas screams at him. "Shut up!" Another kick, harder than the last. Starks yelps.

"Thomas, stop it!" I say.

Starks falls silent, and I think he's passed out.

I turn back to Richard. "Look at me. Focus. This is important. It's part of my long story I promised you. He was threatening us — was about to shoot me — and my brother shot him first. I promise you it was self-defense."

"Call the police," Richard says.

"I can't."

"Why not?"

"Because if they come here, at some point, they'll find out about my connection to a crime from years ago. I didn't commit the crime, but I was there when it happened. I could be considered . . . an accomplice."

"What crime? Alice —"

"It doesn't matter, Richard. The point is I'm not going to prison because this scumbag came hunting for me. I'm just trying to live my life. And I didn't want to involve you, but now you're here, and that can't be undone. You can help him, Richard. Maybe . . . patch him up, at least until we can get him to the hospital later on. We can drop him off. Anonymously."

Richard looks over my shoulder to the bloody mess on the floor.

"Patch him up?"

"I know it looks bad. Maybe you can at least look at him, see how bad?"

"Alice . . ."

"Richard, I'm begging you. Did you . . . did you look at that website from earlier?"

"Yes."

"Then you know I have a hell of a past. Bad things have happened to me, but I'm a *good* person. If I get caught up in this, I don't know what I'll do."

"Alice, how can I even examine him if he's dangerous? I don't even want to get close to him."

"I don't think that'll be a problem," Thomas says from across the room. I look over, and he nudges Starks with his foot. Starks is motionless. "He's out."

"C'mon," I say to Richard. I pick up the planter-box gun from the floor and walk carefully over to Starks. Richard follows but maintains a safe distance.

"Richard, he's unarmed. Unconscious. I'll keep the gun pointed at him if you can just check to see how bad he is. He can't hurt you."

"I don't even have gloves, Alice."

I run into the kitchen and grab a pair of yellow, rubber dishwashing gloves from beneath the sink, then race back and hand them to Richard.

"Are these new?"

"No, but they have to be clean enough," I say. "I use them with soapy water, after all."

He lets out a resigned sigh and snaps on one of the gloves. With his other hand, he reaches out to Starks's neck, tentatively at first. When he feels safe, Richard puts two fingers on Starks's throat and checks his pulse against his wristwatch.

"Pulse is low, but not dangerously so." He leans back and puts on the other glove. The first thing he checks is Starks's head, probing his fingers into the bloody, matted hair.

"Not too deep. But he'll need stitches. Tetanus shot for sure."

"How about where I shot him?" Thomas asks.

Richard reaches over and tries to unbutton Starks's shirt. At first, he fumbles because of the thick gloves, but he finally manages to work his way through all the buttons. He opens the shirt and pulls back as much of Stark's jacket as he can.

I keep my gun pointed right at Starks's head, but I can't help but move my gaze to the hairy belly painted in red. Bile creeps up my throat.

Richard sticks his finger inside the bullet wound on the edge of Stark's abdomen. Now I know Starks is truly passed out, because otherwise he'd be howling in pain.

"I'm gonna puke for real now," Thomas says.

"Then get out of here," I tell him. He does, heading for the kitchen. Once he's there, I hear him spit up into the sink. I force my own bile back down and steel myself against the sight of the gore.

Richard gets up, stands over Starks, then bends over and lifts him onto his side and checks his back. There's another hole, and once again, Richard pokes into it before resting Starks on his back.

"Bullet went through," he says. "About as clean of a wound as you can hope for. No major organs near the path where the bullet went, just muscle and fat. He's lost a decent amount of blood, so that's where we should start. I've got some gauze and large bandages upstairs, along with a suturing kit. Is it okay if I go up and grab them?"

I don't like that he asked my permission. It makes it sound like I'm holding him hostage. Perhaps I am.

I nod, and Richard straightens and takes off his gloves.

"Alice, I don't want to get into trouble over this."

"No, Richard. I don't want you to, either. Let's fix him up the best we can, wait until it's a bit darker, and then I can drop him off at the ER."

Richard nods and heads for the front door.

As he leaves, I wonder if he's going to lock himself into the Perch and call the police. Honestly, that's probably what I would do.

After a couple of minutes, I become very nervous.

Thomas comes back in the room and asks where Richard is.

"We might need to start running," I say. "We'll just have to get in the car and go, because if Richard is calling the police, they'll be here soon."

Then something wonderful happens.

Richard returns.

Starks comes to fifteen minutes later, after we've bound him to one of my dining room chairs with rope from my basement. I have no expertise in knots, but I make up for it with the sheer volume of loops I place around Starks. He reanimates as Richard finishes bandaging the entry wound. Starks gnashes at him with his teeth, like a fox caught in a snare. Thomas rips off a piece of medical tape and covers Starks's mouth.

"I've cleaned both wounds as best I can. The bleeding's stopped, but he'll need fresh blood and sutures. The sooner the better. And to get checked for a concussion."

I look at the clock on the wall. Not even 6:00 p.m., but at least it's dark out.

"I can't believe this is happening," I say.

"Alice, it's not too late to call the police."

"It *is* too late," I say. "That was never an option."

"*Why not?* What exactly did you do?"

Starks looks over with wide eyes and a crimson face. He would be all too happy to tell Richard that I'm a junkie, thief, and murderer.

So I tell Richard. Tell him about that night with Jimmy. But I tell the truth, which was I had nothing to do with the murder. How I ran that night.

"Ran where?"

"To my mom," I say, remembering that rare feeling of wanting to be cared for by her. Of needing her. It lasted less than three days. "Then rehab, then I moved up to Manchester."

"Jimmy never came looking for you?"

"If he did, I never knew it. By the time I left, he was constantly high. His brain was fried. I wouldn't be shocked to find out he didn't care I left."

Richard quietly processes all I've said.

"Wow" is what he finally says. Not even a *holy cow.* I was hoping for more, just as I'd hoped for advice from Thomas. But I don't know what I'd say if I were in their positions. I'd probably want to distance myself as much as possible.

"That's why we can't call the police. Just a little longer, then I'll drop him off at the ER."

"It's not that easy," Richard says. "There are security cameras outside. Besides" — Richard looks down at Starks — "he knows where you live. Where *we* live. He came for you once. How do you know he won't come back?"

All things I've already considered, but for which I have no answer. "I don't know what else to do," I say.

"We could kill him," Thomas says, a little too quickly.

Starks shouts into the tape.

"Thomas, we can't do that."

"Then *what the fuck,* Alice? Richard is right . . . Starks will just come back for you. Is that what you want?"

Starks shakes his head as if to say, *No, I promise I'll never come for you again,* but there's not an ounce of sincerity in his eyes.

"Of course not," I reply. "But we can't

190

just kill him."

Though that's just what Mr. Interested wants. He's nudging me toward very bad things, just as Mister Tender did with his customers.

I turn to Richard. "You don't have to be here anymore. I'm sorry I've dragged you into all of this, and I truly appreciate your help. But you should go. The longer you're here, the more trouble you could be in."

"So, I should just go upstairs, make myself dinner, and forget all this is happening right below me?"

"I know," I say. "I just . . . I don't want to get you too involved."

"Way too fucking late for that," Thomas mumbles.

"He's right," Richard says. "I'm already here. I can't erase that."

Thomas walks around and faces Starks, then leans down and peers deep into his eyes. "I'll bet he knows who Mr. Interested is. Hell, this might even be the creep stalking you, Alice."

"Mr. Interested from the website?" Richard asks.

I sigh. "It's what the glass of wine was going to be for," I say to Richard. "It's a long story, but it sounds like you already know some of it."

"It was hard to glean a lot of information from the Mister Tender. com site. I was pretty confused. Is there a short version of the story?"

I think on that for a second, then almost laugh at how a short version of my story would sound. Then I decide to actually try it out.

"I grew up in England. When I was fourteen, I was stabbed by two of my 'friends' who were convinced they were being commanded by a graphic-novel character named Mister Tender. A character who, by the way, was created by my father. I barely survived the attack. My parents split up afterward, and my mom brought my brother and me to America, at which time I changed my name because of all the media from the case.

"My father was murdered three years ago, yet just this week, I received a book in the mail — an unpublished cover of a book he never finished — which contained a handwritten inscription from him to me. The book is mostly blank but includes some drawings. The drawings depict me here in Manchester. Someone is *watching* me, Richard, and I've found out there's a small online community obsessed with me. The leader is this person calling himself Mr.

Interested."

"Holy cow," Richard says.

"I know."

"I mean, seriously?"

"Seriously."

"So this is Mr. Interested?" Richard asks, pointing to Starks.

"I'm not certain, but I don't think so. He claims Mr. Interested told him where to find me."

Richard thinks about this for a minute. "But how would anyone know about your involvement that night?"

Exactly what I've been wondering.

"Jimmy," I say. "He was there, and he probably could have tracked me down without too much trouble. It has to be Jimmy."

Starks shakes his head again, dying to speak. I walk over to him.

"Okay, I'm going to take the tape off your mouth. If you start yelling or saying things I don't like, I'm going to put it back on and keep it on. Understood?"

An eager nod of the head.

I take one corner of the tape and peel it away from his stubbled cheek. Then I rip. Fast and hard.

"Ah, *goddamn it,*" he says. "I'm going to fucking rip your —"

I grab the roll of tape, which stops his threat.

"Okay, look," he says. "I'll play by your rules. Just . . . just take me to the hospital, okay? I'm not in good shape."

"Actually," Richard says, "considering you've been shot and bludgeoned, you're doing okay."

Starks gives Richard a stare I can only guess means he's been added to his list of future targets, which now includes everyone in this room.

I stand in front of Starks, and as I shift my weight, I can hear the stickiness of blood on the bottoms of my shoes, blood that has spilled over the rug and onto the hardwood floor. Thomas sits in the chair about five feet behind Starks, the gun now in his hand, resting against his thigh. My brother has a glazed look in his eyes, as if he's been on a long, forced march, and his body has gone into some kind of shutdown mode. Maybe he *does* need his medication. Like, right now.

Richard nervously paces to my left, hands in his pockets, head mostly down, but glancing over at Starks every few seconds.

I take a deep breath, count to four, then let it out. I do that three more times, while Starks just watches me. I can only imagine the magnitude of the panic attack that will surely come from this, but in this moment, I feel surprisingly in control of myself.

"What did Jimmy tell you?" I ask him.

Starks smiles, and the smeared blood from his raw lips and cheeks looks like clown makeup. "He had a hard time saying anything with my gun halfway down his fuckin' throat."

"Did he tell you about me?"

"A little. Not much."

"What did he say?"

"He mostly mumbled about not having the money. I don't know. He's just a strung-out junkie. He was tweaked at the time, not even really that scared. He didn't even apologize about killing Nick."

"Did he tell you I left after that?"

"No."

"Did he tell you where to find me?"

"No. I told you I already knew that. That old guy who stopped me on the street told me."

"And what *exactly* did that man say about me?"

Thomas lets out a sigh, and I look at him. He looks completely detached now, as if sleeping with his eyes open. This worries me, but I put that worry in place behind larger ones I own at the moment.

"He said . . ." Starks looks up as if trying to remember, then finally drops his gaze back to me. "He gave me your address, but he said not to hurt you. Didn't care what I did to Jimmy, but didn't want you touched. Said you were *special.*"

"What?"

"That's what he said. Of course, I told him I'd be nice to you, but I had no intention of keeping my word. Why should I? I didn't owe nothing to that faggot."

"Why do you call him that?"

"I don't know. The guy seemed all fancy. Dressed up nice. Faggoty accent."

I lean closer to him.

"What kind of accent?"

"You know, pompous. Like a king."

British?

This brings a flood of questions into my mind, and now I want to know everything about this man who approached Starks on the street. Every detail of his appearance, his features, how tall he was, how he walked, his hair style. Everything.

I'm about to launch into my series of questions, but before I do, Thomas snaps from his reverie, raises the gun to the back of Starks's head, and pulls the trigger.

Starks's skull bursts like shrapnel all over my living room.

■ ■ ■ ■

PART II
THE GLASSIN TWINS

■ ■ ■ ■

TWENTY-SIX

Wednesday, October 21

The clouds outside the dirt-streaked window of the 777 are sunset-kissed, a dull pink-on-white, the sky vast and commanding. Yet even here, in this moment of stillness, I find no beauty. The clouds aren't painted by a setting sun. No, all I see is Starks's blood dissolved into dirty Manchester snow. I don't see the slow rotation of the wondrous earth thirty-eight thousand feet beneath me. I see a ticking clock. A time bomb, the seconds counting down before it explodes.

I lower the shade.

I'm flying to England. Back to my home. I'm not so much heading there as I am fleeing New Hampshire. London was a good choice, because I might find answers there. It's the birthplace of everything bad in my life.

What a mess.

I glance to my right and catch my seat-mate out of the corner of my eye. He's maybe midthirties, a bit shaggy and good-looking in a distressed-leather sort of way, smells vaguely of saddle soap, and, from the flashes I've seen on his laptop screen, works in real estate. He chatted me up a bit upon boarding in Boston, told me he's going to a conference in London, and asked what I did. I told him I owned a coffee shop, and he seemed more interested than anyone should be in that subject matter. He told me his name was Ben, and I shook his hand and told him my name was Mary. Ben doesn't wear a wedding ring. At an appropriate and early lull in the conversation, I put in my earbuds, and Ben faded easily into the background.

Yet Ben is persistent. He says something to me, and I pop my earbuds out.

"What?"

"You never told me what you're going to London for," he says.

"No," I say. "I didn't."

"Work or pleasure?"

I return his gaze. He's probably seven years my senior, but I feel so old in the moment, infinitely older than him. I'm certain I've produced more heartbeats in my life, and that counts for something. His eyes project youth and vibrancy. I feel beaten and worn.

"I had to get away from home, because my brother just murdered a man in my living room. Don't get me wrong; this guy had it coming. He was there to kill me, after all, and we couldn't chance going to the police. Which is another long story."

Ben's mouth is slightly open, that indecisive state in between smile and frown.

Screw it, I think. *This feels good.*

"Do you know how hard it is to dispose of a body?" I continue. "Especially that of a two-hundred-pound man? Massively difficult. And getting bloodstains out of a hardwood floor? Backbreaking. But we did it. But that only covered up the murder. I also have a stalker. He's been obsessed with me since I was nearly stabbed to death in London when I was fourteen. I figured maybe in England I can find a clue as to who this creep is and be done with him once and for all. So, I guess it all depends on how you define it, Ben. Does that sound like work or pleasure to you?"

Ben blinks once. Then twice. A flight attendant passes at that moment, and Ben catches her and asks for a Dewar's and Coke. She disappears up into the galley and then returns with the little plastic liquor bottle and the soda can. Bens pours and swizzles the drink, and at this point, I think he's not going to respond to me at all, which is, I suppose, what I was hoping for. He takes a sip, then clears his throat.

"You know," he says. "If you didn't want to talk to me, you could've just said so. I'll leave you alone."

Ben reaches into a leather messenger bag and pulls out his Bose headphones, plugs them into his laptop, and launches a movie. I recognize it even before the title credits appear. It's *The Martian,* the movie I saw just a few weeks ago. Someone drew an image of me leaving the theater that night, which ended up as a panel in my stalker's book. Everything seems endlessly connected, yet I can't figure a single thing out.

I reach up and turn off the light, pull my jacket over my shoulders, and curl up against the window. I don't bother to listen to music. I just listen to the white noise offered by the plane, and sometime later, I drift into a jagged sleep, where I dream of uncomfortable things.

My bones ache as I disembark from the plane hours later, my body craving exercise. My last true physical exertion occurred three days ago, when Thomas and I dug a grave in the White Mountains. For all the fear I've experienced in my life, none was quite so sharp and visceral as disposing of a body in the middle of the night, horrified that at any moment, brilliant red-and-blue pulses from a police cruiser's lights would wash over us. More likely, it would have been the sweep of a cop's powerful flashlight, illuminating us deep in the woods. Just dragging Starks's body that far was nearly impossible, but that wasn't the truly challenging part. That was reserved for digging into frozen ground, one tiny shovelful at a time. We each had a flashlight, but the light did little more than make me feel exposed. It took nearly two hours to create a hole we thought would keep the scavengers out and roll Starks into it. I was keenly aware that, despite our gloves and amateurish attempts at caution, our DNA could well be somewhere on his body. A hair, most likely. But ridding ourselves of the corpse still didn't compare to the challenge of cleaning up my house, which looked like a Pollock painting.

But even *that* wasn't the real problem.

The real problem was — and still is — Richard.

After Thomas killed Starks, the next thing my brother did was aim the gun directly at

Richard.

"Thomas, what are you doing?" I had asked.

The room was silent, though the concussion of the shot that killed Starks still echoed in my ears.

"He's a problem," Thomas said. "He could turn us in."

"Put the gun down! He's helping us. God, Thomas, you just *killed* Starks. What is wrong with you?"

But Thomas didn't put down the gun. He held it fast with a hand that, incredibly, didn't shake. He was so calm and focused. He was in a video game.

Richard hadn't flinched. He maintained his gaze with Thomas, the two of them locked in to each other. Richard didn't seem scared. He didn't plead for his life, didn't try to convince my brother that he wouldn't go to the police. Instead he stood there for maybe a minute, a forever length of time. I waited for the shot to come, the blood to spray. I think I said something to Thomas again, but I don't really remember.

Then Richard turned and walked to the door. Thomas kept the gun trained on him the entire time but didn't fire. Richard opened the door and left, but he didn't drive away. I heard his weight on the steps leading to the Perch, the door opening and closing, and then nothing. Like he always did, Richard had once again turned into the ghost upstairs.

The police never came. I didn't go to see Richard. I figured if he was going to report what had happened, he would've already. So all Thomas and I could do was get rid of the evidence the best we could.

After we buried Starks, Thomas and I cleaned my car, scrubbing and vacuuming until it was spotless. Back at my house — at this point just after two in the morning — our attention turned to the mess in the living room. We were running on nothing but adrenaline at that point. We created a macabre collection of evidence to be disposed of: the bloodstained area rug, the rope, the pieces of medical tape, the chair Starks occupied, the bloody snow shovel, the shovels we used to bury Starks, our dirt-smeared clothes, the two guns. Worst of all, the three pieces of Starks's skull that had landed on the living room floor near my fireplace. I picked them up with a plastic bag, much like I would a dead bird found in my yard, and added them to the pile.

We scrubbed the floor and walls. Fortunately, most of the blood had been soaked up by the area rug. Though the remaining blood appeared to come out completely with Clorox bleach spray, I'm not so ignorant as to believe our efforts would stand up to a true forensic analysis. If the police came to my house looking for evidence of a crime, they would find it, I'm certain. Probably easily. A few sprays of luminol.

I can only hope no one will be surprised that a Boston drug dealer went missing, and that little effort will be made to find him. At some point, all you can do is pray. This is true whether or not you even believe in God.

Thomas and I built a large fire in my fireplace that night, and on top of the wood, we added all the things that could easily burn. Everything else we bleached and wiped and tossed in three separate Dumpsters later. As for the pieces of Starks's skull, I placed them in a gallon-size ziplock bag, took a hammer, and pounded them into tiny pieces. The powder of an ex-man.

I fought to repress my disgust at this, especially in handling the chunk with a small piece of scalp dangling like a loose tooth from it on one side and a slick coating of blood on the other. I tried to manage the process with the detachment of a field surgeon, just dealing with the bits and pieces and not concerned with the actual human to whom those bits and pieces belonged. Looking back, my overall coolness surprises me. For years, I've suffered panic attacks over memories, but actual blood on my fingers left me relatively calm and focused.

Thomas barfed until there was nothing left but scorching dry heaves.

Once I'd pounded the pieces of skull into manageable pebbles, I flushed them down the toilet. Farewell, Freddy Starks.

Thomas slept for about three hours; sleep did not come for me. When he woke, he put on the one change of clothes he'd brought with him and drove back to our mother's house. He was calm, almost pleasant. I wonder if he would have done what he did had he taken his medication.

"You should get out of here," he'd told me. "Just for a little while."

Once Thomas was gone, I'd checked my laptop for any messages from Mr. Interested. Nothing.

I haven't heard from him since he told me to kill Freddy Starks.

I walk groggily through Heathrow, which is a buzz of activity around me. Swarms of people, all with intense purpose and direction. Ben is gone from my view, and now my life. I queue up at immigration. I maintain dual citizenship, so I choose the shortest line: UK nationals. Signs all around tell me to turn off my cell phone, and as I reach for my mine, I notice a missed text. It's from Verizon, welcoming me to the UK and telling me how much money I will spend if I care to use my phone here. I silence the ringer and slide it back into my purse.

I was doing fine asleep on the plane, but as I stand in this line, my nerves begin to fray. Seven immigration officers are waiting up ahead, and suddenly I wonder if there's an alert out for me. Maybe Richard talked. Maybe Mr. Interested knows everything and sent a tip to the police, just as he tipped off Freddy Starks.

This flood of paranoia slowly builds to the point that I start thinking of proper nouns such as *MI5* and *Interpol*.

I inch forward in the queue, a sea of drained travelers surrounding me. Families, business travelers, students. Scanning their faces, I see no fear. Just fatigue, boredom, impatience. But not guilt. What do they see on mine?

Closer. Now I'm certain this is all a mistake. What the hell was I thinking, coming here? *They know,* I think. Once my passport is swiped, a word is going to appear on the screen in front of the immigration officer. A word like *detain.*

Another agent directs me to a shorter line in front of one of the kiosks. I look at the officer with heightened fear. He's not the one I was hoping for. There was another officer one kiosk over, and he was smiling at the travelers in his queue. Joking, even. Not this guy. My guy is younger, Indian or Pakistani. Maybe thirty. He's been scowling the entire time, as if disappointed every time someone passes through without incident. He spends an inordinately long time with the man in front of me, asking him several questions I can't make out.

I shift my weight back and forth between legs, trying to use my breathing exercises to steady my pulse. It does no good. I look up at all the cameras recording me, and I picture a team of analysts in a room somewhere, leaning into their monitors and studying the live stream, reading the signs of anxiety that are surely evidenced in every bit of my body language. They are alerting my guy something is up with me, that I should be given extra attention. The harder I try to calm myself, the more I feel like screaming. God, I have to get out of here.

But there's nowhere to go. Just forward.

Finally, the man in front of me passes through.

My guy beckons me over with an imperial

flick of the wrist.

I hand him my British passport, and he scans it in the reader. I wait for alarms to begin screaming.

He leans in and squints at his monitor. "You're a U.S. resident, then?"

"Yes."

"What's the nature of your visit?"

The question rattles me. Why does it matter? I'm a citizen of the UK, so it shouldn't be necessary for me to tell him why I'm here.

"Visiting family," I manage to say.

He looks me over, a scowl on his dark, acne-scarred, swarthy face. He holds the passport up and flicks his gaze between my photo and my face.

"When is your return flight?"

It's getting harder to keep the panic from reaching up and squeezing my throat closed.

"Three . . . three days from now."

"What areas will you be visiting?"

Take control, Alice. You're scared, and he smells it. I don't think they know anything, but I don't want to give them reason to question me further.

"I'm sorry, but can you explain to me why that matters?" I ask. "I'm a citizen of this country. Why do I need to tell you where I will be going?"

His scowl deepens for just a second, then quickly melts into a smile. Boyish.

"I live in Clerkenwell," he says. "If you're in that area, maybe we can meet up for a coffee."

Are you fucking kidding me? I'm on the cusp of a heart attack, and this immigration agent is trying to pick me up? Yet my anger is still tempered by relief.

I reach out and pluck my passport from his hand.

"How often does that work?" I ask.

"Virtually nil," he admits. "But given how many people come through my lane, the numbers bear out."

"Can't you get in trouble for that kind of thing?"

He shrugs. "It wouldn't be the worst thing to be sacked from this job."

"Can I go?" I ask.

"So I assume your answer is no."

"The answer is no. Can I go?"

The scowl is back. He flicks me away as brusquely as he'd summoned me, and I become another one of his statistics, a tick in the *no* column. I leave to claim my bag.

At the luggage carousel, I reach back into my purse to check my phone for Wi-Fi. I want to at least let Thomas know I've arrived. We've both agreed not to write anything even remotely incriminating in our emails or texts, but I can let him know I'm here.

As I unlock the screen, I see another text has arrived. Likely another bit of traveler advice from Verizon, but it only takes a second for me to see it's not. It's not that at all.

It's from a blocked number.

Welcome home, Alice.

TWENTY-SEVEN

How, How, How? How can he possibly know I'm here?

I don't reply. Flustered, I turn off my phone and make my way out of the airport to the taxi stand, where I ask my driver to take me to Dollis Hill, a northwestern suburb of London. He asks for an address, and instinctually I begin to give him the address of my childhood home but stop myself.

"Are there hotels there?" I ask.

"There are hotels everywhere, miss. You have one in mind?"

"Something near Gladstone Park."

He reaches two fingers beneath his wool cap and scratches his head.

"Don't know that area all too well," he says. "Give me a minute." He consults his iPhone, then says, "There's a Travelodge nearby. And a Holiday Inn. Both of them too far to walk to the park, I'd say, if the

213

park is where you want to be."

God, is the park really where I want to be? The way he says it makes it sound like Disney World.

"Anything closer?"

He looks again. "There's an inn. Quincey House Hotel. Three and a half stars on TripAdvisor. Right on the south side of the park. That's the closest."

I have a vague memory of that hotel from my youth but can't picture it.

"Can I bother you to phone them and see if they have rooms?"

"My pleasure." He dials, has a brief conversation, then turns back to me. "He's wanting to know how many nights."

I have no idea. "Three," I say, figuring that would be on the long side.

He relays the information, chirps "Very good, then," and hangs up.

"Quincey House Hotel it is, then."

"Thank you."

At least I have some place to stay, though I still have no plan or even much of an idea of what I'm doing here. I have some vague notion of a direction and a strong hope that an invisible current will carry me along until a path becomes clear. Or perhaps it will just dump me out into the ocean, setting me adrift forever. I suppose that's a reasonable end as well.

The driver tells me it will be at least a forty-minute drive. I nod in agreement, and as he pulls from the curb, I close my eyes less out of fatigue and more to prevent conversation, but within minutes, I'm asleep. It's a bumpy, fitful half sleep, but qualifies as sleep because I have dreams.

I dream of the sea.

I'm a little girl, and our family is at Littlehampton Beach, where we would go for a few days every summer. In my dream, I'm running along the small sand dunes, and though I have no concept of how old I am, I see Thomas, and he's just a tiny boy, so I can't be more than about seven. The air is heavy with salt, and the sound of small waves licking the shore is louder than it should be. Crackling, like heavy static on a radio.

I chase Thomas through and over the dunes; he squeals with delight. He scurries behind a dune, and I scale it to reach the other side, only to find he's not there. I look to my right, and somehow he's now a hundred yards away, past the chalky-white sand and out in the water, where my mother holds him fast with both hands. My father is on the shore, building a sand castle, lost in his own world of creation. My father was

215

often lost in creation.

I watch as my mother lowers Thomas into the water, belly first, positioning her arms beneath him. She's teaching him to swim. She's thin here, and quite lovely. Nothing like how she looks now. Thomas kicks and flails his arms, spastic attempts to keep himself afloat, but he starts to sink as my mother pulls her arms away. He panics, and she lifts him up again, reassuring him that *she has him.*

I can hear her so clearly.

I have you, silly boy. I'll never let you go.

Then she repeats the process. Thomas kicks and flails, then slowly sinks until she lifts him from the water once again. This goes on and on, and I just stand on my dune and watch. In the distance, the sad, lonely warble of gulls echoes.

I look to my father, whose creation is suddenly massive and striking, but not a castle at all. He has rendered Mister Tender from a billion grains of wet sand. The bartender is life-size, rising from the ground like some kind of sea creature come ashore to feast. The creation looks at me, just me, smiling as my father fortifies its legs, making it stronger, protecting it against a swirling, rising tide.

Then, in the imagination of the dream ver-

216

sion of me, I picture one of those legs moving. Breaking free of the beach, lifting of its own accord. Coming to life. But it's real. I see it. My father steps back, nervous and proud, admiring what he has brought into this world.

Mister Tender turns to me and smiles.

His other leg lifts.

A small step, then a larger one.

He grows larger as he heads directly toward me, consuming the beach with every pounding step, adding height, weight. Depth. In seconds, he's a tower. My father is gone.

The sand monster is coming to kill me.

Then, a scream. But it's not mine. It's Thomas's. I look past the sand creature closing in and see my mother near Thomas, but this time, she didn't pick him up after he began to sink in the water. She just left him, and the scream I heard was the last he made before he slipped beneath the surface. For a flash of a second, I see his little white hand poking above the top of the shimmering waters, but once it disappears, I see him no more.

My mother calmly walks back to shore, wiping her hands on her hips, back and forth, back and forth. For a moment, she is smiling, and then she wears no expression at all.

Shadows on my face. Then my view is blocked entirely.

The sandman is here.

I jolt awake when the taxi stops at a light, and I'm so disoriented and rattled from the dream that I grab the top of my knees to steady myself. A few deep breaths, then I turn to the window.

The neighborhood isn't familiar to me, but the *look* of things is, as is the smell. Britain has such a distinct scent, I think. There's such an age to it. The smell of centuries-old books.

Ten minutes later, things start to spark memories. The rows of houses, the grocers that haven't changed in all this time, and then, finally, Gladstone Park. It's out my window, and as we travel past, I decide to close my eyes again. It will be there if I want to look, especially since I'm staying nearby, but right now, I don't care to.

The driver pulls up in front of the Quincey House Hotel, a three-story brick building that looks as if it could have been a small school a hundred years ago. I realize I'll need to use my credit card to pay the driver. It makes me nervous, as it will be another part of a trail I'm leaving, but I have little other choice. I could take money from a nearby ATM, and will likely do that, but that's a fingerprint as well. There is no easy way to hide.

As he hands me a receipt, the driver says, "Suppose this park is special to you. Not a lot to it. Most tourists prefer Hyde Park or St. James's."

I don't want to tell him the park is special to me, because that's not the word I would use. But I also don't want to explain why I would use the word *haunts.*

So I simply reply, "I'm not a tourist."

Inside, I tell the front-desk clerk I'm the person who just inquired about a room for three nights. He nods and smiles but thankfully engages in little small talk. I hand him my credit card, and he asks for my passport, which I lightly protest against, but he informs me hotel policy insists upon it. When I hand it over, he proceeds to make a photocopy. Any chance of anonymity is officially gone.

Upstairs, my room is decent if not a little antiseptic, as if whatever charm this building once had was efficiently sanitized away by uninspired hotel architects. But it'll do. Before I bother to do anything else, I collapse on the bed, wriggle my feet under the covers, and sleep.

This time, there are no dreams. My ghosts have decided to get a little sleep of their own.

Twenty-Eight

I wake in darkness so suffocating, I could be inside a coffin. Dizzy seconds pass. I steady my breathing and try to remember where I am. I feel drunk, drugged, confused. A shaded window's outline glows in some sort of distance, a faint rectangle of light. Then, with the fierceness of a bad memory, it all comes to me.

London. I'm in London. *Gladstone Park.*

I'm hungry. God, I am so hungry.

I turn in the bed and look over at the clock, which reads just after 8:00 p.m. *Eight?* I've been asleep for hours.

I sit up, place my feet on the floor. Blood drains from my head, and for a second, I think I'm going to topple. I could easily go back to sleep, but I fight it off. I don't want that. I want to get up. I *need* to get up.

In the bathroom, I splash lukewarm water on my face, pull my hair back and tie it up, brush my teeth. Life begins filling me again.

Grab my bag, double-checking it for my laptop, wallet, phone. Shoes on. In the small lobby, I ask the same desk clerk the closest place for a bite, and at this point, I don't even think I'd protest against fast food. Thankfully, he directs me to a pub down the street. Quick walk. Inside the pub, I nearly faint from the wonderfully heady aroma of a shepherd's pie I order. I rarely drink beer, but here I have a pint, and as the last drops slide down my throat, I admonish myself for not drinking it daily. I order another. As the server drops it off, I ask him to remove the dinner knife from the table, telling him I won't be needing it.

I pull out my laptop, boot it up, and connect to an open Wi-Fi network. There's an email from Brenda. She tells me things are fine at the Stone Rose and asks again if I'm okay. I tell her what I wrote yesterday. *All is good. Just need a few days to deal with some things. Thanks for your understanding.* Nothing else. She has no idea I'm thousands of miles away.

No email from Thomas.

Nothing from Richard.

Most notably, nothing from Mr. Interested since his ominous text. I have a constant sense of his breath on the back of my neck.

I check the online news back in Man-

222

chester, and there's no mention of a body being found in the White Mountains. I search Boston news sites, and there's nothing about a missing drug dealer, though that might not even be newsworthy. But it's not relief I feel. It's more like anxiety, because I know what we've done doesn't just go away forever. Nothing just goes away forever, much less a murder.

I open a blank Word document and start typing.

The book is postmarked London. Dad's handwriting on the inscription, which tells me not to trust anyone. Is he telling me not to trust Mr. Interested? Did he even know him? Or is it all just a forgery?

Why does he call himself Mr. Interested? Because he's interested in every aspect of my life?

I think about this for a moment, staring at the name. Say it aloud. "Mr. Interested." There's something familiar about the lettering, the sounds, the cadence. Then a thought hits me, and I switch over to my web browser. I Google *anagram* and find a site where I can type any word or words, and it will spit out all other possible word combinations based on those letters.

I type:

Mister Tender

Hundreds of results, but only one that isn't nonsense. It's the first result on the list.

Mr. Interested

I sit up straighter and stare at the screen. This feels like a meaningful moment, but I don't quite grasp the significance.

It's an anagram. Okay, I get it. Clever. One minor mystery solved. But does that really tell me anything? Is he telling me he *is* Mister Tender? If so, what the hell does that even mean?

Back to my writing.

What I know about him:
   He's older. Starks called him "fancy." British accent. FIfty or sixty.
   Assume he lives near me, but the book was sent from London — does he travel back and forth? He watches me, but hard to say how often. He's been at my house, maybe even inside it. At least knows what the inside looks like. Says he's been watching me for a long time. Somehow even knows about Jimmy and me and the

night in Boston. Was able to track Freddy Starks.

He can draw like Dad. Maybe even mimic his handwriting.

He has access to guns.

Tech savvy? Maybe. Enough to run a message board, which probably isn't hard. He knows I'm in England. Is he tracking my phone somehow?

I stop, knowing I could write myself into circles. Really, there's only one immediate question, and it's the last thing I type on the page before shutting down the laptop.

Where do I go next?

I already know the answer, even if I haven't fully admitted it to myself. It's why I chose to stay in this neighborhood. Maybe it's the real reason I came to England.

There's a sip of beer left, and I swallow it. For a brief moment, I consider actually ordering another, but instead I pay my bill and provide an answer to my one immediate question.

I walk outside and head deep into Gladstone Park.

Twenty-Nine

Once I step outside, cool, moist air curtains me, creeping down my neck, burrowing under my shirt. Settling on my skin.

I enter the park from the southwest gate, the opposite corner from my old house. The park is nearly a hundred acres in size. I walk briskly, not caring to linger though I have nothing for which to be late. My path is lit by the occasional security light, and a CCTV camera is mounted next to every one of them. I have forgotten about the British obsession with monitoring. All the more reason to suspect Mr. Interested is a product of England. He comes from this culture of surveillance, one that watches every move. Records every breath.

As far as I can see, I am alone, which doesn't at all mean I am. All I hear are my own hurried footsteps on the path and the distant hum of light traffic on nearby streets. I stop once and look directly behind me.

Nothing.

There is a haunting nostalgia here, a childhood familiarity layered with seconds of sheer terror. I used to play in this park. I nearly died in this park. I chased young boys in this park. Over three pints of my blood spilled in this park.

Ahead are the trees I remember so well. They had been planted in such a way that the park seems to turn into a dense forest without warning. Thomas and I used to call this section Hundred Acre Wood, and I would always play Christopher Robin. Thomas would always be Tigger, bounding and bounding about, both reckless and delighted with himself. Sometimes a whole day would pass here, though we'd hardly be aware of more than a few minutes going by. I suppose that's really the definition of childhood. As you age, the day eventually seems as long as it actually is, and toward the end of one's life, I imagine a single day can feel like a lifetime.

I enter Hundred Acre Wood, and immediately I'm swallowed inside the dense covering of trees. The path snakes next to a small creek. The trees loom over me, like a million predators frozen in mid-pounce. Streetlights shine small pools of light on the ground, and it's all I can do to convince myself to make it to the next one. One step after the other, though, these steps are slowing. Getting smaller. Less certain in their purpose.

There. Up ahead. There's the bridge.

What am I doing here?

Closure, perhaps, whatever that really means. The truth is, ever since the moment I chose to come to England, I knew I would come here. To the place it all happened.

It happened, in fact, right *there.*

Up ahead, a small wooden pedestrian bridge crosses the creek, park benches bookending each side. In the fall, we would drop leaves off the bridge and watch them softly float away. Sometimes we'd follow them all the way to the edge of the park, where they would bunch against a grated culvert. I always wondered what was inside that culvert, where it led, and what sorts of things might call that dark, wet place *home.*

Sylvia and Melinda Glassin once said that was where Mister Tender lived. That he'd rise from the depths of the culvert at night and go to the pub, holding court until the last customer went home. Then he'd slither back home, turning his body into a kind of rubber so he could squeeze through the narrow bars of the grate. Of course I knew this wasn't true. My father invented Mister

Tender, after all, and he never wrote about where he lived. As far as anyone could tell, Mister Tender's existence began and ended in a bar, and he never slithered anywhere else in between.

My pace slows as I step onto the bridge. I can hardly see the creek in the faded light of the streetlamps, but I can hear it. The slow-moving water trickling over rocks sounds ghostly in the moment. Empty. Lonely, almost.

At the top of the small bridge, I stop and then crouch to one knee. My fingertips brush the coarse wood planks by my foot, and if I squint in the dark, I can almost picture the blood. But surely it's not here anymore. It's been cleaned up, and perhaps these planks have been replaced altogether.

But here, *right here,* is where it happened.

Melinda took me by the hand, while Sylvia walked behind us. I remember thinking how odd it was that she wanted to hold my hand, or even that the twins had shown recent interest in me at all, considering I was seen as more of a freak than anything as my father's books sold more and more. Mine was otherwise a quiet existence, so when the Glassin twins came over one night and asked if I wanted to "hang out," I could hardly protest.

We'd spent the evening at their house, a few blocks off the south side of Gladstone Park. My parents weren't thrilled with the idea of me spending time with the Glassin twins, going so far as saying the Glassins weren't "their type of people." They never explained what they meant by that. But I was fourteen and desperate for any kind of attention, so I protested loudly enough that my parents buckled beneath the weight of my teenage angst.

At dinner with the Glassins that night, the twins' father asked me about my dad, about where he got all his ideas. *I don't know,* I had replied. It was the truth. How his mind worked was always a beautiful and maddening puzzle.

"Surely you must know," Mr. Glassin had insisted. "Surely he tells you such things. Tells you his inner thoughts."

"No," I had replied. "I don't know anyone's inner thoughts. That's what makes them inner."

Mrs. Glassin told me they used to be social with my parents, long ago. Before I was born, even. But that they'd grown apart once the babies started to come along. "That's to be expected," she'd said. "Hard to find time for anyone else once you pour your life into your children."

This was a surprise to me.

I remember thinking I wanted to ask my parents about their long-ago friendship with the Glassins. I never did.

After dinner, I spent the next few hours in the twins' shared bedroom, where the girls proudly displayed each issue of my father's graphic novels. The books exhibited the battle wounds of well-read volumes. Sylvia and Melinda peppered me with question after question about Mister Tender. Were there things about him I knew that no one else did? What was going to happen in the next issue?

But the question I remember most:
What would you do for him, Alice?

"Nothing," I had said. "Because he's not real."

Oh, the look of disappointment. Anger even, especially on Sylvia's face. Then Melinda calmly said, *Of course he's not real, Alice. But that's not the game we're playing, is it?*

After that, there were no more questions.

We settled into a movie that we watched on a small television in their room. Lights off. I sat on the floor, the twins propped side by side on their bed behind me. I don't remember the movie exactly, but it was scary. Scarier than I was accustomed to, but they had insisted on it, being near Halloween and all. I wasn't very familiar with the concept of Halloween, but I sat there and watched a movie and tried not to close my eyes in fear, all because I wanted these girls to like me.

I could hear them whispering during the moments of silence.

She's scared.

It's okay.

Does she know?

Of course not.

I thought maybe they were planning a prank, something innocent like reaching out and grabbing me during a particularly jolting scene. But in the bedroom, they never touched me.

After the movie, they offered me mushrooms. I didn't understand why we would be eating mushrooms after we'd already had dinner, until they explained these were *magic* mushrooms. Horrible tasting, but mind altering. Illegal mushrooms.

You'll see everything differently, Alice. Everything will be beautiful, and nothing will hurt.

I remember Melinda's words so clearly, because we'd just read Vonnegut's *Slaughterhouse-Five* in school, and that sentence had stuck with me. The little hand-drawn image of the tombstone with the inscription *EVERYTHING WAS BEAUTIFUL, AND NOTHING HURT.* So curious.

Melinda reached out her hand, and I saw little dried-up brown things shriveled in her palm, like the ears of small creatures. I knew some kids at school had access to drugs, or at least claimed to. Pot, mostly. But this was the first time I'd ever seen actual illegal drugs, and it made me feel completely out of my element. I felt older than I wanted to be and had a sudden longing for childhood.

I could smell the mushrooms from two feet away, and the aroma was powerfully bad. My need to be accepted by these girls was overruled by my fear of the unknown. What if the mushrooms made me crazy? What if my parents found out? Could I get addicted?

I declined. Melinda and Sylvia each popped one in their mouths, giggling in their communion.

I always wonder what I would have felt that night had I taken the mushroom. I don't think any drug would have made what happened beautiful, or would have anesthetized the pain.

I recall their energy as we sat in their dark bedroom — energy that, as the drugs took effect, shifted from nervous to confident.

They kept laughing over a joke never shared with me, and after a couple of hours, I no longer felt a part of anything, and I wanted to go home. It was nearly eleven at night, and I was supposed to be home by ten thirty.

They insisted they walk me home. Said I shouldn't walk alone through the park at night.

Melinda and I walked out of the house; Sylvia said she'd be right there. This was the moment, according to testimony at the trial, she went into the kitchen and removed the eight-inch chef knife from the butcher block on the kitchen counter. Sylvia emerged moments later. Melinda took me by the hand, while Sylvia followed behind. I was distracted by Melinda's hand on mine — *Why is this girl holding my hand?* — which I think was the whole point of it. At a normal walking pace, it would have taken less than ten minutes to navigate through the park to my house, but Melinda walked slowly, weaving me around the path, and any time I picked up my pace, she pulled on my arm with just the slightest pressure, easing me back. *What's the rush?* she asked. *Everything is beautiful.* The mushrooms were taking hold of her.

She asked me about my father, echoing

her own dad's line of questioning from dinner. What he was like? Where did he come up with his ideas?

I told her I did not know. That I wasn't even allowed to read the books.

She squeezed my hand and turned to me. In the streetlight, her eyes blazed. *You haven't even read the books?*

No, I told her. Which was a bit of a lie. I had read some, but they disturbed me.

Do you even understand who Mister Tender is?

Yes, I said.

I could hear the trickle of the creek. We had stopped just short of the footbridge. In the far distance came the sound of men laughing. Mates walking home after the pub.

So you know he can make your dreams come true, right? If you do what he says, he'll give you what you want.

He's just a character, I told Melinda. Ink on paper. A cartoon.

But what if he wasn't?

What do you mean?

Sylvia stopped close behind me. She said nothing, but I could feel her presence. Close. Blocking.

What if he was real? Melinda asked.

I don't understand, I told her.

Melinda squeezed my hand hard. At the

time, I took it as a sudden burst of affection, maybe a reaction to the drugs. Later, I realized it was meant to keep me from running.

She leaned in. She wore cheap perfume, and Sylvia didn't, which sometimes was the only way I could tell them apart. *He writes to us,* she said. *He told us to become friends with you. You don't think we'd otherwise care about someone like you, do you?*

Now Sylvia giggled. I could feel her close behind me, but I didn't turn. I should have turned.

Alice, you know what we want? We want to become famous. Look at us. We deserve to be noticed.

I think you're high, I told Melinda.

She grabbed my free hand, and I just let her. She looked at me with so much interest, like I was a newly discovered life form. She leaned in and said, *He can give us fame. We just have to give him what he wants.*

I don't think I ever actually asked the question, but it formed in my head. I think I was too scared to ask, because she might tell me.

But she did anyway.

He told us we had to make a sacrifice. That everything comes with a price, and our price was you.

What?

Melinda looked over my shoulder, and as both of her hands clamped tighter on mine, she nodded. Just the faintest bob of her head, and she held me fast in place. Then she mouthed the word *NOW.*

I turned to look, but Melinda held my hands fast, so the best I could manage was a half turn. But it was enough for me to see the knife high above Sylvia's head — silhouetted in lamplight — its grip held in both her hands. I didn't even see her face. All I could see was that knife, and it seemed suspended above me for an eternity. But in truth, it was there for maybe two seconds. Perhaps there was the slightest hesitation on her part, a millisecond of second-guessing, the briefest splash of reality on her insanity. But that lasted only as long as it took Melinda to shout:

DO IT!

Just as she screamed, I have the vaguest notion of another voice. A man, somewhere in the distance, deep in the trees, screaming one word:

Stop!

This could have been a voice in my own head, or perhaps it was the man who found me bleeding and called for help. Whoever that voice was attached to, it has remained a mystery.

The knife came down in a swift, tight arc. Worse than being stabbed is that instant when you see it about to happen, and you imagine how the cold steel will so easily penetrate your skin, your muscle, even your bones. The inevitability of it all. That's what I still dream about. Not the moment I was actually stabbed, but that breath of time immediately before.

Sylvia stabbed me three times before she handed the knife to her sister. When it was Melinda's turn, I was on the ground at the edge of the bridge, just off the path, with my head in the grass. I remember the burning, sucking pain of that moment, but also the cool of the wet grass on the back of my head. It was soothing, like a cold compress. Melinda stood over me, and there was no doubt in her expression. No second-guessing. And before she plunged the blade five more times into my body, all she said was:

We'll have everything we ever wanted.

I didn't try to move after they left me to die. I couldn't even if I had wanted to. My body had nothing left in it, no energy to expel. Shock settled over me like a heavy lead blanket, a sensation I still feel on the onset of my panic attacks to this day. Now when I feel it coming on, it's terrifying, but at the time, in the moment, my body at the foot of the little pedestrian bridge, that lead blanket kept me safe. Told me everything would be over soon.

The creek kept trickling as I bled to death in the softness of the night. I remembered thinking the sound of the moving water would be the last thing I would ever hear, and in that moment, that was quite all right. There was an eternal element to that sound. Music to carry me away.

I don't remember being found by the man in the park. Whoever he was, he called 999 and left before help arrived. I barely remember the blaring sirens, the police, the ambulance ride, the paramedics desperately giving me fluids and trying to stanch the bleeding. The next thing I recall was regaining consciousness in a gray-and-white hospital room, and my very first thought was an illogical one: I must be someone's captive. Maybe it was because I was hooked up to so many machines and tubes, but I couldn't help feeling that I was someone's prisoner, their science experiment. A keepsake.

And now, all these years later, I feel the exact same way.

Tonight, in Gladstone Park, I look down

and see a few leaves on the top of the bridge, and then I bend and pick one up. I drop it over the edge of the bridge into the small creek below, and though it's too dark to follow its path, I picture it heading downstream, down toward the grate, to the deep, dark tunnel where the unknown creatures live.

THIRTY

Minutes later, I'm standing in front of my old house, continuing my journey of bad memories. I expect to feel something, but I'm hollow inside. Maybe the years of suppressed, mostly good memories here were snuffed by the last few horrible months, which culminated with my mother whisking us to America and my broken father selling the house. Now, I'm left with indifference as I stare at the place where I grew up, not even wondering who lives there now. I stay here only a few minutes, then choose to visit one more memory before heading back to the hotel.

Back in the park, over the little bridge for a second time, across the whispering creek. South, toward my hotel. Three men walk toward me, so I divert my gaze to my phone. Just after 10:00 p.m. They talk loudly, ranting about football. Drunk, from the sound of it. As they pass, one of them murmurs to another. *I wouldn't mind having a go at that.* Another one laughs. My muscles tense, and I visualize a progression of defensive moves I could use against them, but they pass without incident.

Through the south end of the park, across two streets, then a left. It takes a moment, then I realize I have it wrong. Back a street, then left again. Two, three, four houses down on the right. It's not as obvious, because it's dark and all the houses are cuddled together into long strips of brown and white, but after a moment, I have it right: 113 Fleetwood Road.

This was the Glassin house. I had only been there a few times, the last of which was that night almost exactly fourteen years ago. I don't have the same indifference here as I did looking at my old house. Maybe because all the lights are on in this house. There's life inside.

I stand in a yellow streetlight puddle, hardly feeling the chill in the air.

Then, for no reason other than I have an impulse to do so, I walk up and knock on the door. The late hour doesn't stop me. I don't know what I'm looking for or what I will say if someone answers the door — or who that person might even be. Still, here I am.

Footsteps inside, a slow shuffling. A curtain pulls back to the right of the door, but I don't make out the backlit face peering at me before it disappears.

I'm almost relieved when, seconds later, the door doesn't open.

But just as I turn to walk away, it does.

I turn back.

I know this man.

THIRTY-ONE

Charles Glassin looks at me with confused eyes. Deep lines groove his ashen cheeks and forehead, and he looks more like a rock that's been cut by centuries of water and wind rather than a sixty-year-old man. He says nothing, and I say nothing, but it doesn't take too long for his confusion to shift to recognition. When he does, he is the first to speak.

"Alice. Alice Hill. Is it really you?"

I nod. "It's Alice Gray now. But yes. It's me."

He looks as if he's seeing a ghost, and in some ways, I suppose he is.

"What are you doing here?"

"I honestly don't know."

He opens the door fully. "Please, Alice, come in."

"It's late, Mr. Glassin. And I don't even know why I'm here. I don't want to be a bother."

His face scrunches into a scowl. "Alice, you could never be a bother. Now come inside before you're chilled through."

He steps aside, and I pass through the open doorway. The inside of his house smells musty, as if the opening of doors and windows is a rare occurrence.

Charles ushers me into a living room I don't quite recall. There are a small couch, a chair, a coffee table, and little else. What strikes me most is the lack of anything on the walls. There are a few random nail heads and the dusty outlines of where pictures once hung, but the white plaster walls are otherwise bare.

"Can I get you some tea?" he asks.

"I'd rather have whiskey."

He nods. "I might just join you in that."

Charles disappears into the kitchen and emerges a minute later with two tumblers of whiskey.

As he hands me my drink, he says, "Why are you here, Alice? Have you moved back?"

"No. I just . . . I suppose I needed to see this area again."

He nods and says, "I'd tell you I understand, but I could never understand what you went through. How does it feel to be back?"

"Rather unsettling."

"Yes, I suppose that makes sense. So, then, you're Alice Gray, not Hill. You got married?"

I take a sip. The burn is wonderful. "No, I . . . It was just easier to change my name."

He nods at the floor. "Yes, yes. Of course."

"And Mrs. Glassin?"

"Margaret left a long time ago," he says. "In fact, just about the time you left for the United States, she went there as well. To New York. After what happened, things were never really right between us." He takes a sip of his own drink and wipes his lips with the back of his hand. "When a couple suddenly realize they've raised monsters, maintaining a bond to each other is impossible. At least, it was for us."

"I'm sorry."

He waves me off. "Don't be. Don't ever be sorry for the Glassin family, Alice. We took everything from you, and every morning I wake up wishing I'd never had those two girls."

"Mr. Glassin —"

"Call me Charles, please."

"Charles, you didn't do anything to me."

"For better or for worse, Alice, you can never separate yourself from your children. They are an extension of you. I haven't spoken to my girls in over ten years, but they are still a part of me."

"Like a tree," I say. "Branches on a tree."

"No," he answers. "Like a cancer."

A heavy silence falls on us, and Charles uses the quiet to down the rest of his drink. I get the sense Charles and whiskey have been in a long-term relationship for some time.

"You really haven't spoken to them in ten years? You haven't even seen them since their release?"

"No," he says and walks back into the kitchen. He comes out with a fresh drink. "I don't have anything to say to them. I get letters sometimes, though it's been a while. Sylvia doesn't even speak anymore."

"You mean she won't talk to you?"

"No, I mean she doesn't speak. To anyone. At some point in prison, she just stopped talking. I suppose she communicates through writing when she needs to, but she hasn't even written to me in ages. I'm surprised they released her and didn't at least send her to a mental institution."

"And Melinda?"

He sighs, and there's a wet rattle in his chest. "She's found Jesus, that one. I'm not certain what Jesus was doing skulking about Her Majesty's Prison for Women in Holloway, but Melinda found Him there. She writes me a few times a year, and there are a lot of *glorys* and *hallelujahs* in those pages. Not quite sure which of the two of them is crazier."

I take another sip and feel suddenly light-headed, so I sit on the couch. Charles takes the chair.

"Where are they now?" I ask.

"Dover," he says. "Sharing a flat there. They're on some kind of prison-release work program. Strict curfew, that kind of thing. Melinda wrote me recently, asking me to come and visit. But . . ." He shrugs. "But I haven't. Not sure I ever want to." He drinks and changes the subject. "So what else are you planning to do back here?"

"I'm not certain," I say truthfully. "I felt a need to get away for a bit, and there are some things going on right now related to . . . what happened. And I suppose I wanted to come back to see if I could find some answers."

"Answers to what?"

I remain quiet as I decide if this is a question I want to answer. Before I get a chance to say anything, he says, "Alice, sometimes it's best to leave the past alone. We all have things we wish we could take back. I think about some of the things Margaret and I did when we were young. People we associ-

248

ated with. I wonder if some of the decisions we made affected how we raised the girls, but I've learned not to dwell on it, because I can't move a pebble of anything from the past."

He seems lost inside himself, and the look of sadness on his face is painful to see. I wonder what he's talking about, but before I can ask what kind of bad decisions he's referring to, he snaps out of his fugue and says, "How's your mother, Alice?"

The question catches me a bit off guard, so I reply with the first answer that enters my mind.

"Fat," I say, then start laughing. I'm not sure if the tension of the moment makes this seem so funny to me, but I'm overtaken with it. "She's *so* fat, Charles."

Charles seems momentarily appalled but then joins in with the laughing. Finally, as I begin to settle down, he says, "Well, hard to keep the body of one's youth. She was a beautiful woman back then."

"You used to be social with my parents, didn't you? Back before I was born?"

"We were," he says, though he shifts his gaze to the ground. "Went around a few times. Then kids come along, and no one has time for anything. Fell out of touch, but always saw them at school functions. Things like that."

The way he speaks makes me feel there's more to the story, though maybe I'm just trying to find something, *anything,* to propel me forward.

"Did anything happen between you and my parents?"

"What do you mean, Alice?"

"I don't know. Like an argument. Falling-out. That kind of thing."

He looks surprised, but I'm not sure I'm buying it.

"Oh, heavens no, no. Nothing like that. I mean, sure, Margaret and your mum didn't always see eye to eye, but what two women do?"

"What do you mean?"

He's clearly uncomfortable. "It was a long time ago, Alice. I don't remember all those things." Then, he deftly changes to a topic I can't brush off. "And I'm so sorry to hear about your father. What a horrible, horrible shame. I mean, I could hardly believe it. You know, because . . ." He loses his words.

"Because I was stabbed and he was stabbed?"

Another sip. "Yes. Something like that."

The whiskey is starting to take hold of me. "I miss him," I say. "I feel like . . . like he was the biggest thing I lost."

"Good man, he was. Sweet natured. And, of course, immensely talented."

"That talent got him killed. And me nearly."

A deep, lonely sigh. "I never understood the obsession," he said. "I mean, for God's sake, it was just a *cartoon*. And yet the girls were plain obsessed. I didn't think much of it. Hell, fourteen-year-old girls get obsessed by any number of things; it's wired into their brains that way. But I think the fact they actually went to school with the daughter of the creator . . . Well, that turned it into something else entirely."

But it was more than an obsession, I know. There's another layer in explaining the depth of the twins' love of Mister Tender. There were the *notes*. Melinda even mentioned as much seconds before Sylvia stabbed me.

He writes to us, Alice.

Typed letters, as were later shown in court. Source unknown. A total of three of them, each one mailed to the girls with no return address. The content was similar: *You will be famous, but you need to sacrifice someone. Signed, Mister Tender.* It wasn't until the third letter that the target was identified: me.

The Mister Tender graphic novels were a

sensation at the time, and nowhere was their popularity greater than at my school. Rather than featuring superheroes or extravagantly overdrawn villains, the Mister Tender stories were simple, dark, psychological studies, all centered around one man and his power of persuasion. A man obsessed with the question of *How far would you go?* Mister Tender didn't have to lure his pawns in. They simply walked up to the bar and started talking — and everyone at Mister Tender's bar had a story. All he had to do was listen. He had intense charm, bottomless empathy, and the ability to ask the right questions at the exact right times.

He spoke in veiled hypotheticals. *What would you do to get rid of that boss you hate? How badly do you need ten thousand quid? If you had to hurt someone innocent to save someone you love, would you do it?* The person with the problem would leave the bar, often drunk, mostly dismissing the ideas that had been planted in their head. But there was still a trace. The thinnest of roots. And then there would be notes, left for them at their workplace or on their doorstep. Simple, typed notes, messages of vague inspiration.

Today is the first day of the rest of your life.
Dream big, act big.

*You can't get what you want if you don't
even try!*

Everyone who talked to Mister Tender
ended up listening to him. Sometimes the
recipient of his advice ended up dead or in
prison. Sometimes they got away with
murder and were rewarded with everything
they wanted. In all cases, none of them ever
saw Mister Tender again, for he wandered
from pub to pub, and rarely could anyone
who knew him in those brief periods quite
remember what he even looked like. *Handsome* was all the detail most could sum-
mon. Mister Tender was more a ghost of
one's conscience than anything else, a
mirage of want, greed, fear, and all things
desperately human.

The novels were especially popular among
teenage girls, who are avid readers but not
the typical graphic-novel demographic. But
rather than the novels making me popular, I
was seen as a bit of an outcast, the daughter
of a warped mind, and no one really wanted
much to do with me, though they loved talking *about* me. So when the letters came into
evidence in court, and since no author was
ever connected to them, it was widely accepted they were written by a fellow student
who knew the Glassin twins were already
deep into Mister Tender fandom. Whoever

wrote them signed my death warrant, either wittingly or not.

"Did you know about the letters?" I ask Charles. I know what answer he had given at the trial, but I want to hear it again.

"Heavens, no, Alice. If I had known those letters were being sent, I would have gone to the authorities."

I expected this.

"So, did you ever . . ." How do I word this? "I mean, was there ever an indication?"

"What? That my daughters were capable of doing what they did?"

"Yes."

"That is the cursed question I've asked myself for fourteen years. Was there a sign? If there was, I could never figure out what it was. To me, they were normal girls. *Normal.* Not seeing any warning signs makes me more of a failure as a parent than anything else."

"It's not your fault."

"Well, Alice, that's kind of you to say. But you don't really know that, do you? Besides, I'm not to be pitied. Not with you sitting here in my living room." Charles swirls the last licks of his second whiskey around in the tumbler. Then he says, "Alice, I never got to tell you how sorry I am, not really. If there's anything I can do to help you out in any way, please let me know. It would . . . help me as well."

I know just what to ask for.

"I want to see them," I say.

"Who, the girls?"

"Yes."

He considers this. "Why?"

"Because someone is following me. Has been for some time. Years, I think. I thought I had finally left my past behind me, but it turns out there's a small community dedicated to my every movement, and there's one person who seems to be leading the charge."

"Good lord. And you think it's one of the girls?"

"No. Well, I suppose it could be, but that's improbable since this person has actually been to my house, and your daughters have been in prison until recently. Anyway, I think it's a man. He goes by the screen name Mr. Interested. But your daughters might have an idea who he is. There's a connection to England, to my father, to his artwork. But this Mr. Interested knows everything about me."

Charles swallows what's left in his glass and then just stares at it. He remains this way for several seconds, and I know the glass is just something to keep him from looking at me. He seems to be considering his next words carefully.

Then he says, "And what will you do when you find this person?"

"Well, in a way, I have found him. Or at least communicated with him. He even knows I'm here."

"Where?"

"In England."

It suddenly occurs to me perhaps *he* is Mr. Interested. That Mr. Glassin has somehow orchestrated everything, and in his perfect predictability of my thoughts, he somehow even lured me to his very doorstep. A very cunning spider.

I try to shake off my paranoia, knowing thoughts like this one make everything more dangerous. Whoever Mr. Interested is, he's only human. I can defend myself against him, and if I can find him, I can attack. But the *mental* threats against me know no bounds. They are capable of far more lingering damage than fists or blades. If I begin suspecting everyone around me, I'm only helping Mr. Interested's cause.

Charles thankfully interrupts my thoughts. "If it helps you, Alice, I can take you to see the girls."

"Tomorrow," I say.

He exhales so forcefully that I can smell

the whiskey from my end of the couch.

"It scares me," he says. "I haven't seen them in so long. I don't have any relationship with them."

"Just take me to them, Charles. You don't need to see them. Just wait for me while I talk to them. *Please.*"

Charles sets down his empty glass, stands, and smooths the front wrinkles of his blue oxford shirt with his palms. "Well, hell, Alice, if *you're* going to see them, I have no excuse not to. I can't imagine how difficult that will be for you. Tomorrow, then. We'll go tomorrow. Are you staying close by?"

"I'm just over at the Quincey House Hotel."

"Okay, good, yes, I know it. I'll pick you up at, say, ten in the morning. All right?"

"Good. Thank you, Charles." I'm thankful for his help, but the idea of actually visiting the twins suddenly fills me with dread. It will be a long night tossing in my bed, and the jet lag will only make it worse. I swallow the last of my whiskey and flirt with the idea of asking for more but decide to leave.

I stand and walk over to the front door. Charles follows, and I can feel him close behind me. When we reach the door, I open it, and the outside world feels like a relief. I suddenly feel the heaviness of this house, the staleness, the sense it's little more than a shoe box holding a bug hostage for as long as it takes that bug to die.

I turn. "Charles, why don't you have anything on the walls? Photos, keepsakes, artwork. Anything."

Charles Glassin puts his hands deep into the front pockets of his corduroy pants and offers me the simplest of shrugs.

"There's nothing left I want to remember."

THIRTY-TWO

Thursday, October 22

We drive in silence, which suits me fine. Charles seems lost inside himself, and I try to wonder what it must be like to see his daughters for the first time in a decade. My wondering doesn't last long, as I have my own host of emotions to manage.

It's a two-hour drive, and we rumble along the M2 in Charles's silver Fiat. The shades of gray in the clouds number nearly as many as the shades of green in the patchwork of the landscape. It's so unmistakably English, that contrast of green to gray at the horizon. I find myself almost hypnotized by it as we drive, and for a little while, I'm happy. Nostalgic, perhaps, for the innocence of my childhood, but behind the melancholy is nervous excitement. As if maybe I can get another try at all of this. A new life waiting ahead of me, where there are no memories of anything horrible chewing at me every day. I don't want to end up sixty years old with bare walls.

That positive feeling is fleeting, as it always is, and I shift my gaze out the front window and think about what I'm going to say to the twins. I get as far as *hello* in my mind, then visualize myself grabbing one of their heads and twisting her neck until the vertebrae offer a satisfying *crack.*

So I distract myself with my phone, which is freshly equipped with a local SIM card I picked up this morning. Now I can get data, plus I'm unreachable at my normal phone number. No more texts from Mr. Interested. I thumb through the news, focusing especially on New Hampshire happenings. Still no stories about a body in the White Mountains. I check in with Thomas, wording my email carefully. No red flags there either. Even my mother's Facebook account has been blessedly free of pleas for attention. Brenda tells me all is well at the Rose, and I even send Richard a light *How are you?* email, though I don't expect an answer.

In this moment, everything is quiet. Everything is still. It's the kind of silence I imagine two opposing battalions experience as they fix their bayonets and eye one another across a long, grassy expanse. It's a wonder I haven't had a panic attack since

Starks's murder. Perhaps attacking real threats rather than memories is doing wonders for my psyche.

Sometime later, Charles speaks. "Almost there," he says. We've just passed the first sign for Dover, and the clouds, fittingly, have darkened. "Do you want to stop for lunch first?" he asks.

"I don't think I could hold anything down."

He nods. "Me neither."

He fiddles with the GPS on his phone as he slows upon entering city limits. "Just up ahead."

"What time are they expecting us?" I ask.

"They're not."

"What?"

He shoots me a sidelong glance.

"I figured it might be best not to announce ahead of time I'm coming, since I'm bringing you along."

"Why?"

His hands seem to grip the steering wheel a little tighter. "I don't know. Don't suppose there's a real reason to it. Maybe I felt like had I called and told Melinda we were coming, I wouldn't have the ability to change my mind."

"Do you feel like changing your mind, Charles?"

He thinks on this for a moment. "Not really sure what I think," he says. "But . . . this sounds crazy. I feel a little *scared.*"

"That doesn't sound crazy at all," I say. I know exactly what he means. Then something occurs to me. "Am I even allowed to see them? I mean, would this be a violation of their parole or anything?"

"Huh," he says. "Guess I hadn't thought of that. I suppose if you're the one who wants to see them, should be okay. But I suppose they'll tell us if it's a problem."

The British voice of the GPS tells us to make a right turn, and then a left. Finally, she commands us to make another left turn on Noah's Ark Road and that our destination will be ahead on the left.

"Noah's Ark Road," I say. "There's a metaphor in there somewhere."

Charles pulls the car over to the curb and looks up at the clouds, which struggle to hold back a heavy, powerful storm.

"This is it," he says, and though I know he's referring to the address in front of us, he may as well be talking about some point of no return in my life. *This is it, Alice. No going back now.*

I look at the row of flats outside my window.

"Which number?" I ask.

"Two twelve. They share the same flat."

"We don't even know they're there."

"They're not allowed many freedoms outside of going to work, which they don't do on Thursdays. I expect they're there."

"Only one way to find out."

I open the car door and step out. As I do, I feel the first of a billion rain drops.

Charles gets out, and we walk to the door together, slowly, as if marching in a funeral procession. A few feet from the door, we both stop, as if allowing the other person to take the final step forward. After a long moment, Charles moves first.

He rings the doorbell.

I don't hear the footsteps. There's no warning. Just the sudden rattle of a lock being unlatched. The doorknob turns, then the door opens.

The woman looks first at Charles, and then her gaze locks directly on me.

I stare directly back at Melinda Glassin.

"Praise Jesus Christ," she says.

THIRTY-THREE

Like her father, Melinda Glassin has aged beyond her years. She's not even thirty, but her long hair has stray, kinked strands of white, and her pale face looks, ironically, as if it's weathered in the sun for far too long. Fierce blue eyes blaze against the dark bags beneath them. In one look at her, I immediately think of black-and-white images from America's Dust Bowl years, of the hardscrabble farmers' wives, wiry and beaten down, strong but ultimately helpless, working the fields until the ground has no more to give.

But yet in all this severity, she smiles, and her teeth are a dull yellow, the color of white plastic aged by the elements. It's the smile that unnerves me the most.

She reaches out with bony arms to hug her father. Charles seems surprised but steps forward and lightly wraps his arms around her back.

"Daddy," she says. "You came. I'm so happy you came."

Her voice is similar but not identical to the one that haunts me. The one I hear in my head has more of a malevolent hiss to it.

"I . . ." Charles finally breaks the hug and stares at the ground. "Yes, I came. I brought someone." Then he turns to me, as does Melinda's attention.

"Yes, I see that."

The first words I say to Melinda Glassin in fourteen years are "Do you know who I am?"

"Yes," she says. "You're an angel."

"What?"

She smiles again, not quite as widely as before. "Jesus brought you here so you can forgive me. I've been waiting so long to see you, Alice."

Whatever I was expecting to happen here, this wasn't it.

"I'm not here to forgive you."

"You are," she says. "You just don't know it yet." Then Melinda steps back inside the house and beckons us. "Come inside. Oh, please come inside."

Charles looks at me, saddened by the whole scene, then turns and enters the house. I hesitate, then decide to follow. As I pass Melinda, she stops me and places a palm on my cheek. Her skin is cool.

"Oh, Alice," she says. "It is really you."

I remove her hand, fighting the temptation to snap her twig-like wrist. "Don't touch me. Ever."

She nods, keeps smiling. I walk inside.

The Glassin family seems to share the desire for closed-in spaces, because Melinda and Sylvia's flat is as dark, musty, and suffocating as their father's house. Shades are drawn against an already gray day. Few lights are on. Perhaps after a decade and a half in prison, one becomes rather agoraphobic.

There is no sign of Sylvia, though I imagine her lurking within these shadows.

Charles says, "I didn't tell you we were coming. You must be rather surprised."

"I'm not surprised in the least," Melinda says. "God is mysterious, but He is also reliable. He has delivered, quite literally to my doorstep, two people who will forgive me. And when you forgive me, you will see the full extent of His beauty, maybe for your very first time. I first saw it five years ago, in prison. And now . . ." She clasps her hands together like a little girl watching a butterfly land nearby. "I see it everywhere."

Melinda reaches out and places her hand on her father's chest, closes her eyes, and takes a long, deep breath, as if transferring her energy to him. For his part, Charles looks confused and embarrassed.

"I missed you, Daddy."

He softens a bit.

"I just couldn't come to that place to see you anymore," he says. "Living like that. And knowing what . . . what you two had done. I wasn't even planning to come now, but then Alice showed up on my doorstep."

"Yes," she said. "Of course. I never blamed you for anything. I was a demon then." Now those bright eyes flash at me. "But I'm a different person now. That will never excuse what I did, but God guides me now, so I can never stray off the path of righteousness." She smiles again at me, and I wish she wouldn't. "Come. Please come in to the living room. I will fix us all some tea."

Charles says, "Where's Sylvia?"

"Quite likely sleeping," Melinda answers. "She doesn't come out of her room much when we're at home. She fatigues easily, I'm afraid. And you know that —"

"That she doesn't speak," Charles says. "Yes, you've written me about that. Is it a condition?"

"No. I think she simply has nothing to say."

"How do you communicate with her?" I ask.

"Well, Alice, that's the thing about twins: we do quite a good job of knowing what the other one is thinking."

What a horrifying thought.

"Of course," she continues, "Syl will write things down when she needs to, use hand gestures, that kind of thing. Please sit, Alice. You're making me feel like a bad hostess."

This is so surreal, I think. I'm having tea with Melinda Glassin. She's my *hostess.* I want to feel rage at her. For years, I've been studying martial arts, almost as if preparing for this very moment, a moment where I can dominate her, hurt her. Make her bleed. But now that I'm here, I don't want that. I just want to get out of here.

She seems to have lost a bit of her mind, and that seems to be wildly comforting to her. What a different experience from mine. My mind is a prison of memories, and hers is an open field of delusion. It almost makes me jealous.

I sit on a lumpy couch, and Charles takes a nearby chair. He looks at me without saying anything as Melinda prepares tea in the kitchen. I look around and wish for more light. There are too many dark corners.

She comes back a few minutes later, carrying a basic tea set with four cups. She pours a cup for me, which I'm in no mood to drink. Still, I sip to be polite, and then immediately think:

Polite? What the hell?

I place the cup down.

"Melinda," I say. "You need to understand something. I'm not here to forgive you. Maybe you've found Jesus, but you will never have my forgiveness. You have no way of understanding how what you and your sister did to me continues to haunt me. I've turned to drugs. I've considered suicide. I've spent countless nights awake and horrified. The panic attacks, the neuroses. It's all never ending. If it were my decision, you'd be in prison for the rest of your life."

"Oh, my dear Alice . . ." she starts, still smiling.

"And if you don't wipe that fucking smile off your face, I'll smash your teeth in, you *cunt.* And don't think I'm not capable. You have no idea how satisfying it would feel."

That does it. The smile disappears, and for the briefest of moments, there's a flash of something on her face. Not quite anger, but perhaps resolve. Whatever it is, there's not an ounce of Jesus in it.

"Of course, Alice. You have every right to be angry. So why, exactly, are you here?"

Charles remains quiet. I wonder how he feels about me calling his daughter a cunt. Mixed emotions, I suspect.

"I'm here because someone is stalking me. This person is dangerous."

"Oh my," she says. "Well, that must be awful."

"Yes, it is."

"And what does that have to do with me?"

"Because this person is part of a small group of people obsessed with me. And the reason for their obsession is your crime. These people know where I live, where I work, where I go. They've taken pictures of me *while I'm sleeping.* They've spoken to people from my past — people I've wanted to avoid — and told them where to find me."

"That's terrible," she says. "You should call the authorities."

I've brought my backpack with me, and I pull out the book.

"I got this in the mail," I tell her as she delicately takes the book from my hand. "It was postmarked London. The cover and the inscription come from my father. The other panels were drawn by someone else."

She doesn't open the book. She's too mesmerized by the image on the cover.

"This was never published," she whispers.

270

It's like I'm showing her a lost book of the New Testament.

"No, it's the beginning of an unfinished book by my father."

She runs her fingertips along the page, as if she could caress the soft, stubbled cheeks of Mister Tender. In her eyes, I can see the remnants of a deep wanting. Then she shuts her eyes, shakes her head, and thrusts the book back at me.

"Take this," she says. "I can't see it. I'm not allowed to even be looking at things like that. That was . . . that was a long time ago, anyway." I don't reach for the book, so she drops it to the coffee table as if it were in flames. "I'm very sorry for your situation, Alice. But I can't help you. I don't know who's doing this to you. You should go to the police."

"They can't help me. You *must* know something, Melinda. Maybe they've contacted you. There's a leader of this group. He goes by the name Mr. Interested. It's just an anagram for Mister Tender."

I sense a flicker of recognition in her eyes.

"Do you know that name?"

"No, I . . ."

"What? What is it?"

"I did get some letters. A long time ago. Years ago. I didn't keep them."

"Were they from him?"

"Yes."

Then Charles speaks for the first time since we've sat down. "What did the letters say, Melinda?"

She looks over to her father, and her eyes hint at a vulnerability I hadn't seen before. "They were the exact same letters I received . . . back then."

"You mean the three letters you got in the mail fourteen years ago? The ones telling you to target me?"

She nods. "But these weren't signed Mister Tender. They were signed Mr. Interested."

"Do you have any idea who sent you the original letters?"

Her words are very slow and measured. "No. I mean . . . at the time. Things were so different back then. *I* was so different. I truly thought they were sent by Mister Tender. Some manifestation of him at least. That Sylvia and I would be famous."

"But you know he's not real."

"Yes," she says. "Of course I know that now. I'm sure the letters were some kind of prank. Someone from school. But then I got the other ones in prison, and it just . . ."

"Just what?"

"There was something else that was sent.

272

It was in the last letter from Mr. Interested."

"What was it?"

"A drawing."

Charles says, "What sort of drawing?"

Melinda's eyes seem to ice over as she stares deeply into my face. "It was a picture of you, Alice. From that night in Gladstone Park."

I want to ask *before or after you stabbed me,* but I don't. But now I know there's at least one other picture of me, this time from years ago. I reach forward and flip the pages of the book until the four panels of me appear.

"Look at this, Melinda. Just look. It's okay."

She glances down.

"Did it look like these drawings? Could the drawing you saw have been done by the same person as these?"

She looks at the panels for maybe a second.

"I don't know," she says. "Perhaps."

"Has Mr. Interested written to you again? Or Sylvia?"

"No. Not me, at least. I don't believe to her, either."

"Melinda, is there anything else you can remember? Do you have any idea who could have sent you those letters? I need to find out who's doing this to me in order to have any chance at finding peace. You understand that, right?"

"You can always find peace in God, Alice."

"Just answer me."

"I don't know anything else."

I lean back into the couch, frustrated. Dust motes drift in schools, floating through weak, filtered sunlight, swirling and dancing.

"Melinda," I say. "Why did you do it? Just tell me why."

"*Forgive* me, Alice."

"I'm not forgiving you. I just want to understand."

I don't think she's going to answer, but she finally says, "I believed I was being commanded. We both were. I can't explain it any better than that, Alice."

Her words reveal the soul of a fragile and fractured woman. So easily lured. So wanting to believe. To be a part of something bigger. Significant.

"Don't you see, Melinda?" I say.

"See what?"

"You just want someone to tell you what to do. Fourteen years ago, it was Mister Tender. Now, it's Jesus. You can't think for yourself."

"Don't blaspheme Jesus in my house."

Now I feel anger at her. Anger that this person, who is just a simpleminded follower, changed the course of my life.

"Your life is devoted to imaginary characters, Melinda. You live in the world of fantasy, but your actions have real consequences. You're pathetic."

"You have to leave now, Alice."

Charles says, "Alice is just expressing her feelings."

But Melinda ignores him. "I'm asking you to leave. Now."

Fine by me. I get up from the couch and start to walk to the door, then turn to see if Charles is coming. He remains seated quietly next to his daughter on the couch; Melinda stares away from him and wears a sullen expression, all traces of her smile gone. His hand is half outstretched toward her arm, as if he wants to touch her, make a connection to the girl he once knew. But his fingers hang in midair for only a few seconds before Charles pulls his arm back.

I hadn't considered his true pain until this very moment; I'd been too absorbed in my own. Maybe I haven't dwelled on it because it's not something I can even comprehend. His loss is different from mine. The twins took away who I was. But Charles had spent fourteen years raising and loving his girls, committing his soul to their happiness and well-being. And with a few flicks of the wrist, a few slashes with a kitchen knife, they destroyed everything he'd built. In a span of seconds, they made Charles a failure as a parent and, by proxy, as a human being. The twins took away my childhood, but they had utterly decimated their parents' souls.

He leans in to her and, with the gentlest voice I've ever heard used by a man, says, "I can never see you again."

Melinda lowers her chin into her chest and begins to cry. Soft, soft weeping, barely a sound. Heartbreaking.

His final gesture is to commit to that touch after all. He stands, bends down to her head, and places a light kiss on the top of it. He stays there for a moment and breathes her in, perhaps hoping for a familiar scent, a flash of a good memory, maybe. Then straightens, turns to me, and nods.

"Let's go," Charles says to me.

We shuffle side by side out of the living room and toward the front door. The sunlight streaming through the small window in the door is tantalizing, and I'm suddenly eager to smell the sea when we pass through to the outside. Just before we reach the door, there's a sound. Then a movement.

Next to me, a door opens.

The room behind the door is pitch-black, as if it's nothing more than a windowless cell. It takes a moment for my eyes to focus, but then Sylvia Glassin steps forward into the muted light, and I see her clearly.

It's as if there was only one Glassin girl, and at some point, someone split her into two people. One of those two found religion and, though still quite mad, figured out how to exist on a day-to-day basis — how to cook, clean, shop, care for herself. The other one was sent into the wild to live the rest of her life as a feral creature.

This latter one looks at me with wide, glowing eyes, like a cat that's suddenly spotted a small creature scurrying near the baseboards. Her long hair is wild and kinked, extending outward almost as far as down. She wears a thin robe that hardly conceals her bony frame, and with a quick glance, I see that her fingernails are unnaturally long and sharp, like claws. She doesn't move, but her eyes dart back and forth between Charles and me.

I say nothing. The truth is, I'm scared in a way I didn't feel at all with Melinda. I can almost smell the danger on Sylvia, the unpredictability, the rawness of her being. She says nothing but rather holds up a sheet of paper.

It's a drawing, and instantly I realize it's the one Melinda told me about. It's a scene of Gladstone Park at night, the wan light beautifully shaded by an expert hand — the same hand, very clearly, that drew the other panels sent to me. Dark, towering trees, the arched footbridge, the trickling, haunted stream glimmering under the moon. This could be a scene from a gorgeously illustrated Winnie the Pooh book, the Hundred Acre Wood at night, except for one small but gruesome detail. At the foot of the bridge, fourteen-year-old Alice lies crumpled and bleeding, a pool of black spreading beneath her, and little, perfectly inked puncture wounds peppering her body. In this image, Alice's eyes are open. Wide.

Sylvia holds the image higher, nearly to my face, as if gesturing for me to take it from her. I reach for it, but the moment I do, she backs away a couple of feet into her cave. She keeps holding the picture out, as if to taunt me.

I move inside her room, just a few inches, smelling her for the first time, and though her scent is not powerful, it's unmistakable. This woman hasn't bathed in some time, nor made any attempt to hide her stench with perfume.

She takes another step back.

I look to Charles, who stares at his other daughter with shock.

"Come on, Alice," he says. "We need to leave."

I turn back to Sylvia, and we lock in to each other. She says nothing. Just as I'm about to turn and leave, she holds the picture against her chest and smiles.

It's not the plastic, brainwashed smile of her sister. No, this is the smile as it was first ever invented by humans. Not one to convey joy or happiness, but simply to show the enemy your fangs.

I turn away, slightly conscious of having my back to Sylvia Glassin. I walk to the front door and open it, and I drink in the salt air as if it's the only thing that will save me in this moment. I step outside, and Charles follows, having never said a word to his other daughter.

The door closes behind us, and the Glassin twins return to being the ghosts of my mind.

THIRTY-FOUR

Charles drops me off at my hotel after a silent ride back to London. He seems shell-shocked. Whatever he was expecting to find in Dover, it wasn't there. He sat hunched forward over the steering wheel during the drive back, both hands curled tightly over the worn leather grip, as if he needed every ounce of focus and determination to escape the event horizon of where we'd just been.

I get out of his car, turn, then lean back down to him.

"You're not a failure, Charles. You raised your girls the best way you knew how. Some people just turn out . . . broken. Not everyone can be saved."

He neither accepts nor rejects this. "Goodbye, Alice."

I close the door, knowing I have likely seen the very last of the Glassin family.

Up to my room. I grab my laptop, navigate to the forum on MisterTender.com, and direct message Mr. Interested, telling him I want to talk. I've come to realize a few things during my visit here, but the one thing that stands out the most is that I'm being very inefficient in achieving my objective. I'm trying to find Mr. Interested and going to great lengths to do so, but the one thing I'm not doing is reaching out to him directly.

I wait a few moments with no reply, so I decide to take a shower. I'm feeling the need to scrub the visit with the twins off my skin. I stand for a long time beneath the jets, letting the steaming water beat against me. When I finally get around to soaping up, I take extra time massaging my scars. They seem bigger today, more pronounced, like ropes of worms breaching the surface of my skin.

I wrap a towel around myself, then check my laptop again. Now there's a message in the center of my screen.

Are you enjoying your holiday?

I sit on the bed and perch over the keyboard.

How did you know I was here?

Technology, Alice. Your phone gives everything away. Though I have lost track of you. Switched out your SIM card, I suppose, haven't you?

Of course.
Another message appears.

I haven't been well.

Good, I think. But I don't type this. I want to keep him engaged so I can learn enough to find him.

What's wrong with you?

I'm dying, Alice.

The words sit there on my screen. I stare at them, not knowing if I can believe anything this person tells me. He writes more before I can reply.

Thus, the nature of my urgency.

You mean why you're stalking me?

I've never stalked you. I've just wanted to be a part of your life.

Why?

Because you're special to me.

I don't understand. Who are you?

Soon, Alice.

I need to get answers, and he does nothing but write in circles. I visited the twins, I write.

Did you, now? That must have been quite something.

They said you wrote to them. In prison.

Yes, I did. That was a long time ago.

Did you write the original letters to Melinda and Sylvia? Fourteen years ago?

He doesn't answer, though I give him several minutes. Then I write:

Did you know my family?

Silence.
Finally, he writes:

Did Melinda mention the artwork I sent her?

Okay, at least he's still here.

I saw it. Sylvia showed it to me. Why?

He's gone again, and I don't know if he will answer. I think about the picture, the accuracy with which it depicted me bleeding to death on the footbridge.

Something nags at me. Something I'm not quite get —

And then I know. Oh my God, I think I know.

It was you, I write. You were the one who found me that night. You were the one who called the police.

His reply is immediate this time.

Yes.

That's why you're obsessed with me. You were there.

I think back to the trial, to the muffled, anonymous voice on the 999 call. It was definitely male, and the caller said little more than "There's a girl badly injured in Gladstone Park." The call had come from a nearby pay phone, from which no useful prints had been recovered.

I saved your life, Alice. I took care of you. I protected you. Every breath you've taken since that night is due to me.

And then a horrible, chilling thought: What if he hadn't found me by accident? What if he knew what was about to happen and wanted to be there? Maybe he *wanted* to find me, dead or alive.

My chest tightens in that awful, familiar way, and I have a sudden sense he's watching me. I jump off the bed and check the peephole of the door, but my fish-eye view of the hallway shows nothing. I walk to the other side of the room and peel back the edge of the closed curtain, but see nothing more than the midafternoon bustle on the street. Though if he were out there somewhere, tucked away with a pair of binoculars, I suppose I wouldn't really know.

I close the curtains, then pace the thin, patterned carpet in front of the television. *Calm down, Alice. He doesn't know where you are. He hasn't been able to track you after you switched out the SIM card.*

Back to my laptop. Enough of this bullshit.

Where are you? I want to meet.

You will meet me before I die. That I promise.

Why not now?

He doesn't answer my question. Rather, the last thing he writes to me is:

You should visit the site of your father's murder.

Then, before I can even react to this, a message flashes on my screen. Not from him, but from the private messaging software.

Mr. Interested has left the conversation.

THIRTY-FIVE

Monday, October 26

Three days pass in which I focus on nothing but myself. Three days of pushing Mister Tender away, of communication with no one. I switch hotels, trading Gladstone Park for Regent's Park, spending my days walking the hectic streets of London, pretending, just for a time, that perhaps I'm someone else. A tourist, seeing the sites. The last two days, I worked out in a local boxing gym, finding joy in throwing fists and feet at a well-worn heavy bag for nearly an hour. The expulsion of sweat and energy left me deliciously drained, and for three nights, I've actually slept well. Okay, not well. But not terribly.

But today I leave, heading back home to a world of uncertainty. I have several hours before I catch the Heathrow Express train from Paddington Station to the airport, and after an intentionally long lunch, I take a taxi to Southwark. I give my driver the address, which I only know because I Googled it. He takes me over Blackfriars Bridge, and I get a chill just looking at the cold, gray waters of the Thames. Dirty whitecaps. In the distance, I see Tower Bridge, both majestic and imposing, and think back to school tours of the Tower of London as a little girl. It was the first time someone pointed out to me the exact spot where a person had died.

I remember the tall and burly Beefeater commanding the attention of my entire fourth-grade class as he pointed to Tower Green — a lush stretch of impossibly green grass with a small square of granite in the center — and told us that was where the scaffolds once stood. He explained how only the privileged had the honor of being executed in the privacy of the Green, away from the screaming and gawking commoners, and that at least seven people lost their heads at that exact location. How thirty-year-old Anne Boleyn, blindfolded and kneeling, received just a single blow from the executioner's blade. The strike — delivered by an expert swordsman imported from France for the occasion — was swift and precise, and the queen's head fell cleanly from her torso.

Had I known how my own family's relationship with sharp objects would unfold, I might have taken more cautionary interest in the field trip that day. Instead, I stood there and simply pictured heads on the Green, eyes wide open, gazes fixed far beyond the gunmetal clouds cloaking the two-thousand-year-old city.

Across the bridge, left on Southwark Street, another left on Hopton, around a bend that approaches the Tate Modern. The taxi slows.

"36 Hopton," the driver says.

I look out the window. The building is completely unremarkable. The street quiet for a late-morning weekday.

"This right?" he asks when I only stare at the building.

"Yes," I say. "I think so."

I pay him and get out, and as he drives off, I suddenly wish I hadn't come.

Standing on the sidewalk with my backpack and my one piece of luggage, I'm unsure what to do next. I have been avoiding this moment for three days, trying to ignore the last thing Mr. Interested wrote to me. But now I'm here, because maybe there's something to learn. There must be a reason he told me to come here.

The building at 36 Hopton Street is

residential, with street-floor retail and office space. There's a coffee shop I eye with interest, simply because it seems to be independent. Not many of those left, especially in the large cities. *Good for them,* I think. Next to it is a grocery store about the size of my basement back home.

Next to that is Unit C.

Currently occupied by Thomas & Evans, Solicitors.

Formerly occupied by Harding Publications.

This is where my father worked until his death, which occurred, as best as I can tell from the articles I've read, about where I'm standing on the sidewalk. He was stabbed to death soon after the publication of his satirical drawings of Mohammed. The blade pierced him four times: twice in the chest, once in the stomach, and the fatal blow to the neck.

An Islamic extremist was the presumed attacker, but no suspect was ever caught, and no group took credit for the killing.

I stare deeply into the grains of the sidewalk, grimly looking for any sign of faded bloodstains. My stomach clenches at the memory of the police photos, which I regret ever having seen, for they provided me the last memories of my father. His body slumped on this sidewalk, his face pressed to the ground and the ocean of blood pooling around him. I wonder how much pain he felt. If it was at all like my attack, there wouldn't have been much, because shock would have rapidly quelled it. There would only have been an intensely cold feeling at the entry wounds, a shattering sense of vulnerability, and then finally darkness. Deep, deep darkness, a night of forever sleep.

I see no trace of blood. There is, in fact, nothing abnormal about this location at all, no sign that anything horrific ever happened here. They simply took his body away, washed off the pavement, and the world kept spinning. The publisher closed, these solicitors moved in, and if my father's ghost is here, he simply joins the millions of others in a city long accustomed to death.

I look up, my attention grabbed by a flyer taped to the solicitor's window. I noticed it briefly when I first walked over but now stare at it intently, suddenly knowing it holds more significance than I first realized. With small, cautious steps, I walk up to the window. To anyone but me, the flyer appears nothing more than an advertisement for a band or some kind of performer. Exquisite hand-lettering shouts off the top of the page:

Directly below is a hand-drawn image, and I immediately know the artist. This image was penned by the same hand that drew the panels of me, the scenes from Manchester, the moments of my stark aloneness. And here I am again, drawn neatly on this flyer, the familiar strokes and inking that mimic but don't quite duplicate the telltale works of my father. Here is a single panel depicting me on a street, leaning into a window, staring at a flyer — this *same* flyer. In fact, the image is this very scene occurring right this moment, and though my outfit is different, everything is captured exactly as it is happening right now, so accurately that when I step back away from it in shock, I almost expect the Alice in the drawing to do the same.

Below the image, more lettering.

Alice, Looking Through the Glass
October 31
Mister Tender's Pub

What is happening here?

I look up and see a man staring down at me through the second-story window of the solicitor's. He's very nicely put together and wears a very British look of tight concern on his face. I don't get any immediate sense he's part of this, which is perhaps naive of me, but that feeling is reinforced with the words he mouths to me.

Are you all right?

I nod, which he accepts after a few seconds and then disappears inside the office space, his duty done.

But I'm not all right. Not nearly at all.

And then I see someone else.

Another man. Not inside the office space, but outside. In fact, at this moment, he's the only other person aside from me standing on this narrow side street.

He's fifty feet away and not moving. He's just standing, staring at me, his muscled arms hanging by his sides.

I assess him as quickly as I can, as my defenses have taught me. If you view everyone as a threat, you can never err on the wrong side of caution.

He's perhaps my age, give or take a few years. Too young to be Mr. Interested, based on Freddy Starks's description, but there's something not right about him. He wears a long-sleeved, tight brown T-shirt tucked into the darkest of blue denim. Brown work boots, the kind used for actual work and not fashion. He wears a long, wiry beard, the kind that in America suggests hipster bartender, but on him, it appears anything but. It's more like he's trying to cover as much of his identity as possible, an idea further confirmed by a gray wool cap pulled over his forehead and gold-rimmed aviator sunglasses with coal-black lenses. This man is in shape, but not gym shape. He's in real-world, I-can-be-a-problem shape.

And he just keeps staring at me.

The familiar swell of panic fills my chest, and I battle it by taking a step forward. Toward him. *I can be the aggressor as well.*

Normally I might look at this kind of person with curious caution, a potential threat easily avoided by dodging into the coffee shop or the office space.

But not today. Not here on the sidewalk where my father was slaughtered. Not with this man staring me down in a brazenly predatory fashion.

And not after Mr. Interested told me to come here.

This man might not be Mr. Interested, but I'm certain he's a part of everything. Maybe one of the message board minions, another pervert obsessed with daily updates about me. A groupie, under the direction of Mr. Interested. Maybe he's the one who taped the flyer on the window.

I'm struck with an immediate blaze of fury. White-hot, almost blinding. There's no sense to it, but it's the most powerful, freeing, releasing sensation I've ever known. A fucking rage orgasm. With no thought, I do what I've been meaning to do for fourteen years.

I attack.

I release my backpack and luggage and sprint toward this man at full speed, closing the gap in seconds. He doesn't react fast enough, and as I lunge in the final feet before reaching him, his eyebrows arch high above the rims of his shades, his disbelief total.

There is no thinking now. There is just training.

Impact.

I take him down easily despite his size, not hoping to hurt him yet, just to get him off balance. We both fall to the ground, but I roll and bounce to my feet, and I have him exactly how I want. Slowly getting to his feet.

"Wait," he says, rising. "Just —"

He's in perfect position as he tries to get up. His head is just about at my level, and I do what I do best.

I kick.

A beautiful, perfect arc of a roundhouse

kick. The kind you can only dream of, the thing of movies. The top of my left foot connects perfectly with the right side of his jaw, the blow crushing. The force begins to spin his body to his left, which is exactly what I want. I pull my left foot down, push forward on my right, and drive my right fist toward the exposed left side of his face. My knuckles smash his jaw, and glorious, blinding pain shoots through the bones in my hand and all the way up my arm. The combination of punches is textbook, exactly how I trained, and something so rare to actually execute. Even if I've broken my fingers, I know the damage to him is much worse.

He collapses to the ground in a heap, his head taking one bounce off the pavement before coming to a stop. I kneel, yank off his cap, grab a fistful of hair with my left hand, and pull my right arm back. His glasses have scattered to the ground, revealing deep-brown eyes, wide and full of fear. I cock my arm back more, knowing I could smash his nose into pieces with one punch.

"Wa . . . wait . . ." he gasps.

He tries to hold up his arms, but I leap on top of him, pinning his elbows to the ground with my knees. He's strong, but inexperienced fighters who get punched first spiral quickly out of control. He's too stunned to react, which puts me in charge.

"He tol' me to come 'ere and watch for you," he says, spitting up a thin tendril of blood. "P-p-paid me two hundred quid! Just had to give you a little spook, is all. *Fuck!*"

"What?"

"Get off me, for Chrissake! I think you knocked my fucking tooth out."

"Who told you to come here? *Who?*"

"I dunno," he says. "I met him online. I do . . . odd jobs. Security work, that kind of thing. He found me. Said he was havin' a scare at someone, is all. Just wanted me to stand 'ere and watch you. Nuthin' more."

I raise my fist as if to strike, and he closes his eyes. So I place my thumbs over his closed eyelids, applying just enough pressure to let him know I could press hard enough to burst his eyes inside their sockets.

"Did you put that flyer there? Did you tape it to the window?"

"Wha . . . what flyer? Don't know about no flyer."

"How long have you been watching for me?"

"I haven't been. Got a call just a few minutes ago. Christ, you're *mad.*"

Mr. Interested is close. Was watching for me. He put the flyer up himself, probably not too long ago. I look up and see no one, but he could be anywhere.

The man struggles beneath me, testing my weight. He's bigger than me, and unless I attack him again soon, he'll push me off. So I push off him voluntarily, get to my feet, and assume a defensive stance a few steps back. Now I have space to work with. He scrambles to his feet and faces me.

"Loon," he says. Then he spits a wad of blood, and a tooth clinks along the pavement next to his feet. "Bloody fucking *hell.*"

"Did he tell you anything else?"

"Just told me to stand there and stare at you a bit. Thought it'd be easy money. Was wrong about that. Should make you pay to get my tooth replaced." He spits again, and this time, the bloody wad lands close to me. *"Bitch."*

I take one step toward him, and that's all it takes. He turns and runs.

"Bitch," I whisper.

My hand throbs, and I try to ignore the pain. I look around and see three faces in the coffee shop window, all eyes trained on me. No doubt someone has alerted the police by now.

I run back and fetch my backpack and luggage, then wheel down the street and into an even smaller alleyway. I peer each way and look for signs that someone is following me but see nothing unusual.

Back on busier Southwark Street, I find a taxi and ask the driver to take me to Paddington. If he notices my heavy breathing and my sweat-streaked face, he says nothing about it. It takes several minutes to slow my heartbeat, and when I finally do, I have an urge to dive completely back into my world. Back into the hunt, back on the grid. I swap out the local SIM card I purchased for my phone and put my old card back in. If Mr. Interested is truly tracking me through my SIM card's GPS location, he'll know my location again. Fine by me. Let him come.

The phone boots. Two texts waiting for me.

The first is from my mother, dated two days ago.

Thomas says you're in London?? What on earth are you doing there?

And the second one is time-stamped five minutes ago, the number unknown to me.

You are strong. But in the moments you're weak, I'll be there to save you.

THIRTY-SIX

Tuesday, October 27
Manchester, New Hampshire

Alice, what did the penguin always tell you?

That simple sentence rattles around my head, refusing to leave. I stare out my bedroom window, scanning the dark for movement, but this does no good. If someone is out there watching me, they know enough to do it from a distance. They won't close in on me until I'm asleep, and the combination of jet lag and paranoia ensure sleep won't come anytime soon.

So now I keep watch and wonder why my father wrote those words to me.

He wrote them at some point before he died, perhaps as long as fourteen years ago. He was planning to give me the book with that inscription. Did he give up on it entirely, or was it still a work in progress when he died? And, more importantly, how did Mr. Interested get his hands on it?

What did the penguin always tell you?

Not to trust anyone.

I open the bedroom window and invite in the frosty air, which heightens my senses. The hum of a car in the distance rises and then falls, then is eventually replaced by another. The New England air is so distinctly different from that of Old England, and as I take it deep into my lungs, I feel happy to be home. Even if uncertainty waits for me here.

This is no use. It's just after four in the morning, and since I've never been the type to sleep past six, I give in to the day. I dress, grab my purse, and head out the front door.

I turn and look at my house, consider how it's changed in such a short period of time. It has the same shape and look as always, but we murdered a man inside there, so the energy of it is forever mutated. Depending on how my future unfolds, perhaps my little home will one day be part of a ghost tour for New England haunt-seekers.

All is dark in the Perch. I haven't seen Richard since I arrived home yesterday, and

I have no doubt he's not eager to reconnect with me. But I sense ours is a relationship that is far from over. There are things to be said, assurances to be made. When you cover up a homicide with someone, that's a bond not easily broken.

I walk down the street, feeling the weight of the black morning on me. My breath steams the air, and I squeeze my fists inside their gloves, keeping the blood in my fingers flowing. It's a short distance to the Rose, and I'm certain I will hear anyone following me. But it's as quiet as if I were strolling through a graveyard, which, seeing all the neighborhood Halloween decorations in the light of the streetlamps, it almost seems I am.

I reach the Rose and enter through the alley door. Brenda should be opening today, which means she'll be here sometime before five. I'm looking forward to seeing her; she'll be a splash of normality I desperately need.

I turn on the lights, which buzz to life and trap me in their harsh glare. It takes a few seconds to adjust, and then I move behind the counter and fire up the espresso machines, which hum and purr as they slowly wake.

I first hear the noise as I'm reaching for an apron. The sound is unmistakable, and

I'm certain it didn't come from the espresso machines. I freeze, cock my head, and wait.

There, again.

A knock.

I abandon the apron and take a step forward, closer to where I think the sound originated. It was so brief, it's hard to tell, but I think it came from there. Above me.

Again.

Two knocks, and this time, they're louder.

Rap. Rap.

Could be water pipes heating up, or any other sounds common to the creaking bones of an old building. But there was something very deliberate to the rapping I heard, something that was trying to command my attention.

Then it happens again, not ten seconds after the last.

Rap. Rap.

It's the sound of a heavy-knuckled fist knocking on a thick wooden door. Not desperate, not pounding, but *insistent*.

Let me in.

But there is no wooden door here, just a glass one in the front, and though I turn to assure myself no one is there, it's unnecessary. The sound isn't coming from either side of me.

It's definitely coming from the ceiling. As

if someone is trapped there, telling me they want out.

I think of Simon, the ghost Brenda insists is real. She usually opens the shop and is so far the only one to hear Simon, so maybe he's only active at this early hour. I'm less afraid there's a ghost in here than another person.

I don't move. The silence is so electric that I sense the slightest sound will jolt me to death. I suck in a deep breath and hold it, doing my best to push the fear down. I've had a lot of practice lately.

Then, again. This time, a single, deep pound against the ceiling. A closed fist rattling the floorboards in the space above. Then, after I remain completely still for what must be several minutes of ensuing silence, one solitary thought loops in my mind.

It doesn't matter.

If it is a ghost, it doesn't matter. What can I do about it anyway? And if it's a person, then it's probably just someone in the space above. The worst thing in the world is certainly not a hundred-year-old ghost animated by the smell of cappuccino.

Then, just as I'm having this thought, a loud hissing sound rattles me. A thousand-pound snake rearing to strike. I snap my head around and see a cloud of steam pouring from the espresso machine, and as I walk over to it, I find the valve open. You have to turn the valve to open up the steam, and I certainly didn't do that.

I close the valve, and the hissing stops.

Standing there for a moment, my nerves are begging me to give in to their desire to fray. But then again, I think, *it doesn't matter.*

"Happy Halloween, Simon," I say aloud, and the sound of my voice soothes me. Then I laugh, and soon I can't stop myself, laughing so hard, I almost have to kneel on the floor. Of all the true horror in my life, all the terrors of the terrestrial world I face, *now* I have to deal with a goddamn ghost?

If that isn't funny, then I might as well give up on any chance of a happy life.

I make myself a mocha, and it's delicious.

The morning hums along, and it feels good. There are things I must do, but here I'm in a safe place, ghosts notwithstanding. I spend time with Brenda, who doesn't ask me much about my recent absence other than to see if I'm okay. *I am,* I tell her and, for the time being, mean it. She doesn't even mention my bruised and swollen fingers, which aren't broken but still ache terribly.

We are both in good moods, and I'm feeling very fortunate to have her. There are things I must do, the first of which is go see Thomas and check in on him, but for the next few hours, I just want to serve my customers.

I relish the normalcy.

But then, during a lull in customers a couple of hours later, the normalcy disappears with a single sentence from Brenda.

"I forgot to tell you. Someone came in to see you yesterday."

I wipe down the steamers on the espresso machine with a damp rag, pretending not to react to the words.

"Who?" I ask.

"Said his name was Jimmy."

Fucking Jimmy.

"Are you sure that was his name?"

"Yeah, I'm sure. Said you used to go out."

"That was a long time ago."

"He seemed . . . I don't know." Brenda seems to be searching for what to say. "Tweaked, almost. Nervous as hell. Real edgy. Looked like he'd gotten into a fight. Freaked me out, to be honest."

I finally turn and look at her. "It took you two hours this morning before you remembered a tweaked-out ex-boyfriend of mine came looking for me?"

Brenda shakes her head. "No. I wanted to tell you right away, but you seem to have so much shit to deal with right now. And you looked relaxed and happy. I didn't want to unload it on you. But he might be coming back, and I thought you should know. Is he trouble?"

"I don't know," I say. "Did he say what he wanted?"

"He said he misses you. But he said it in a weird, nervous way. Didn't seem like the kind of guy who suddenly finds himself pining for an old flame."

I'm sure. And I know how he found me. The same way Freddy Starks did: Mr. Interested. But why does he want to see me now? When Jimmy shot that dealer, it was an irrational burst of violence, one born of a drugged, chaotic mind. But I know Jimmy. He never would have methodically tracked me down in order to kill the sole witness to his crime, as good of an idea as that might have been. Jimmy likely just accepted that I was gone and moved on with his desperate existence.

Yet, he's here now.

"I'm sorry you had to deal with him," I tell Brenda. "He won't be a problem."

"I'm just worried for you, Alice. I went to that website you showed me. That's all true?

I mean, about your past and those creepy twin girls?"

"Yes. It's all true."

"That's so messed up. And that group of people in the forum, all stalking you?"

"Also true. And also messed up."

Her questioning gains momentum.

"Does this have anything to do with where you just were?"

I let out a heavy breath. "I went back to England. I actually just met with the girls who stabbed me. They're women now, of course. Just got out of prison."

"Oh my God. What was that like?"

"As unsettling and bizarre as you might expect. One is a Jesus freak, and the other is a mute. I'm trying to find this person who's stalking me and thought they might know him."

"And?"

"And nothing. My world is spiraling out of control because of one sick bastard who has apparently been obsessed with me for fourteen years. It's the person who found me — and saved me, ironically — after I was stabbed."

"You know him?"

I shake my head. "No. He found me that night and called the police, then disappeared. I don't remember him."

"And this all has to do with the comic your dad made?"

At the mention of my father, I feel the energy of the story drain from me. I want to tell Brenda everything, but there's no way I can, not here and now. And I don't want to tell her bits and pieces just to satisfy her hungry curiosity. After all, once my storytelling is done, she gets to leave my world and go back into her own, which is assuredly a cozier place.

"It's a long story, and some of it I can't tell you," I tell her. "The other parts are better told over a bottle of wine." It occurs to me I said the same thing to Richard, but before that wine could be had, death interrupted.

"Of course," she says. "I'm sorry . . . This all has to be horrible for you. But I'd be lying if I didn't say it's fascinating. I guess that makes me pretty shallow."

"You're not shallow. I just need to be in the right space to unload all of this."

"So . . . sorry, one more question. So you can't go to the police with any of this?"

Would that it were all that easy.

"We'll have that bottle of wine soon," I reply. Brenda smiles and nods, giving me the look that she's so good at, the one that makes you feel you're the only person important to her in the world at that moment. If I bothered to write a will, I'd surely leave the Stone Rose to her.

I stay until noon, the longest I've lasted here in what feels like years. I even found myself humming to the eighties music throughout the morning, nostalgic for a decade in which I barely existed.

As I take off my apron and grab my purse, I make a promise to myself. When all of this is over, assuming I come out the other side, I'm changing my last name back to Hill. I don't know why, but it's now a goal that holds importance. It's my father's name, and it should be mine. And, apparently, changing one's name does little to hide you from the world.

I need to see Thomas, to make sure he's okay. I haven't heard much from him in days, for which I'm mostly to blame. I haven't even told him about my visit with the twins. And then there's my mother, who I need to talk to sooner or later, but she'll have a million questions and opinions about my trip to London, none of which I'll likely ever be in the mood for.

Mr. Interested has been silent since his last cryptic message to me, which promised he'll be there to save me. Nor have I sought him out. I know that doesn't make him go away, but we all need to pull the sheet up over our faces and hide every now and then. The monster will still be under the bed when I go looking.

It doesn't take more than a block of driving out of Manchester when I spot the car behind me, as obvious and jarring as a shark fin cutting through the ocean surface.

It's a 1970 charcoal-gray Dodge Challenger. Sleek and slippery, so dark, it seems as if light just disappears into it. But I see it. I see it clearly, and even if the illegal tint job obscures its driver, I know who's behind the wheel.

Jimmy.

The Challenger rumbles up close behind me at the next traffic light. My rearview angle doesn't show me his face clearly, but I can make out his spiked blond hair. Hasn't changed that style since I last saw him shooting our dealer in that parking lot three years ago.

Despite the fact Jimmy's low on the list of things freaking me out at the moment, I'm still consumed with nervous tension. But I can take him, no problem. He's a waify little thing, and I can take care of myself. Unless he has a gun.

He said he misses you.

Then, while we're still at the red light, he bumps into me. Not hard, not even what you'd consider a love tap, but this is something incomprehensible, because his car is the only thing Jimmy ever cared about besides heroin. He'd go days without a shower, but his Challenger always glowed like it was surrounded by some kind of force field. He actually used to garage the thing in winter, paid to *garage* a car in Boston, because of the weather. He washed that car more often than we had sex, and I don't know if that's a sorrier statement about his priorities or my taste in men.

He would *never* purposefully tap another car with his Challenger. Yet, he just did. And with that one little bump, I know I'm not avoiding him. So when the light turns green, I move forward a block and turn into the parking lot of the Hannaford Market, the place where Jesus the butcher precuts all my meat.

It's midday. Decent number of people pulling in and out of the lot, and I'm highly visible to the nearby street traffic. A safe place. I stop, get out of my car, and watch him park behind me.

Come on, Jimmy, I think. *Come tell me what you want. I'm looking for a problem to cross off my list, and you'd be a good start.*

312

He gets out of the car, and I get a look at my old lover for the first time in three years. The first thing I notice is his bruised and battered face, compliments of Freddy Starks. In contrast to the black-and-purple hue of his beaten face are his baby blues, the eyes that drew me in from the moment I met him in that Boston bar. With one look, I can tell Jimmy isn't tweaked. I've seen him tweaked; hell, there wasn't much time we spent together *not* tweaked, and those eyes are not ones glazed with heroin.

No, it's something else.

Jimmy is scared.

He takes a step toward me, an uncertain one, as if wondering if there's a live mine under the pressure of his foot.

"Alice," he says. *"Help me."*

"Jimmy, what the hell? Why are you here?"

Then I notice a small . . . *something* in his left ear. He puts a hand up over his ear, cups it, and nods.

"I know, I know, *okay*?" he says. But he's clearly not talking to me. If I had a normal life, I'd think this man was just talking to himself. A schizophrenic drug addict. But my life is not normal, and with instant certainty, I piece it together.

In his ear is a wireless headset.

Someone is talking to him through it.

And that someone has to be Mr. Interested.

Jimmy has been working with him the whole time.

I move to get back in my car, and he yells out, "Alice! Please, wait!"

He stops to listen to the voice in his ear again.

"What?" I ask. "What, Jimmy?"

Then Jimmy pulls back the flap of his jacket and flashes me the gun tucked into his waistband.

"You have to listen to me, or I'll kill you," he says.

Nothing seems right here, including Jimmy's threat. Jimmy killed a man once, yet despite that truth, I know violence is not typically part of Jimmy's nature. When we were together, he was sweet, sometimes even goofy, a good-looking junkie with boyish charm. Any agitation came from his need for a fix. He killed for drugs, and he killed because of drugs. After I left, I never worried he'd come looking for me, wanting to eliminate a witness — that just isn't Jimmy. So now, here, as he threatens me with a gun, it feels hollow. Forced.

"Jimmy, who's talking to you?" Though I probably know more about that person than Jimmy does. Jimmy likely doesn't even know the name Mr. Interested.

"I can't," he says. "But I need to deliver a message to you, and then it'll be okay."

"Jimmy, what is going on? How is he controlling you?"

Jimmy looks on the verge of tears. He seems so weak, so fragile, and I think one swift kick to his torso would snap him in half. I don't think he really wants to hurt me. Still, he has a gun.

I take a step toward him.

"Jimmy, it's okay. He doesn't want you. He wants me."

His face is a mixture of confusion and imminent panic. "Stay back, Alice."

But I don't stay back. I take another step, and his eyes grow wider in fear as I close in. I almost feel sorry for him.

"What's the message, Jimmy? Tell me."

"Stay back."

Another step. I'm nearly in arms' reach of him.

"Tell me, Jimmy."

He nods, but not to me — to the voice in his ear. Jimmy's right hand shakes as it moves to the butt of the gun.

"It's okay, Jimmy," I say. I begin to shift my weight to my back foot, finding the balance that puts me in the best position to strike.

"I loved you once," he said. There is no emotion to this.

"That's your message?"

"I loved you once," he repeats. "But I didn't deserve you. I didn't . . . didn't know how special you truly are." These aren't Jimmy's words. They are clearly being fed to him through the earpiece. What the hell is going on?

"And now I'm taking you with me."

"Stop. You don't even know what you're saying."

He mouths something to me. If I had to guess, he said *I have to.*

"If you don't come with me, Alice, I'm going to kill you."

"Jimmy, stop it already."

"Alice, just do as I say, *please.* Get in the car."

This whole thing is some kind of private performance staged just for me, but I don't want to be part of it anymore.

"I don't care what he's telling you. I'm leaving."

Jimmy takes out his gun and holds it by his side. He's shaking so much, I'm not sure he could shoot me even from this short distance. But that's a risky assumption to make.

"Why are you doing this?" I ask, trying to

keep my voice as calm and even as I can. "What's he threatening you with?"

"I never deserved you," he said. He sounds on the verge of tears, and a spit bubble rides his lower lip. "Now get in my car, Alice."

"No, Jimmy. I'm not getting in your car."

He pauses just a moment, and I can tell he's listening to the voice in his ear. Waiting for his next set of instructions.

Seconds later, as he raises his arm and points the gun at me, I know my chance to attack is gone. I had it, right there, in that brief space of time. I could have pounced, but with the gun now trained on me, I've lost all the opportunity.

"I don't want to do this, Alice."

I chance a quick look around. There must be someone seeing a man pointing a gun at a woman, but if there is, I don't notice them.

"Put the gun down, Jimmy. You don't have to listen to him."

He nods. Quiet, desperate, defeated. Then, with his free hand, he softly taps his chest.

"What?" I say. "What are you trying to tell me?"

"Get in the car, Alice. I'm going to count to three."

Is this how it's supposed to end, with Jimmy the proxy shooting me? Mr. Interested is a coward. He can't even kill me face-to-face. I'm not getting in that car, not going anywhere.

"One," Jimmy says. His face is twisted in anguish, like someone is bending his arm to the point of the bone snapping.

"You don't have to listen to him, Jimmy. Just drive away."

"Two . . ." he says. Then he mouths something to me, something he doesn't want the person controlling him to hear. I think I understand. I think he said *Who are you talking about?*

This makes no sense. I'm talking about Mr. Interested. Who does he think I'm talking about?

"Two . . ." he repeats, drawing it out.

He won't do it. He won't. This is Jimmy. He's not the greatest example of a human being, but he's not pure evil. He wouldn't shoot me.

Then, in a sickening jolt of realization as he steadies his quivering hand, I think:

He's going to kill me.

I pounce, knowing it's too late, but it's the only thing I can do. He's going to kill me, but I won't be running away when he pulls the trigger.

The sound of the gunshot is not as loud as I expected. Just a muffled *pop,* but I hear it. Jimmy's eyes widen as I launch my body at him, and in midair, I expect my world to go black.

It doesn't.

I tackle him, and he falls to the ground with no resistance.

He missed me, I think. No pain. No blackness. He *missed* me.

He's already released his grip on the gun, and I waste no time making sure he'll stay incapacitated. I raise my fist and deliver a quick blow to his trachea.

He should be gasping, struggling for breath against blinding pain. He should be reaching for his throat.

But Jimmy does none of these things. He just lies on the cold asphalt parking lot of Hannaford Market.

I rise from him and immediately see the blood on his dirty, gray T-shirt. The stain blossoms as I stare at it, growing until his whole chest is a deep crimson.

"Jimmy?"

He doesn't answer. He doesn't move. His eyes — wide open and staring into the gray skies — don't blink.

I reach down and lift his shirt, pulling it above his chest. There's no way he could have shot himself — the gun was pointed right at me.

It takes a moment to understand what I'm

looking at. A thin metal band, around an inch wide, strapped around Jimmy's chest so tight, his skin pushes out around it. I don't want to see, but I have to see.

I grab under his arm and roll him halfway over, and that's when I see the little black box — the size of a cigarette pack — held in place by the metal band. It's positioned directly behind his heart.

"Oh my God!"

The voice is behind me.

I turn and look up at the woman staring down at me. I am suddenly aware of the warmth of Jimmy's draining blood onto my fingertips.

She drops a grocery bag at the same moment she starts screaming.

A jug of milks breaks on the asphalt, and a pool of glossy white collects around Jimmy's lifeless feet.

■ ■ ■ ■

PART III
MR. INTERESTED

■ ■ ■ ■

THIRTY-SEVEN

Whatever decision I make in the next few moments will have a cascade of consequences. I have no idea what to do.

The woman can't do anything but stare at Jimmy's body as she continues to scream. A man runs over and looks down as soon as he's in full view of the scene.

"Jesus," he says. "Did someone call 911?"

"I just did," I lie. I begin sidestepping toward my car.

"What happened?"

The woman tries to speak but only manages a muttering of syllables. The milk has moved up from around Jimmy's feet all the way to his thighs, making him appear painted on canvas. The other groceries have scattered around the woman's feet, and I can't picture her calm enough to ever pick them up.

"I saw him waving a gun," I say. "He yelled at me to get out of my car, which I did. I think he's just some strung-out homeless guy. Then, there was a bang, and he just fell over." I look over to the woman to see if she immediately contradicts my story, but I don't even think she's processed my words.

"He shot himself?" the man asks.

"I don't know," I say. "I think so."

The gun rests a few feet from Jimmy's hand, next to the front left tire of the Challenger.

The woman finally speaks.

"Is . . . is he dead?"

I don't answer.

Three other people are coming our way, and I know I have to make a decision soon. A quick glance at the parking lot lights tells me there aren't any security cameras out here. For all I know, this woman is the only person who even saw me attack Jimmy, and she couldn't have heard our conversation.

I realize I have Jimmy's blood literally on my hands, and then add, "I tried to help him, but I don't have any medical training. I didn't know what to do."

The man nods at me and then puts his arm around the hysterical woman and squeezes her shoulder. His close-cropped hair, square jaw, and solid build assign him an authoritative look. Military, even.

"Come on," he tells her. "You don't need to be looking at this. There's nothing we can do . . . The police are on their way." He turns her away from Jimmy, then bends down to pick up her groceries.

"Look," I say to him, "I don't want to be involved in this."

"I think you have to wait for the cops to come," he says. "They'll need statements."

This is when I make my decision. I like to think it's a calculated one, that I'm playing to odds I've fully weighed, but the truth is I'm scared. I'm getting the hell out of here.

"Sorry," I tell him. "I'd like to help but I can't talk to the police. I . . . . There's someone looking for me, and I don't want him finding me. If I'm in the paper, he'll know I'm here. I can't keep running."

My words are only half lies. As I walk to the car, I half expect this man to stop me, yet he lets me go. But as I pull away, I look in the rearview mirror and see the man holding up his phone at eye level. He's taking a picture or video. Of my car. My license plate.

My hands start to numb as they grip the steering wheel, an icy flow that starts at my fingertips and makes its way up my arms, through my shoulders, and then finally fills my chest, making it difficult to breathe. My limbs begin with that familiar, prickly tingling. Panic attack coming. I can feel it as much as I can feel the stickiness of Jimmy's blood on my fingertips. I'm due for one. *Overdue,* really. I made it through the events in London without one, and I was beginning to think that confronting my fears head-on was curing me. Seeking Mr. Interested in earnest, visiting the site of my attack, taking control for once — that somehow those were steps to freeing myself of constant fear.

But now I feel it all slipping away with every shallow, gasping breath.

I'm on the highway before I even consider the idea of going back home. I can't be alone for this. Not this time. This is going to be a bad one. I keep going, gaining speed, focusing only on the road, the white lane markers slipping by in a blur, knowing after thousands of them I'll be at my mother's house. I've never wanted to be taken care of as much as I do in this moment. I want to surrender and have someone there to hold me when I do.

My phone buzzes, pulling me out of my trance. A text. I glance down at the console where the phone sits. It could be anyone, but of course it isn't. I know exactly who it is. I can't not look at it, just as I can't stop any of this anymore. I reach for the phone and flip it over, and there's only a one-sentence text waiting for me from an unknown number.

I'll always be there to save you, Alice.

These words fill me with dread, because the pattern is now both obvious and insane.

Mr. Interested forced Jimmy to threaten me, just so he could then kill him.

Yes. All the same pattern.

He told Freddy Starks where to find me, then planted a gun to let Thomas and me kill him.

He sent a man to confront me in London, and probably would have done something to stop him, had I not attacked the man first.

And it all started the moment he called the police when I was bleeding to death in Gladstone Park.

I'll always be there to save you, Alice.

It's a circle, a demented, fourteen-year-long cycle of abuse and rescue. Mr. Interested has a savior complex. He's been tracking me for years, probably fantasizing about the high he got rescuing me. But only recently did he finally act on it.

Because he's sick, I tell myself. He said he was dying. So now he's living out his fantasy before he no longer has the chance.

I fall back into a trance, trusting instincts

327

to guide me to my mother's house. I'm slipping away, and I'm not sure any amount of breathing exercises will keep my car from careening over the median into oncoming traffic. Or even if I want it to.

Focus. Keep focusing. One mile at a time. Don't think of anything. Clear your mind. Let go.

I am in control, I tell myself. Then I say it again, this time aloud.

"I am in control."

Over and over again, hundreds of times, each aloud, and it's just enough to get me to the exit at Arlington. I weave through the small city streets, past Mount Pleasant Cemetery, until finally I jolt to a stop in front of my mother's house. The second I open my car door, all the focus and control I've clung to spills from me. The dam has burst. I nearly collapse as I stagger up the steps and grab the doorknob.

Locked.

I pound weakly on the door, then ring the bell over and over again. What if they aren't here?

Then I hear movement inside, and I lean against the sun-warmed door, using it to heat my freezing bones.

The door opens, and I fall into the house, weakly bracing myself with my hands as I hit the hardwood floor.

My mother stands over me, and for the first time in a very long time, I'm happy to see her face. She is my mum, and she'll take care of it.

"Alice, dear. My God."

Then I slip beneath the surface into the silent, deep, dark waters.

THIRTY-EIGHT

Wednesday, October 28

I wake with a jolt, unsure of where I am, how I got here, and even very nearly who I am. It's very dark. Hot. A dry, static hot, and my tongue swells in my mouth, begging for water. Yet my skin is covered in sweat.

In seconds, bits and pieces flash back to me. I was driving to my mother's house, racing against the onset of a very bad panic attack. She opened the door, and I collapsed inside the house.

I'm in my mother's house.

In a bed, must be the guest room upstairs. My body is so tightly spooled by sheets that I feel mummified. I try to lift my arms but my movement is restricted, and this alone makes me want to scream in fear. *Relax. Move slowly.* And when I do, I free my right arm, and then my left.

More memories flood in.

Of my mother taking me upstairs by the

time the attack took complete control of me. Of being in a ball on the bed, immersed in the blackest of thoughts. The absence of all hope. The desire, the *thirst,* to kill myself, and the thought that even death wouldn't provide me relief. The hell of everything.

I sit up and stare into the darkness long enough that I can finally make out the cracks of light around the windows and door. No idea what time it is, or even what day. I can hear the familiar sound of a space heater whirring somewhere nearby. My mother always uses these, because she thinks they cost less than the central heat, and the one in this room has raised the temperature to a thousand suffocating degrees.

I remember sobbing uncontrollably, crying until my lungs hurt.

There's something else.

I was saying something, over and over.

It was . . .

I miss Daddy.

Rocking back and forth in the bed, crying into the dark like a scared, little girl, sobbing *I miss Daddy.*

More images from last night slowly take focus. My mother entered the room. Her hand on my back, *there there*-ing me, telling me she had a glass of water. Me, reaching for it, gulping it down greedily, feeling that it didn't taste right.

Her telling me she'd put a little something in it. Just to help me sleep. Just a little special powder she sometimes gives Thomas when he's upset.

Then it's all a blur. But there was sleep. Sleep like death, deep and shapeless, dark and vulnerable.

And now I'm awake. Alive, I think. Feeling like I've been hit by a truck.

I get out of bed, stand with unsteady legs. Move to the wall, flick on the light, brace against the brightness. My eyes adjust, and I scan the room. No purse, no phone. Still in all my clothes.

Open the door, head into the hallway. Hazy light streams from the far windows, but it's soft and weak, the light of morning. Thomas's room is next to mine. I crack open the door and peek in. He's asleep, headphones on, a bottle of prescription pills and a Mountain Dew can on the dresser next to him. I'm about to leave him alone, let him sleep, then choose instead to go inside. I'm pulled to him out of some emotion I can't quite define, but its closest relative would be sadness.

I watch him sleep, listen to his heavy, heavy breaths. I feel weak just looking at him, knowing how much he struggles just to live a normal life. But Thomas isn't normal; he exists in a state of arrested development, and the growing chasm between his biological and emotional years will forever define him. We are all defined by something, and in this moment, I think how I've been solely focused on my own labels, not considering nearly enough that Thomas's struggles are no less real or significant than my own.

I never should have left him alone.

It's a sudden, jarring thought, one as clear as if being spoken directly into my ear.

He should not be here.

I should not be here.

I came here seeking my mother's comfort, and she responded by drugging me.

My gaze flicks to the bottle of pills on Thomas's nightstand, the white, plastic cap resting, but not secured, on its top. I pick it up, remove the lid, and find the bottle half-filled. The capsules are the blue of a robin's egg. So simple and pretty, in their own way. The label lists the drug name; it's long, stuffed with vowels, and unfamiliar to me. Must be one of the meds for his bipolar schizoaffective disorder. Who knows what effect, good or bad, it's having on him? I have an urge to take the rest of these and flush them down the toilet, along with the past fourteen years.

"What are you doing in here?"

My mother stands in the doorway, her frame filling a good portion of it.

"I don't know," I say. My throat is painfully dry. "I just wanted to see him."

"He needs his sleep, Alice. As do you. You had quite a night. Poor, poor dear."

I gave the pill bottle a little shake. "What are these for?"

She lets out a breath with effort. "They calm him down."

"They're a sedative?"

"Alice, please don't come here and start judging. You don't understand the needs your brother has."

I put the pills back down on the side table. Thomas hasn't stirred an inch. That whispered voice is back in my ear.

Don't leave him here, Alice.

"What did you give me last night?" I ask. "I can't remember much, and I feel like I weigh a ton."

She takes a step inside the room and crosses her meaty arms against her chest.

"Something to help you sleep."

"You sedated me?"

"You were quite a mess. I *helped* you. That's why you came here, right, Alice?

Because you needed your mother, and I helped you."

It's true. I didn't want to be alone. The visions of yesterday afternoon stab at me.

The parking lot.

The fear in Jimmy's eyes. His gun pointed at me.

The explosion. The screaming woman.

The blood.

I hold my hands up and see the faded red stains of Jimmy on my hands. Did my mother see the blood?

"You were in fits, Alice. What happened yesterday?"

"Where's my phone?" I ask.

"Downstairs," she answers. "Alice, what set you off yesterday? You were screaming, you know."

Screaming? I close my eyes and concentrate. Before she moved me to the bedroom, I was on the living room floor. Thomas was there. Trying to comfort me, I think. My mother told him to leave me be, that she would handle it.

Then Thomas was yelling. At her, I think. Telling her *It's all your fault.*

Then she moved me. Gave me the water with the powder. Then there was just darkness until I woke this morning.

"I don't remember much," I tell her.

"God, I could go right back to bed. Sleep for a week."

Her eyes widen at this. "Alice, yes, of course, dear. Go back to bed. Take as much time as you want. You could stay here for a bit, you know."

"I can't. I just can't."

"You're falling apart at the seams, Alice. I can see it. You look terrible, you know. Does this all have to do with that book you received in the post? Is that why you went to London? You never tell me anything, and all I can do is sit here and worry."

Thomas still hasn't moved an inch, but I don't want to wake him by continuing the conversation in his bedroom.

"Can I get some coffee?"

She wipes her hands on the front of her pants. "Yes, of course, dear. Come on, then."

I follow my mother down the stairs, watching her take each tread carefully.

In the kitchen, she prepares a pot of coffee and offers me crumb cake, which smells the way God must. I take only a small piece, knowing too much sugar will make me want to crash even harder than I already do.

"I went to see the twins," I say.

"The twin what?"

"The *twins*. The Glassin twins."

Her eyes widen, and her fleshy cheeks immediately redden. "Jesus and Mary. Why on earth would you care to do such a thing?"

"I'm trying to figure out who sent me the book."

When she puts her hand on her hip, it sends me back to every argument we've ever had. "So you flew to England and went to a prison to see those wretched girls?"

"No. I went to their home. They just got out."

"They're *out*? How are they allowed back into society?"

I shrug. "I don't make the rules, Mom."

"You don't even seem upset," she says.

"Well, I'm sure you wouldn't have said that last night," I say. "Right now, I don't have the energy to be bothered by anything. Pour me a cup, and maybe that'll give me the strength to work myself up a bit."

The coffeemaker has spit out just enough to fill a mug, which my mother does and hands it to me. Dark and delicious.

I take a deep breath and try to find a solid, balanced center within myself. When I feel I'm close enough, I look down to the countertop and say, "Mom, whoever sent me that book — whoever did those drawings — has been following me. Stalking me. Is obsessed with me and the stabbing. I think he's been following me for years. In fact . . ."

When I look up, I find my mother staring straight at me, the kind of stare that is so focused, it can only be used as an effort to keep from shouting.

But very softly, she does speak. She says, "In fact *what*?"

I let another long breath out. "In fact, this person *might* be the same person who found me that night. The one who called the police."

"That's ridiculous. That person was just a bloke who didn't want to be involved. He saved your life."

"I know he did. And now he seems to be obsessed with the idea of continually doing that."

"Meaning what?"

"I don't know," I say, not wanting to reveal to her how deep this all goes. I don't know if I'm trying to protect her from the truth or just don't want to have to manage her reaction to everything. God, if she knew about Thomas shooting Freddy Starks . . .

"Wait, have you had contact with this person?"

"Some," I admit. "A few emails. He's baiting me, and I'm trying to find him."

"Why in the world would you want to do that? What would you do if you even found him?"

That's the question, really. What happens if you find Mr. Interested, Alice? Just tell him to please leave you alone? Or would you do what you did to that poor British man and nearly beat him to a pulp?

"I don't know. But I can't keep living my life knowing he's out there."

She shovels a generous piece of the crumb cake in her mouth, swallows quickly, then says, "Alice, you needn't pursue bad things. Enough bad things have found you without any effort on your part. Leave the past in the past. Ignore this person . . . I'm sure he'll soon leave you be."

"I don't understand why you want me to sit back and be a victim." Although I do understand. It's the role in which she excels.

"I just want you to be safe."

"I think I'm past that point now." I allow a moment of silence between us, then say, "I also saw Charles Glassin."

"Charles Glassin? I haven't thought of that name in ages." She takes another bite.

"He said you all used to get together way back when. Before I was even born."

She looks startled, and for a moment, I think the crumb cake has perhaps cut off her airway. But she regains composure, swallows, then says, "We did a few social things, but not much. I hardly knew them, and what I did know of them I didn't much care for. The mother's a bit of a tart."

"What did you used to do together?"

She seems to be filtering through her mind for the right thing to say. She decides on, "Drink, mostly. That's more or less what everyone did back then. Drink and smoke."

I accept this answer as at least some of the truth and press her no more.

"How did you find Charles?" she asks.

"He's still in the same house."

"You went back to the neighborhood?"

"Yes. The neighborhood. The park. I just knocked on his door, and he was home. He's a very sad man. His wife left a long time ago. I think he said to New York."

"What else did he tell you?"

I think back to my time with Charles in his suffocating little house with bare walls. "He talked about how they split up after what happened. How it felt to fail in doing the only job that's important: raising your children. He took a lot of responsibility for what happened."

My mother turns her back to me and starts wiping an already-clean counter with a dish towel. "Understandable, I suppose. He did raise those little monsters."

The word strikes me. "Yes. *Monsters*. He said that, too. I remember thinking how very sad it was to hear someone call their own children monsters, even if that's what they are."

She stops wiping, turns, and walks directly to me, and then finally takes me into her arms and pulls me hard against her. I don't know if she's shielding me or if I'm shielding her. She holds me tight and says, "You need to let go of the past, Alice. Whoever is stalking you will surely tire of their little games. You should come home. Live here. Let me take care of you. It would be good for all of us."

I gently push away from her. "Mom, this doesn't all go away. He's not going to tire of me. He's been watching me for years, as far as I can tell, and now he's slowly making himself known. He's not going to stop until he gets what he wants."

Or until he dies of whatever ails him, I think. But waiting that out is dangerous, if it's even true. I suspect he wants some kind of closure with me before his life ends.

"Your father created him," she says, and I don't know what *him* she's referring to, the character or the real-life stalker. Perhaps she means both. "He destroyed everything, and I'm left to deal with all the pieces. Thomas is a zombie, and you're just a little bag of nerves."

This is where it all turns. It's like she switches into another role, or perhaps the exterior dissolves and the real her is exposed. But it's always ugly, because all she can focus on is *her.* I don't want to engage, so I need to leave.

"Mom, thank you for taking care of me last night. I do love you for it. But I have to go."

"That's right," she says. There's a fierceness in her tone. "Because that's what you do best, Alice. You run away. Just like your father, you don't look behind you to see the mess you've left."

"I can't do this, Mom. I can't do this."

"Then go, Alice." She wipes her hands on her hips, back and forth, back and forth.

Then I see her from my dream, the one where she was teaching Thomas to swim. That awful, sickening moment when she lowered him into the water and calmly walked away, letting him drown, wiping her hands on her hips as her son's lungs filled with water. I will get him out of here, I resolve. I don't know how I'm going to do it, but I will take Thomas from here.

She shuffles after me as I grab my purse and phone and walk out the front door.

She stands in the doorway, and I can hear her huffing. She wants to shout something,

342

and I'm waiting for it.

Maybe she can't think of anything to say, or maybe it's just all been said before, because, for a rare time in my mother's life, she chooses to be silent.

I pull out of the driveway as she is swallowed back inside the house, back into her world of self-pity and control. As I drive, the tears well up in my eyes, and I begin to softly cry as I head back to Manchester. I cry not because of everything happening in my life, but for things that aren't happening.

I miss my dad more than ever.

THIRTY-NINE

Thursday, October 29

Today was so close to being a normal day that it felt oddly peaceful. A storm chaser would liken it to the eye of the hurricane, and soldiers would recognize it as a temporary truce on opposite sides of a battlefield. Calm, quiet. A sense of the rare, delicious ordinary.

I worked a full day at the Stone Rose, spending more time than usual chatting with the regulars. Charlie told me how his grandchildren bought him a La-Z-Boy chair for his eightieth birthday and even mentioned he'd missed seeing my face lately. Jim and Linda ordered matching macchiatos and told me about their CrossFit gym, which they refer to as "the box." I listened not so much with interest as with pleasant comfort.

Brenda signed up the Rose to be a part of a Halloween window-decorating contest, and for two hours, a troop of ninth-graders painted away. Their amateurish strokes turned into something quite impressive: a pumpkin patch under a full midnight moon, overlooked by a ratty, old scarecrow whose face conveyed a profound loneliness, an expression I would not have thought possible with window paint. Brenda chooses a window all to herself, where she paints a mesmerizing depiction of Simon, a beautifully imaged vapor of a ghost, rising up in the form of steam from a coffee cup. Simon is smiling and holding in his left, ethereal hand a blueberry scone, just like the ones we sell at the Rose.

Before leaving the shop for the day, I check the news online once again for anything about Jimmy. The story seems to have remained local, and there's been nothing more detailed about his death other than a small explosive charge killing him. Nothing being ruled a homicide, and no mention of a woman fleeing the scene. Just the all-encompassing term *ongoing investigation.* Jimmy's behavior was described as "erratic" by witnesses, and I wonder who those witnesses are since really I was the only one to whom he spoke. Still, I'm grateful nothing has led the police to my door. Yet.

Back home, the sun sets through my

kitchen window as a cold October wind whips up the trees in my front yard. I build a fire and prepare a simple dinner, which I eat sitting on the floor in front of the flames. It feels good, the heat on my face and arms, and I try not to think too much about the evidence of Freddy Starks's murder burning to ash in this very fireplace. I try to sustain a sense of normalcy, of comfort, but don't try too hard, for often that's when it slips fastest through my fingers.

Then the doorbell rings, and in an instant, all feelings of security disappear. My body tenses against my wishes, a Pavlovian reaction. It's just after six o'clock, and I can't imagine who's on the other side of the door.

But I can imagine, can't I?

Is it so hard to picture Mr. Interested at my door, in whatever form he takes shape? In a brief, strange moment, I picture a man at the door in a tuxedo, getting on his knee and flashing me an engagement ring. I don't know why that enters my head, but it's nicer than picturing a maniac with a knife and a rope.

I slide an iron poker from its hearthside harness and grip it in my right hand. It feels wonderfully assuring, an extension of my own hand. My brain instantly processes the amount of damage I could do with this, which makes me think of all the blood that's already been spilled and cleaned in this room.

I creep up next to the door and slide the curtain an inch away from the window, then pecr outside.

Richard.

The tension drains from my body, causing my shoulders to slump. I lean the poker against the wall, deactivate the security system, and open the door. Richard seems even taller and more gaunt than usual, and his cheeks are a gray, ashen hue.

He holds up a bottle of wine.

"Can we talk?" he asks.

I take the bottle.

"Sure. Guess we never did have that bottle of wine earlier, did we?"

"No, we didn't."

He walks inside and looks around, as if expecting to find I'm not alone.

"I know you were gone for a few days and just got back. You sure this is a good time?"

I close the door and lock it. "I'm surprised you want to talk to me at all."

"I just . . . just need to work through some things. Out loud."

"Of course," I say, a little worried about what he means. "Do you want to take off your coat?"

"Sure." He shrugs off his bulky army coat, revealing his long, wiry frame beneath a black T-shirt and faded jeans. His arms are even paler than his face, and blue, ropy veins track down his biceps and into the crooks of his elbows. For the first time, I notice the bottom of a tattoo poking out beneath his right sleeve.

"I didn't know you had ink," I say, pointing to his arm.

"Oh, yeah, yeah." His left hand goes up as if to cover his tattoo for a moment, but then he pulls up his sleeve, revealing what looks like the pi sign, only with a line along the bottom as well. "It's my birth sign. Gemini. I know, it's stupid. I was young and drunk. Suppose I could've gotten something much worse."

"I like it," I say, not sure if I mean it or not.

He pulls his sleeve back down.

"Have a seat on the couch," I tell him. "I'll go open the wine."

He does, and a minute later, I return with two glasses and set them on the coffee table, then go back to grab the bottle. I pour us each a glass, place the bottle on the table, and then sit, leaving a cushion of distance between us. For a brief moment, I have a flash of sharing a couch in a dark room with

Melinda Glassin, which feels like a year ago. Or maybe it didn't happen at all.

"I haven't been sleeping much lately," he starts. "I can't get what happened here out of my mind. I mean, did that all really take place?" He runs his fingers through his hair as he looks down at the floor.

"Yeah, it did," I say. "What happened was terrible. I think about it, too. But you had nothing to do with it, Richard."

"I know, I know."

"You were trying to help. I didn't expect Thomas to do what he did. I didn't want that, but it happened. That man was going to kill me, Richard." The last thing I need is a guilt-torn Richard going to the police to wipe his conscience clean. "Even if we'd dropped him off at the hospital and he got fixed up, he was going to come back for me. I know that doesn't make what happened in here any easier, but it's the truth."

"Alice —"

I talk over him. "And no matter how you feel, you weren't involved, but if the police find out, it could make things very tricky. We need to make sure this stays with us. God, how you must hate me for making you a part of this."

"Alice, you aren't listening to me."

I lean back on the couch.

"What?"

He leans forward and sets his wine on the coffee table.

"I don't hate you. I want to help you. Any way I can."

I shift my weight just a fraction away from him.

"I don't need you to save me, Richard."

"I didn't say that. I said I wanted to help."

"Why? If you were smart, you'd move out. Get as far away as you could."

"It's hard to explain," he says.

And for a moment, I have a flash of what he's about to say. It's something ridiculous, like he's falling in love with me. Or that he feels we're supposed to be together.

"What is it, Richard?"

"It's just . . . Well, this is going to sound strange. But I don't feel guilty or bad about what happened. And maybe I should. Hell, I'm a nurse, aren't I? But I feel just the opposite. He was going to hurt you, and then . . . what Thomas did. Once I got over the shock, I realized . . . I realized it gave me a *rush,* you know? The power of that moment. That man came here with a plan, thought he was in control. And then, *bam.*"

Richard grabs his wine and takes a larger gulp, either to steady his nerves or to keep his lips from speaking more.

"Wow," I say. "I was not expecting you to say any of that."

"I know. Maybe that makes me a freak."

"No, it doesn't. I just wasn't expecting it."

"I don't know what to do now," he says. "My life is so boring. I just do the same thing every day. And then . . . what happened, *happened*. It was like someone injected adrenaline right into my heart. I couldn't sleep for nearly three days. My mind is constantly spinning. And then you disappear for a few days, and I don't know what's happening, and I worry about you."

"I'm fine, Richard."

"I know, I know. You can take care of yourself. But even . . . with all the stuff going on in your life, you at least have this excitement going on."

"Excitement? Are you kidding me? I would trade the *excitement* of having a maniacal stalker and panic attacks for a thousand boring lifetimes."

"I know. I don't mean it like that. It's just that . . ." He lifts his arm and points to the middle of my living room. "He died right there. A man was tied up and bleeding, and then Thomas just killed him. *Right there.* And I saw the whole thing. I was part of it. I suppose I'm still trying to process all of it, and part of what I've learned in the past week is how incredibly insignificant my life is."

"Richard, my life is a constant struggle for air. None of it is fun, or exciting."

"I'm not trying to make light of it," he says, and I can see in his face he means it. "But I want to help. I want to be a part of it."

"There's nothing you can do."

"How do you know that? I mean, have you found the guy who's stalking you?"

"No."

He drinks more, and I feel the need to catch up.

"Well," he says, "at least tell me what's happening. I know a little from what you told me, but . . ." Then he lifts the bottle of wine. "Here we are."

I've always felt unusually comfortable around Richard, which is to say *somewhat* comfortable. And now, in his eagerness to talk, there's something almost boyish about him, a quality I'd never expect to shine through his hallmark seriousness.

I lift my now almost-empty glass. "Pour us some more, and I'll catch you up on the latest episode of Mister Tender's Girl."

Richard smiles, and though his teeth are far from perfect, in this moment, he's lovely.

He fills my glass.

■ ■ ■ ■

A bottle and a half later, my head spins comfortably, like I've just walked off a scary roller coaster and survived. Somehow I've managed to do all the talking and kept up my share of drinking.

The wall clock chimes eight thirty, and we've had nothing more than smashed grapes for dinner. But I'm not hungry. I just feel a lulling, heavy pull toward sleep. Richard is more awake than ever, energized by my stories.

"I can't believe that about your ex-boyfriend," he says. "I read about that online."

"I'm constantly worried my name is going to come up in connection with it. I don't know how I can keep in front of this much longer. I just want to . . . disappear."

"Seems that's not an easy thing to do. You tried it before. This Mr. Interested still found you."

"All I did was change my name when I moved here, and I wasn't even aware at the time someone was already watching me. God, I just want a do-over. A fourteen-year do-over."

Richard leans his head back on the couch,

which is the most comfortable position I've ever seen him assume. "But that's not going to happen, of course. And you don't really want to keep running, do you? I can't imagine."

"No," I say. "It's a fantasy, disappearing. Creating a whole new world for myself. But it wouldn't matter. I can never escape what happened to me. What's in my mind. Moving again and getting a new social security number won't change any of that. Besides, there're good things in my life, and I don't acknowledge that enough. I love my coffee shop. The people I work with. My house. And Thomas. I can't leave Thomas."

"So then, if you can't get a do-over, and you're not going to disappear, your only other option is to find Mr. Interested and stop him."

I nod, almost amused by how simple this all sounds. "And somehow not get tied to the deaths of three people: the drug dealer three years ago, Freddy Starks, and Jimmy. Mr. Interested knows about all of them, and God knows how he plans to use that information."

Richard briefly touches my arm, and the graze is so light, it could be an accident.

"And you think he's the person who found you the night of your stabbing?"

"He told me as much."

"And that maybe it wasn't an accident he happened to be there at that time?"

"It's hard to say. I mean, could I actually have known him back then? How would the twins know him? According to Melinda, he sent her letters in jail, and she had no idea who he was. But she's crazy, so who knows what to believe?"

Richard *hmmmms* and we both sit and stare forward, each of us slumped on the couch, relaxed, casual, and with less space between us than at the first glass of wine. I never would have thought discussing my stalker with my tenant would lead to a pleasant evening. A day ago, I was curled in a ball in my mother's house, succumbing to whatever drugs she thought I needed.

After a long, comfortable pause, Richard says, "There's something not right."

"Not right?"

"Yeah, from your story. Something's missing."

"I told you everything that happened," I say. Which is true. Richard now knows as much of what's happening to me as I do. I told him what we did with Starks's body, my flight to London, my visit to Gladstone Park. Charles Glassin. The twins. My messages from Mr. Interested. Jimmy. My panic

355

attack last night and my conversations with my mother. Everything.

"Don't you think it's weird your parents used to hang out with the twins' parents?"

"Everything about all of this is weird, that included," I say. "But on the scale of weirdness, I'd put that way over on the side of not so much. I mean, it sounds like they just got together socially a few times."

"It's hard to wrap my head around," Richard says, "but there seem to be connections to Mr. Interested and your past. I mean, you even said you think he's the guy who found you in the park, and maybe he knew what was going to happen. That maybe he wrote the original letters to the twins telling them to hurt you. You're right in what you told me: he seems to have some kind of hero complex. Hurt you, then help you."

"Keep going," I say. I've been through this in an infinite loop in my head, so I'm anxious to see if he has a different perspective on everything.

"Your father writes the warning message in the book, telling you basically not to trust anyone," he continues. "You only know he wrote that sometime after your stabbing, but you don't know who or what he was talking about."

"Right. I'm fairly certain it's his handwriting, and the cover art and first panels are his. But not the other panels."

"He was drawing out the adventure story he used to tell you?"

I nod. "When we were kids. Chancellor's Kingdom. It's where Mister Tender came from. I don't know, maybe he was drawing the whole backstory as some form of closure or something. He only drew the first few panels."

"But Mr. Interested somehow got ahold of it. Doesn't that mean he maybe knew your father?"

"I thought about that," I say. "He could have, but he could also just be an obsessed fan and ransacked my father's place after he died. I have no idea."

"There was something your father wanted to warn you about, but he never sent you that book. He never warned you of anything in the time you spent with him before he died."

"No."

"So maybe whatever your father was referring to was either not an imminent threat, or he didn't really believe it himself."

"I have no idea. It could be nothing," I say. "I mean, it was a quote from a penguin, after all."

My hand is just next to his leg, the knuckles lightly grazing. It's barely perceptible, but it feels nice to touch someone.

"You said Charles referred to bad decisions he's made. With his wife."

"He said . . ." I close my eyes and see Charles in his little house, wearing his painfully sad expression. "He told me not to chase ghosts. That he and Margaret made some bad decisions. I think he even said *associated with the wrong people,* or something like that, and he wondered if it affected how they raised the girls. But he never said what those decisions were."

"You didn't ask?"

"I wanted to, but he seemed so upset. Then he changed the subject. Asked about my mother."

Richard sits up, and I take my hand off his leg.

"I think there's something in their past that's connected to all of this. What was your mom's reaction when you told her you saw Charles?"

"Fairly dismissive. But she was surprised, for sure. Said they used to go drinking together, but that she didn't really care for them. Especially Margaret."

"Why Margaret?"

"I don't know," I say. "She was like Charles. Quick to change the subject."

"So Charles was cryptic and your mom was dismissive when talking about their past. Do you know where Margaret is now?"

Close, I remember. "Charles said she moved to New York soon after I came to the States myself. But I have no idea if she's still there."

"Let's find out," he says. Richard reaches into the front pocket of his jeans and slides out his phone. "Glassin, right?"

"Yes," I say, then spell it for him. "But I can't imagine she kept the same name. She might have remarried, or just changed it because of the association."

He stares at the screen, and I lean over to catch a glimpse, and as I do, my hair falls forward against his chest. It's a small, intimate moment. It catches me off guard for just a second, but I'm soon pulled back into the search results on his phone.

"A number of hits," he says, thumbing down through the results. He refines the search to *Margaret Glassin New York.*

The very first result is a *New York Post* article, dated four years ago. It's an arts-and-entertainment piece about the gentrification of certain sections of Brooklyn and the efforts to keep the character of existing establishments while appeasing millennial tastes. There are several examples of local business owners bemoaning the changing neighborhood.

One of those business owners is Margaret Glassin, who, according to the article, moved to New York from London over a decade earlier.

"Holy shit," I say, reading what kind of business owner Margaret Glassin is. "She owns a bar. A *bar.*"

Richard reads from the piece. " 'Margaret Glassin came to New York over a decade ago, hoping for a fresh start after a painful divorce.' "

"There's nothing in there about the stabbing," I say. "No one bothered to look her name up."

"No need to," he says. "Just a fluff piece, really." He keeps reading. " 'She's currently the owner of Maggie's on Franklin Avenue, in a building where a bar in one form or another has operated for over fifty years. Glassin told us her drink menu consists solely of ale, gin, whiskey, and beer, and she actively resists all hipster demands for elaborate mixed drinks.' "

This is the extent of Margaret's mention in the article, but it's enough to make me certain it has to be the same person. Charles and my mother never referred to her as Maggie, but still, it lines up perfectly.

"Google the bar," I say.

He does. "Still there," he says. "What are you thinking?"

I rest my hand on his arm. "I'm thinking I should go talk to Maggie," I say.

He smiles and nods, and I expect him to ask to come along. But he doesn't. Then, as I look back down at my fingers on his forearm, I once again notice his tattoo peeking out from under his sleeve.

Gemini.

Then another word suddenly pops in my head.

Twins.

Isn't that the symbol for Gemini? Twins?

I remove my hand and straighten on the couch, no longer feeling quite as comfortable as I was a moment ago. It's a stupid tattoo, and it doesn't mean anything other than his astrological sign, and I would normally think nothing of the association with twins. But there's that always-present question, the one etched in my memory with my father's perfect, flowing script.

Alice, what did the penguin always tell you?

FORTY

Friday, October 30
Now then, if you get the sudden urge to start
trusting someone, be smart and do away with
it.

That's what Ferdinand the penguin would
tell the Thomas and Alice of the Chancellor's Kingdom adventures. And he was
right, because in my father's stories, there
were many occasions where any degree of
trust was eventually used as a weapon
against anyone who dared to trust in the
first place. And though he had a relatively
minor role in the bedtime tales my father
wove, there was no more duplicitous character than Mister Tender, who would pour you
a special elixir and, as you sipped and
slipped into a place of deep, trusting comfort, would slowly extract your most personal stories, know your deepest hidden
fears, and, most importantly, discover what
you most desired. The one thing you wanted

more than anything else, the thing you were certain would make you *complete*. Then, as your head swirled with thick, intoxicated dreams, Mister Tender would place his elbows on the bar, lean in to you with a jackal's smile, and always ask the same thing:

What would you be willing to do for it?

And no matter the patron, under the deepest of Mister Tender's spells, the answer would also always be the same:

Anything.

As I drive to New York City on Halloween eve, I wonder what I most desire. The one thing I need to make me complete. The easy answer is what I told Richard: a do-over for the last fourteen years. A normal life, a body without scars, even just a single night of eight peaceful hours of sleep. I would wish my father never came up with the idea of Mister Tender, and that my family remained intact in London.

But I don't live within the pages of the graphic novel, and dreams of rewinding the past can't come true, even if I would have to do some very bad things to make them so. Instead, I've had to do some very bad things just to keep moving forward with my broken life, and the idea of some kind of mental peace continues to live on the other side of a wall that grows a brick taller by the minute.

I left early this morning, knowing it would take four and a half hours to get to Brooklyn, making no arrangements other than telling Brenda I wouldn't be at work, which she's so used to at this point, she sounded surprised I even bothered to let her know.

Richard did finally ask if I wanted company for this trip, and I turned him down.

Cars whoosh past me, and I have a vague sense of going too slowly on the interstate, but my mind is occupied with a thought that has kept coming back, over and over, taking little nibbles out of me until last night it finally started drawing blood.

Is Richard part of the community?

He's not Mr. Interested — he's far too young. But is he involved? Could he be one of the small legion of fans tracking the movements of Alice Gray?

My instincts tell me he isn't, though logic forces me to consider otherwise. Richard sits right above me in the Perch. He's so close. Maybe he's figured out my alarm code and has broken into my house. Taken pictures of me sleeping. Maybe Richard is the documentarian, and he sends the photos to Mr. Interested in London, who renders them into illustrations in the style of my father.

How messed up would all *that* be?

But how does that explain the one photo I saw on the website, the photo of my home in summertime, which clearly shows Richard looking down from the Perch. Richard didn't take that photo. Who did?

In an attempt to stop the cycle of obsessive thoughts, I scroll through the playlists on my phone and shuffle my classic rock compilation. Janis Joplin starts breathlessly screeching at me, and any escape into her world is immediately halted by the refrain, a metaphor to her, but something potentially literal in my life.

Take another little piece of my heart now, baby . . .

I skip to the next song, grateful for Dire Straits.

I roll into Brooklyn just a little after eleven in the morning. Franklin Avenue is flanked by four- and five-story brick buildings, all varying shades of sun-stripped tan and white, pockmarked by time and neglect, piles of garbage bags heaped on the sidewalk like sandbags trying to hold back an imminent floodwater breach.

I don't see the bar yet, but I take advantage of an open parking spot and ease into it. When I step out, I'm greeted by a stiff New York wind, cold and hostile.

Three doors down, I find Maggie's, a sliver of a brick building shared with a shoe-repair shop and a Chinese takeout restaurant. The upper floors of the building hold apartments. An old man leans out an open window — not caring about the cold — and surveys the street like a crow, ready to caw out a warning if it senses danger. He watches me with a furrowed brow and wrinkled forehead but says nothing as I walk up to the building.

The sign for Maggie's is attached to a ground-level railing, but the bar itself is below ground. With each of my descending steps, the world around me grows darker. At the bottom is an old wooden door with iron bars over a small, eye-level window. Another larger window is next to the door, its shade closed from the inside. A small neon sign buzzes the word *OPEN,* and a faded black-cat cutout decoration, taped to the door, represents the extent of Maggie's Halloween decorations.

I push the door open and take my first step into Maggie's, and in this instant, I feel like I'm entering another time, one in which I don't belong.

It's dark, not just from the sheer lack of any natural light, but from Maggie's use of as few lightbulbs as necessary to keep the bar operational. Maybe it's a cost-saving decision, though I suspect it's more of an effort to smooth the wrinkles of time. Darkness is Maggie's makeup, though even with it, I can see she's old, tired, and long set in her ways.

Everything in here is wooden: tables, chairs, floor, bar. I can smell the unmistakable aroma of moisture mixed with the wood, and there's a sense of boarding an old sailing vessel, the planks solid but squeaky beneath my weight.

There are a total of three other people in here, two of whom have their backs to me. Day drinkers (actually, late-morning drinkers), both men, sitting on rickety barstools. Their spines seem permanently curved toward and over their drinks, and they sit in silence, a stool between them, not bothering to turn as the heavy door closes behind me. Old warthogs at the watering hole.

The third person is a woman who stands behind the bar, and it doesn't take me any time to know this is the person I've come to see. This is Margaret Glassin, proprietor of Maggie's, mother of twin monsters. The memory I have most of her is from the trial, where she sat and watched every minute from the gallery. This is the same woman, though her long, kinked brown hair is now streaked with gray. She looks thinner than I remember, and tougher, with the kind of strength not found in a gym rat, but from a woman who has to fight for everything she gets. Even in the dim light, I can see the crow's-feet around her eyes and the veins in her lean, sinewy arms.

"What're you havin'?"

Her voice stops me dead. It's the same voice that pleaded mercy for her girls directly before sentencing. No apology for what happened to me, just a beg for leniency for her little psychos.

I take a step forward, and her eyes narrow in a focused gaze before widening with recognition. The same experience I had with Charles.

"Well, fuck me," she says.

"I guess you go by Maggie now," I say.

She recovers quickly, probably used to dealing with surprises in this dark basement of a bar. "When I moved here," she says. "Fresh start and all that."

"I understand that," I say. "I went from Alice Hill to Alice Gray." I scan the bottles behind her. "Gin and tonic."

She reaches behind her and grabs a bottle

of Tanqueray, but I tell her to use Hendrick's.

"Two dollars more," she says.

"I think you can buy me a drink," I reply.

She thinks about that for a moment, then shrugs. As she mixes my drink, she says, "I heard you moved to the States. Boston, is that right?"

"Close enough."

"And I don't suppose you just happened upon my pub here by accident."

"No. No accident at all." She slides the drink to me, and I take a sip. It's stronger than it needs to be, and I wonder if she's just a generous pour or is hoping to dull me enough to leave me vulnerable. Just like Mister Tender would.

"Is there a place we can talk in private?" I ask.

She points to the day drinkers. "Need to stay here for my customers, dear." She says it *coostomahs,* the same as my mother would. "We can talk in front of them — no secrets in Maggie's. 'Sides, Pete and Mikey can't spread gossip because they're always here."

I look at both men and know Maggie is likely right. These men are here just waiting for death, which they're bringing about one dirty shot glass at a time. One of them raises his empty glass and gives it a little shake, to which Maggie responds with a double pour of whiskey. No words are exchanged.

"Okay," I say.

She leans her elbows on the counter and looks at me with something bordering on excitement. There's no pain on her face, no sense of regret as there was with Charles. I wonder if she feels sorry for what happened, but I know I won't ask her. That's not why I'm here.

"Well, then, Alice Gray. Tell me, what's so important you came all this way to search out the likes of me?"

And so I tell her, and in the process, I also indirectly tell Pete and Mikey. I've gotten good at this story, this past of mine I assumed would always be locked away deep inside me. Once again, it feels oddly good to tell it, as if I can place just a small piece of my burden on someone else for a little while. It takes some time, and I don't stop, though at one point I notice one of the men looking over at me, head cocked, gaze drilled on me. I pause just for a moment, and then he nods, beckoning me to continue. So I do. I leave out the parts about Freddy Starks and Jimmy, but otherwise I tell these three people the tale of the last two weeks of my life, and I would expect that, even for a bar that has likely been host to thousands of intriguing tales, mine is one to remember.

When I finish, Maggie pours me another gin and tonic and then asks me, "So, how do they look? The girls, I mean. How do they look?"

"That's what you want to ask?"

"Well, they are my girls, after all. 'Suppose I still have an attachment, loose as it may be."

I'm on a stool at this point, and I straighten to soothe the muscles in my back. "Well, Melinda is put together enough to be passable," I tell her. "But glassy-eyed, in a brainwashed kind of way. But Sylvia looks like a feral cat. She'd seem right at home gnawing fish bones out of garbage cans."

Maggie nods at me and gives me a little squint, and I wonder if she's hurt by my words. I kind of hope so.

"I don't believe you." The man — who is either Pete or Mikey — looks at me with an empty gaze. This man could be in his sixties, but more likely he's a very hard-earned fifty.

"Excuse me?" I say.

"I don't believe a word of your story."

"I don't care what you believe," I tell him.

"Oh, shush you'self, Mikey," Maggie tells

him. "And not that it's your business, but her story is all true. At least about what happened to her years ago. I was *there.*"

Mikey looks me over, and then his face breaks into something close to a smile. "Well, I'll be goddamned," he says. "Show me a scar then, will ya? Never seen a stabbing scar before. Lift your shirt a little. Ha!" His fetid breath washes over me. "You can even show me more if you want. Looks like you got a nice pair under there."

I've practiced for fourteen years ignoring people, disappearing into my own world, walking away from comments designed to provoke me. I'm good at it, and it would be very easy to ignore this old piece of crust. But I've recently learned the joy of taking control, making the other person blink.

So I get off my stool, grab the back of Mikey's unwashed, clumpy hair, and press his face deep into the glossy bar top. He instinctively reaches out with his left arm, which I easily twist behind his back with my free hand. God help him if he has brittle bones, because some of them will soon shatter, especially if he puts up a struggle.

"Goddamn it!" he grunts. "Get off me, *bitch.*"

I pull his head back just a few inches off the bar, then slam it down. Hard. The sound of his skull connecting with lacquered oak is immensely satisfying.

"Try that again," I say. "This time, ask nicely."

Mikey squeezes his eyes shut as a few bubbles of spit form on his cracked lips. "Get off me . . . *please.*"

I let go, and Mikey nearly tumbles off his barstool, just managing to catch himself before he spills to the floor.

"You have any other comments for me?" I say.

"You're fuckin' crazy," he mumbles.

I move for him, but he immediately leans back and puts his hands up in surrender.

"I thought so," I say.

Mikey peels himself off the stool and wobbles a bit before collecting himself. "Maggie, you've let this place go to shit," he says, then turns and staggers out the door.

Maggie yells out after him. "Need to settle your tab before another drop!" All I can see are Mikey's legs as he wobbles up the concrete steps to the world above.

She turns to me and says, "Well, aren't you full of piss?"

"I didn't come here to chitchat with drunks," I say. I look over to the man who must be Pete, but he hasn't moved. He's a

Madame Tussauds wax figure of an aging alcoholic, eternally posed over his bottomless glass.

"No, you certainly didn't," Maggie says. She lets out a laugh that's just shy of being pleasant. "But you did come here for some reason, more than just bringing me up to date with a past I moved here to forget. So what is it, dear? What do you want with me?"

"I want to know who's stalking me," I say.

"I would think you would. But I certainly couldn't tell you that."

"But I think you do know something. Something about when you and Charles and my parents used to get together. Before I was born. Both my mother and your ex-husband told me you used to be social."

"Is that what they said?"

"Yes."

"That all?"

The way she asks makes me nervous. "More or less. Said you and my mother didn't always get along. I got the impression you all went out together a handful of times, and that's it." I lock onto her. "But there's something more, isn't there? Charles and my mother . . . they both quickly dismissed the subject. As if there was more to say but they didn't want to talk about it."

"Aye," she nods. "There's good reason your mum didn't want to talk about it. And Charles? Well, he's just too British to say anything."

I have no idea what she's talking about, but whatever she knows, it's big.

"And you, Maggie? Are you too British? Or are you going to tell me what you know?"

She places each hand on the edge of the bar and leans in.

"So your mum never told you? All this time. Imagine that."

"Maggie, I'm losing my patience here. What is it I don't know?"

Maggie seems immensely pleased with herself, and she takes her time drawing the words out.

"Yeah, all right then. Your folks and us, we used to go out, and more than just a few times. Charles and me had just moved into the area, lived just a few houses down from your parents at the time, not across the park back then. Didn't have kids. Young. We all got on. Sort of, that is. Never did quite take with *her,* actually. Always thought she was a bit of a *highness.* But the four of us together could keep ourselves entertained. Your father . . . brilliant, I'd say, imagination and charm. Circles around my Charles, anyhow."

Maggie leans closer, just an inch. Perfume heavy, cloaking the aroma of spilled beer. "Used to go 'round to a pub, the Tender Arms it was called. Go there maybe once a week, 'round a Saturday night more often than not. Have a few pints. Gossip a bit." She winked at me. "Flirt a bit with your father, if I'm being honest with you. He'd flirt right back. But real subtle-like. I think just enough to poke your mother a bit. Just for fun, right?

"But the main reason we went to the Tender Arms was the barman," she continued. "Lord Jesus, what a charmer, as dashing as they come. Beautiful head of black hair. Deep, olive skin. Green eyes, devilish the way they'd look at you. A smile that'd melt any woman's heart, and intimidate most men's. His name was Jack."

She stops and holds her gaze on me, waiting for something to sink in. It doesn't.

"Jack," she says, "was all about mischief, you see. He'd listen all day to his customers, and he was a *good* listener. They'd complain about an unfaithful wife, or an 'orrible boss. Maybe a spoiled brat or a shitty love life. And he'd look at them and say, 'Now then, if all that could be fixed, what would you be willing to do?' It was his game, understand. He wanted to know what a person would be willing to do to make their lives better. What a person's price was for happiness, or fame and fortune."

This is it.

Mister Tender didn't come from my father's imagination at all. By the time Mister Tender made his debut in the stories of Chancellor's Kingdom, he'd been around for quite some time.

"Mister Tender was a real person," I say.

"Well, now, not *real* real. But based on a real person, that's for sure."

"How did I not know this?"

Maggie shrugs. "Why would you know?"

"But it was never brought up at the trial."

"No reason for it. Jack didn't do those things to you."

But he's real, I think. He inspired my father to create the character that made us comfortably rich and desperately sad.

"That can't be all," I say. "I mean, I had no idea, but you're not telling me this as some big secret, just that this Jack person was a loose inspiration for Mister Tender."

She reaches for a clean glass and wipes it with a dirty rag.

"No, Alice, dear. That's not all."

"Tell me," I say.

She stops polishing the glass. "Good lord. You really don't know, do you?"

I begin to rise from my stool. I'm coiled, ready to spring.

"Tell me."

It's the moment she seems to have been wanting for years, because the excitement in her eyes is that of a little girl seeing a shooting star for the first time.

"Well, dear, it seems Jack *fucked* your mum."

FORTY-ONE

Maggie holds up a hand of innocence. "Of course, that's what people say. Hard to know for sure. But they *changed,* your parents. Something happened. Didn't want to go to the Tender Arms anymore, then didn't want to see the likes of us. It's not like they told us so, exactly, but they just stopped comin' round. Ignored our calls." Maggie seems desperately trying to sound casual. "And then, suddenly, your mum was *pregnant.*"

This last sentence is a finishing blow. I knew it was coming, and all I could do was sit helplessly and watch the fist arc toward my jaw. It smashes the life out of me.

There is a reality here I don't want to believe. An answer that perfectly fits the question, a question I'm now wishing I'd never asked. And it all explains one thing about me, a feature that people remark on from time to time, always in a complimentary way. A feature I didn't inherit from my mom or dad, though I was told a grandparent on my mother's side had it. A trait singular, in my immediate family, only to me.

My green eyes.

"What year?" I ask. "What year was that?"

She looks at the ceiling, as if she didn't know the exact year already. "Oh, who can say for sure? Late eighties or so, I suspect."

Right around when I was born.

I can't talk, so she does.

"You wanted to know, Alice. Like I said, all I know is rumors and innuendo. I can't tell you what's fact and what isn't."

"Jack," I finally whisper. "What became of Jack?"

Maggie shrugs. "He was just a bartender, dear. Disposable, like the rest of us. Probably moved on to different bars until settling down to grow old and lonely." Her eyes lit up once again. "But that smile. I will never forget that smile." She stares vacantly past me, into a long-ago time. "If I'm being truthful, I think I was a little jealous of your mum. I was attracted to Jack. Might have even had a go at him myself. But he never seemed to be interested in me. Much more enchanted with your mother."

"You knew," I said. "This whole time, you knew."

"Like I said, Alice. Just rumors and innuendo. I never knew anything for certain."

Is this true? Is my father really not my father?

It's too much.

How can any of this make sense? I try to think it through, to fit the pieces, but everything moves too fast and frantically in my brain.

"But my father didn't create Mister Tender until a decade later."

"So?"

I struggle to speak, to find logic when my mind spins out of control. Maggie sees this and, in a moment of pity, pours me another drink. I sip, then slowly say, "Do you know anything else?"

Maggie crosses her arms, and in this pose, I can see her strength, muscles pressing out against the taut skin of her arms.

"There's nothing else."

"You never asked my parents directly about it? Talked to Jack?"

"No, Alice. I got pregnant myself with the twins near then and stopped going to bars. Stopped socializing with your parents. We all went into our own little suburban cocoons."

"But he kept track of you," I say. "He must have. He knew your girls followed Mister Tender. He wrote them letters, telling them to stab me."

She takes a deep breath that seems to take all her energy to hold, then lets it out. "There was one time," she said. "One other time I saw Jack. After your father's books had come out. The most random thing, really. I was out with a friend at a bar in London, and there he was, barely looking a day older, working the bar just as before. I recognized him immediately, as he did me. Even remembered my name. Put me at ease immediately, which is what that man can do. Even my girlfriend lit up at the sight of him."

"Did you talk to him?"

"For a few minutes," she says, "though I could have gone the whole night listening to him. Chitchat mostly, but he was keen on asking about our kids. Specifically about you, but I told him we fell out of touch with your parents. Then he asked about Charles and me, and I told him we had twin girls. Twin girls who, in fact, were more than obsessed with your father's books."

"So he didn't know about the novels?"

"No, I don't believe so, or at least didn't seem to know. I even told him the plot of the books, and that, in fact, they were perhaps based on Jack himself. He got real quiet after that."

Picturing this conversation is all too easy to do.

"Did he act angry?"

"Not that rubbed off on me, anyway. Was cool as ever, just quiet. But he did ask me again about my girls and what I meant about them being obsessed with the books. I told him . . ."

Maggie looks up, searching her memory.

"What did you tell him?"

"Said something to the effect that they were in love with a charming bartender, and I understood them. That I knew what it meant for a man to be able to talk you into just about anything. Anyway, I think at that point my girlfriend got a little worried and steered us to a table. She probably thought I was going to bring him home with us."

"Was that it?"

She holds a hand up, as if taking an oath. "Never talked to him again."

I ask one last time. "Any other detail you remember?"

She sighs. "I've told you what I remember. But mostly, I don't try to remember things any more. My life was over the night my little girls tried to kill you, and since then

I've just been waiting to die, holed up in a bar every day, spraying weeds with poison."

Just like Charles. Living life from one bleak moment to the next, waiting for all of it to end. The little brown-haired twins had ripped through many lives.

"You should talk to your parents," Maggie says.

"My dad is dead," I say.

The pained look in her face seems beyond her acting skills. "Oh, that is a shame. Nice man, your father." She sighs. "Dust to dust, I suppose."

Maggie doesn't ask what happened to him, and I don't offer to tell her. Our time here together is ending, and I use the momentary silence to swallow the rest of my drink. It burns, which is at least momentarily distracting.

"Talk to your mum, then. If you want to, ask her about Jack. She's the only one who knows it all."

But my mother has had years to tell me everything, while this relative stranger revealed so much in only minutes. Whatever else my mother has to say about the past, it's locked deep inside her. She's convinced herself of new truths by now.

A silence falls on this unhappy, stale place. Maggie waiting for my next words. Me, too dizzy with gin and reality to speak.

Then the man on the barstool to my right lifts his head from his drink and turns to me. Pete, I remember. He's been silent the whole time, and though he sits only a couple of feet from me, I'd forgotten he was even here.

"Alice Hill," he says. "I think I remember that story. So long ago, but I remember it." His voice is dry and scratchy, as if years of flowing alcohol have carved canyons in his throat. "I sold insurance back then. Whole life. Term. Umbrella. That was the last job I ever had." He lifts a softly quivering hand and sips out of his shot glass, preserving the last little bit. "And I remember reading the story about you, Alice Hill. And I remember thinking, what a goddamn shame everything is." He grimaces as if passing painful gas, then looks at me with his ghost-blue eyes. "But you know what? You're just one story out of millions. One tragedy out of all the countless tragedies that fuel the world. Just a speck of sorrow on this whole shitbed of a planet."

With that, Pete de-animates back to his drink, gaze returned to the bar top, dormant once more.

Of everything I've heard today, his is the truth most pure.

FORTY-TWO

My mother's car is in her driveway. They're home. They're always home.

My chest rattles as I exit my car and walk up the path to the house. The rattle spreads through my body, chilling me, and I envision all the ghosts from the cemetery rising from their graves and snaking into my bloodstream, voodoo heroin.

It's not rage that fills me as I let myself into the house. I don't think I have any space left in me for that. I don't even know what I hope to accomplish here. But I need to know who my mother is, because she is a stranger to me.

I cross the living room, dark and dusty. Curtains drawn against the daylight, stillness abounds. For a moment, I think of the twins' flat, that insulated capsule damming the evil inside, the musty smell, shadows in the corners.

I don't announce myself.

Murmuring. Soft. Coming from the kitchen.

My mother's voice is faint and pleasant, singsongy, a nanny reciting nursery rhymes while tucking the little ones tight beneath the sheets at bedtime. She's talking either to herself or maybe on the phone. I don't hear anyone else.

She's in the kitchen. I can just make out the slightest whiff of spice in the air. Tea.

I start walking again, which is now more of a creep. I'm afraid to find her in a vulnerable moment, doing something we only do when we think we're completely and totally alone. Yet somehow that's what I want. I want to see her, if even for a second, as who she really is. Catch her without her mask on.

Another voice.

Thomas.

He's not really talking, just a few monotone syllables.

A couple more steps. I'm as quiet as I can be, because part of me wants to keep the option of spirting away without her ever having known I was here.

"There you go. That's my boy."

I'm close to the kitchen now, and these are the first words I make out clearly.

Seconds later, I'm standing just outside

the opening to the kitchen, and I angle myself so I can just make out the sight of my mother at the kitchen table. She's sitting with her side to me, and both her arms are resting on the tabletop. Spread out in front of her is an array of different-colored pills, scattered along the gleaming wooden tabletop like a child's Halloween loot.

She picks up a pill.

"This one makes you happy, do you remember that, dear?"

She's talking to Thomas, who must be sitting across from her, though I can't see him from my viewpoint.

"Uh-uh."

"Oh, yes, it does. Especially if you take it with one of these." She picks up another pill and places them both now in her right palm, holding them out to my brother.

"But that happiness doesn't last long, does it? It never does with you. You're a very sick boy, Thomas. I don't know why God doesn't love you, but that's what *I'm* here for."

"Yes, Mother."

His words are slow and slurred, as if sleep talking.

"Only I know the right combination of these pills to keep you alive. You know that, right? The doctors think they know, but there's not a soul on this earth who knows my boy like I do."

"No one."

"So it's very important you take only the pills I tell you to take. You understand?"

"Yes."

As I watch in stunned silence, one thought loops over and over in my head. *I'm witnessing a murder.* Just like in my dream, where my mother drowns Thomas. Only this is a slow, torturous drowning, years in the making.

"I calmed you down, didn't I?" she asks. "You were out of control, Thomas, and if I hadn't given you the right medication, you could've hurt both of us. I know you're tired and weak, but isn't that better than being full of hate?"

"I just want to sleep."

"I know, love. But first you need to take these. You're always going to be sick, but they'll make you happy for a little while."

"I don't . . ." His voice trails into a whisper.

"Do as I say, Thomas." She places the pills back on the table and pushes them across the table. "Then you can go to sleep."

I step into the kitchen.

"Thomas, don't."

My mother jumps in her chair.

"Alice, for the love of God, you *scared* me."

I ignore her and focus on my brother, who is now in full view. He's dressed in sweat-pants and a red hoodie, which hangs loosely over his head. Face pointed to the table, like a schoolboy receiving a stern lecturing. He doesn't even look over at me. He's aware of nothing beyond the pills in front of him.

"Thomas, don't take any more pills."

"Alice, what are you —"

My brother gingerly plucks two pills from the table and uses his other hand to lift the can of nearby Coke.

"No!" Now I dash, and it takes only three strides to reach the table and smack the pills from his hand. Thomas drops the Coke, which tumbles onto its side and spills its contents over the tabletop.

My mother leaps to her feet. "Alice! I don't know what's gotten into you, but you can't —"

I swipe my arm along the tabletop, send-ing all the rest of the multicolored pills fly-ing, along with a rain of soda.

"Alice," Thomas says in a voice that's hauntingly calm. "I need those."

My mother is screaming at me, but I block her out. Instead, I grab Thomas by the shoulders and force him to focus on me.

"Thomas, Thomas, please listen to me. She's poisoning you. She has been this whole time. Everything she says is a lie, and it's ending now. Right now. Okay? You're coming with me. It's all going to get better."

A force slams into me. My balance is gone, and I'm tumbling to the floor. As I land hard on the tile, I look up at my mother. She *shoved* me. She's never in her life laid a hand on me until now.

"You watch your mouth, you insolent little girl. You've gone mad again."

Thomas says nothing.

I leap to my feet, and she looks ready to charge. I look at her as I never have before, as a physical threat, and my body instinctively responds. Defensive stance, right foot back for balance. Hands raised to face level, core tight. I will not attack her, but I won't let her attack me, either.

She is shaking with rage, face glistening with sweat. But she doesn't move.

"You brat," she says. "You spoiled, ungrateful *fucking* brat."

"Thomas," I say, keeping my gaze fixed on my mother. "Everything is a lie. I found out Dad isn't even my real dad. I found out Mister Tender is based on a real person, and I'm his *daughter*."

"Shut your mouth," she says.

"She never told us. That's why they were always fighting. Dad knew about Mom's affair but never left her. He should have."

She starts to move toward me, and I brace for her. "Don't," I say. "Do you really think you can hurt me? You wouldn't stand a chance."

"You don't know what you're talking about. You're insane, always have been."

Thomas says nothing.

An electric silence crackles between us. Her chest heaves up and down, and I'm vaguely hopeful she's on the verge of a massive heart attack.

"That's it," she says. "I'm calling the police. Let them take you to the looney bin." She turns toward the phone on the counter.

"Good idea," I say. "Call the police. They'll want to see all these pills. You have prescriptions for all of these?" She freezes. "I know what Thomas has been diagnosed with, and I know he hasn't been prescribed all these different medications. You're keeping him as a drugged prisoner just so you can tell all the world about the burdens of your life."

The dream comes back again. My mother walking calmly from the surf to the shore, as little Thomas sinks beneath black waters. To him, I say, "I don't think you were ever sick, Thomas. That's why the doctors could never figure out what was wrong. Don't you see? She got addicted to all the attention she received after I was attacked, but that faded. She needed something else to feed into, something that could last a long time. She poisoned you and has been doing it ever since you were fifteen."

"You bitch," she hisses. Another first for her. "You diseased little bitch."

Now Thomas looks at me for the first time. His eyes are clouded with hopelessness.

"I know," he says.

My heart shatters in the echo of those two words.

"I know what's she's doing, Alice. But I need her."

"Thomas . . ." I start. I don't even know what to say. His innocence kills me. He's so far gone. Maybe too far gone.

His gaze goes back to the table, and he takes his index finger and starts slowly dragging the tip of it through the spilled Coke, creating sticky caramel whiskers along the wooden surface.

"You have to come with me, Thomas," I say. "Tonight. Right now."

"I need my pills, Alice." He says this to the table. "You've seen what happens when I go a day without them. *Murder.*"

"What is he talking about?" my mother asks.

"I don't know," I lie. Thankfully, Thomas doesn't explain.

"Well, he's not going anywhere," she says. "You're not fit to even take care of yourself."

She's facing me again, and rather than take a defensive posture, I take a step until I'm only inches from her. Then I act on an impulse, powerful and unexpected. I reach out and take her in my arms, hug her, hold her tight. She's burning up, and her heat transfers to me. She stiffens, resists at first, but I hold fast, anchor myself to her, and as I start to hear her cry, my mother finally holds me back.

Then she breaks down. Her legs buckle just enough to make me work to keep us both upright, and from her emits a long, low wail, the most sorrowful sound I've ever heard. Pure, uncloaked desperation. After that, the tears pour, and I keep holding. I can't even think of the last time I've heard my mother cry. This lasts minutes.

Finally, she composes herself enough to wonder aloud, "What have we all become?"

I press my face into her shoulder and say,

"I feel like I don't even know what's real anymore. But the only thing I'm certain of is I need to get Thomas out of here. You know that."

I pull back, and she stares at me with wide, tear-filled eyes snaked with blood vessels. She nods at me. Actually nods.

"I know. I know."

"I'm taking him now, Mom. Okay?"

I recognize the detached expression on her face. I've seen it in the mirror, on the far side of a panic attack. There's utter honesty there. Self-assessment that burns like acid. I'm not sure she's ever been to this place before.

"Okay," she says. "Take the yellow pills. He does need those. At least for a while."

"I will, Mom. Okay, I will."

She's distant now, just like Thomas. Floating in some other realm. I wonder what that feels like for her.

"He ruins everything he touches. Don't let him touch you, Alice."

I don't ask her *who.* I don't need to. I know she's not talking about Thomas.

"I won't."

"I'm a terrible person," she says. "And yet I'm not. Does that make sense to you?"

"Yes. Yes, it does."

"I hurt him just so he had to rely on me.

I'm a monster."

I don't reply to this. I don't even think she's talking to me.

I lean in and kiss her on the cheek. To my recollection, I've never done that in my life.

"I don't think I'll ever see you again," I say.

A fresh tear escapes down her cheek. Another nod.

"I might kill myself tonight," she says. There's a chilling stillness in her words, and I can tell, for once, she's not looking for attention. She's stating a fact. "Maybe I'll take enough of the pills, and that will be that."

God help me, I don't try to dissuade her. Instead, I reach to the table and scoop all the yellow pills I can find that haven't been dissolved by the Coke, then slide them into my pocket. I reach down and touch my brother on the shoulder.

"Thomas, come on."

He looks at me, and those hopeless eyes have just a glimmer of a spark.

"Where are we going?"

I think about that for a second, and then answer the way Dad would.

"We're going for a ride on the back of a giant penguin."

FORTY-THREE

We arrive home just past four in the afternoon. As soon as I lead Thomas inside my house, my phone buzzes with a text.

Where have you been?

It's from *him.*

There is so much loaded into those four words. He's making me think he actually lost sight of me, which may or may not be true.

Finding out who you are, I reply.

A pause, and then:

What have you learned?

I get Thomas to my couch, then get a blanket and drape it over him. I sit next to his feet, and as he slips further into the stupor from whatever my mother gave him, my own heart starts racing. It's all too much.

Another text.

I've always been with you, Alice. I'm the one you were always meant to be with.

Chest cramping, cheeks flushing. Impending panic attack. God, I'm such a *victim.*

Then, I see it all in front of me as I stare at his words on my phone. Even when I didn't know he existed, he was still in control of my mind. For fourteen years, he's been in control, and all I have to do to escape my mental and emotional shackles is get rid of him. I don't care if he's my biological father or some random lunatic. I was never sure what I would do if and when I finally found Mr. Interested, but it's suddenly and beautifully clear to me.

I am going to kill him.

There can be no hesitation. When I find him, I will kill him, no matter the consequences. I'd rather be in actual prison than the mental cell to which I've been confined for so long. I'll never be free as long as he's alive.

I reply to him.

Where are you? It's time for this to be over.

He doesn't write back.

A headache comes full force, and now my whole body heats up. Breathing comes with more effort, as if I'm slowly climbing into thinner and thinner air. The attack is coming, and I know there's no stopping it.

Let it come.

Why not?

Come, take me.

Move to the kitchen. Grab a bottle of wine and pour a large glass, which I gulp down in seconds. If I'm going through this to-night, I'm going through it damaged. Dulled and beaten. Pour another glass and think about the yellow pills I brought home with me. Three or four pills, I think. That's all it would take, washed down with the rest of this bottle of wine. Death by merlot. It would be so easy. In fact, it would be the easiest thing I've ever done. All the struggles would be gone. Screw killing the man who's stalking me — I'll just kill myself. Falling asleep would finally come with no effort at all. I would just slip away, like a small boat pulled out by the tides into the vast ocean.

But then Thomas would be utterly alone.

A knock at the door.

Please be him, I think. *Him or me. Right now.*

My pulse is pounding.

Back to the living room. Grab the fireplace poker. To the door. I don't even bother to look out the window. I just raise the weapon in my hand and yank the door open.

Richard.

"Alice, take it easy," he says. He takes a half step away from me.

The ache in my head turns into a fire.

Richard has about five seconds to live unless something can convince me he's not part of everything.

"I just wanted to see what happened in New York," he says.

I raise the poker higher.

"Alice, it's okay. It's okay." Richard stands on my porch, hands held up in a gesture of peace, his dark eyes wide with more than just fear. There's concern. "All I want to do is help you."

Smash his brains in. Do it, Alice.

But against that logic rises a belief, one that is powerful as much as it's baseless.

It's not him, Alice. He's not a part of this.

The two warring factions inside me are ripping me apart mentally and, it feels, physically. God, I just want to be left alone.

I lower the poker.

"Go away," I say.

I don't wait for him to answer. I shut the door in his face, then go to my security system and arm it in Stay mode. I remain holding the poker as I head back to the kitchen, grab my bottle of wine, then walk through the house and close all the blinds.

I'm guessing I have thirty minutes until I'm in a fetal position on the floor.

I go over to the couch and lean toward my brother's face. His eyes are open, but just barely.

"Are you going to be okay, Thomas?"

He murmurs. "I think so."

"I'm starting to have an attack," I say. "It's going to be a horrible night, but we'll both be better in the morning."

A slight nod.

"Can you just stay here on the couch?"

"Yes."

I stand.

Thomas whispers, "I love you, Alice."

All my defenses fall, leaving me completely exposed. "I love you, too, Thomas."

I swig from the bottle, gulping wine like water, then head up to my bedroom. I make space for myself on the floor, where I surround myself with the wine, the fire poker, and my laptop — this is where I will spend the night. I want to feel the hardness of the wooden floor against my bones. Another drink, then I open up the laptop and head back to MisterTender.com.

I scour the website, looking for anything new, but there hasn't been a post for two weeks. Not since the day I first found Mister Tender on the dating site. So I look through old posts, hoping to find something, anything that will help me hunt down Mr. Interested.

I go back to when the first post appeared

two years ago. I look at pictures I hadn't seen before, read all the things about me. A time capsule of horror.

How I look. What clothes I like. How often I cut my hair.

More pictures of my house.

Me, driving in my car. Springtime. I'm actually smiling in that photo, and I wonder why.

Links to articles about the twins.

An old interview with the detectives who worked the case. One of them describes the twins as "soulless."

I read and read, descending deeper into the reality show of my life. I get lost in this world until I can no longer keep my hands from shaking. I manage one more gulp of wine, and then the bottle falls from my grip, spilling its final drops of blood on the hardwood floor. A stain to match the one left by Freddy Starks in the room beneath me.

I collapse on the floor and pull my knees into my chest. The floor chills my cheek. I touch the front pocket of my jeans.

Thomas's pills are right in there.

So easy.

The chill spreads to my body. I think of being in deep, icy waters. The fierce pain of the cold before the heavy numbness sets in.

I shift my gaze back to the computer, to the last post I'd opened on the site. A photo of me, posted by Mr. Interested. Dated a couple of years ago. I'm in the Stone Rose, wearing my apron, standing behind the counter, my eyes looking directly at whomever is snapping a photo of me. I look surprised but not scared. Curious, perhaps.

My mind clears for a second, long enough for me to understand the importance of what I'm seeing.

I remember that moment. We were hosting a fund-raiser for a local school. I remember a few specific people taking pictures. I remember faces. In fact, I remember one specific face.

Can it be?

The fear is back, ravaging me. I'm desperate to ease the terror, even if that means death.

I call out to my dad.

"Help me. Please help me."

He doesn't answer.

Dad never answers.

I'm suddenly overwhelmed with a series of images, a mental slide show firing at a rapid pace, and one over which I have no control. Sometimes this happens in these moments, as if it's some weird kind of defense mechanism my brain launches to protect itself. I see an image in my head, clear as a movie screen, but that image lasts less than a second before another one replaces it.

I close my eyes, as if that might help. It doesn't.

Tonight's feature is a collection of blood and bone, each one more horrifying than the last. Bombing victims. Battlefield gore. Medieval heads on spikes. A body in a bathtub, half dissolved by acid. Twin babies, throats equally cut, distant gazes of death.

This won't stop until I pass out.

I no longer even have the strength to pull myself to the bathroom, to the pills. I lack even the tiny amount of power needed for suicide.

So I lie here, shaking and cold, and make a promise to myself. I repeat this promise in my head, over and over, and it soon becomes the soundtrack to the gore-filled slide show.

This is the last time.

This is the last time.

This is the last time.

FORTY-FOUR

Saturday
Halloween

The morning wears heavy on me, like an oppressively thick-layered coat that keeps the chill out and allows only the slowest, smallest movements. Showering and getting dressed saps the only ounces of energy I had to spare, and afterward, I sit in my kitchen and sip coffee, staring at nothing, trying to build back up a reserve.

The mantra comes back, just for a moment, and I feel the same commitment in the words as I did last night.

This is the last time.

I'm done being controlled. I'm done being a victim. The only way I can stop the panic attacks is to stop running. To stop the person after me. To shut down the Mister Tender.com website. To end the peep show that is my life.

Which means, starting right now, I'm in charge.

The phone rings, and my mother's number flashes on the screen. So it seems neither of us killed ourselves last night. Knowing she's alive doesn't make me upset or fill me with relief. It's simply a piece of information, about which I feel very little. And for now, I want nothing to do with her.

A swipe of my thumb rejects her.

Thomas is awake, rummaging in the kitchen.

"Good morning," I say. "Happy Halloween."

"Oh yeah. Is that today?"

He is reanimated after his drug-induced stupor from last night.

"It is."

"You have any bacon?"

"I think so. Bottom drawer of the fridge. You know how to cook that up?"

He speaks into the refrigerator. "I'm not a kid, Alice. I know how to cook."

"Okay." I look at him, a skinny puzzle of bones still draped in yesterday's clothes. He looks like some kind of refugee, which I suppose is sort of what he is.

"Thomas, I want to restart our lives. Together."

"Mmm-hmm."

"Seriously. I don't want you here just for the night. I want you away from Mom. We'll go to a new doctor, get proper treatment, get off the pills."

"Sure," he mumbles. He finds the bacon, peels off three spongy strips, and places them in a small frying pan. "When you fry bacon, you don't need oil," he says. "The bacon fat takes care of that."

He's not connecting with me. Maybe he doesn't believe my intentions, or perhaps he's only capable of living in the immediate moment. Which makes me wonder.

"Thomas, do you remember when I came over to get you last night? At Mom's?"

"Not much. I remember you spilling my Coke."

"The argument with Mom, do you remember that? What we said?"

"Screaming, fighting, same old shit. I block out the details."

He doesn't remember — the drugs probably clouded everything. Which means he doesn't know the truth about my real dad, and that Mister Tender is based on an actual person. He's just simple, blissfully ignorant Thomas, and I have no desire to change that now. I don't have the energy to tell him everything at the moment.

"Let's talk later," I say. "I have to go to

work. Stay here, okay? There's plenty of food, and I want you to lock the door after me. If Mom comes, don't let her in, okay?"

"Okay."

"Seriously, Thomas. I don't think you remember a lot from last night, which is okay. But it's clear you need to be with me now. No more Mom." I watch for his reaction to this, but if there is one, I can't perceive it. "Where's your cell phone?"

"Back at Mom's. I don't have anything of mine here but the clothes I'm wearing."

Though he's a grown man, in the moment, all I see in Thomas is the little boy he insists he isn't. It's hard to reconcile this person with the man who shot Freddy Starks in the next room. With the man who helped me bury a body deep in the woods.

"Do you . . . I brought some of the yellow pills home. I don't even know what they are. Do you need any to keep steady today?"

Now he looks at me for the first time with interest.

"Yes. Where are they?"

"On my counter, in the bathroom." I don't like the hunger I see in his eyes. "How often are you supposed to take them?"

"One every twelve hours. So I need one now."

I turn, walk out of the kitchen, head

upstairs. I take one pill from my bathroom counter and hide the rest in a pillowcase in my closet. Downstairs, back in the kitchen.

"Here," I say, handing him the pill.

He knows I've hidden the rest; I can see it in the way he looks at me. "Thanks."

"You okay?" I ask.

He doesn't need time to think about it. "No. Are you?"

I shake my head. "No. But we both will be."

Thomas shrugs, which is probably the best I could hope for.

"See you this afternoon, okay? Make yourself at home, be comfortable. Relax."

"Okay."

I turn and leave him. I feel some trepidation, like leaving a puppy home alone for the first time. I'm excited and scared for our future together.

I slip into my wool coat and grab my car keys. Though I won't be driving, I don't want Thomas getting any ideas. Outside, the morning clouds are low, just a few stories higher than a thick fog, and I picture reaching up and stirring the sky as if it were a thick witch's brew.

A Halloween sky.

As I walk from my house, I shoot a brief glance back and look up at the Perch. Richard's car is still in the driveway, which means he's still up there. I wonder if he's watching me. If he heard me call out last night. I don't even remember if I screamed out or not. The last sound I remember is calling out for my dad. The first thing I recall after that is waking in a pool of sweat and sticky wine drops.

I stumble the few blocks to the Rose, my head pounding from a lack of water and sleep combined with an excess of wine and adrenaline. But now I need to focus, because this won't be a normal day at work. Not after the photo I saw last night.

I pass the usual shops and antique stores, window displays heavily cobwebbed, windows painted with pumpkins and ghosts, a safe kind of fright.

I walk into the Rose, and instead of feeling the immediate comfort I usually do, an unease builds in me. I know these people, but how many do I actually trust? How many gazes on me have wicked thoughts inside the minds controlling them? Just one, I think. Just one.

The Ramones are singing "Pet Sematary," and I know the playlist for today will be all eighties Halloween songs. Scanning the room, I see my usual customers, and instead of giving them my usual nod and smile, I go up to each of them and chat for a few moments. These short, simple moments make me aware of how incredibly alone I am. Aware of the barriers I've built around me for fourteen years. No more. I'm going to make connections, real connections. I'm going to have friends. A normal life, or none at all.

The whole time I'm greeting my regulars, my stomach muscles are so tight, they could stop a bullet. *Be calm, Alice. Be normal.*

When I see Brenda, she tells me, "Simon was active this morning when I opened. Maybe it being Halloween and all."

"This must be like Christmas to him," I say, not telling her I've had my own recent encounter. "Does it scare you to hear things like that?"

"No," she says. "Because he's never done anything scary. He just makes sounds. So I figure he's not trying to hurt me."

"That's a good outlook," I say, not adding, *Though when harm suddenly comes, it's usually too late for second-guessing.*

She sweeps her gaze over me. "You look like you've had a rough night."

"Yeah, not a lot of sleep. But a lot hungover."

"Can I assume you were with someone?"

I smile. "I wish."

411

"Are you still having . . . you know, issues? With the creep who sent you that book?"

I dig my nails into my palms, but I don't think she notices. "Yeah, still having issues. I just . . . I just need one normal night. A pleasant dinner, good conversation. I'm just so tired of this cycle."

And then Brenda does what I hoped for.

She wipes her palms on her apron and looks straight at me with a determined expression. "Okay, that's settled, then. You're coming over for dinner tonight. Unless you already have plans?"

I need to make sure Thomas is okay, but I'm sure he can take care of himself for another few hours if I go out tonight. I need this. "I . . . No. No, I don't have plans. But —"

"I don't have plans, either," she says. "I'm not much of a cook, but we can order takeout. We'll have that good conversation and hand candy out to trick-or-treaters. Maybe watch a scary movie."

"No scary movie," I say. "But I can certainly tell you some scary stories."

"Of course, of course. So it's settled, then?"

I pause a moment, then nod. "It sounds great. Thank you, Brenda."

"Cool. Come over at seven?"

"See you then."

Brenda flashes that smile and holds her gaze on me a moment longer. It's quite magnetic, though suddenly different from all her smiles of the past. Everything is different now. Then she twirls around and walks up to a customer approaching the counter. She moves her magical gaze to the man, and I expect that, for a few seconds, he feels like he is the only person in Brenda's world. The man smiles.

I'm home by three. I'm relieved to see Thomas asleep on the couch, the blanket pulled all the way up to his chin. A white plate stained with bacon grease and holding a half-eaten English muffin sits on the floor next to the couch, though there's a coffee table that would have easily accommodated it. Water glass, half full. Dirty socks, crumpled in wads. As I look down at him, all I want to do is sleep. My body craves it, and when I head upstairs and collapse on my bed, it comes fast. Deep and dreamless. My alarm buzzes at 6:00 p.m. I'm dizzy and confused, and for a few moments, I can't remember where I am or what day it even is. When it all suddenly rushes back at me, I feel an instant yearning for those fleeting

413

seconds when I couldn't remember. Amnesia must be the ultimate high.

I stumble to the window, stretch, and look out onto the now-dark streetscape. I see a few groups of people on the street, parents with young kids, making their way from house to house. The early rounds of trick-or-treaters are always the ones with the chaperones. By eight, it'll be the middle schoolers out on their own, and by nine, high school kids will be the only ones left on the prowl.

I haven't a single piece of candy to give out.

A hot shower injects life back into me, and when I'm dressed, I go downstairs to Thomas.

He's still on the couch, which worries me. I walk over and give him a gentle nudge.

"Thomas."

He says nothing.

I push harder.

"Thomas, wake *up.*"

This time, he moves, just a little. Lets out a low moan.

I give his face a light slap.

"Thomas."

Eyes closed, he grumbles, "Wha . . ."

"Thomas, what's wrong? Can you get up?"

"Let me sleep."

Then it hits me. "Did you take anything? Anything besides the yellow pill?" Maybe he found the other ones, but how? Or . . .

Of course. I'm such an idiot. I run back upstairs to my bathroom and yank open the medicine cabinet. Thomas isn't the only one with medication. I have my own, but since I rarely take any, I'd forgotten all about it. Two bottles, one with Xanax, the other with Ambien. They are out of place. I snatch up both bottles and hide them in a pair of boots in my closet.

Back downstairs. "How much did you take, Thomas?" My mouth is next to his ear, and I gently slap his face a few more times.

"Leave me alone," he moans, then flips to face away from me.

"I need to know how many pills you took. *Tell me.*"

"Two . . ."

"Two what, Thomas? Two of which medication?"

His words are muffled into the couch cushion. "One of each."

Okay, one Ambien and one Xanax. That'll deliver a good knockout punch, but I don't think it's enough to be dangerous.

"What time, Thomas? When did you take them?"

No answer.

415

"Thomas, answer me!"

"I don't fucking know. *Earlier.* Now leave me alone."

His sharp reply tells me he's going to be fine, but he might be sleeping for a while. He's due soon for another yellow pill, but I have no idea what that could do combined with what else he took. Better to wait until tomorrow.

As I stand, I spy a small devil walking up my driveway.

"Thomas, I have to go out tonight. It's important. Otherwise I'd stay here with you."

"Okay, just go." The devil knocks on my door, but I don't answer.

"It's Halloween. There are going to be trick-or-treaters, but I don't have any candy. Just ignore them, okay?"

His only reply is a soft snore. He's out again.

A second knocking at my door, but I don't answer it.

I put on my coat and wool hat, then grab a bottle of wine from the kitchen. After a few seconds of thought, I decide to grab the folding wine opener and slide it into my coat pocket. With its coiled steel needle and inch-long foil cutter, it's the closest thing to a knife I own.

I move about the house, turning off most of the lights. I usually leave them on, because I don't like arriving to a dark house at night, but a dark house might let the trick-or-treaters know not to bother with this property.

I walk outside, then lock the door behind me. Richard is sitting on the nearby porch steps. He's handing out candy to the devil and another kid dressed as something from Star Wars. He cranes his head around as he hears me approach from behind.

"I heard them down here. Wasn't sure if you were handing out candy, so I came down."

I flip my collar to the cold. "Thomas is inside, but he's sleeping. I'm headed out. So feel free."

The kids scamper back down the driveway as their parents wave a *thank you* to Richard.

"Your brother is here? How's he doing?"

There are several easy, bullshit answers I could give to this, but I choose an honest one.

"He's broken."

Richard seems to accept this.

"And what about you, Alice? Are you broken, too?"

"I'm just trying to control the damage at

this point."

Just last night, I held a fire poker high in the air, ready to brain him with it. That feels so long ago.

"Let me know if I can help," he says. "I can be good at damage control."

I snap my head to him. "Why do you want to help me?" Then my hands burrow into my coat pockets, and my thumb runs up and down the cool metal of the wine opener. "I pulled you into something you never should have been a part of. I'm a mess. My life is falling apart around me. You should want nothing to do with me."

"Yet here I am," he says. "Telling you I want to help if I can. I never claimed to be logical. I'm just telling you how I feel."

The clash between logic and emotion seems to define whatever kind of relationship this is. It's that same clash confusing me about whether I should trust Richard. So far, I keep leaning toward trust, though my logic keeps poking at me, reminding me of what can happen when you trust too much. Or at all.

Still, he *could* help me. I revisit a thought I had earlier in the day.

"Okay, want to help me? Download an app called Find My Phone."

"Why?"

"I'll tell you if it gets to that point. Just install that app on your phone, okay?"

He shrugs. "Sure, okay, Alice. If that helps you."

I pull my own phone from my purse and check the battery. Ninety-two percent. Good.

"You just going to sit out here in the cold and hand out candy?" I ask him.

"It's not that cold. Figure I'd do it until I ran out. I don't have that much."

"Have fun."

As I reach the sidewalk, Richard calls out. "Happy Halloween, Alice."

I raise a hand in acknowledgment but don't call back. I feel him watch as I walk away, his gaze boring into me, until I deepen and darken, eventually becoming another indistinguishable picce of blackness in the night.

FORTY-FIVE

Brenda lives south of Bridge Street, the less desirable part of Manchester. There's no real line of demarcation, no obvious shift in the environment, no sudden appearance of graffiti-tagged buildings or vagrants wandering about. Yet there is a sense of fatigue south of Bridge Street. Houses are more tired and worn than their counterparts just a couple of blocks to the north. Yards less kempt. Sidewalks more cracked. It's as if this section of the city simply cares a bit less.

It's only a ten-minute walk for me, and the cold both chills and wakens me, giving me the energy I need. I pass packs of trick-or-treaters, some with their parents, others by themselves. Older kids buzz with excitement, the thrill of being out alone at night, approaching strangers' doors with no real fear. The fun kind of scared.

On High Street, there is less activity. More

darkness. The electrical line hanging over the sidewalk crackles and hums, and as I pass under it, I feel a soft heat rise on the three-inch scar above my clavicle. I check my phone and confirm the house in front of me is Brenda's. I've never been here before.

A massive evergreen stands heavy and old in front of Brenda's house, its thick, sagging branches nearly blocking the path to the door. Needles sweep my cheeks as I pass. Tiny, bony fingers. Three concrete steps up to the entrance, each one heaved in different directions, victims of expanding underground roots. When I get to the door, I see there are, in fact, two doors, and then realize the house is subdivided into apartments. I check the address once more and confirm Brenda's is the one on the left. Her apartment has lights on. The apartment on the right is dark enough to almost fade into the night.

I ring the bell.

Deep breath. Count to four. Exhale.

Brenda answers a moment later, greeting me with a bowl of candy. She smiles and opens the door.

"I figured it was either you or my first customer of the night," she says.

"You haven't had a single one?"

"Not yet. I think that tree keeps everyone

away. I need to have my landlord trim it back. Such a pain."

She holds the door open, and as I pass, I notice her perfume, not strong but more present than I've ever noticed in the Rose. Lavender. A scent meant to relax and calm. I've tried lavender incense at night to help me sleep. It didn't work.

I walk in a few feet, turn, then pull the wine bottle from my purse.

"Might as well drink since I'm not driving," I say.

"You live close?"

"Close enough."

She takes the bottle. "Thank you. I don't know very much about wines, but it looks good."

"It's red, and it'll get you buzzed. That's about all I know."

I get Brenda's top-shelf smile, which pulls me in like a tractor beam.

I follow her into the kitchen, where she takes an opener from a drawer. The opener I brought remains in my jacket pocket, and I slide my jacket off and hook it over the back of a chair at the kitchen table. There are two place settings, and the aroma of Chinese takeout fills the air.

"I already ordered," she says, pouring me a glass. "Hope that's okay. Got a little bit of everything."

"Of course," I reply. I have zero appetite. I reach for my purse. "Here, let me give you some money for the food."

Brenda instantly waves me off. "Please, you already pay me more than what my position deserves. It's the least I can do."

"Thank you," I say. "But truly, you deserve more. You're basically running the Rose solo, Brenda. I've hardly been there the past two weeks."

"You know I'm happy to help. Besides, ever since you fired Dan, it's been a lot more peaceful." She turns and hands me a glass of wine, and for the first time, I notice she has a little bit of makeup on. Not much, but since she never wears any, it's notice-able. Brenda has the kind of simple, time-less beauty makeup rarely augments.

She raises her glass.

"Happy Halloween," she says.

It's the last thing I want to toast, but I clink her glass anyway, adding, "and to things taking a turn for the better."

"Yes, absolutely." She takes a sip. "Things have been pretty rough, haven't they?"

The wine is heavy and full, warming my chest after I swallow. I have to remind myself to take it easy.

"Yes, pretty rough."

"Sorry," Brenda says. "I don't mean to pry. We really don't need to talk about any of that." A sip, a doe-eyed glance. "If you don't want to."

"It's fine," I reply, then walk into her living room — just a few steps away — and take a seat on a tired leather couch. "It's good for me to talk about it, because I almost never do."

This elicits another smile from Brenda, but not of her usual variety. This seems more a knowing smile, the kind used by a person who just got what they wanted. She walks over and sits on the couch directly next to me, leaving a whole cushion of space free on the other side of her. She lightly touches my knee with her fingertips.

"I'm glad you said that," she says. "Because ever since you told me about that website, I've had a million questions for you."

Good, I think. *This is why I'm here.*

"I almost don't know where to begin," she adds.

I lean back into the cushion. "Take a stab."

FORTY-SIX

The minutes quickly melt into an hour, which itself turns into two. At some point, we moved to the table, and Brenda brought forth an array of takeout boxes she'd been keeping warm in the oven, and I manage to eat enough food to soak up some of the wine.

There have been a grand total of three groups of trick-or-treaters, to whom Brenda was very generous with fistfuls of candy. She dispatched them quickly, returning to me with more questions. I've been very open with her, even more than I was with Maggie. I didn't say anything to her about Starks, but I did tell her about Jimmy, mostly because I wanted to see how she reacted.

She acted surprised. Wide-eyed and wanting to know everything Jimmy said to me.

My glass has been empty for some time, as is hers, as is the bottle. She must have noticed me looking at my glass, because she says, "I don't have another bottle, but I do have some bourbon. A friend gave me a bottle of small batch."

"I'm good, thanks."

She stands from the couch directly in front of me.

"You sure? I think I'm going to have some. Come on. Join me."

I'm not even a little buzzed, so I think I can afford a bit more. I sense if I stop drinking, the night here will end, and I'm not ready for that. I have work to do.

"Okay, just a little."

"Good."

When she joins me back on the couch, she's even closer than before, and she leans back into a brief stretch and emits something close to a purr. Then she refocuses on me.

"I can't believe everything you've told me," she says. "I still don't understand why you don't just go to the police."

She keeps her gaze trained on me as she sips her bourbon, watching for my reaction.

"I've got some . . . some other stuff in my past that makes me hesitant to contact the police," I say. "That's a story for another night."

"Wow, you *are* full of surprises." Her hand

finds my arm for a moment.

I try to reconcile what I know about Brenda with how she's acting, and I keep coming to a conclusion that fits a theory that's been poking at me since last night. I remember that day a couple of years ago, that fund-raiser at the Stone Rose. There were a lot of people taking pictures that day, but I specifically asked *Brenda* to take pictures as well in case we wanted to put them up on the website. We never did, but she *did* take pictures. I remember it clearly because she actually used a proper camera, while everyone else just used their phones.

I'm almost certain it was Brenda's photo of me on the MisterTender.com website. Even if it was hers, that doesn't mean she was the one who uploaded it, but I'm not leaving here until I find out.

Through this lens, I try to interpret Brenda's behavior tonight. She's not reacting to my stories the way Richard did, which was with complete shock and an earnest attempt to help. Instead, she looks at me with what seems sincere surprise, but I've learned Brenda is very good at practical emoting. It's so difficult to understand what is real and what isn't with her, because Brenda's talent at being a good listener is at an Olympic level. There's a real skill in deftly feigning emotions where none exist. I believe it's called psychopathy.

I take a sip of my bourbon, and if there's water in it other than the two ice cubes, I can't sense it. The liquor bites my tongue, then scorches down my throat. I need to be careful.

Then there are the light touches she's been giving me all night. In the time I've known her, I can't think of her ever mentioning a partner, a date, or a romantic interest of any kind, man or woman. She's always been very private. And she never touches. It's as if she's readying to consume me.

The doorbell rings.

"Wow, it's late for another trick-or-treater," Brenda says.

"Last call, perhaps," I say.

She sighs, then rises and grabs the candy bowl, which contains only a few remaining pieces.

Once she's near the door, I walk back to my purse, grab my phone, and text Richard.

If I'm not back in a few hours, use that app to find me.

I then tab to the app itself and send Richard a request, which gives him permission to locate my phone.

428

I silence the phone and slide it back into my purse, knowing I've now shifted a huge responsibility onto him. But he wants to help. This is how he can.

I reach into my jacket pocket, still hanging on the back of the chair, and fish the wine opener from inside. It fits snugly in my front jeans pocket.

As I walk toward the hallway, Brenda intercepts me.

"Are you looking for the bathroom?"

"Yes, please," I say.

"Down the hallway, past the staircase. Left door."

Inside a cramped bathroom that it would be fair to call dingy, I turn on the light and the fan, then shut the door as I step back into the hallway. There, I have two options. A set of stairs leading to the second floor and likely her bedroom. Or one other door, directly opposite the bathroom. A closed door.

My chest begins to tighten, my breaths shorter. Heartbeat like a rabbit's.

Upstairs is too risky. The wooden steps may creak as I walk on them, or she could hear me moving around up there. So I choose the nearby door instead. One quick glance down the hall to make sure Brenda's not in view, and then I take a step to the door and try the handle.

It's unlocked. I've got maybe a minute, tops.

I open it a crack and see only darkness.

That alone is nearly enough to drive me back to safety. But screw it. I'm committing to this, whatever happens.

I turn on the light and step into the room.

FORTY-SEVEN

It's a small room, maybe ten by ten at most, and the light comes from a floor lamp in the far corner, which creates long shadows from all the towers of clutter inside. This is a closet, I think. It's a room, but it's being used as a closet, a dumping ground. Clothes, still on hangers, stacked in piles on boxes. Books in loose arrangements on the floor. I scan a couple of titles, seeing a range from mysteries to academic texts. An area rug, tightly rolled, stands on end and leans against the wall. A lamp on its side, a tear zigzagging along its shade. In one corner, a heap of shoes, like bodies thrown in a mass grave.

Each second in here is a risk. If she's just Brenda, the girl at work whom I've always known, then getting discovered in this room will be awkward at worst. But if she's someone else entirely, I may have a real problem.

431

My body heats. Sweat beads on my fore-head, and the panic is starting to turn into actual nausea. My mouth is slick with saliva, the precursor to a good bout of puke.

Keep calm. You can do this. It's okay.

I touch the wine opener through the front pocket of my jeans, suddenly realizing what little use it is. I quickly scan the room, see-ing nothing immediately suspicious. There's just too much stuff in here, and I need time to pick through things.

Thirty more seconds. Then leave.

I suppress my urge to vomit and focus my efforts on one thing that stands out in this claustrophobic space. Near the far wall is a drafting table, its surface positioned at a working angle, with a single, backless stool in front of it. There is nothing stacked on the table or chair, which makes me think both might be used on a regular basis.

A wave of dizziness sweeps over me as I make my way to the table. My left foot hits a tower of precariously stacked books, and they crumble to the floor.

"Damn it." I don't have time to put them back.

I reach the table and sit on the stool, and the sudden support beneath me makes me realize how unsteady I actually am. I lay my palms on the smooth, white surface of the table, which is angled up toward me. There are no pens, pencils, or paper in sight, though there are a few stray, colored marks on the table, evidence of its use. I should be searching elsewhere, through the various half-open boxes or piles of books for something that will give me insights. But I'm pulled to this table. There is something here. I can feel it.

I run my hands along the top and the sides of the table as my head feels lighter by the second, as if slowly being filled with helium.

What the hell is happening to me?

I flick my gaze to the open door and confirm Brenda's not there. Just a few more seconds.

My hands go beneath the table, and at that moment, my fingertips find a drawer handle. I look down, seeing the drawer isn't necessarily hidden, but it's tucked flush under the base of the table, and it's only a couple of inches deep, so not obvious to the eye. The drawer is nearly as wide as the table, and as I slide it open, a clutter of colored markers and pens rolls toward me.

The colored tips begin to blur, and in this moment, I know something is very wrong.

I'm aware of paper: thick, heavy white sheets. Blank. I reach inside the drawer and grab the one on the top.

My stomach roils. A sudden, stabbing pain in my side, like a very large bee stinger. Or a very small knife.

I'm sick, I think. Food poisoning. Bad Chinese. And if I don't make it back into the bathroom, I'll be sick in this office. On this table.

Go back, logic insists. *Get out of this room.*

I pull the sheet out and hold it up. It's a dull white, the color I imagine my face must be right now.

It's blank.

Leave this room.

My disappointment is quashed by my sudden, commanding need for a toilet. I'm not even sure I'm going to make it.

My body starts shaking, and the heat that mere moments ago filled my body is replaced by jagged, stabbing ice, which saws at me from the inside out.

This is beyond food poisoning.

This is *poisoning.*

My legs turn numb, and I have to brace myself on the top of the table to keep from collapsing. As I do, the paper falls from my hand and twists in the air.

When it lands, it's turned over, and this side isn't blank. Not at all.

Artwork. Heavy black lines outline a shape I know very well, even though he's only half drawn, and only partially filled with rich, brilliant, piercing colors. Mister Tender is leaning over the top of his bar and whispering into the ear of someone who looks very much like me.

And suddenly I see the similarity. The bold strokes, the confident outer lines of a first sketch. This artist is undeniably the same as the one who chalked up daily specials and images of coffee cups on the chalkboard at the Rose. The same person I always thought should be in art school, rather than working in a simple coffee shop.

My legs give up entirely, and I fall to the ground, crumpling the page beneath.

I look up.

Brenda stands in the doorway, smiling at me. It's a genuine smile, top-shelf, and I know beyond question there's nothing more important in her world right now than me.

She says something, but I don't understand. My mind tells me I'm reaching for the wine opener in my pocket, but my limbs don't respond. My only thought is that I'm now the one thing I promised I'd never be again: helpless.

Then, as much as I try to fight it, darkness comes.

FORTY-EIGHT

I wake. No, that's not the right word. What I do is emerge from one state into another. The last state was, I think, unconsciousness. This is lucid unconsciousness. Awareness through some senses, others deadened.

Sight.

I have none. The limited, weak atmosphere circling my head is hot and thin, trapped in by something with mass. A bag, I think. There's a bag on my head. Fabric, perhaps. A sack.

Smell.

Horrific. Vomit. There's no other aroma like that. I don't know if the puke is inside or outside this bag on my head. The vomit is certainly mine.

Touch.

I'm sitting in a chair, feet on the floor. I move to take the bag off, but my wrists are bound to the arms of the chair. Each ankle bound to a chair leg. There's a dampness on the top of my thighs.

Taste.

Bile. Puke and Chinese food. Acid.

Brenda poisoned me.

Pounding headache. Any coherent thought lasts only moments before vaporizing.

Sound.

There wasn't any until now, but I hear it. Another room. My mind comes back into focus for a moment, and I hear Brenda talking. On the phone, perhaps. Short words. Clipped sentences. I hear something like

Everything's ready

and

Do you want to watch?

I'm able to focus my mind a little more, and now I feel the first true pangs of panic. There will be a moment when she'll lift this bag off my head, and then I'll understand what her plan is. But I can't be the victim. I might be bound and helpless, but I *won't* be the victim.

I make a promise.

If I die tonight, I will face it with deep, long breaths. A clear mind. And I won't beg for anything.

Nothing.

The wine opener is still in my front pocket, pressing against my thigh. But that's worse than bringing a knife to a gun fight.

It's like bringing a letter opener to a battle-field.

Richard.

Did he get my text? How much time has passed? The nausea from earlier is gone, replaced with a headache. That should have taken hours.

Then:

Footsteps on hardwood floors.

A door opening, hinges squeaking. A brief rush of air on my face.

Light floods my eyes, but I only see an inch in front of me. Everything is a hazy tan, and I have no sense of depth. It's like looking onto an endless expanse of sand, stretching forever.

Then the sand disappears.

The hood is yanked from my head, and my eyes recoil against the light. But it takes only seconds to adjust, and then I see I'm in the same room as before. In front of me is the drafting table. The light in the corner. I look down. I'm in a chair from the dining room. Vomit cakes the tops of my jeans. The stench is stronger, and though I gag, every-thing stays down. Maybe there isn't even anything left to come up.

The hood falls to the floor next to my feet, and I see it's just a pillowcase. A light tan pillowcase with brown spots on it. Puke stains. Maybe blood.

My focus is watery. Feels like I'm viewing everything through a swimming pool.

Brenda materializes into view. She peers down at me, like a little boy inspecting an insect he's just about to squash. No more smile.

"He wants to talk to you," she says.

I open my mouth to talk and then realize it's completely devoid of all moisture.

"Water," I manage.

Brenda furrows her brow at the request, leaves the room, then returns with a glass. She holds it to my lips and pours faster than I can drink, and most of the water ends up all over me. But I get a few swallows, which douses the fire in my throat.

After a few gasping coughs, I ask, "Who wants to talk to me?"

"You know who."

I sit up as straight as I can, and my spine protests with a sharp pain. I've been slouched for too long.

"You took the pictures," I say. "All those pictures."

"For two years," she says.

"Why?"

"Because you're all I have, Alice."

"What does that mean?"

She leans down and places her hand on

my cheek, pats it once.

"I started reading Mister Tender when I was very young. All sorts of graphic novels, really. But Mister Tender was the one I couldn't get enough of. And then . . . then you were stabbed. I was twelve when that happened, and I suppose I got a little obsessed over the story."

Then Brenda steps back, unzips her jeans, and slides them down her legs. She is wearing just a tiny strip of red underwear that tightly hugs her hips. Her legs are strong, toned, and milky white, and as she steps out of her jeans, I realize this isn't some kind of bizarre sexual advance. She wants to show me something.

Her legs are covered in scars.

Hundreds of them. It's like looking at the surface of the moon, in an area covered in the eternal, dusty tracks of rovers. Straight lines, zigzag lines, some not longer than inch, others the length of her thigh. Crossing, parallel, diagonal. Up the calf, across the knee, some as far up as her panty line. Most of them are whiter than her skin, old scars. A few are a dull red, more recent. One, a two-inch incision across the shin, is bright red and puffy. It could have been made yesterday.

I say nothing. There is nothing to say. Brenda is insane.

FORTY-NINE

"I'm running out of room," she says. Brenda slowly turns around, letting me view the extent of her carvings. "I don't want to cut above my waist, but it's getting harder to keep myself from it." Then she reaches out and thrusts her left arm toward me. I don't understand what it is she wants me to see, and then I spot the small scar on her forearm. A single ski track on virgin snow. I remember the Band-Aid on her arm from last week. When I had asked her about it, she told me she was cut by a nail sticking out of the wall in her apartment.

"I've been cutting since I was a teenager, but my scars are nothing compared to yours. You are the queen of scars, Alice." She steps into her jeans, pulls them up, and buttons the waist. "And then I found . . . found the community."

"The website."

"Yes. The website. I realized I wasn't the

only one interested in you."

Yes. *Interested* is the right word.

"Brenda, this is crazy. You *drugged* me. You'll be arrested. You need to stop this now before you make things worse for yourself."

"You're the queen of scars, Alice," she repeats. "But I'm the queen of *you.* I get to be next to you all the time. Do you know how exciting that is?"

I won't be able to reason with her; that is quite clear now. But maybe I can keep her talking until I figure something out.

A fresh wave of vomit stench attacks my nostrils, and I suppress a gag.

"You moved to Manchester just to work with me?"

She smiles. God, she's *excited.* "From upstate New York."

"So, what, you just want to be close to me? Take pictures of me so you can tell your fellow online psychopaths what I'm doing?"

The smile disappears. I don't care for her serious face.

"You don't understand, Alice. I'm the number two fan. I'm very important."

"So you're the one who draws all the pictures?" I feebly nod toward the drafting table.

"Some. But Mr. Interested does most. I do the inking. He's in charge of everything, though."

He's in charge of everything.

"Like Jimmy? He told you to kill him? Showed you how to do that?"

She lets out a frustrated sigh, almost angry that I don't immediately understand her delusions.

"I didn't do that. I mean, I had to help. I followed my instructions, found Jimmy, got him high, and put the strap on his chest. Gave him the wireless. But I didn't kill him. That was Mr. Interested. It wasn't my *privilege.* Mr. Interested is the number one fan, after all."

"Why? Why do you let him be in charge?"

She looks as if I just asked her the most basic question in the world. "Because he was there from the beginning. And he's always been there."

Does she actually know who Jack is?

"So that makes him the number one fan?"

"Of course." She takes a deep breath of satisfaction. "But tonight, he's letting me be in charge."

Her voice — so pleasant, almost singsongy — makes this pronouncement all the more horrifying.

"Is he here? In Manchester."

"He was. He's back in London now," she

adds. "He relies very heavily on me for things."

"Like placing a gun in my planter box," I say.

"That. And other things."

"So . . . so you take pictures of me, send them to him to draw, then he sends you the artwork to ink?"

"We are very busy."

Keep her talking, Alice.

"Why? What's the point of any of this?"

Brenda takes a step toward me, and for a moment, I smell her perfume rise above my own stench. Then she leans down and kisses me on the lips, the lips with remnants of my own puke still on them. It's little more than the slightest brush on the lips, but it's sensual and disturbing.

"The point," she says, "is tonight."

Brenda leaves the room.

FIFTY

I have no idea how long she'll be gone, so I use the time to whip my head around and try to find anything that can help me. It's still dark outside, which means morning has not yet come. How long was I out? Did Richard even get my text? And what the hell do I expect him to do, come kick the door down and wrestle this lunatic to the ground?

Everything in the room is what I remember from before. Nothing I can obviously use as a weapon, even if I could free myself. Moving my feet is impossible. I yank against the tape binding my wrists, and it twists a little. There's a little room there. Maybe, with time, I could make some progress. But there is no time.

Brenda reappears, grabbing the stool next to the drafting table and setting it in front of me. Then she sets a laptop down, and with the flair of a magician revealing the surprise under a handkerchief, she yanks open the screen. Skype.

A man stares directly at me.

Then Brenda says, "Alice, meet your number one fan."

FIFTY-ONE

What if some of the people you meet in the world already know you? Know everything about you, have been studying you, stalking you? And you have no idea. Like you're a bug trapped under their glass lid, and all you do is wonder stupidly why you keep running into invisible walls.

I had this thought two weeks ago in the Stone Rose and attributed it to my long history of paranoia. I had this thought, in fact, when a stranger ordered a drink. Older man, salt-and-pepper beard, deep-green eyes, the color of jade. Charcoal suit, no tie. All he did was order a cappuccino, but when he handed me the cash, he just stared at me. It lasted no more than a few seconds, but there was endless longing to it. I remember the name I wrote on the cup, the name that he paused before giving me, as if I had asked him a deeply personal question. *John.* But I also know there's a common nickname for John. Something less formal, the name of a barman.

"Jack," I say.

"You remember me," he says.

"You came into my shop. Twice."

"It was all I could do to only order a drink from you and not talk more than that. I couldn't even manage to give you the name everyone knows me by, only my birth name."

His British accent betrays just the slightest hint of Cockney, as if he's worked years to put traces of hardscrabble roots behind him. I immediately feel his pull, a gentle gravity, and realize I'm actually leaning toward the laptop screen. I'm trying to see any of me in him. And as much as I want to see nothing, our eyes could be interchangeable. Exact same shade of green.

This is my father.

Jack leans back in his seat. The room he's in is dark, with just a small lamp providing the only light. He wears a loose oxford shirt, a cerulean blue.

"You have no idea what it means for me to finally talk to you," he says. "You have grown into such a beautiful woman. Strong, flawed, wondrous."

There's too much happening, and the smell of my vomit hits me again, threatening to overload my senses. I close my eyes, shutting my view of this man, and take in a deep breath, hold it to four, then let the air trickle from me.

Keep calm. Figure out what they want, and use it to your advantage. Focus on nothing but escape.

"Tell her to let me go," I say. The words sound so impotent, but I have no idea what else to say.

"She won't do that," Jack says. "This is a very important night for her. For all of us, really."

I won't ask why. I can't ask why.

Now when I move my wrists, I sense the slightest bit more wiggle room. If I could even get one hand free, maybe I could reach into my pocket and get the wine opener without Brenda seeing. There's the sharp little end used for cutting the foil. Perhaps I could saw through the rest of the tape. But Brenda would have to be out of the room. There's no way I could do it without her seeing me. Still, there's a chance. *Keep them talking. Just keep them talking.*

"How many fans are there?" I ask. "You are the number one and two fans. How many more? How many have the username and password to the website?"

"Dozens." The voice is Jack's. I look at the

screen, and he's smiling. "And the only thing they all have in common is an obsession with you, Alice. Isn't that wonderful?"

"It's disgusting."

"It's not uncommon, actually. I call it victim fetishism. We read about crimes all day, don't we? Every leading news article is one horrific event after another. Most of the stories wash over us, leaving us feeling very little about them. But once in a while, a particular crime affects us deeply, and not necessarily because we're saddened by it. Sometimes a crime is so cruel and horrifying that it forces us to sit up and take notice. To honor it, in a way."

"I've never had that feeling," I say.

"Perhaps not, but many people do. And when the victim survives, the fascination deepens. And for a small number of people, that fascination sucks them in and doesn't let go."

Brenda's voice, cool and distant. "I cut myself because of you, Alice."

Jack continues. "The crime against you ensnared many of these people. They read the story and wonder, *What was that like for her? What was going through her mind the moment those little girls began stabbing?* And, most of all, they wonder, *What's her life going to be like now?* They want to know

451

what it's like to be Alice, all these years later."

"It's a nightmare," I say. "Just one long, unending nightmare."

"But not all the people who follow you are the same," Jack continues. "It's a diverse group — we have members from around the world. IP addresses from Turkey, Indonesia, Japan. Most just want to watch you, study you, follow you as if you're a character on their private stage, which, in a way, you are."

"Why?"

"Because you fascinate them, Alice. You've experienced horror like very few ever have — as a mere child, no less — and now you're trying to lead a normal life, push away the past. Perhaps that's not very interesting to most people, but to members of our website, the life of Alice is the best show around."

I don't want to ask, but I need to keep them talking.

"So, why . . . why this? If everyone just wants to watch me, why are you doing this to me?"

Brenda purrs. "Some of us want more."

"She's right," Jack says. "Not everyone has the same motivation. Brenda has a hunger for you that cannot be sated by simply chronicling your life."

Oh God, I knew I didn't want to ask. I keep facing the screen, afraid to look over to Brenda.

"And what about you, Jack? What is it you want?"

"You'll know the answer to that soon enough," he says.

The room falls silent, and my head spins, trying to think of more questions, anything to stretch the time. Time represents hope, and I sense both are quickly fading.

Just as I'm about to speak, Jack says something that rips away any remaining hope.

"Go get the knives, Brenda."

FIFTY-TWO

If I'm breathing, I'm not aware of it. I'm not moving, not even shaking with fear. I'm scared frozen.

Go get the knives.

My catatonic moment lasts a year, or maybe five seconds. All I know is when my brain snaps back into a functioning mode, my only thought is:

Not like this. It can't end like this.

It's easy to think of bravery in theory. But when you're strapped in a chair and the man who's been stalking you for fourteen years tells his partner in crime to *go get the knives,* any sense of bravery evaporates. Raindrops on sizzling desert asphalt.

I can't help it. My bladder just releases, and the hot urine filling the seat of my jeans is almost a welcome relief. Maybe if I can let go of my bladder, I can let go of my mind. Maybe death will feel as strangely relieving as soiling myself.

"Stay with me, Alice," Jack says.

It's just him and me. Brenda has left the room.

"I don't deserve this," I say.

"We are all dying, Alice. Just at different rates."

The internet connection stammers, and Jack's face blinks into a digital void for a second, then reappears.

Tears well in my eyes, but I refuse to let them fall.

"Are you really my father?"

"Yes, darling."

"Then how can you let this happen?"

Before he can answer, Brenda reappears. She carries a soft piece of rolled velvet, which she places on the top of the drawing table. When she unrolls it, three pieces of metal catch the light of the lamp. A cutter's tool kit.

"No," I say.

I don't add *please.* I'm not going to beg. I'm covered in my own puke and piss, but I'm not going to fucking beg for my life.

I struggle against the tape and realize there's no way I can get my hands free in time. The binds dig into my wrist, and I almost relish the pain.

"If you kill me," I say to Brenda, "then what? You'll have nothing left. You'll be all alone. No purpose."

Brenda removes and holds up a blade. A scalpel. An instrument meant for cutting, not stabbing. For carving.

I gag, but there's nothing left to come up.

Then I scream. I scream as loudly and as frantically as I can. Maybe if someone is outside, they'll hear me. I'm hysterical, my voice screeching until it hurts my ears.

Brenda slashes my forearm with the scalpel, and the skin immediately opens. I stare down at the wound in horror, and Brenda has succeeded in silencing me. As I watch, I think for a moment that it's not too deep. There's no blood.

And then there is.

It pours from my forearm, slicking my skin. More blood than seems possible from the little cut. I can't look any more.

"I know how to cut without pain," Brenda says. "I've done it for years. Stop screaming, and I'll make this as painless as I can. Or, I can put tape over your mouth, and take out pieces of you one by one. Then you can scream all you want."

Close your eyes, Alice. Go to another place. A soft, warm place. A place where you can't feel.

As I close my eyes, I'm aware of the word that escapes my lips.

"Daddy."

Then, Jack's voice.

"I'm right here, Alice."

"You're not my daddy," I whisper. Over and over. I say it until I have a thought. Maybe my daddy is out there telling me what to do.

I thrash in the chair enough that I ultimately tip over onto my left side, pounding my shoulder into the floor. Brenda immediately kicks me in the ribs. Pain roils me, but I can take a million kicks. Anything but the blade.

"Goddamn it," she says. I catch a glimpse of her looking at the screen.

"Now what?"

"Get her upright, and then continue," he answers.

I don't have any expectation of escaping just by falling to the floor. But I rock myself enough to direct the flow of blood from my forearm down toward my right hand. It works. Hot, sticky liquid oozes around my wrist, making it slippery. I yank my lubricated right hand, and a bit more of it slides out from the tape. I'm close. There's a chance.

Brenda stops my rocking and yanks up on the chair, but she isn't strong enough to lift me.

"Okay then," she says, releasing the chair so I'm back on my left side. "I guess we'll have to do this on the floor."

"No," I hear Jack saying. "I need to watch. It's very important."

She doesn't seem to hear him. Brenda is in her own world, the world of a cutter making the intoxicating leap from the canvas of one's own skin to that of another.

"I've wanted you for so long," she says. "And now I get to have you."

She's sideways on the floor now, wedged in front of me in the clutter and filth of this tiny, dingy room. Her nose is close to mine, and when she breathes, it fills me. Now she wears the Brenda look, the one that makes you feel like you're the only thing in the world that matters. For years, I've wondered if this look was sincere, and in this moment, I know it is. I am her focus. Her reason.

I pull and twist my right hand. Pull and twist. It's looser within the tape. Just another few minutes. That's all I need.

This can't happen. Not like this. Keep them talking.

I twist my head toward the laptop screen, hoping I can get Jack to tell her to stop. I can only make out the top half of the screen from the floor, but one thing is very clear.

Jack is no longer there.

Back to Brenda, who now holds the blade up to my face. Very slowly, she places the tip on my nose, and I go cross-eyed looking at it.

"I could start here," she says. "Work my way up to your scalp, or down to your lips. Do you want to choose, Alice?"

This is it. Fourteen years ago, I didn't see it coming. Now, with the blade hovering in front of me, I have a chance to control the moment. Control my mind. Steel it against the pain. If I can just shut my mind down for a bit, it'll all be over.

I just need to make it to the other side.

One last yank of my wrist. It's not enough. I can't get my hand free.

I close my eyes. As I do, I decide not to scream.

"Daddy," I whisper. I don't ask him to save me. I think I'm telling him I'll see him soon.

That will be wonderful.

There's the slightest pressure on the tip of my nose.

FIFTY-THREE

Everything is gone in a moment, and all that exists is a singular memory. This must be death, because no memory has ever been as clear, as potent. Real.

I see, smell. Hear perfectly. Touch. I'm aware of my life as it is both now and as it was then. I am not reliving this. This is reliving me.

I'm in a twin bed wedged against one side of a very small room, a room I know. I grew up here. Thomas's bed is next to mine, separated by a narrow nightstand holding a Winnie the Pooh lamp, Hundred Acre Wood. But Thomas is not there. He's next to me in bed, the soft flannel of his pajamas rubbing against my arm.

He laughs, high-pitched and musical. He is maybe four years old and looks nothing like the man he will eventually become. I must be eight.

"And then what?" Thomas says. "Do they

find the keys?" His little voice has a British accent, one that will disappear by his mid-teens.

"Well, I think that's enough for tonight."

I turn and look away from Thomas to the voice.

Daddy.

He sits on the edge of my bed, larger than life. He's so young. Dark hair sweeps over his forehead, disheveled, wavy, and wiry. Stubble grows like moss on his narrow, pale cheeks, and his eyes, his light-brown eyes — the color of a melted chocolate bar — hold a weariness that's more than just fatigue. His hand rests on my stomach.

"No, please," I say, grabbing his arm. My voice also holds a high-pitched accent, a tone I haven't heard in a very long time. "Just a little more, please, Daddy."

"Yes," Thomas says. "Do Alice and Thomas find the keys?"

"You'll find out tomorrow night," my dad says.

He's telling us the story of Chancellor's Kingdom, the epic adventure made up on the spot and revealed in little chunks every night over the course of several months. Little Alice and Thomas only wanted to find their way home but were continuously swept into the bizarre and alien lands of the

461

Kingdom. Lands where creatures roamed.

"Please, give us a hint," I say.

"I'm tired, love," he says. "And sometimes telling this story takes more energy than I have. This is one of those nights."

I smell the alcohol on him. Feel it on my eyes.

"I know what happens next," Thomas says. "I think Mister Tender gives them the keys."

My father looks down at him. "Is that so? Don't you remember the story, Thomas? For them to get the keys, they would have to betray Ferdinand to the king. Do you think Alice and Thomas would do that?"

"Yes!" Thomas giggles. "Bye-bye, Ferdinand."

"No," I say, taking the question as seriously as my father intended. "They wouldn't do that. They would have to find another way."

"But what if there is no other way?" my father asks, shifting his gaze to me. I feel delighted and pained to see him, to feel him so close. I continue holding on to his arm, and if I could, I'd stay like this forever. Maybe that's my heaven.

I challenge him. "There has to be another way."

"But what if there isn't? What if the only

way for them to get what they want is to betray the thing they love?"

"I don't like that idea," I say.

He pulls his arm from my grasp, and I feel panic rise in my little chest, a helpless sense of falling down, down. Forever. But he then moves his hand to my cheek and instantly grounds me. His energy flowing into my blood.

"I don't either, Alice. Yet, there it is. Life is fragile."

"What does fragile mean?" Thomas asks.

"Fragile is like an egg," I tell my brother. "Easily broken."

"Yes," my father says. "Like that, Alice. Life can be like an egg. Beautiful, perfect, smooth. But it just takes one thing, one event. A little too much pressure, and that eggs breaks. And it's never the same way, not ever again." His voice is so sad, and it scares me.

"I don't think I want the story if it doesn't have a happy ending," I say.

This seems to snap my father from his melancholy. He smiles down at me. In this moment, he is impossibly beautiful.

"I'll do my best," he tells me. "I'm sure Alice and Thomas will find a way. They just have to be very clever, and very careful. And they need to remember the very important thing Ferdinand told them."

I hear myself whisper, repeating words like a Bible passage.

"If you get the sudden urge to start trusting someone, be smart and do away with it."

"That's right, Alice." He strokes my cheek. "That's right. Under the covers, then, and Thomas, back to your bed."

Thomas scurries away and dives into his bed, yanking the covers up over his body. I worm my way under mine, going slowly, knowing the faster I move, the sooner my father will leave. I'm able to delay maybe an extra twenty seconds.

Then my father leans over me and kisses my forehead, and in my mind, I fight back tears I'm incapable of producing. This little girl knows nothing, and I know everything. I know all about the fragility of life, and how the three of us, this little family in this little room illuminated by a Winne the Pooh lamp, how each of us eventually breaks, after which we will never be the same. Cracked, spilled open. Forever changed.

"Good night, Alice," he says.

"Good night, Daddy. I love you."

Another smile. "I love you."

He rises and kisses Thomas, then reaches down and pulls the cord on the lamp, sending the room into darkness. Footsteps to the door, and as he opens it, the light from the hall silhouettes him. He is long and slender, a shadow with no weight, a ghost of the night.

And I desperately, painfully, want to go with him, because if I don't, I think this is the last I will ever see of him.

FIFTY-FOUR

The vision doesn't last, and my dream for death is denied long enough to feel myself pulled back into reality. Back to Brenda.

I'm still strapped to the chair, lying sideways on the floor. My stomach turns into rock, solid granite. Eyes squeezed shut. The sense of cool steel on my burning skin, the tip of my nose, no idea which direction the blade will travel.

It's okay, it's okay, it's okay.

A flash of a thought. A hope for a quick death. The knife across my throat, carotid artery. Bleed out fast, and then it will be over.

I don't want pain.

No more pain.

Just let me die in peace.

I start to hyperventilate as the blade travels up my nose, splitting the skin. Hot blood spills sideways down my cheek, to the floor. I think of tears. So many tears for so long, and now everything pools beneath me.

Goodbye, Thomas.

Goodbye, Mom.

"Oh God," I mutter.

But I don't tell her to stop.

I won't beg.

Soon, Dad. Soon.

She's nearly to my forehead. I try not to imagine the sight of me with my scalp untethered from my skull.

But I can't do it. It's all I can think of.

There's no pain yet, but there will be.

Please just let me die.

Then:

A sound. Two sounds, actually.

Soft, like air puffing from a compressor.

Pop pop

A third sound. Wet, spongy.

Mist on my face. Something hits me in the chest, then falls to the floor.

The blade is gone. A dull thud.

I open my eyes.

Brenda is still on the floor next to me, eyes wide open.

The top of her skull is missing.

FIFTY-FIVE

My brain is focused, clear. I can't see the door from where I lie, but I know Richard has found me. He's come and saved me. Or called the police and they came here, broke into the house, shot Brenda.

I start to cry, my tears mixing into the blood. God, there's so much blood, and I can't tell where my blood ends and Brenda's begins. She stares right at me, and in death, she maintains her same look, like I'm the most important thing in the world to her in this eternal moment.

"Please help me," I say. "I'm bleeding badly. My . . . my nose."

Footsteps toward me. Not rushed. Calm, determined. Only four or five of them.

I sense someone behind me, leaning down.

Then, a voice. A voice with a British accent.

"That was close. I told her I'd let her kill you, but I was always going to save you.

Then the video feed went out, and I couldn't see what was happening. I was afraid I'd be too late."

I crane my neck, and the blood flows up my face, into my eyes. My world becomes a blurred, wavy red. I'm swimming in it.

No, no, no.

He lifts the chair upright, and now the blood drips down my nose, onto my thighs. For a moment, my eyes clear enough to see him. Just as he was on the screen a moment ago.

This is Mister Tender. This is the father I never knew existed. This is Jack.

"You're a right mess," he says. "Give me a moment."

He disappears, and I frantically start moving my hands. The tape is especially loose on my right hand, and if I have enough time, I have a chance.

I sneak a look at Brenda's body. Sweet God, I can see her brain.

Eyes back up. *Just focus on the tape, Alice. Get your hand free.* I stare at the ceiling as I work my wrist, ignoring the stench and trickling of blood flowing from open wounds. These cuts won't kill me, so I must ignore them. *Focus.*

Minutes later, he returns. I can't not look at him.

Jack carries a handful of bandages, and he makes quick work of sticking cotton pads onto my nose and wrapping gauze around my head, securing the pads in place. He does the same thing with my forearm, and I pray he doesn't notice how stretched the tape is around my right wrist. All it would take is another loop of tape to destroy the progress I've made.

"There," he says, stepping back and looking at me. "You look a bit mummy-like, but it'll work until we can get you properly cleaned up." Then he looks at the floor. "Suppose there's a lot of cleanup to do overall. Long night ahead, I'm afraid."

My head is light as a balloon, and I'm on the verge of passing out. I can't let that happen. Close my eyes. Deep breath in, count to four, exhale. Open my eyes.

Focus on Jack.

"Where did you come from? She said you were in London," I say. *Keep your voice calm. Steady. Don't show fear.*

"That's what I told her. I wanted her to think she was in control, that she could do whatever she wanted with you."

"Why?"

"Because it makes it all so much more *real*," he says. "Real passion, real fear. If I was here in the room, Brenda would have deferred to me, and I didn't want that. I had to be able to save you, and in order to do that, Brenda needed to fully have your life in her hands, at least for a moment. But I was here the entire time." A soft chuckle. "The flat next door is unoccupied. I broke in earlier today. Needed to be close, you understand." He looks down at the woman he just murdered. "And that was a little *too* close, if I say."

All this orchestration. All this obsession.

"You . . . you killed Jimmy."

"I didn't kill Jimmy," he says. "I saved you from him."

"Just let me go," I say. I won't say *please.*

Jack looks silently at me for a long time. His eyes are as beautiful as his gaze is fierce, and it's not hard for me to imagine him holding court in his bar, extracting the most personal of stories from strangers.

"I think you know we're beyond that point, Alice. I don't have much time left, and I want to spend it with you. I want to be a proper father."

"You're not my father," I say.

He leans in and pats my cheek, just as Brenda had. "Oh, yes, love. I am. And I haven't been a good one, so I need to make up for that."

"I want nothing to do with you."

Now he turns into something altogether different. The calm, dashing demeanor evaporates as he screams, his reddened face pulled tight in rage. "How 'bout a fucking *thank-you* for saving your life? Ungrateful bitch!"

The suddenness of it hits me like a shock wave, and all I can do is stammer a response. "I'm . . . yes . . . I'm sorry. Thank you."

He straightens. Face softens. "Yes, that's better. Right then."

He turns for a moment, and I work my right hand. I nearly have my thumb free.

"Where to start," he mutters, scanning the mess in the room.

"Why don't you have much time left?" I ask. I have a sense that if I let him control everything that happens next, I'll end up disappearing with him, and then God-knows-what will happen after that. So I need to ask questions. Lots of them. Keep him from doing what he came here to do. "You told me earlier you were sick. What's wrong with you?"

He points to his head. "Brain tumor, diagnosed a few years ago. About the size of a walnut, but slowly growing. Inoperable, apparently. I wasn't supposed to last this long, yet here I am. Causes terrible headaches, and at some point, one of those headaches will be my last. Could be tonight, could be a few more years from now. Who knows?"

"I'm sorry," I say, not meaning it in the least but aware I need not antagonize him anymore.

The effect of my words is astounding. He takes a knee in front of me — soaking his pants in Brenda's blood — and places his hands on my arms.

"Alice, darling, I can't tell you how much that means to me. Thank you. Yes, you see? We do need to spend time together." Jack stands. "I was a fool to wait this long. I won't waste any more time."

This is a desperate man. I need to be very careful here.

"You saved me," I say. "In Gladstone Park."

"Yes," he says, his eyes filled with hope, as if I now understand him. What I know is he was the one who told the twins to stab me, just so he could be the one to save me.

"You saved me from Freddy Starks. From Jimmy." He found Jimmy and somehow managed to get him to talk about that night three years ago when Jimmy shot our dealer. He spent considerable time and effort finding Freddy Starks just so he could point him in my direction, only to save me from him.

"Yes," he says.

I nod to the body on the floor. "Her motivation was to cut me. But you're different. You don't want to hurt me or just to watch me. You want to save me. You saved me from her."

"Yes, yes, yes." His voice cracks with emotion. "They all wanted to hurt you, and would have if it weren't for me." He reaches out and lightly touches the gauze on my nose, which sends a fresh burst of pain through my head. "She would've killed you."

Just keep talking. "You had an affair with my mother. She got pregnant. But you . . . you wanted nothing to do with me, did you?"

He looks at me in stunned silence, as if a mask he's worn his entire life has just been removed. "Alice, I'm so sorry. I was so scared. She was ready to leave Reggie for me. We could have had a proper family. A home of our own. And I-I said no. I was a stupid man. I shunned her. I shunned you. And I've never forgiven myself for it."

"Don't call him Reggie," I say. "Only his friends called him that."

"Is that so? Well, then, at some point, I must have been his friend, because that's what I called him at the pub."

"I don't care. Don't call my father by any name."

"Alice, love. You can juggle semantics all you want, but it doesn't change the fact that *I'm* your father."

My mind buzzes. I think about my mother, my father. How they always acted around me, around Thomas. The fights. The drinking.

He *knew.* My dad knew I wasn't his child. He loved everything about me, except where I came from. He didn't leave my mother; he didn't leave me. But he knew the truth, and it poisoned everything from the time I was born.

"You destroyed my family long before you told the Glassins to stab me. My mother turned into another person entirely because of you."

I think this is quite probably true. I never knew my mother before I was conceived by her and Jack. Was she a wonderful, selfless person at some point in her life?

"And what did she become, Alice?"

"She . . ." It hits me in its sudden incredible simplicity. "She became just like you."

"Is that so?"

"Of course it is. She keeps Thomas medicated just so she can be his savior. This . . .

this whole fucking inflated sense of self-worth. The thought that only she can make things right. *She's just like you.* She's addicted to saving him." So many realizations dawning on me that I'm beginning to lose sense of what's happening. Lose sense of the fact I'm still taped to a chair, covered in my own blood, vomit, and piss. "She creates pain just so she can get the credit for healing."

"I haven't had any contact with your mother in a very long time."

If nothing else, I will survive this night for Thomas. We will be together, and we will go far away. I have to live, if for no other reason than that. I look at Jack and strive to see any part of him that will be merciful, or even the slightest bit sane, but I see none. I came from a monster. A fairy-tale villain. A manipulating demon. My father must have seen this as well, spotted it through the handsome, engaging shell of a simple bartender. And when he found out about my mother and Jack, it must have shredded his guts. When my father told Thomas and me the stories of Chancellor's Kingdom, he didn't just create Mister Tender on the spot. He'd been thinking about him for some time. He'd been thinking about Jack.

But this man before me is not just a

simple bartender with whom my mother had an indiscreet affair. He is a ticking bomb, a collection of synapses blindly firing. If I had to guess, he's always been unhinged, but something made him more so. Something made him obsessed with me. With *saving* me.

Of course.

My father's books.

"My father created Mister Tender to hurt you."

"*Reggie* was a hack," he says. "He was never good enough for you. Or your mother."

"Don't use his name."

"Knowing I had a daughter out there who I couldn't see was agonizing enough," he continues. "But I accepted it. I made a decision and couldn't go back. Your mother refused to allow me to see you. I respected her decision."

My mother. All the secrets. And how could she not tell me about this man, especially after she knew I was being stalked by someone? She's just concerned with her own world, with self-pity and suffocating caregiving. As sick as him, maybe.

"But then your father created that awful comic. He made me into the devil, a source of evil. He mocked me, and it made him rich."

"We were never rich."

He lashes out again. "You had more than I had! I was in my thirties and working in whatever pubs would have me. I wanted my rightful family and couldn't have it, and all I could do was watch you grow up." He rubs his forehead, as if struck by a sudden burst of pain. "And I watched you, you know. For a long time, a lot longer than you realize. Where you went to school. I knew things about you, knew you weren't popular. Knew you wanted friends."

Here is where I have to choose whether or not to engage. None of his logic is rational, except to him. He feels justified in everything he's done, including bringing me to the edge of death and back more than once. Nothing I can say will convince him he's anything other than heroic.

He stalked the Glassin girls after hearing from Maggie they were obsessed with the Mister Tender novels. He convinced them to do what they did.

He created a site dedicated to following me for years, amassing a twisted collection of fans. Fans like Brenda.

He told Freddy Starks where to find me. He killed Jimmy.

He told Brenda to cut me, saving me only in the last moment.

He . . .

Oh God.

It has to be.

"You killed my father."

"Alice —"

"You did, didn't you?" I openly yank against the tape, not bothering to hide my intent any more. I'm going to get free, and then I'm going to rip him apart. Gouge his eyes, bite off his nose. "*You* did it."

"Alice, calm yourself."

"Be a fucking man and admit it, then. That's how you got his drawings, isn't it?" My mind spins, trying to fit everything together. "You hated him all along, but you didn't do anything about it until you found out you were dying, isn't that right? You killed him, then ransacked his flat. You found that book with the inscription, didn't you? He meant that for *me.*"

There's a hint of panic on his face, as if he's losing me. He thinks there's a chance I could see him as something more than he actually is. He puts his hands on my shoulders to calm me, which enrages me further. "But he never sent it to you, did he, Alice? He kept that book locked away, and only I gave you the chance to see it. I even added my own drawings. *I* gave you that gift. Not him."

"So you don't even understand the inscription."

"No, of course not. What would I know about some penguin?"

A small satisfaction. Jack doesn't know about Chancellor's Kingdom. That's something special, known only by a dead man and his two broken children. Jack doesn't know about Ferdinand's advice: trust no one. Now I see what my father meant by it. He was referring to Jack. He was referring to my own mother.

"Alice, enough," Jack says. "Please understand the considerable efforts I've made in protecting you. Now that you're finally safe, you need to be with me. I'm the only one who can keep you from further harm, but we don't have much time. We need to get you cleaned up and out of here."

"Then get me out of this tape," I say. "I'll go home, take a shower, and then we'll go wherever you want."

It's my only hope, but Jack has impulses only a dying man can feel. He killed my father, and now, on borrowed time, he's come for me. The idea of being someone's final wish fulfilled is a chilling one.

He softly shakes his head and gives me

the slightest smile. I can feel his pull again, his allure, even as a man who must be almost sixty. There's a genuineness to him, which is all the more tragic when coupled with an obsessive personality. As much as Jack disavows Mister Tender, I can see what my father surely must have seen. Jack *is* Mister Tender, through and through.

"Alice, I know I still need to earn your trust, though you must see by my efforts how much I love you. Still, I'm not convinced you're willing to accept me as your family. It will take time, and until then, I'm afraid your freedoms will be limited."

"So what are you going to —"

"I'll be back."

He leaves again, and it's perhaps my final chance. When he comes back, he's going to do something to incapacitate me. When I come to, who knows where I'll be? A cell somewhere? Chained to a wall? He's had years to plan this very moment. If he takes me, I'll never be seen again.

I bend at the waist, enough so I can get my face near my fingers. When I'm at my limit and can go no further, I reach and pull the gauze and pads down over my nose. There is pain now. Much of it. My wound begins bleeding again, unrestricted, a fresh burst of bright-red blood, which I direct over my right wrist. Soon, my wrist and hand are coated in it, and I start yanking once more against the tape. The fresh blood relubricates, and I pull and pull, not caring how much skin comes off in the process. I'm a fox in a bear trap.

Finally, it works. My right hand slips past the tape, the flesh around my wrist and the base of my thumb stinging raw. Frantically, I reach in my front pocket for the wine opener, pulling it along the inside pocket of my tight jeans. The second it's free, I lose my grip and it falls to the floor, next to Brenda's head. I reach, leaning, stretching my fingers as far as they can go. I can't help but look at her, and once again, I feel my body starting to shut down at the sight and smell of all the gore.

Grab the opener. Sit back up. I try to work the foil cutter open, but it's impossible with one hand, so I put the opener in my mouth and hold it fast between my teeth. With my free hand, I pull out the cutter.

It looks remarkably dull and ineffective, but there's the slightest serrated edge to it.

He's coming back soon. Any second. I'm so close.

Saw through the tape on my left wrist, which takes an eternity. Sweat-stained hair falls over my face. Blood drips onto my jeans, which now contain nearly every bit of fluid that can come out of my body.

Left hand free. I just need to do the ankles. That's all I need.

Reach down.

Door opens.

I look up.

Richard.

FIFTY-SIX

"Oh my God. Alice."

He drops his phone at the sight of me and doesn't even seem to notice.

"Richard," I whisper. "Hurry. He's coming back. Help me get out of this."

Richard doesn't move. He just stares. This man who works nights in an emergency room can't comprehend the carnage in front of him.

"Richard, *help.*" My whisper is now a hiss.

Suddenly, he gasps, as if just emerging from a full minute under water. I think the smell just hit him, because he bends over and heaves.

Damn it.

I need to do what I've always done. Rely on myself. I lean over and saw at the tape on my left ankle, then see something I curse myself for having forgotten.

Brenda's scalpel.

It's close to her hand. I can't reach it

without tipping myself over.

"Richard, listen to me. *Listen to me.* Hand me the scalpel from the floor. That's all you need to do. Then get out of here and call the police."

Richard looks at me, a wave of guilt washing over his face. Then he smacks his own face. Actually hits it, hard. Shakes it off, and suddenly he's in control of himself. He takes three steps, reaches for the scalpel, but doesn't hand it to me. Instead, he quickly slices through the tape on my left ankle.

He moves to the tape on my right ankle and is just about to cut it off when Jack comes in and shoots him.

FIFTY-SEVEN

Richard spins to his left and collapses. He tries to push himself up, but his arm gives out, and he lands with a thud against a stack of banker's boxes, the top one of which wobbles but doesn't fall over.

The scalpel is still in his right hand, and he's just close enough to reach out and hand it to me. I grab it before Jack can make another move, then I stand. My muscles scream in protest, and it's difficult with one ankle still shackled to a leg of the chair, but I need to be standing right now.

I hold up the blade. Jack's gun is pointed at my face. He's ten feet away.

Richard moans. He's on his back now, and he grabs his left shoulder with his right hand. I can see the red blossoming through his dull-olive army jacket. Brenda is only a few feet away. This room is a slaughterhouse.

"Your tenant," Jack says. Of course Jack

knows who Richard is. Jack knows everything. "How did he know to find you?"

I guess not everything.

"Fuck you," I say.

Jack shifts his aim. The gun is now trained
on Richard.

"Alice, please know I don't want to kill
him. But I will."

Richard looks at me with frightened eyes.
Not quite panicked, but fearful.

"It's a GPS app," I say. I'm starting to
become light-headed again, my feet unsteady. Blood continues to drip from the tip
of my nose. How much do I have left in me?
"I suspected Brenda was a part of this from
a photo on the website. I told Richard to
come find me if I wasn't home in a few
hours."

"Who else knows?"

"No one."

Jack takes a step forward and lowers the
gun even closer to Richard's head.

"I swear," I say. "No one."

Jack holds something in his left hand. A
small, white plastic box, and I think it's a
first-aid kit. This is what he went to the
other apartment to retrieve when Richard
came in.

"We need to go," Jack says. "This isn't
how I wanted it to be. I didn't want Brenda

to actually hurt you. I didn't want to shoot your friend. But this is where we are, and now we need to leave."

I continue to hold the scalpel in front of me, but my arm quickly grows tired. My feet reflexively want to assume a fighting stance, but it's all I can do just to keep my balance.

"I'm not going anywhere," I say.

"Alice, love. Please understand you're hurt and I need to help you."

"He's more hurt than I am," I say, nodding at Richard. "Help him first."

"He'll get help, I promise. But you must cooperate." He opens the kit with one hand, revealing a needle and a small glass vial of liquid. Realizing he can't fill the plunger with just one hand, he takes a step back into the doorway, sets his gun down, then sticks the needle into the top of the vial and sucks the liquid into the plunger.

Richard shifts on the floor, but only in pain, not in an effort to attack. He's too hurt. He's not an option.

I could throw the scalpel at Jack, but I can't see that working. It's not balanced like a throwing knife, and even if the blade managed to strike him, it'd have to kill him, because I'd lose the only weapon I have. I'd put those odds at next to nothing.

But I'm not letting him near me. That needle is meant to knock me out, and then I become his. Maybe forever.

"Alice, I need to do this. So put the knife down."

"No," I say.

"Darling." There's an edge to his voice. "I'm doing this for you. You have to understand that. I'm a bit disappointed at your lack of appreciation for all I've done. But once we leave, once we have time together, you'll see. You'll see that I'm the father you always deserved."

"I'm not going anywhere with you."

Jack sighs, shakes his head, picks up the gun. He takes two steps back into the room, gun in his right hand, needle in his left. Once more, he aims the gun at Richard's skull.

"I'm afraid you have no choice, darling."

What follows is a profound moment of stillness. It's a religious kind of moment, where the silence seems heavier than possible, the air containing so much weight that the deafening noise of an explosion seems the only possible outcome. And in this moment, in this silence, I am calm. I feel all my history wash over me, all the things that have happened, the pain I've allowed, the fear I've cultivated, the panic I've embraced.

It's all gone. And all that's left remaining is *me.* A woman with a choice.

I put the tip of the scalpel against my throat.

"Alice, no."

Both Jack and Richard say this.

I don't want to die, but if I'm going to, it will be on my terms. Jack is an addict, and his drug is me. His obsession is saving me, and if I go with him, at some point, he'll hurt me badly enough that he won't be able to bring me back. Whether he'll mean to or not, he'll kill me. I'm certain of it. The only way to stop him is to take away the source of his addiction.

"Sorry, Jack. You can't have me."

"I'll kill him, Alice. I promise you I will. Put the knife down."

I look down at Richard, and his dark, fearful eyes are closed. Which is good. I don't want him looking at me.

"I'm sorry, Richard," I say.

Then, to Jack, I say, "If you shoot him, I'll cut my throat. And you won't be able to stop the bleeding. You won't have me anymore, Jack. You won't have anything."

Jack keeps the gun in position. Richard keeps his eyes closed. I keep the blade against my skin.

"You won't," Jack says. "You're a survivor."

I take a deep breath. Count to four. Let it out. And then I softly nick the base of my throat with the edge of the blade, enough to start a trickle of blood. For fourteen years, I've gone without holding a knife in my hand, and here I am, using it to do the one thing that has haunted my nights for all that time. And there is a beautiful sense of power and control to it all. I *choose* to do this.

"Stop!" Jack says. "Alice, darling, please don't."

"Then give me the gun, Jack."

"I love you, Alice. I've always loved you." He is shaking. He is broken.

"Give me the gun." I draw the blade just a fraction more across my throat, with little awareness how close I actually am to my artery. But that's okay. It's all okay.

Jack lowers the gun.

And then, rather than hand it to me, he walks out of the room. Seconds later, I hear the front door open and close.

I am motionless, and it takes a moment to realize I'm still holding the blade against my throat. As I lower it, a muffled bang jolts me.

A gunshot. Unmistakable.

491

I strain to listen but hear nothing else.
Jack is gone.

FIFTY-EIGHT

"Alice."

I look up at my father. Arlington, Massachusetts. The last time I ever saw him alive.

What is happening to me?

We're finishing our dinner in a restaurant. He's just called my mother a fucking devil. With one exception, we eat the rest of the meal in a thick and dreary silence.

"I wish I could live *now*," he says, tossing his napkin onto his empty plate.

"What do you mean?"

"*Now*. Right now. Not in the past. Not thinking about anything else. Just here. You. This." A considered pause. "Forever."

"I don't understand," I say.

But I do.

He means a world without a past, the one thing I've always wanted. The ability to Be Here Now.

Forever.

493

FIFTY-NINE

Jack is gone, and I feel every moment before this one slipping away, dirt crumbling from a cliff's edge, deep into the void. No definition of past or future. It feels like a blissful injection of morphine directly into my bloodstream. This is either heaven or insanity, or perhaps the two are the same.

Moments exist in a fog.

No, not a fog.

An opening. A clearness that feels as foreign as anything I've ever known.

There is no fear. No sense of time.

Things are finally bright. Clear. A light shining down on a life I'm supposed to have, and the colors overwhelm me. I've never seen them before.

I'm vaguely aware of reaching down and cutting the tape from my ankle. I'm aware of Richard's eyes opening, of me telling him it's okay. I slowly walk over, feet unsteady, and pick up Richard's phone. Hand it to him. Tell him to call for help. To get himself to the hospital. I say all these things in a voice I barely hear. It's like hearing myself talking underwater.

Richard is beautiful. I've never noticed that before.

I leave the room.

He calls out, "What's wrong with you?"

Into the kitchen. To my purse. I don't even bother to take it with me. Just the keys inside.

I leave the house. The door to the adjacent apartment is closed. There's no sign of Jack anywhere, but I am certain he is gone.

In this moment, a piece of time that might only last minutes, an hour at most, I have control. I choose what to do.

In the comforting darkness and silence of Manchester streets, I walk.

SIXTY

Sunday, November 1

I enter the Stone Rose and flick on the lights. As I do, I see the clock on the wall.

Just after two in the morning.

November first. Day of the Dead, when all souls come back to earth.

I walk over and turn on the espresso machine, which whirs and hums in its satisfying, predictable way. As I stand layered in my blood and urine and vomit, there's nothing so satisfyingly normal as the slow wakening of my espresso machine.

To my office, my comforting tree house with its wood paneling and tight, snug spaces. I soak in it, breathe of it. It is home. It is me. In a corner drawer, I have a pair of sweats, a T-shirt, and training shoes — gym supplies. I strip out of my stained and vile clothes and into these fresh ones. I even lace up the shoes.

Then I bring down the first-aid kit, which

I think has been used perhaps twice since I opened the Rose. Grab the Band-Aids, head to the bathroom.

Turn on the light. Look in the mirror.

I am a mess.

I am beautiful.

I turn on the water and let it become comfortably warm, then lightly splash some on my face. The sink turns pink with the blood still flowing from the tip of my nose. I rinse the wound on my arm. The nick on my neck. These will all become more scars I can add to my collection. More parts of me, queen of scars. Hash marks of life. All perfect.

I bandage everything in a piecemeal fashion, layers upon layers, piecing myself back together.

I think of Sally from *The Nightmare Before Christmas*. The Sally who needed the Jack to love her.

Back into the shop. A cloud of steam suddenly pours from the espresso machine, and as I walk over to it, I find the valve open, which I'm certain it wasn't just a few minutes ago. I find comfort in this. Ghost in the machine.

I pull a double shot of espresso. It comes out as always a gorgeous shade of black, topped with a silky, caramel crema. One packet of sugar. Stir. Sip. I think of rich soil from a faraway land, one I might have been told stories about when I was a little girl.

Then I move back to the front of the store, turn off the lights, sit on the floor cross-legged. I cradle the espresso with both hands — soaking in the heat of the porcelain cup — and absorb the silence around me. Wrap myself in the darkness.

I think of my father. Of all he taught me without even knowing, perhaps, what he was saying. I need to have his name again, *my* name. I will be Alice Hill again, leaving the Gray forever behind.

I think of Thomas, waiting for me to come home. I'm not going to be his savior, because I refuse to fall into that role after everything I've been through. But I will give him a chance to experience life free from medication, free from a forced and violent coddling. I can't promise to keep him from drowning, but I won't hold his head under the water.

I think of my mother, but not for long. Perhaps she is also somehow a victim, but I struggle to see it. I wonder if I will ever see her again.

I think of Jack, and then Maggie, and then of myself. Of our commonality. How we all sought a profession of serving drinks, of slaking particular thirsts while standing behind a counter. I glance to the Rose's counter and wonder how much of it is just a barrier that I had hoped would separate and protect me from those who wander into my space.

My search for clarity, for sanity, for normalcy, is over. None of these things exist, at least not in a way I could ever seize and keep hold of them. There is both profound sadness and relief in knowing this. Maybe that's true for all of us. Searching, searching. Those moments when true ugliness surrounds you, and it makes you want to burst out, search for brilliant, bright existence, run along the grasses of sweet mountains, finding God or whatever exists in His place. You say, *Tomorrow I will do that,* tomorrow I will do something unexpected, unpredictable, and the shell around me will crumble. I'll be free. Fucking free. And you can imagine how you'll smile when that happens. You see it in your visions, drink of it until it's just enough for you to make it through the night.

But the tomorrows of your thoughts are so very different from the ones that actually come. This is what I am just now realizing.

The concept of tomorrow is an illusion, a sweeping gesture of time. Marketing.

At some point — and here I arrive in this very moment — you realize it's about the nuances of *today*. Those tiny moments, some of them hardly perceptible, that define what it means to take each breath, one by one, until they are all used up. For me, for all I've experienced, it was never so much about finding a life unburdened by the things that have haunted me. It was about that initial, warm breeze of springtime, where you smell the sun for the first time in months. The soft resistance of your pillow after an eternal day. The touch of your father's hand on yours, leading you forward, guiding you through a place you could never navigate on your own, even if that place is nothing more than a cheap carnival, a crowded movie theater, a playground teeming with strange children. Or the wondrous, frightening world of Chancellor's Kingdom.

Now, in this place, *my* place, I know it's about the *moments,* and to strive for something greater might be worthy, but for me unnecessary. I'm free now, because the scent of coffee tells me so. I breathe in, hold it four seconds, then release. Repeat.

There's a knock on the ceiling. One knock, no more.

I smile, because this time, there's no other excuse for it.

It's not Simon.
It's my dad.
He's telling me I've got it all figured out.
Deep, deep in the night, sirens.

READING GROUP GUIDE

1. *Mister Tender's Girl* is inspired by the real case of two teenagers and the iconic internet monster Slender Man. After reading the book, what comparisons can you make? How do they differ, and how are they similar?
2. How does it make you feel to know there is something close to nonfiction in *Mister Tender's Girl*?
3. Is there a character in *Mister Tender's Girl* that resonates more strongly with you than others? If so, why?
4. What similarities did you see between Alice's mother and Jack?
5. Alice feels a connection to her father whenever she remembers Chancellor's Kingdom, the childhood story he used to tell her and Thomas. Do you have any special books or stories from your childhood that remind you of a special person, and how do they still influence you today?

6. Did you guess the identity of Mister Tender before the end of the book, and if so, what are the clues that led you to your conclusion? If you did not, who did you think was stalking Alice?

7. The Glassin twins were very young when they committed their crime and were heavily influenced by a dark, persuasive figure. Do you still hold them accountable for Alice's attack? If not, who do you think is ultimately responsible, and why?

8. What did you make of Richard's involvement in Alice's situation? Why do you think he went out of his way to save her from Mister Tender?

9. The internet has a lot of shadows that can endanger privacy, shield abuse, and allow anonymity. Has this book made you think differently about online life? In what ways has it made you more curious or cautious to explore?

10. Without the medication, how do you feel Thomas will cope? In what ways has he shown he can thrive (or not) throughout the book?

11. How do you think Alice fares after the story ends? Did you interpret her triumph as strength, or something more fragile or sinister? Do you think it's even possible to

let go of something so formative — and do you think she would even want to?

A CONVERSATION
WITH THE AUTHOR

Mister Tender's Girl **pulls from a real true crime story. When did you first hear about it, and in what way did it plant the seeds for your book?**

I remember first reading about the Slender Man case online, soon after the crime took place. I was both horrified and drawn to the story. About three paragraphs in, I stopped reading because I knew that idea was going to form the basis for my next book. I didn't want to read any more because I didn't want to be too tainted by the actual series of events. To this day, I still haven't read very much about the Slender Man crime or the girls involved.

How did you come up with the character of Mister Tender and his chilling means of persuasion?

He took a few different incarnations, but I

knew his name was going to be Mister Tender — that name just popped in my head and felt right. And after a while, it occurred to me that Tender could mean he was a bartender. And what are bartenders good at? Listening and giving advice. So then I thought about those characteristics being attributed to someone evil, and Mister Tender eventually took shape.

What research did you do to further understand the effects of posttraumatic stress disorder and panic attacks, both of which play a large part of Alice's development?

Fairly extensive online research, and in particular, I remember an article where sufferers of PTSD were asked to write down what a panic attack felt like to them in just a sentence or two. It was harrowing, powerful stuff and really painted a dark picture more effectively than any clinical analysis. I thought back to those images quite a bit when writing about Alice.

What draws you to the thriller genre?

A few things. I enjoy tension, because without it, stories wouldn't be all that interesting. And I love personal stakes. The idea of an everyday person in an extraordinary situation. I want the reader to be able to put themselves in the protagonist's place and think, "What would I do? How would I get out of this?" And, more than anything, I love writing paranoia. That sense of *all is not right here.* Taken together, all the things I love to write point very directly to the thriller/suspense genre.

Are you an outliner or a "panster"? *(warning — spoilers ahead!)*

I'm the very definition of a pantser. I never outline — I just start with an opening scene that intrigues me and take it from there. I have no idea what the story is about for about the first one hundred pages, and certainly no clue of how it will end. It's all a huge puzzle that I try to figure out as I go along. A great example in this book is Brenda's involvement with everything. She was a character I had written in as a friend to Alice, and I had no idea she was going to be a part of the sinister side of things until the chapter where that is actually revealed. It just happened, and I was surprised as anyone by it.

Your book is full of fantastic twists! Do you have any advice for aspiring writ-

ers hoping to keep readers on their toes?

Well, again, I ascribe that ability to my pantser nature. If I don't know what's going to happen next, usually the reader won't know either. That makes for terrific twists (and often a lot of editing). But my advice for aspiring writers is not to lean toward too much structure. If a good idea for a twist suddenly pops in your head, pursue it, even if it takes you on a different course from what you were planning. It won't always work, but when it does, the results may be better than you'd ever hoped.

What does your writing space look like?

Mostly like a Starbucks. Sometimes I write at home, but I do 90 percent of my writing in the mornings in my hometown coffee shop — I like having the energy of people around me, even if I pop on my headphones and dive into work.

I order a double espresso every day, and they even have a special little cup for me. I'm quite fancy.

What author inspires you, and why?

If I had to choose one, I'd be hard-pressed not to say Stephen King. He's masterful both in his scope of work and his ability to capture nuances of characters with an efficiency of words. I've always been impressed with his ability to create tension and fear with just a few choice phrases. His books are long, but they're not overwritten. They always feel edited to just the point they need to be, which is a really difficult thing to do.

Besides writing, what else are you passionate about?

Family, exercise, and travel. The hard part is trying to balance everything.

If there's one thing you'd like readers to take away from *Mister Tender's Girl*, what would it be?

I suppose more than anything I want the readers to feel that they got their money's worth from my story. That they read something different, something a bit out of the ordinary, and with characters who stick with them even after they've finished the book. The best compliment I've ever received is when readers tell me about a character they keep coming back to in their mind. That's pretty satisfying.

ACKNOWLEDGMENTS

This book is dedicated to Ed Bryant, a brilliant writer, Nebula Award winner, Hugo finalist, and friend. Ed dedicated much of his time and soul to helping writers like me by running critique groups throughout Colorado. Our group — Old Possum's — has been around about fifteen years. We still convene monthly, and up until his death in 2017, Ed was in charge of every meeting. Ed's privilege was being the last to critique a piece, to have the final word. He'd clear his throat, look down at the manuscript in hand, and in his low, professorial, so-distinctly-Ed voice, would always begin, "Well . . ." Sometimes he'd praise, sometimes he'd admonish, though usually it was a bit of both, done with just the right amount of care as to not break your spirit. Ed truly helped to shape me as a writer, and I miss him and his wisdom constantly. To the other members of Old Possum's —

Dirk, Linda, Sean, and Abe — I am so grateful for your advice on this manuscript, as well as your friendship.

I am, as ever, endlessly thankful to my agent, Pam Ahearn, who keeps pushing me harder to be a better writer. I was thrilled with her reaction to the first draft of this manuscript, and she worked tirelessly to help me improve it and then make sure it found the right home. That home turned out to be Sourcebooks, who has embraced me in a way an author can only dream. Anna Michels, my wonderful editor, made this story better with her keen insights and clocked countless hours shepherding the book through the long road of production (all the while being a new mom!). And thanks to the entire Sourcebooks team for putting so much of your time, effort, creativity, and boundless enthusiasm into this title. You are an impressive team.

This was the first time I went "on location" to research a book, and I thoroughly enjoyed my time skulking about Manchester, New Hampshire, a city I'd never before visited. In particular, I want to thank Margit and Rob, proprietors at the beautiful Ash Street Inn. If you're ever in Manchester, I highly recommend staying at their five-room bed-and-breakfast — it's a gem.

Dad, you are ever-present in my thoughts and in my writing; I suspect some will see that reflected in these pages. Mom, thank you for all your help with proofing and giving me your feedback on the story. I'll try to use the word *fuck* less in the next book, I promise.

Jessica, your love and support mean everything to me, and I couldn't do any of this without you. Ili and Sawyer, you make me a proud dad, and I love laughing with you. Henry, your energy and creativity continue to inspire. Sole, I truly appreciate our friendship over all these years.

A special thank-you to my longtime friend Craig Gerber, who let me bounce some ideas off him when figuring this story out. You're a smart man, Mr. Gerber.

Thanks to Tim Booth and the rest of the Manchester, UK, band James for allowing me to reprint the lyrics at the beginning of this book. I have traveled across oceans to see James perform, and if you aren't aware of them, I'd like to suggest a few songs to try out. "Sound," "Born of Frustration," "Sometimes," "Out to Get You," and "Moving On" are good starters, but don't stop there. The music of James constitutes a good chunk of my Spotify playlists and is my go-to whenever I need some inspiration.

To all readers, thank you for picking up this book. There are so many forms of entertainment competing for your eyes and ears these days, and I appreciate you carving out some of your time for me. None of this works without you.

Lastly, if you've finished the book and were wondering if the website Alice discovers is real or not, you might want to give it a try.

And make sure you have the password.

Carter Wilson
Erie, Colorado
October 2017

ABOUT THE AUTHOR

Carter Wilson is the *USA Today* bestselling author of *Final Crossing, The Boy in the Woods, The Comfort of Black,* and *Revelation.* He is a two-time winner of both the Colorado Book Award and the International Book Award, and his novels have received critical acclaim, including multiple starred reviews from *Publishers Weekly* and *Library Journal.* He lives in a spooky Victorian house in Erie, Colorado. Visit him at carter wilson.com.